HERO TALES FROM MANY LANDS

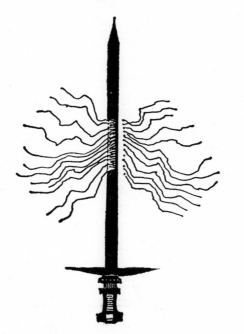

HERO
TALES

FROM MANY LANDS

Selected by ALICE I. HAZELTINE

Illustrated by GORDON LAITE

Nashville   ABINGDON PRESS   New York

The compiler and publishers wish to thank individuals and publishers for their permission to use copyrighted material as follows:

Beling, Mabel Ashe. "This Hound Hath Loved Me" from *The Wicked Goldsmith,* copyright, 1941, by Mabel Ashe Beling. Used by permission of Harper and Brothers, publishers, and the author.

Buck, Alan Michael. "Deirdre" from *The Harper's Daughter,* by Alan Michael Buck, copyright 1940 by Henry Z. Walck, Inc., reprinted by permission of the publishers.

Church, Alfred J. "The Sack of Troy." This selection from Alfred J. Church, *The Aeneid for Boys and Girls,* copyright 1908, by The Macmillan Company, and used by permission of The Macmillan Company and Seeley Service and Company, Ltd.
"The Slaying of Hector." This selection from Alfred J. Church, *The Iliad for Boys and Girls,* copyright 1907, by The Macmillan Company, and used by permission of The Macmillan Company and Seeley Service and Company, Ltd.

Crane, Louise. "The Empty City." From *The Magic Spear and Other Stories of China's Famous Heroes.* Copyright 1938 by Random House, Inc. Reprinted by permission.

Colum, Padraic. "The Return of Odysseus." From *The Adventures of Odysseus,* copyright 1918 by Padraic Colum. Used by permission of the author.
"The Dream of Ronabbway." From *The Island of the Mighty,* copyright 1927, by Padraic Colum. Used by permission of the author.

French, Allen. "Grettir Becomes an Outlaw." From the book *The Story of Grettir the Strong* by Allen French. Copyright 1908 by E. P. Dutton and Company, Inc. Renewal, 1936, by Allen French. Reprinted by permission of the publishers.
"Njal the Lawyer." From *Heroes of Iceland,* copyright 1925 by Little Brown and Company. Used by permission of Aletta L. French.

Hatch, Alice. "Frithiof's Journey to the Orkneys." From *Bag O' Tales* by E. L. Powers. Copyright 1935 by E. P. Dutton and Company, Inc. Used by permission of Alice Hatch and E. L. Powers.

Hosford, Dorothy. "How Sigurd Awakes Brynhild upon Hindfel." From *Sons of the Volsungs* by Dorothy Hosford. Copyright, 1932, by the Macmillan Company. Copyright, 1949, by Dorothy Hosford. By permission of Henry Holt and Company, Inc.

Hull, Eleanor. "How Cuchulain Wooed His Wife." From *The Boy's Cuchulain: Heroic Legends of Ireland* by Eleanor Hull. Thomas Y. Crowell Company, New York. English rights, George S. Harrap and Company, Limited.

McNeer, May and Ward, Lynd. "Shizuka's Dance." From *Prince Bantam,* copyright 1929 by the Macmillan Company. Used by permission of the authors.

Morris, Kenneth. "Manawydden Son of the Boundless." From *Book of the Three Dragons,* copyright 1930 by Longmans, Green and Company. Used by permission of the publishers.

Mukerji, Dhan Gopal. "The Search for Sita." From the book *Rama, the Hero of India* by Dhan Gopal Mukerji. Copyright, 1930, by E. P. Dutton and Company, Inc. Renewal, 1958, by Mrs. Dhan Gopal Mukerji. Reprinted by permission of the publishers and J. M. Dent and Sons, Ltd.

Pyle, Howard. "The Tournament in Ireland." From *The Story of the Champions of the Round Table.* Reprinted with the permission of Charles Scribner's Sons. Copyright 1905 Charles Scribner's Sons; renewal copyright 1933 Anne Poole Pyle.

Seredy, Kate. "Attila the Conqueror." From *The White Stag,* by Kate Seredy. Copyright 1937 by Kate Seredy. Reprinted by permission of The Viking Press, Inc.

Sherwood, Merriam. "The Wedding of the Cid's Daughters." From *The Tale of the Warrior Lord: El Cantar de Mio Cid,* copyright 1930, by Longmans, Green and Company. Used by permission of the publishers.

Tietjens, Eunice. "Antar the Hero." From *The Romance of Antar* by Eunice Tietjens. Copyright 1929 by Eunice Tietjens. Published by Coward-McCann, Inc. Used by permission.

Young, Ella. "The Lordship of the Fianna." From *The Tangle Coated Horse and Other Tales: Episodes from the Fionn Saga,* copyright 1929, by Longmans, Green and Company. Used by permission of the publishers.

Zeitlin, Ida. "Yoro Reveals Himself as Gessar Khan." From *Gessar Khan,* copyright, 1927, by Ida Zeitlin. Used by permission of Rinehart and Company.

ISBN 0-687-16943-7
Library of Congress Catalog Card Number: 61-5096

This book is dedicated to the memory of
A<small>LICE</small> I. H<small>AZELTINE</small>
by all those who have had a part in its making

———————

ALICE I. HAZELTINE
An Appreciation
by Frederic G. Melcher

This collection of hero tales has been brought together
by an experienced maker of anthologies, Alice I. Hazeltine. It
has proved to be the final test of her taste and skill in gathering
and arranging poems and stories for children's use as well as
for those who serve children with books in home, school or
library.

The making of anthologies requires a vast background
of reading, a tenacious memory, a delicate sense of literary
values and a thorough acquaintance with the uses and the users
of such books. Alice Hazeltine had just such needed background
and experience and she has put these to use in the preparation
of a dozen volumes from her "Christmas in Legend and Story"
and the "Easter Book of Legends and Stories" to "We Grew Up
in America" and this present book. Her books are found, used
and reused, in thousands of libraries where they serve to delight
readers, aid writers, and enrich story hours. To each user of her
books, there must always come through something of her rich
personality flavored as it was by the long library and teaching
experience which carried her career from distinguished posts at

Carnegie Library, Pittsburgh, and St. Louis Public Library, to twenty years of spreading influence at Columbia University.

To hundreds of librarians Miss Hazeltine was friend as well as beloved teacher. Characteristic of her understanding and initiative was my own first contact with her, which proved to be both pleasant and fruitful. In 1921, then director of children's work at the St. Louis Public Library, she was chairman of the Children's Librarians Section of A.L.A. and she invited me to speak on "Children's Book Week—A National Movement," at the annual meeting of the Association at Swampscott. Children's Book Week had been launched two years before, but there were those who feared that, in cooperating, libraries might be taking a step toward the commercialization of their profession. Miss Hazeltine thought otherwise, and her cordiality to cooperative ideas led me to ask the opportunity to present to the business meeting of the Section, the idea of an annual award for a distinguished book for children. The John Newbery Medal was the name that visualized the idea. Her interest in the potential possibilities of Children's Book Week and her recognition of the part that libraries might play by becoming judges of current books, thus giving encouragement to new writers, led to important developments in the annual book week and in the medal awards.

In her long life Miss Hazeltine was always in the forefront of movements for more and better books for children. Her anthologies will extend her influence through the years.

CONTENTS

FOREWORD

Here are heroes and heroines of great stature from long ago and from the ends of the earth; from warm, sunny Mediterranean shores; from the colder regions of the North; from regions like France and Spain; from English, Irish, and Welsh soil; from Persia, India, and Tibet—even one from the plains of America. These great stories have been told and retold by a long line of storytellers and writers. The versions reprinted here are especially suitable for the twentieth century reader.

To know what happened in the story before or after the selection in this book, readers may wish to find the books from which these stories have been taken or other books which tell them in a different form. Some of these tales readers will find have been published in many versions, but others are available in only one or two editions.

ALICE I. HAZELTINE

A Cause of War

by James Baldwin

from *A Story of the Golden Age*

When Menelaus, King of Lacedaemon, a city-state in Greece in the early days of Grecian glory, married the beautiful Helen, his rivals for her hand, the rulers of other parts of Greece (Hellas), promised that they would help him if at any time Helen was taken from him. Some time later Menelaus made a pilgrimage to Troy to carry out a command of the gods of Greece. When he returned, he brought with him as his guest, Paris, the son of Priam, King of Troy. Paris wanted Helen for himself, and when Menelaus was away, Paris persuaded Helen to return to Troy with him. Menelaus was, of course, very angry when he returned and found Helen gone. He went at once to see Nestor, a neighboring king and wisest of the Greeks, to determine what should be done. And there plans were laid for the siege of Troy.

A CAUSE OF WAR

James Baldwin

———— ◆•◆ ————

THERE was silence in the golden halls of Menelaus, and guests sat no longer as of yore around the banquet tables. Anger and grief and uneasiness were plainly seen in every face. Men gathered in the streets, and talked in wild, excited tones about the strange things which had lately happened in Lacedæmon; and the words "Helen," and "Paris," and "Troy," and "Ilios" seemed to be on every tongue, and repeated with every sign of love and hatred, of admiration and anxiety.

Meanwhile, with troubled brow and anxious heart, Menelaus sat in Nestor's halls, and told the story of his wrongs. Before him, seated on a fair embroidered couch, was the aged king, listening with eager ears. Behind him stood his brother Agamemnon, tall and strong, and with eye and forehead like mighty Zeus. Close by his feet two heroes sat: on this side, Antilochus, the valiant son of Nestor; and on that, sage Palamedes, prince of Eubœa's distant shores. The last had just arrived at Pylos, and had not learned the errand which had brought the king of Lacedæmon thither.

"Tell again the story of your visit to Troy," said Nestor. "Our guest, good Palamedes, would fain understand it all; and I doubt not that he may be of service to your cause."

Then Menelaus began:

"There is no need that I should speak of the long voyage to Ilios, or of the causes which persuaded me to undertake it. When I drew near the lofty citadels of Troy, and through the Scæan gates could see the rows of stately dwellings and Athené's marble temple, and the busy market-place of that great city, I stopped there in wonder, fearing to venture farther. Then I sent a herald to the gates, who should make known my name and lineage, and the errand upon which I had come; but I waited without in the shade of a spreading beech, not far from the towering wall. Before me stood the mighty city; behind me the fertile plain sloped gently to the sea; in the distance I could see the tomb of Ilus and the sparkling waters of Scamander; while much farther, and on the other side, the wooded peak of Ida lifted itself toward the clouds. But I had not long to view this scene; for a noble company of men led by Paris himself, handsome as Apollo, came out of the gates to welcome me. With words of kind greeting from the king, they bade me enter within the walls. They led me through the Scæan gates and along the well-paved streets, until we came, at last, to Priam's noble hall. It was a splendid house, with broad doorways and polished porticos, and marble columns richly carved. Within were fifty chambers, joining one another, all walled with polished stone; in these abode the fifty sons of Priam with their wedded wives. On the other side, and opening into the court, were twelve chambers, built for his daughters; while over all were the sleeping-rooms for that noble household, and around were galleries and stairways leading to the king's great hall below.

"King Priam received me kindly, and, when he understood my errand, left naught undone to help me forward with my wishes. Ten days I abode as a guest in his halls, and when I would return to Lacedæmon he pressed me to tarry yet a month in Troy. But the winds were fair, and the oracles promised a pleasant voyage, and I begged that on the twelfth day he would let me depart. So he and his sons brought many gifts, rich and beautiful, and laid them at my feet,—a fair mantle, and a doublet, and a talent of fine gold, and a sword with a silver-studded hilt, and a drinking-cup richly engraved that I might remember them when I pour libations to the gods.

" 'Take these gifts,' said Priam, 'as tokens of our friendship for you, and not only for you, but for all who dwell in distant Hellas. For we too are the children of the immortals. Our mighty ancestor, Dardanus, was the son of Zeus. He it was who built Dardania on the slopes of Ida, where the waters gush in many silvery streams from underneath the rocky earth. To Dardanus a son was born named Erichthonius, who, in his time, was the richest of mortal men. And Erichthonius was the father of Troas, to whom were born three noble sons, Ilus, Assaracus, and Ganymedes. Ilus had a son, famous in song and story, named Laomedon, who in his old age became my father. He, though my sire, did many unwise things, and brought sore distress upon the people of this land.

" 'One day Apollo and Poseidon came to sacred Troy, disguised as humble wayfarers seeking some employment. This they did because so ordered by mighty Zeus.

" ' "What can you do?" asked my father, when the two had told their wishes.

" 'Poseidon answered, "I am a builder of walls."

" 'And Apollo answered, "I am a shepherd, and a tender of herds."

" ' "It is well," answered Laomedon. "The wallbuilder shall build a wall around this Troy so high and strong that no enemy can pass it. The shepherd shall tend my herds of crook-horned kine in the wooded glens of Ida. If at the end of a twelvemonth, the wall be built, and if the cattle thrive without loss of one, then I will pay you your hire: a talent of gold, two tripods of silver, rich robes, and armor such as heroes wear."

" 'So the shining archer, and the shaker of the earth, served my father through the year for the hire which he had promised. Poseidon built a wall, high and fair, around the city; and Apollo tended the shambling kine, and lost not one. But when they claimed their hire, Laomedon drove them away with threats, telling them that he would bind their feet and hands together, and sell them as slaves into some distant land, having first sheared off their ears with his sharp sword. And the twain went away with angry hearts, planning in their minds how they might avenge themselves.

" 'Back to his watery kingdom, and his golden palace beneath the sea, went great Poseidon. He harnessed his steeds to his chariot, and rode forth upon the waves. He loosed the mighty winds from their prison-house, and sent them raging over the sea. The angry waters rushed in upon the land; they covered the pastures and the rich plain of Troy, and threatened even to beat down the mighty walls which their king had built. Then, little by little, the flood shrank back again; and the people went out of the city to see the waste of slime and black mud which covered their meadows. While they were gazing upon the scene, a fearful monster, sent by angry Poseidon, came up out of the sea, and fell upon them, and drove them with hideous slaughter back to the city gates; neither would he allow any one to come outside of the walls.

" 'Then my father, in his great distress, clad himself in mourning, and went in deep humility to the temple of Athené, where stands the heaven-sent statue which we call Palladion. In sore distress, he called unto the goddess, and besought to know the means whereby the anger of Poseidon might be assuaged. And in solemn tones a voice came from the moveless lips of the Palladion, saying,—

" ' "Every day one of the maidens of Troy must be fed to the monster outside of the walls. The shaker of the earth has spoken. Disobey him not, lest more cruel punishments befall thee."

" 'Then in every house of Troy there was sore distress and lamentation, for no one knew upon whom the doom would soonest fall. And every day a hapless maiden, young and fair, was chained to the great rock by the shore, and left there to be the food of the pitiless monster. And the people cried aloud in their distress, and cursed the mighty walls and the high towers which had been reared by the unpaid labors of Poseidon; and my father sat upon his high seat, and trembled because of the dire calamities which his own deeds had brought upon his people.

" 'At last, after many humble victims had perished, the lot fell upon the fairest of my sisters, Hesione, my father's best-loved daughter. In sorrow we arrayed her in garments befitting one doomed to an untimely death; and when we had bidden her a last farewell, we gave her to the heralds to lead forth to the place of sacrifice. Just then, however, a noble stranger, taller and more stately than any man in Troy, came down the street from the Scæan gate. Fair-haired and blue-eyed, handsome and strong, he seemed a very god to all who looked upon him. Over his shoulder he wore the tawny skin of a mighty lion, while in his hand he carried a club most wonderful to behold. And the people, as he passed, prayed him that he would free our city from the dread monster who was robbing us of our fair loved ones.

" ' "I know that thou art a god!" cried my father, when he saw the stranger. "I pray thee, save my daughter, who even now is being led forth to a cruel death!"

" ' "You make mistake," answered the fair stranger. "I am not one of the gods. My name is Heracles, and like you I am mortal. Yet I may help you in this your time of need."

" 'Now, in my father's stables there were twelve fair steeds, the best that the earth ever knew. So light of foot were they, that when they bounded over the land, they might run upon the topmost ears of ripened corn, and break them not; and when they bounded over the sea, not even Poseidon's steeds could glide so lightly upon the crests of the waves. These steeds, my father promised to give to Heracles if he would save Hesione.

" 'Then the heralds led my fair sister to the shore, and chained her to the rock, there to wait for the coming of the monster. But Heracles stood near her, fearless in his strength. Soon the waves began to rise; the waters were disturbed, and the great beast, with hoarse bellowings, lifted his head above the breakers, and rushed forward to seize his fair prey. Then the hero sprang to meet him. With blow upon blow from his mighty club, he felled the monster; the waters of the sea were reddened with blood; Hesione was saved, and Troy was freed from the dreadful curse.

" ' "Behold thy daughter!" said Heracles, leading her gently back to the Scæan gate, and giving her to her father. "I have saved her from the jaws of death, and delivered your country from the dread scourge. Give me now my hire."

" 'Shame fills my heart as I tell this story, for thanklessness was the bane of my father's life. Ungrateful to the hero who had risked so much and done so much that our homes and our country might be saved from ruin, he turned coldly away from Heracles; then he shut the great gates in his face, and barred him out of the city, and taunted him from the walls, saying, "I owe thee no hire! Begone from our coasts, ere I scourge thee hence!"

" 'Full of wrath, the hero turned away. "I go, but I will come again," he said.

" 'Then peace and plenty blessed once more the land of

Ilios, and men forgot the perils from which they had been delivered. But ere long, great Heracles returned, as he had promised; and with him came a mighty fleet of white-sailed ships and many warriors. Neither gates nor strong walls could stand against him. Into the city he marched, and straight to my father's palace. All fled before him, and the strongest warriors quailed beneath his glance. Here, in this very court, he slew my father and my brothers with his terrible arrows. I myself would have fallen before his wrath, had not my sister, fair Hesione, pleaded for my life.

" ' "I spare his life," said Heracles, in answer to her prayers, "for he is but a lad. Yet he must be my slave until you have paid a price for him, and thus redeemed him."

" 'Then Hesione took the golden veil from her head, and gave it to the hero as my purchase price. And thenceforward I was called Priam, or the purchased; for the name which my mother gave me was Podarkes, or the fleet-footed.

" 'After this, Heracles and his heroes went on board their ships and sailed back across the sea, leaving me alone in my father's halls. For they took fair Hesione with them, and carried her to Salamis, to be the wife of Telamon, the sire of mighty Ajax. There, through these long years she has lived in sorrow, far removed from home and friends and the scenes of her happy childhood. And now that the hero Telamon, to whom she was wedded, lives no longer, I ween that her life is indeed a cheerless one.'

"When Priam had finished his tale, he drew his seat still nearer mine, and looked into my face with anxious, beseeching eyes. Then he said, 'I have long wished to send a ship across the sea to bring my sister back to Troy. A dark-prowed vessel, built for speed and safety, lies now at anchor in the harbor, and a picked crew is ready to embark at any moment. And here is my son Paris, handsome and brave, who is anxious to make voyage to Salamis, to seek unhappy Hesione. Yet our seamen, having never ventured far from home, know nothing of the dangers of the deep, nor do they feel sure that they can find their way to Hellas. And so we have a favor to ask of you; and that is, that when your ship sails to-morrow, ours may follow in its wake across the sea.'

"I was glad when Priam spoke these words, for, in truth, I was loath to part with Paris; and I arranged at once that he should bear me company in my own swift ship, while his vessel with its crew followed not far behind.

"And so with favoring winds being blessed, we made a quick voyage back to Lacedæmon. What followed is too sad for lengthy mention, and is in part already known to you. Need I tell you how I opened my halls to Paris, and left no act of courtesy undone that I might make him happy? Need I tell you how he was welcomed by fair Helen, and how the summer days fled by on golden wings; and how in the delights of Lacedæmon he forgot his errand to Salamis, and cared only to remain with me, my honored guest and trusted friend? One day a message came to me from my old friend Idomeneus. He had planned a hunt among the mountains and wooded vales of Crete, and he invited me to join him in the sport. I had not seen Idomeneus since the time that we together, in friendly contention, sought the hand of Helen. I could not do otherwise than accept his invitation, for he had sent his own ship to carry me over to Crete. So I bade farewell to Helen, saying, 'Let not our noble guest lack entertainment while I am gone; and may the golden hours glide happily until I come again.' And to Paris I said, 'Tarry another moon in Lacedæmon; and when I return from Crete, I will go with you to Salamis, and aid you in your search for Hesione.' Then I went on board the waiting ship, and prospering breezes carried us without delays to Crete.

"Idomeneus received me joyfully, and entertained me most royally in his palace; and for nine days we feasted in his halls, and made all things ready for the hunt. But, lo! on the evening of the last day, a vision came to me. Gold-winged Iris, the fleet-footed messenger of the gods, stood before me. 'Hasten back to Lacedæmon,' she cried, 'for thou art robbed of thy dearest treasure!' And even while she spoke, one of my own ships came sailing into the harbor, bringing trusted heralds whom the elders of Lacedæmon had sent to me. They told me the fatal news. 'No sooner were you well on your way,' they said, 'than Paris began to put his ship in readiness to depart. Helen prayed him to tarry until your return, but he would not hearken. "I will stay no longer," he said. "My seamen rest upon their oars; the sails of my ship are spread; the breeze will soon spring up that will carry me to my own fair home across the sea. But you, beauteous Helen, shall go with me; for the deathless gods have spoken it. Aphrodite, long ago, promised that the most beautiful woman in the world should be my wife. And who is that most beautiful woman if it is not yourself? Come! fly over the sea, and be my queen. It is the will of the gods." '

"It was thus that the perfidious Trojan wrought the ruin of all that was dear to me. At first, Helen refused. But Paris is a handsome prince, and day after day he renewed his suit. Then on the sixth day she yielded. In the darkness of the night they went on board his waiting vessel, carrying with them the gold and jewels of my treasure-house; and in the morning, when the sun arose on Lacedæmon, they were far out at sea.

"You know the rest: how in wrath and great sorrow I hurried home from Crete; how I first counselled with my own elders, and then with my brother Agamemnon of Mycenæ. And now, O noble Nestor, we have come to Pylos, seeking thy advice. On these two things my mind is set: Helen must be mine again, and Paris must suffer the punishment due to traitors."

When Menelaus had ended, sage Nestor answered with many words of counsel. "Keep the thought of vengeance ever before you," he said. "Yet act not rashly. The power of Troy is very great; and, in case of war, all the tribes of Asia will make common cause with Ilios. But an insult to Lacedæmon is an insult to all Hellas, and every loyal Hellene will hasten to avenge it. More than this, the chiefs of almost every state have already sworn to aid you. We have but to call upon them, and remind them of their oaths, and all the mightiest warriors of our land will take up arms against the power of Troy."

Then Palamedes spoke in like manner, and his words had great weight with Menelaus; for among all the heroes there were few who equalled him in wisdom.

"Nestor has spoken well," he said, addressing Menelaus, and it behooves us to follow his advice. Now do you and Agamemnon return at once to Argos and Lacedæmon, and call upon the fighting men along the eastern coast to join you in the war. In the meanwhile, Nestor and myself will do the same, here on the western coast and along the islands of the sea."

"By the way," said Nestor, "there is Odysseus, king of Ithaca, —the rarest and bravest of men. Did he but know of this affair, he would be a host within himself, to lead us to sure victory."

"That is true," said Palamedes, "and we must seek his aid first. My ship lies now at anchor, just off the beach; and if noble Nestor will be my comrade, we will sail to-morrow to Ithaca, and make sure of his valued aid."

"Most surely I will go with you," said old Nestor. "And I will never rest nor give up the fight, until Helen is returned to Menelaus, and Paris has received his due reward."

The Slaying of Hector

by Alfred J. Church

from *The Iliad for Boys and Girls*

For ten long years the Greeks besieged Troy. The story of this siege is told in the Iliad, said to have been written by a blind poet, Homer. The Greeks were not strong enough to invade the city; and the Trojans were not strong enough to drive the Greeks away. There were many battles; many men on both sides were slain; and many heroes were acclaimed. Noblest of the heroes of Troy was Hector, son of King Priam and brother of Paris. The greatest warrior of the Greeks was Achilles, who was protected by the gods and could be killed only by a wound in the heel. The story of the battle between these two and of the death of Hector, reveals not only the courage and strength of the two men, but also the ways in which the gods interfered with the battles. Apollo, God of the sun, and Zeus, king of the gods, favored Troy. But Athene, goddess of wisdom and war, Juno, wife of Zeus, and other gods and goddesses favored Greece.

THE SLAYING OF HECTOR

Alfred J. Church

K ING PRIAM stood on a tower of the wall and saw how Achilles was driving the men of Troy before him, and his heart was much troubled within him, thinking how he could help his people. So he went down and spoke to those who kept the gates: "Keep now the wicket-gates open, holding them in your hand, that the people may enter by them, for they are flying before Achilles." So the keepers held the wicket-gates in their hands, and the people made haste to come in; they were wearied with toil and consumed with thirst, and Achilles followed close after them. And the Greeks would have taken the city of Troy that hour but that Apollo saved it, for the gates being open they could enter with the Trojans, whereas the gates being shut, the people were left to perish. And the way in which he saved the city was this. He put courage into the heart of Agēnor, son to Antenor, standing also by him that he should not be slain. Agēnor, therefore, stood thinking to himself: "Shall I flee with these others? Not so: for Achilles will overtake me, so swift of foot is he, and shall slay me, and I shall die the death of a coward. Or shall I flee across the plain to Mount Ida, and hide myself in the thicket, and come back to the city when it is dark? But if he see me, he will pursue me and overtake me. Shall I not rather stand here and meet him before the gates? For he too is a mortal man, and may be slain by the spear."

Therefore he stood by the gates waiting for Achilles, for Apollo had given him courage. And when Achilles came near Agēnor cast his spear, and struck his leg beneath the knee, but the greave turned the spear, so strong was it, having been made by a god. But when Achilles rushed at him to slay him, Apollo lifted him up from the ground and set him safe within the walls. And that the men of Troy might have time to enter, the god took Agēnor's shape and fled before Achilles, and Achilles pursued him. Meanwhile the Trojans flocked into the city through the wicket-gates, nor did they stay to ask who was safe and who was dead, so great was their fear and such their haste. Only Hector remained outside the city, in front of the great gates which were called the Scæan Gates. All the while Achilles was fiercely pursuing the false Agēnor, till at last Apollo turned and spoke to him: "Why do you pursue me, swift-footed Achilles? Have you not yet found out that I am a god, and that all your fury is in vain? And now all the Trojans are safe in the city, and you are here, far out of the way, seeking to kill one who cannot die."

Achilles answered him in great anger: "You have done me a great wrong in this. Surely of all the gods you are the one who loves mischief most. If it had not been for this many Trojans more have fallen; but you have saved your favourites and robbed me of great glory. Oh that I could take vengeance on you! truly you would have paid dearly for your cheat."

Then he turned and ran towards the city, swift as a race-horse when it whirls a chariot across the plains. And his armour shone upon him as bright as Orion, which men call also the Dog, shines in the autumn, when the vintage is gathered, an evil light, bringing fevers to men. Old Priam saw him and groaned aloud, and stretched out his hands crying to Hector his son, where he stood before the gates waiting to fight with this terrible warrior:

"O my son, wait not for this man, lest he kill you, for indeed he is stronger than you. I would that the gods had such love for him as I have. Soon would he be food for dogs and vultures. Of many sons has he bereaved me, but if he should bereave me of you, then would not I only and the mother who bore you mourn, but every man and woman in Troy. Come within the walls, my dear son, come, for you are the hope of the city. Come, lest an evil fate come upon me in my old age, that I should see my sons slain with the sword and my daughters carried into captivity, and the babes dashed upon the ground."

So spoke old Priam, but he could not move the heart of his son. Then from the other side of the wall his mother, Queen Hecuba, cried to him. She wept aloud, hoping that she might so persuade him. "Come, I beseech you, inside the walls, and do not wait for him, or stand up in battle against him. For if he conquers you, then not only will you die, but dogs and vultures will eat your flesh far from here, by the ships of the Greeks."

But all her prayers were in vain, for he was still minded to await the coming of Achilles, and stand up to him in battle. And as he waited many thoughts passed through his mind: "Woe is me, if I go within the walls! Will not they reproach me who gave me good advice which I would not hear, saying that I should bring the people within the walls, when the great Achilles roused himself to the battle? Would that I had done this thing! it had been by far better for us; but now I have destroyed the people. I fear the sons and daughters of Troy, lest they should say: 'Hector trusted in his strength, and he has brought the people whom he should have saved to harm.' It would be far better for me to stay here and meet the great Achilles, and either slay him, or, if it must be so, be slain by him. Or shall I lay down my shield and take off my helmet and lean my spear against the wall, and go to meet him and say: 'We will give back the Fair Helen and all the riches which Paris carried off with her; also we will give all the precious things that there are in the city that the Greeks may divide them among themselves, taking an oath that we are keeping nothing back, if only you will leave us in peace'? But this is idle talk. He will have neither shame nor pity, and will slay me as I stand without defence before him. No: it is better far to meet in arms and see whether Zeus will give the victory to him or to me."

These were the things which Hector thought in his heart. And Achilles came near, shaking over his right shoulder the great Pelian spear, and the flashing of his arms was like to fire or to the sun when it rises. But Hector trembled when he saw him, and his heart failed him so that he turned his back and fled. Fast he fled from the place where he stood by the great Scæan Gate, and fast did Achilles pursue him, just as a hawk, which is more swift than all other birds, pursues a dove among the hills. The two ran past the watch-tower, and past the wild fig tree, along the wagon-road which ran round the walls, till they came to the springs from which the river rises. Two springs there were, one hot as though it had been heated with fire, and the other cold, cold as ice or snow, even in the summer. There were two basins of stone in which the daughters of Troy had been used to wash their garments; but that was in the old days, when there was peace, before the Greeks came to the land. Past the springs they ran; it was no race which men run for some prize, a sheep, maybe, or an ox-hide shield. Rather the prize was the life of Hector. So they ran round the city, and the Trojans on the wall and the Greeks upon the plain looked on. And the gods looked on as they sat in their palace on the top of Olympus. And Zeus said:

"Now this is a piteous thing which I see. My heart is grieved for Hector—Hector, who has never failed to honour me and the other gods with sacrifice. See how the great Achilles is pursuing him! Come, let us take counsel together. Shall we save him from death, or shall we let him fall by the spear of Achilles?"

Athené said: "What is this that you purpose? Will you save a man whom the fates appoint to die? Do this, if you will, but the other gods do not approve."

Then said Zeus: "This is a thing that I hate; but be it as you will." All this time Hector still fled, and Achilles still pursued. Hector sought for shelter in the walls, and Achilles ever drove him towards the plain. Just as in a dream, when one seems to fly and another seems to pursue, and the first cannot escape, neither can the second overtake, so these two ran. Yet Apollo helped Hector giving strength to his knees, else he had not held out against Achilles, than whom there was no faster runner among the sons of men. Three times did they run round the city, but when they came for the fourth time to the springs Athené lighted from the air close to Achilles and said: "This is your day of glory, for you shall slay Hector, though he be a mighty warrior. It is his doom to die, and Apollo's self shall not save him. Stand here and take breath, and I will make him meet you."

So Achilles stood leaning on his spear. And Athené took the shape of Deïphobus, and came near to Hector and said to him: "My brother, Achilles presses you hard; but come, we two will stand up against him." Hector answered, "O Deïphobus, I have always loved you above all my brothers, and now I love you still more, for you only have come to my help, while they remain within the walls." Then said Deïphobus: "Much did my father and my mother and my comrades entreat me to stay within the walls, but I would not, for I could not bear to leave you alone.

Come, therefore, let us fight this man together, and see whether
he will carry our spoils to the ships or we shall slay him here."

Then Hector said to Achilles: "Three times have you pursued me round the walls, and I dared not stand against you,
but now I fear you no more. Only let us make this covenant.
If Zeus gives me the victory to-day, I will give back your body
to the Greeks, only I will keep your arms: do you, therefore,
promise to do the same with me?"

Achilles frowned at him and said: "Hector, talk not of cove-
nants to me. Men and lions make no oaths to each other, neither
is there any agreement between wolves and sheep. Make no delay; let us fight together, that I may have vengeance for the
blood of all my comrades whom thou hast slain, and especially
of Patroclus, the man whom I loved beyond all others."

Then he threw the great spear, but Hector saw it coming and

avoided it, crouching down so that the spear flew over his head and fixed itself in the ground. But Athené snatched it up and gave it back to Achilles; but this Hector did not see. Then said Hector to Achilles: "You have missed your aim, Achilles. Now see whether I have not a truer aim." Then he cast his spear, and the aim, indeed, was true, for it struck full upon the shield; it struck, but it bounded far away. Then he cried to Deïphobus: "Give me another spear"; but lo! Deïphobus was gone. Then he knew that his end was come, and he said to himself: "The gods have brought my doom upon me. I thought that Deïphobus was with me; but he is behind the walls, and this was but a cheat with which Athené cheated me. Nevertheless, if I must die, let me at least die in the doing of such a deed as men shall remember in the years to come."

So he spoke, and drew his great sword, and rushed upon

Achilles as an eagle rushes down from the clouds upon its prey. But never a blow did he deal; for Achilles ran to meet him, holding his shield before him, and the plumes of his helmet streamed behind him as he ran, and the point of his spear was as bright as the evening star. For a moment he doubted where he should drive it home, for the armour of Patroclus which Hector wore guarded him well. But a spot there was, where the stroke of spear or sword is deadliest, by the collar-bone where the neck joins the shoulder. There he drove in the spear, and the point stood out behind the neck, and Hector fell in the dust. Then Achilles cried aloud: "Hector, you thought not of me when you slew Patroclus and spoiled him of his arms. But now you have fallen, and the dogs and the vultures shall eat your flesh, but to him the Greeks will give honorable burial."

But Hector said, his voice now growing faint: "O Achilles, I entreat you, by all that you hold dear, to give my body to my father and mother that they may duly bury it. Large ransoms will they pay of gold and silver and bronze."

"Speak not to me of ransom," said Achilles. "Priam shall not buy thee back, no, not for your weight in gold."

Then Hector said: "I know you well, what manner of man you are, and that the heart in your breast is of iron. Only beware lest the anger of the gods come upon you for such deeds in the days when Paris and Apollo shall slay you hard by these very gates."

So speaking, he died. And Achilles said: "Die, dog that you are; but my doom I will meet when it shall please the gods to send it."

Then did Achilles devise a cruel thing. He pierced the ankle-bones of the dead man, and fastened the body with thongs of ox-hide to the chariot, and so dragged it to the ships.

The Sack of Troy

by Alfred J. Church

from *The Aeneid for Boys and Girls*

The Trojans did not let the body of Hector remain in camp of the Greeks. King Priam himself went to the Greek leaders and his pleadings eventually recovered the body. But with the death of Hector, and later the death of Paris, who himself killed Achilles, the Trojans lost some of their will to fight. They no longer ventured out of the city for battle, but remained inside their high city walls. These walls the Greeks could not capture; but the Trojans were like prisoners inside. What happened in the end is told by the Roman poet Virgil in his epic poem the Aeneid. *Aeneas, the hero of this story, is said to have escaped from Troy and made his way to the area that later became the city of Rome.*

THE SACK OF TROY

Alfred J. Church

————— ◆•◆ —————

W E CAN easily believe that Priam, King of Troy, and his people were very glad to hear that one day the Greeks had gone home. Two Trojans, who had left the city two weeks or so before on a message from King Priam to one of his allies, came back saying that they had gone to the camp of the Greeks and had found it empty, and that there were no ships to be seen.

Every one who was not ill or too old to move about made all the haste they could to get out of the city. The gates were opened wide for the first time during ten years, and men, women, and children hurried out to see the plain where so many battles had been fought, and the camp in which the enemy had lived, and the place where the ships had been dragged up on the shore. As you may suppose, those who had fought in the battles had a great deal to say about what they had done and what they had seen.

There were many things to see, but the strangest one of all was a great Horse of Wood, which was standing not far from the walls of the city. No one was quite sure what it was, or what it meant.

One man said: "It is a very curious thing. Let us drag it into the city that it may be a monument of all that we have suffered for the last ten years."

Others said: "Not so; we had better burn it, or drag it down
to the sea that the water may cover it, or cut it open to see
whether there is anything inside."

Of these no one was more vehement than Laocoön, priest
of Neptune. "Take heed what you do, men of Troy," he cried.
"Who knows whether the Greeks have really gone away? It may
be that there are armed men inside this Horse; it may be that
it has been made so big to overtop the walls of the city. Anyhow
I am afraid of these Greeks, even when they give us gifts." And
as he spoke, he threw the spear which he had in his hand at
the Horse of Wood, and struck it on the side. A great rattling
sound was heard, and the Trojans, if they had not been very
blind and foolish, might have known that there was something
wrong.

While the dispute was going on, some shepherds came up,
bringing with them a man whose hands were bound behind
his back. He had come out from a hiding-place, they said, of
his own accord, when they were in the field. The young Trojans crowded round him, and began to mock at him, but he
cried out in a very piteous voice: "What shall I do? Where shall
I go? The Greeks will not let me live, and the Trojans cry out
for vengeance upon me." Then they began to pity him, and
they bade him say who he was and what he had to tell.

Then the man turned to King Priam, and said: "I will speak
the truth, whatever may happen to me. My name is Sinon, and
I will not deny that I am a Greek. Perhaps you have heard of
one Palamedes. The Greeks put him to death, saying that he
was a traitor; but his only fault was that he wanted to have
peace. Yes, they put him to death, and now that he is dead, they
are sorry. I was a cousin of his, and my father sent me with
him to Troy. So long as he prospered, I prospered also; but
when he was done to death by the false witness of Ulysses, I fell

into great grief and trouble, nor could I be silent; I swore that if ever I got back to Argos, I would have revenge on those who had brought him to his death. So Ulysses was always on the look-out to do me some harm; and at the last by the help of Calchas the prophet—but why do I tell you of these things? Doubtless you hold one Greek as bad as another. Kill me, if you will; only remember that this is the very thing which the two sons of Atreus wish, the very thing which Ulysses himself would give much money to secure."

Then the Trojans said: "Tell us more."

And he went on. "Many times would the Greeks have gone home, for they were very tired of the war, but the sea was so stormy that they dared not go. Then they made this great Horse of Wood which you see, but the storms grew worse and worse. Then they sent to ask Apollo what they should do. And Apollo said: 'Men of Greece, when you came here you had to appease the winds with blood, and you must appease them with blood again when you go away.' Every one trembled when they heard this, for every one feared that it might be his blood that would be wanted. After a while Ulysses brought the prophet into the assembly of the people, and said: 'Tell us now who is it that the gods will have for a victim?' Then many thought that it was I against whom Ulysses was plotting. For nine days the prophet said nothing: 'He would not give any Greek,' he said, 'to death.' These were his words, but in truth he and Ulysses had plotted the whole thing between them. On the tenth day he spoke, and said: 'Sinon is the man.' To this all agreed, every man thinking, 'Well, it is not I that shall die.' So they fixed a day on which I was to be sacrificed, and made everything ready. But before it came, I broke my chains and escaped, hiding myself in the reeds of a pond, till they should set sail. And now I shall never see my own country again; no, nor my wife and children, and, doubtless, these cruel men will take vengeance on them because I escaped. And now I beseech you, O King, to have pity on me, for I have suffered much, though, indeed, I have not done harm to any man."

Then King Priam had pity on him and bade them unbind his hands, saying: "Forget your own people; from to-day you are one of us. But tell us now, why did the Greeks make this great Horse of Wood that we see?"

Then Sinon lifted up his hands to the sky and said: "O sun and moon and stars, I call you to witness that I have a good right to tell the secrets of my countrymen. Listen, O King. From the beginning, when the Greeks first came to this place, their hope has been in the help of Minerva (Athené). But she was angry with them for this cause. Ulysses and Diomed made their way into your city, and climbed into the citadel, and killed the guards. And then with hands all bloody from the slaughter, they laid hold of her image and carried it away.[1] It was this that made the goddess angry, that they should dare to touch her with hands stained with blood. I saw with my own eyes how the eyes of the image, when these two brought it into the camp, flashed with anger, and how the drops of sweat stood upon it; yes, and how it leapt three times from the ground, shaking shield and spear.

"Then the prophet said: 'You must go back to Greece, and come again, and begin the war again, if you wish to take the city of Troy'—and this they are doing now; they have gone back to Greece, and they will soon return. Furthermore he said: 'You must make a Horse of Wood to be a peace-offering to Minerva. Make it, I advise you, very great, so that the Trojans may not take it within their walls. For, if they do so take it, then you will never conquer their city. Nay, they will come

---

[1] It was said that as long as the image of Minerva remained in the Temple Troy could not be taken.

to our own land, and lay siege to our cities, and our children will suffer the things which we have sought to bring on them. But if they hurt the thing, then they themselves shall perish.' "

This was the tale that Sinon told, and the Trojans believed it. Nor is this to be wondered at, because the gods themselves took part in deceiving them. For while Laocoön, the priest of Neptune, the same that had thrown his spear at the Horse, was sacrificing a bull on the altar of his god, two great serpents came across the sea from a certain island that was near.

All the Trojans saw them come, with their heads raised high above the water, as is the way of snakes to swim. And when they reached the land they came on straight to the city. Their eyes were red as blood, and blazed like fire, and they made a dreadful hissing with their tongues. The Trojans grew pale with fear, and fled. But the serpents did not turn this way or that, but came straight to the altar at which Laocoön stood, with his two sons by him. And one serpent laid hold on one of the boys, and the other on the other, and they began to devour them. Then the father picked up a sword, and tried to help them, but they caught hold of him, and wound their folds round him. Twice did they wind themselves round his body and his neck, and their heads stood high above his head. And he still tried as hard as he could to tear them away with his hands, and the garlands which he bore, being a priest, dripped with blood. And all the time he cried aloud as a bull roars when the servant of the temple strikes him unskilfully, and he flies from the altar.

And when the serpents had done their work, and both the priest and his sons were dead, then they glided to the hill on which stood the Temple of Minerva, and hid themselves under the feet of the image. And when the Trojans saw this, they said to themselves: "Now Laocoön has suffered the due reward of his deeds, for he threw his spear at the holy thing which belongs to the goddess, and now he is dead and his sons with him."

Then they all cried out together that the Horse of Wood should be drawn into the citadel. So they opened the great gate of the city, pulling down part of the wall that there might be more room, and they put rollers under the feet of the Horse, and they fastened ropes to it. Then they drew it into the city, boys and girls laying hold of the ropes, and singing songs with great joy. And every one thought it a great thing if he could put his hand to a rope.

But there were not wanting signs of evil to come. Four times did the Horse halt as they dragged it, before it passed through the gate, and each time there might have been heard a great clashing of arms within. Also Cassandra opened her mouth, and prophesied the fate of the city; but no one took any heed of her words, for it was her doom that she should speak the truth and not be believed. So the Trojans drew the Horse of Wood into the city. That night they kept a feast to the gods with great joy, not knowing that the end of their city was now close at hand.

Now the Greeks had only made a show of going away. They had taken their ships, indeed, from the place where they had been drawn up on the coast of Troy, but they had not taken them farther than a little island which was close by. There they hid themselves, ready to come back when the signal was given. When it was quite dark the signal was given; a burning torch was raised from the ship of King Agamemnon, which was in the middle of the fleet. When the Greeks saw this they got on board their ships, and rowed across from the island. The moon gave them light, and there was a great calm on the sea. At the same time Sinon opened the door in the Horse of Wood, and let out the chiefs who were hidden in it. And all the time the Trojans were fast asleep, not thinking of any danger.

Now Aeneas, who was the chief hope and stay of the Trojans, had a dream. He dreamt that he saw Hector, the brave chief who had been killed by Achilles. He saw him not as he was in the old times, when he came back from the battle, bringing back the arms of Achilles, which he had taken from Patroclus; not as he was when he was setting fire to the ships, and the Greeks could not stand against him, but as he was when he lay dead. He was covered with dust and blood, and his feet were pierced through with thongs, for Achilles had dragged him at the wheels of his chariot three times round the walls of Troy.

When Aeneas saw him, he forgot all that had happened and said: "Why have you been so long in coming? We have missed you much, and suffered much because you were not here to help us. But why do you look so miserable? Who has given you these wounds?"

To these questions the spirit made no answer. All that he said was this: "Fly, Aeneas, fly, and save yourself from these flames. The enemy is inside our walls, and Troy is lost. The gods would have it so. If any one could have saved the city, I should have done it. But it was not to be. You are now Troy's only hope. Take, then, the gods of your country, and flee across the sea; there some day you shall build another Troy."

And Aeneas woke from his sleep, and while he lay thinking about the dream he heard a great sound, and it seemed to him like to the sound of arms. So he rose from his bed, and climbed on the roof, and looked at the city. Just so a shepherd stands upon a hill and sees, it may be, a great fire blown by a strong wind from the south, and sweeping over the corn-fields, or a flood rushing down from the mountains. As he looked he saw the fire burst out first from one great palace and then from another, till the very sea shone with the light of the burning city.

Then he knew that what Hector had told him in the dream

was true, that the Greeks had made their way into the city. So he put on his armor, though he did not know what he could do. Still, he thought to himself: "I may be able to help Troy in some way; anyhow, I can avenge myself on the enemy; at the least I can die with honor." Just as he was going out of his house the priest of Apollo met him. He was leading his little grandson by the hand, and on his other arm he was carrying an image of the god.

When he saw Aeneas he cried out: "Oh Aeneas, the glory is gone from Troy; the Greeks have the mastery in the city. Armed men have come out of the Horse of Wood, and thousands have got in by the gates, which that traitor Sinon has opened."

While he was speaking, others came up, one of them being young Corœbus, who had come to Troy, hoping to get the prophetess Cassandra for his wife. Aeneas said to them: "Brothers, if you are willing to follow me to the death, come on. You see what has happened. The gods who used to guard our city have gone from it; nowhere is any help to be found. Still, we may die as brave men die in battle. Ay, and it may be that he who is willing to lose his life may save it." Then they all followed him, and they went through the city as fierce as hungry wolves when they come down from the mountains.

The first thing that happened was this. A certain Greek chieftain, who had many men with him, met them, and mistook them for his own countrymen. "Make haste, my friends!" he cried; "why are you so late? We are spoiling the city, and you have only just come from the ships." But when they made no answer, he looked again, and saw that he had fallen among enemies. So a man comes upon the snake among the rocks, and when it rises with great swelling neck, he tries to fly. So the chieftain turned to fly; but the place was strange to him, and he and many of his company were killed.

Then Corœbus said: "We have good luck, my friends. Let us now change our shields and put on the armour of the Greeks. Who can blame us for deceiving these Greeks?"

Then he took the shield and helmet of the Greek chieftain, who had been slain, and his sword also. The others did the same, and so disguising himself he killed many of the Greeks. Others fled to the ships, and some climbed up again into the Horse of Wood.

As they went through the city they met a number of men who were dragging the prophetess Cassandra from the temple of Minerva, in which she had taken refuge. When Corœbus, who, as has been said, hoped to marry Cassandra, saw this, and how she lifted up her eyes to heaven—her hands she

could not lift because they were bound with iron—he was mad
with rage, and rushed at the men, seeking to set the girl free,
and all the other Trojans followed him.

Then there happened a very dreadful thing. There were
many Trojans standing on the roofs of temples and houses close
by; these men, when they saw Corœbus and the others with
the Greek armour on them, which they had taken, took them
for Greeks, and threw spears at them and killed many. And
the Greeks also began to fight more fiercely than before, and
those who had fled to the ships came back again. Altogether
they gathered a great company together, and the Trojans, of
whom there were but very few, could not stand up against them.
Corœbus was killed first of all, and then almost all the others,
good and bad, for it was the day of doom for the Trojans. At
last Aeneas was left with only two companions, one of them
an old man, and the other hardly able to move for a wound
which Ulysses had given him.

As he stood thinking what he should do, he heard a great
shouting, and it seemed to come from the palace of King
Priam. So he said to his companions: "Let us go and see
whether we can help." And when they got there they found
a fiercer battle than any that they had seen before in the city.
Some of the Greeks were trying to climb up the walls. They had
put ladders against them, and they stood on the steps high
up, grasping the edge of the roof in one hand, and holding
their shields with the other. And the Trojans, knowing that
there was no hope of escaping, tore down the battlements and
threw the big stones at the heads of the Greeks. Now Aeneas
knew of a secret way into the palace. By this Hector's wife
Andromaché had been used to come from Hector's palace,
bringing her little boy with her to see his grandfather King
Priam. So he was able to climb up on to the roof, without being
seen by the Greeks, and to join his countrymen who were de-

fending the palace. There was a high tower on the roof, so high that all the city of Troy could be seen from it, and the camp of the Greeks, and the ships. The Trojans broke away the foundations of this tower with bars of iron, and toppled it over, so that it fell upon the Greeks, and killed many of them. But the others pressed on just as fiercely as before, throwing javelins and stones and anything that came to their hands at the Trojans on the roof.

While some were trying to climb up on to the roof, others were breaking down the gates of the palace. The leader of them was the son of Achilles, Pyrrhus by name. He wore shining armour of bronze, and was bright as a great snake which has slept in his hole all the winter, and when the spring begins, comes out with a new shining skin into the sunshine and lifts his head high and hisses with his forked tongue. He had a great battle-axe, which he held in both his hands, and with this he hewed through the doors; the very door-posts he broke down with it, making what one might call a great window, through which could be seen the great palace within, the hall of King Priam and of the kings who had reigned in Troy before him. And those who were inside also could see the armed men who were breaking in, and they made a great cry; and the women wailed and clung to the doors and pillars, and kissed them, because they thought that they should never see them any more.

There were men who had been put to guard the gates, but they could not stop the son of Achilles, for he was as fierce and as strong as his father had been. He and his people were like to a river that is swollen with much rain and bursts its banks, and overflows all the plain. Just so did the Greeks rush into the palace.

When old King Priam saw the enemy in his hall he put on his armour. He had not worn it for many years, so old he was, but now he felt that he must fight for his home. And he took a spear in his hand, and would have gone against the Greeks. But his wife, Queen Hecuba, called to him from the place where she sat. She and her daughter and the wives of her sons had fled to the great altar of the gods of the household, and were clinging to it. They were like to a flock of doves which have been driven by a storm into a wood. The altar stood in an open court which was in the middle of the palace, and a great bay tree stood by, and covered it with its branches. When she saw how her husband had put on his armour, as if he were a young man, she cried to him, saying: "What has bewitched you that you have put on your armour? It is not the sword that can help us to-day; no, not if my own dear Hector, who was the bravest of the brave, were here. It is in the gods and their altars that we must trust. Come and sit with us; here you will be safe, or at least, we shall all die together."

So she made the old man sit down in the midst of them. But lo! there came flying through the hall of the palace one of the sons of the king, Polites by name. Pyrrhus had wounded him, but the lad had fled, and Pyrrhus was close behind with his spear. And just as he came within sight of his father and his mother he fell dead upon the ground.

When King Priam saw this he could not contain himself, but cried aloud, saying: "Now may the gods punish you for this wickedness, you who have killed a son before the eyes of his father and his mother. You say that you are a son of the great Achilles, but when you say it you lie. It was not thus that Achilles treated me. For when he had slain my son Hector, and I went to him to beg the body for burial, he gave it to me for due ransom, and sent me back to my own city without harm."

So did King Priam speak; then he took up a spear and cast it at Pyrrhus, but there was no strength in his blow. It did but shake the shield, not piercing it at all, and falling idly on the ground. Then said the son of Achilles: "Go, tell my father of his unworthy son, and of the wicked deeds which he doeth. And that you may tell him, die!" And as he spoke he caught the old man's white hair with his left hand and dragged him, slipping as he went in the blood of his son, to the altar, and with his right hand he lifted up his sword and drove it, up to the very hilt, into the old man's body. So died King Priam. Once he had ruled over many cities and peoples in the land of Asia, and now, after he had seen his city taken and his palace spoiled, he was slain and his carcass was cast out upon the earth, headless and without a name.

The Return of Odysseus

by Padraic Colum

from *The Adventures of Odysseus*

Odysseus, King of Ithaca, or Ulysses as he is sometimes called, was one of the Greeks who besieged Troy. He angered the sea god Poseidon and, therefore, was not allowed to return home after the capture of Troy. Instead he was forced to wander from place to place always trying to reach Ithaca but never succeeding. Meanwhile, his wife Penelope was besieged by suitors who wanted to marry her and claim Odysseus' throne and fortune. The story of the wanderings of Odysseus and the faithfulness of Penelope is told in the Odyssey, also written by Homer.

Finally after many years Odysseus, Homer tells us, did return to Ithaca and was reunited before he reached home with his son Telemachus. From Telemachus, Odysseus learned of the suitors. He knew that he would be killed if he appeared before them unexpectedly so he went on in disguise. As he wandered about his grounds he found that Eumaeus, the swineherd, and Philoetius, the cattleherd, longed for his return. But they did not recognize him, and neither did Penelope when he spoke to her, supposedly bringing news of Odysseus. Only his old nurse and his faithful dog recognized their master.

THE RETURN OF ODYSSEUS

Padraic Colum

———◆●◆———

WHEN Odysseus was spoken of, the heart of Penelope melted, and tears ran down her cheeks. Odysseus had pity for his wife when he saw her weeping for the man who was even then sitting by her. Tears would have run down his own cheeks only that he was strong enough to hold them back.

Said Penelope, "Stranger, I cannot help but question thee about Odysseus. What raiment had he on when thou didst see him? And what men were with him?"

Said Odysseus, "Lady, it is hard for one so long parted from him to tell thee what thou hast asked. It is now twenty years since I saw Odysseus. He wore a purple mantle that was fastened with a brooch. And this brooch had on it the image of a hound holding a fawn between its forepaws. All the people marvelled at this brooch, for it was of gold, and the fawn and the hound were done to the life. And I remember that there was a henchman with Odysseus—he was a man somewhat older than his master, round-shouldered and black-skinned and curly headed. His name was Eurybates, and Odysseus honoured him above the rest of his company."

When he spoke, giving such tokens of Odysseus, Penelope wept again. And when she had wept for a long time she said:

"Stranger, thou wert made welcome, but now thou shalt be honoured in this hall. Thou dost speak of the garments that Odysseus wore. It was I who gave him these garments, folding them myself and bringing them out of the chamber. And it was I who gave him the brooch that thou hast described. Ah, it was an evil fate that took him from me, bringing him to Troy, that place too evil to be named by me."

Odysseus leaned towards her, and said, "Do not waste thy heart with endless weeping, lady. Cease from lamentation, and lay up in thy mind the word I give thee. Odysseus is near. He has lost all his companions, and he knows not how to come into this house, whether openly or by stealth. I swear it. By the hearth of Odysseus to which I am come, I swear that Odysseus himself will stand up here before the old moon wanes and the new moon is born."

"Ah, no," said Penelope. "Often before have wanderers told me such comfortable things, and I believed them. I know now that thy word cannot be accomplished. But it is time for thee to rest thyself, stranger. My handmaidens will make a bed for thee in the vestibule, and then come to thee and bathe thy feet."

Said Odysseus, "Thy handmaidens would be loathe to touch the feet of a wanderer such as I. But if there is in the house some old wife who has borne such troubles as I have borne, I would have my feet bathed by her."

Said Penelope, "Here is an ancient woman who nursed and tended that hapless man, Odysseus. She took him in her arms in the very hour he was born. Eurycleia, wash the feet of this man, who knew thy lord and mine."

Therefore the nurse, old Euryclea, fetched water, both hot and cold, and brought the bath to the hearth. And standing before Odysseus in the flickering light of the fire, she said, "I will wash thy feet, both for Penelope's sake and for thine own. The heart within me is moved at the sight of thee. Many strangers have come into this hall, but I have never seen one that was so like as thou art to Odysseus."

Said Odysseus, "Many people have said that Odysseus and I favour each other."

His feet were in the water, and she put her hand upon one of them. As she did so, Odysseus turned his face away to the darkness, for it suddenly came into his mind that his nurse, old Eurycleia, might recognize the scar that was upon that foot.

And now, as Eurycleia, his old nurse, passed her hands along the leg, she let his foot drop suddenly. His knee struck against the bath, and the vessel of water was overturned. The nurse touched the chin of Odysseus and she said, "Thou art Odysseus."

She looked to where Penelope was sitting, so that she might

make a sign to her. But Penelope had her eyes turned away. Odysseus put his hand on Eurycleia's mouth, and with the other hand he drew her to him.

"Woman," he whispered. "Say nothing. Be silent, lest mine enemies learn what thou knowest now."

"Silent I'll be," said the nurse Eurycleia. "Thou knowest me. Firm and unyielding I am, and by no sign will I let anyone know that thou hast come under this roof."

So saying she went out of the hall to fetch water in the place of that which had been spilt. She came back and finished bathing his feet. Then Odysseus arranged the rags around his leg to hide the scar, and he drew the bench closer to the fire.

"Ah," said Penelope, "the day of my woe is at hand. I am being forced by my parents to choose a husband from the wooers, and depart from the house of Odysseus."

"And how wilt thou choose from amongst them?" said Odysseus.

"In this way will I make choice," said Penelope. "My husband's great bow is still in the house. The one who can bend that bow, and shoot an arrow through the holes in the backs of twelve axes set one behind the other—him will I choose for my husband."

Said Odysseus, "Thy device is good, Penelope, and some god hath instructed thee to do this. But delay no longer the contest of the bow. Let it be tomorrow."

"Is that thy counsel, O stranger?" said Penelope.

"It is my counsel," said Odysseus.

"I thank thee for thy counsel," she said. "And now farewell, for I must go to my rest. And do thou lie down in the vestibule, in the bed that has been made for thee."

So Penelope spoke, and then she went to her chamber with her handmaidens. And in her bed she thought over all the stranger had told her of Odysseus, and she wept again for him.

In the morning Odysseus stood outside the hall until Telemachus went to him and brought him within to the hall where the wooers were gathered.

Now there was amongst the wooers a man named Ctesippus, and he was the rudest and the roughest of them all. When he saw Telemachus bringing Odysseus within he shouted out, "Here is a guest of Telemachus to whom some gift is due from us. It will be unseemly if he should get nothing to-day. Therefore I will bestow this upon him as a token."

Saying this, Ctesippus took up the foot of a slaughtered ox and flung it full at Odysseus. Odysseus drew back, and the ox's foot struck the wall. Then did Odysseus smile grimly upon the wooers.

Said Telemachus, "Verily, Ctesippus, the cast turned out happily for thyself. For if thou shouldst have struck my guest, there would have been a funeral feast instead of a wedding banquet in thy father's house. Assuredly I should have driven my spear through thee."

All the wooers were silent when Telemachus spoke these bold words. But soon they fell laughing at something one of their number said. The guest from Telemachus' ship, Theoclymenus, was there, and he started up and went to leave the hall.

"Why dost thou go, my guest?" said Telemachus.

"I see the walls and the beams of the roof sprinkled with blood," said Theoclymenus, the second-sighted man. "I hear the voice of wailing. I see cheeks wet with tears. The men before me have shrouds upon them. The courtyard is filled with ghosts."

So Theoclymenus spoke, and all the wooers laughed at the second-sighted man, for he stumbled about the hall as if it were in darkness. Then said one of the wooers, "Lead that man out of the house, for surely he cannot tell day from night."

"I will go from the place," said Theoclymenus. "I see death approaching. Not one of all the company before me will be able to avoid it."

So saying, the second-sighted man went out of the hall. The wooers looking at each other laughed again, and one of them said:

"Telemachus has no luck in his guests. One is a dirty beggar, who thinks of nothing but what he can put from his hand into his mouth, and the other wants to stand up here and play the seer." So the wooers spake in mockery, but neither Telemachus nor Odysseus paid heed to their words, for their minds were bent upon the time when they should take vengeance upon them.

In the treasure-chamber of the house Odysseus' great bow was kept. That bow had been given to him by a hero named Iphitus long ago. Odysseus had not taken it with him when he went to the wars of Troy.

To the treasure-chamber Penelope went. She carried in her hand the great key that opened the doors—a key all of bronze with a handle of ivory. Now as she thrust the key into the locks, the doors groaned as a bull groans. She went within, and saw the great bow upon its peg. She took it down and laid it upon her knees, and thought long upon the man who had bent it.

Beside the bow was its quiver full of bronze-weighted arrows. The servant took the quiver and Penelope took the bow, and they went from the treasure-chamber and into the hall where the wooers were.

When she came in she spoke to the company and said: "Lords of Ithaka and of the islands around: You have come here, each desiring that I should wed him. Now the time has come for me to make my choice of a man from amongst you. Here is how I shall make choice.

"This is the bow of Odysseus, my lord who is no more. Whosoever amongst you who can bend this bow and shoot an arrow from it through the holes in the backs of twelve axes which I shall have set up, him will I wed, and to his house I will go, forsaking the house of my wedlock, this house so filled with treasure and substance, this house which I shall remember in my dreams."

As she spoke Telemachus took the twelve axes and set them upright in an even line, so that one could shoot an arrow through the hole that was in the back of each axe-head. Then Eumæus, the old swineherd, took the bow of Odysseus, and laid it before the wooers.

One of the wooers took up the bow and tried to bend it. But he could not bend it, and he laid it down at the doorway with the arrow beside it. The others took up the bow, and warmed it at the fire, and rubbed it with lard to make it more pliable. As they were doing this, Eumæus, the swineherd, and Philœtius, the cattleherd, passed out of the hall.

Odysseus followed them into the courtyard. He laid a hand on each and said, "Swineherd and cattleherd, I have a word to say to you. But will you keep it to yourselves, the word I say? And first, what would you do to help Odysseus if he should return? Would you stand on his side, or on the side of the wooers? Answer me now from your hearts."

Said Philœtius the cattleherd, "May Zeus fulfill my wish and bring Odysseus back! Then thou shouldst know on whose side I would stand."

And Eumæus said, "If Odysseus should return I would be on his side, and that with all the strength that is in me."

When they said this, Odysseus declared himself. Lifting up his hand to heaven he said, "I am your master, Odysseus. After twenty years I have come back to my own country, and I find that of all my servants, by you two alone is my homecoming desired. If you need see a token that I am indeed Odysseus, look down on my foot. See there the mark that the wild boar left on me in the days of my youth."

Straightway he drew the rags from the scar, and the swineherd and the cattleherd saw it and marked it well. Knowing that it was indeed Odysseus who stood before them, they cast their arms around him and kissed him on the head and shoulders. And Odysseus was moved by their tears, and he kissed their heads and their hands.

As they went back to the hall, he told Eumæus to bring the bow to him as he was bearing it through the hall. He told him, too, to order Eurycleia, the faithful nurse, to bar the doors of the women's apartment at the end of the hall, and to bid the women, even if they heard a groaning and a din, not to come into the hall. And he charged the cattleherd, Philœtius, to bar the gates of the courtyard.

As he went into the hall, one of the wooers, Eurymachus, was striving to bend the bow. As he struggled to do so he groaned aloud:

"Not because I may not marry Penelope do I groan, but because we youths of to-day are shown to be weaklings beside Odysseus, whose bow we can in no way bend."

Then Antinous, the proudest of the wooers, made answer and said, "Why should we strive to bend the bow to-day? Nay, lay the bow aside, Eurymachus, and let the wine-bearers pour us out a cupful each. In the morning let us make sacrifice to the Archer-god, and pray that the bow be fitted to some of our hands."

Then Odysseus came forward and said, "Sirs, you do well to lay the bow aside for to-day. But will you not put the bow into my hands that I may try to bend it and judge for myself whether I have any of the strength that once was mine?"

All of the wooers were angry that a seeming beggar should
attempt to bend the bow that none of their company were able
to bend; Antinous spoke to him sharply and said:

"Thou wretched beggar! Is it not enough that thou art
let into this high hall to pick up scraps, but thou must listen
to our speech and join in our conversation? If thou shouldst
bend that bow we will make short shrift of thee, I promise. We
will put thee on a ship and send thee over to King Echetus, who
will cut thee to pieces and give thy flesh to his hounds."

Old Emmæus had taken up the bow. As he went with it to
Odysseus some of them shouted to him, "Where art thou going
with the bow, thou crazy fellow? Put it down." Eumæus was
confused by their shouts, and he put down the bow.

Then Telemachus spoke to him and said, "Eumæus, beware
of being the man who served many masters." Eumæus, hearing these words, took it up again and brought it to Odysseus,
and put the bow into his hands.

As Odysseus stood in the doorway of the hall, the bow in his
hands, and with the arrows scattered at his feet, Eumæus went
to Eurycleia, and told her to bar the door of the women's apartment at the back. Then Philœtius, the cattleherd, went out of
the hall and barred the gates leading out of the courtyard.

For long Odysseus stood with the bow in his hands, handling
it as a minstrel handles a lyre when he stretches a cord or
tightens a peg. Then he bent the great bow; he bent it without
an effort, and at his touch the bow-string made a sound that

was like the cry of a swallow. The wooers seeing him bend that mighty bow felt, every man of them, a sharp pain at the heart. They saw Odysseus take up an arrow and fit it to the string. He held the notch, and he drew the string, and he shot the bronze-weighted arrow straight through the holes in the back of the axe-heads.

Then as Eumæus took up the axes, and brought them outside, he said, "Thou seest, lord Telemachus, that thy guest does not shame thee through foolish boasting. I have bent the bow of Odysseus, and I have shot the arrow aright. But now it is time to provide the feast for the lords who woo thy lady mother. While it is yet light, the feast must be served to them, and with the feast they must have music and the dance."

Saying this he nodded to Telemachus, bending his terrible brows. Telemachus instantly girt his sword upon him and took his spear in his hand. Outside was heard the thunder of Zeus. And now Odysseus had stripped his rags from him and was standing upright, looking a master of men. The mighty bow was in his hands, and at his feet were scattered many bronze-weighted arrows.

"It is ended," Odysseus said, "my trial is ended. Now will I have another mark." Saying this, he put the bronze-weighted arrow against the string of the bow, and shot at the first of his enemies.

It was at Antinous he pointed the arrow—at Antinous who was even then lifting up a golden cup and who was smiling, with death far from his thoughts. Odysseus aimed at him, and smote him with the arrow in the throat and the point passed out clean through his neck. The cup fell from his hands and Antinous fell dead across the table. Then did all the wooers raise a shout, threatening Odysseus for sending an arrow astray. It did not come into their minds that this stranger-beggar had aimed to kill Antinous.

But Odysseus shouted back to them, "Ye dogs, ye that said in your hearts that Odysseus would never return to his home, ye that wasted my substance, and troubled my wife, and injured my servants; ye who showed no fear of heaven, nor of the just judgments of men; behold Odysseus returned, and know what death is being loosed on you!"

Then Eurymachus shouted out, "Friends, this man will not hold his hands, nor cease from shooting with the bow, until all of us are slain. Now must we enter into the battle with him. Draw your swords and hold up the tables before you for shields and advance upon him."

But even as he spoke Odysseus, with a terrible cry, loosed an arrow at him and shot Eurymachus through the breast. He let the sword fall from his hand, and he too fell dead upon the floor.

One of the band rushed straight at Odysseus with his sword in hand. But Telemachus was at hand, and he drove his spear through this man's shoulders. Then Telemachus ran quickly to a chamber where there were weapons and armour lying. The swineherd and the cattleherd joined him, and all three put armour upon them. Odysseus, as long as he had arrows to defend himself, kept shooting at and smiting the wooers. When all the arrows were gone, he put the helmet on his head and took up the shield that Telemachus had brought, and the two great spears.

But now Melanthius, the goatherd—he who was the enemy of Odysseus, got into the chamber where the arms were kept, and brought out spears and shields and helmets, and gave them to the wooers. Seeing the goatherd go back for more arms, Telemachus and Eumæus dashed into the chamber, and caught him and bound him with a rope, and dragged him up near the roof-beams, and left him hanging there. Then they closed and bolted the door, and stood on guard.

Many of the wooers lay dead upon the floor of the hall. Now one who was called Agelaus stood forward, and directed the wooers to cast spears at Odysseus. But not one of the spears they cast struck him, for Odysseus was able to avoid them all.

And now he directed Telemachus and Eumæus and Philœtius to cast their spears. When they cast them with Odysseus, each one struck a man, and four of the wooers fell down. And again Odysseus directed his following to cast their spears, and again they cast them, and slew their men. They drove those who remained from one end of the hall to the other, and slew them all.

Straightway the doors of the women's apartment were flung open, and Eurycleia appeared. She saw Odysseus amongst the bodies of the dead, all stained with blood. She would have cried out in triumph if Odysseus had not restrained her. "Rejoice within thine own heart," he said, "but do not cry aloud, for it is an unholy thing to triumph over men lying dead. These men the gods themselves have overcome, because of their own hard and unjust hearts."

As he spoke the women came out of their chambers, carrying torches in their hands. They fell upon Odysseus and embraced him and clasped and kissed his hands. A longing came over him to weep, for he remembered them from of old—every one of the servants who were there.

Eurycleia, the old nurse, went to the upper chamber where Penelope lay in her bed. She bent over her and called out, "Awake, Penelope, dear child. Come down and see with thine own eyes what hath happened. The wooers are overthrown. And he whom thou hast ever longed to see hath come back. Odysseus, thy husband, hath returned. He hath slain the proud wooers who have troubled thee for so long."

But Penelope only looked at the nurse, for she thought that her brain had been turned.

Still Eurycleia kept on saying, "In very deed Odysseus is here. He is that guest whom all the wooers dishonour in the hall."

Then hearing Eurycleia say these words, Penelope sprang out of bed and put her arms round the nurse's neck. "O tell me—if what thou dost say be true—tell me how this stranger slew the wooers, who were so many."

"I did not see the slaying," Eurycleia said, "but I heard the groaning of the men as they were slain. And then I found Odysseus standing amongst many dead men, and it comforted my heart to see him standing there like a lion aroused. Come with me now, lady, that you may both enter into your heart's delight—you that have suffered so much of affliction. Thy Lord hath come alive to his own hearth, and he hath found his wife and his son alive and well."

"Ah no!" said Penelope, "ah no, Odysseus hath not returned. He who hath slain the wooers is one of the deathless gods, come down to punish them for their injustice and their hardheartedness. Odysseus long ago lost the way of his returning, and he is lying dead in some far-off land."

"No, no," said Eurycleia. "I can show thee that it is Odysseus indeed who is in the hall. On his foot is the scar that the tusk of a boar gave him in the old days. I spied it when I was washing his feet last night, and I would have told thee of it, but he clapped a hand across my mouth to stop my speech. Lo, I stake my life that it is Odysseus, and none other who is in the hall below."

Saying this she took Penelope by the hand and led her from the upper chamber into the hall. Odysseus was standing by a tall pillar. He waited there for his wife to come and speak to him. But Penelope stood still and made no steps towards him.

Then said Telemachus, "Mother, can it be that thy heart is so hard? Here is my father, and thou wilt not go to him nor question him at all."

Said Penelope, "My mind is amazed and I have no strength to speak, nor to ask him aught, nor even to look on him face to face. If this is indeed Odysseus who hath come home, a place has to be prepared for him."

Then Odysseus spoke to Telemachus and said, "Go now to the bath, and make thyself clean of the stains of battle. I will stay and speak with thy lady mother."

"Strange lady," said he to Penelope, "is thy heart indeed so hard? No other woman in the world, I think, would stand so aloof from her husband who, after so much toil and so many trials, has come back after twenty years to his own hearth. Is there no place for me here, and must I again sleep in the stranger's bed?"

Said Penelope, "In no stranger's bed wilt thou lie, my lord. Come, Eurycleia. Set up for him his own bedstead outside his bed-chamber."

Then Odysseus said to her, speaking in anger: "How comes it that my bed can be moved to this place and that? Not a bed of that kind was the bed I built for myself. Knowest thou not how I built my bed? First, there grew up in the courtyard an olive tree. Round that olive tree I built a chamber, and I roofed it well and I set doors to it. Then I sheared off all the light wood on the growing olive tree, and I rough-hewed the trunk with the adze, and I made the tree into a bed post. Beginning with this bed post I wrought a bedstead, and when I finished it, I inlaid it with silver and ivory. Such was the bed I built for myself, and such a bed could not be moved to this place or that."

Then did Penelope know assuredly that the man who stood before her was indeed her husband, the steadfast Odysseus— none other knew of where the bed was placed, and how it had been built. Penelope fell a-weeping and she put her arms round his neck.

"O Odysseus, my lord," she said, "be not angry with thy wife. Always the fear was in my heart that some guileful stranger should come here professing to be Odysseus, and that I should take him to me as my husband. How terrible such a thing would be! But now my heart is freed from all doubts. Be not angry with me, Odysseus, for not throwing myself on thy neck, as the women of the house did."

Then husband and wife wept together, and Penelope said, "It was the gods did this to us, Odysseus—the gods who grudged that we should have the joy of the days of our youth."

Next they told each other of things that happened in the twenty years they were apart; Odysseus speaking of his own toils and sorrows, and Penelope telling what she had endured at the hands of the wooers. And as they told tales, one to the other, slumber came upon them, and the dawn found them sleeping side by side.

Attila the Conqueror

by Kate Seredy

from *The White Stag*

Nimrod, the mighty hunter, had two sons, Hunor and Magyar. Hadur was their god. He appeared to them, when it was necessary, in the form of a white stag. The people of Nimrod, and later of Hunor and Magyar, lived, according to legend, in Europe, somewhere north and east of the Danube River. Life for them was hard and full of struggle, and they longed for a new and promised land.

Just before Nimrod died, he foretold that someday a great leader would come who would be called "The Scourge of Hadur." Many years later the son of Hunor, Bendeguz the White Eagle, became the leader of the people now called the Huns. As he led them across Europe, they conquered all in their path. Bendeguz was married and much in love with his wife, but she died the night their son Attila was born. From that moment on, Bendeguz, and Attila after him, lived only for war and conquest. With their coming and the coming of the Huns, the Roman Empire fell, and the dark ages began in Europe.

The deeds of Attila are told not only in Hungary where people still claim proud descent from the Huns of old, but also in the great German epic the Niebelungenlied.

ATTILA THE CONQUEROR

Kate Seredy

———◄●►———

ON a summer night in the year 408 a flaming red comet
appeared over Europe striking terror into the hearts of
all who saw it; a menacing omen, a flaming red comet
shaped like a tremendous eagle with a sword in its talons.

In that year, when the walls of Rome were cracking before
the onslaught of the Goths led by King Alaric; when the Vandals were invading Hispania led by King Gunderic; when
Roman Britain was fighting a losing war against the terrible
barbarian pirates, the Saxons—on a summer night of that year
was Attila born.

And on that night did pity, tenderness, and love die forever
in the heart of Bendeguz. The thousands who had heard his
reckless challenge and had witnessed the dreadful punishment
could and did shed tears of pity for him. The eyes of Bendeguz
were dry, his face a cold mask, for the heart within him had
turned to stone. He did not see the hand of Hunor held out to
him with pity and love. He did not feel the restraining hand
of Damos as he made his way once more to the now cold and
dark altar. He did not see that even the most reckless and ruthless of his men covered their eyes and fell to their knees when
he again mounted the steps and lifted his face to the sky, when
he uttered these words:

"Hadur, Powerful God, Thou hast indeed turned the sword against me. Thy sword, Hadur, not mine! But Thou hast given me a scourge in its place and I swear to Thee, I, Bendeguz the White Eagle, that I shall use that scourge, that I shall make it into the most dreadful weapon ever known to men. Thou hast given me a son, Hadur, he will be that scourge! My son, Attila the Red Eagle, the Scourge of God!"

And at that hour, Flavius Honorius, the Roman Emperor, gazed out of the window of his palace in Milan long and fearfully at the flaming red comet. He knew that the great structure of the Roman Empire was trembling and cracking under his feet . . . might this fearful omen herald the end? From afar came the sound of tolling church bells, from below came the sound of people praying in the streets and the droning voice of a friar:

"Woe unto you! for ye build the sepulchres of the prophets, and your fathers killed them. . . . That the blood of all the prophets, which was shed from the foundation of the world, may be required of this generation . . . verily I say unto you, It shall be required of this generation."

"And there shall be signs in the sun, and in the moon, and in the stars; and upon the earth distress of all nations, with perplexity; the sea and the waves roaring; men's hearts failing them for fear and for looking after those things which are coming on the earth: for the powers of heaven shall be shaken. . . ."

At that hour Christians and pagans all over Europe prayed that this dreadful thing approaching from the East might be averted from them.

And in a dark tent, between the river Rha and the river Tanais, a new born child cried bitterly, cried for comfort and warmth and tender love, cried for the things he was never to know.

Early in the fall of that year in the month the Romans

called September the great army of the Huns stood ready. It was night. Thick white mist hung close to the ground, but above, countless stars glittered in the dark blue sky. The full white moon looked down on what seemed to be the reflection of countless stars on the ocean of white mist: glittering tips of helmets, spears, and javelins, phalanx upon phalanx of them. The great army of the Huns was waiting, listening to the last words of old Magyar whom they were leaving forever. For the Magyars refused to go on farther, refused to follow Bendeguz whose face was stone, whose eyes were ice, and whose voice was like the lash of a whip.

The stars and the moon were listening too and the moon summoned a wisp of cloud to hide its face behind it. The glistening drops of water on the hard faces of warriors might have been drops of rain from that cloud, might have been their own tears—who knows?

When the moon looked again, the sparkling helmets and spears were hidden in the rising mist. All the moon could see was the flag of the Red Eagle floating in the wind, moving slowly westward.

Slowly, very slowly, for the whole of Europe rose up in arms against that flag. More and more armies gathered to check, to stave off the implacable doom that poured out of Scythia. The fertile prairies, the plowed fields, and green pastures of Samatia became a battleground where a fresh field of glittering spears grew for each that death had mowed down, where brooks and rivers ran red with blood.

Samatians, Dacians, Goths, Franks, and Romans rallied in desperate effort to stop the Huns, in vain. Month after month, year after year, the Huns pressed forward gaining two victories for each minor defeat.

"They are not human!" spread the rumor in the camps of opposing armies. Survivors of battles and escaped prisoners whispered strange tales, tales which struck terror into the hearts of listeners. Tales about the man Bendeguz who knew no pity and would tolerate none; Bendeguz whose face was stone, whose eyes were ice, and who would ride into the most frightful slaughters always without a sword, without armor, carrying a small child on his shoulders. Later there were tales about Attila, the child, whose narrow slanting amber-colored eyes were like the eyes of an eagle, who, always in the van riding a coal-black horse, laughed at death, for death was powerless against him; Attila whose shrill voice rang out above the tumults of thousands like the scream of an eagle.

"The Huns call him the Red Eagle," ran the rumor far and wide, "and his father calls him Attila the Scourge of God."

"The Scourge of God!" echoed the cry from land to land.

"Flagellum Deii," whispered Pope Innocentius and sent his priests into far countries to preach Christianity with renewed zeal, to remind people of the words of the angry Lord:

"The lion is come up from his thicket, and the destroyer of the Gentiles is on his way; he is gone forth from his place to make thy land desolate; and thy cities shall be laid waste without an inhabitant.

"For this gird you with sackcloth, lament and howl: for the fierce anger of the Lord is not turned back from us."

And indeed it seemed as if the Huns were superhuman. Joint armies of many nations became panic-stricken rabble, wrecked, scattered, trodden down to the dirt by this merciless avalanche of horsemen. The Huns themselves were like possessed fanatics in whose souls the vision of the promised land burned with such a blinding white flame that they could not even see the perils on their path. Their eyes were on Attila, Attila the fearless, Attila the invulnerable. They feared Bendeguz but they worshiped his child. To them he was a symbol—a promise fulfilled by Hadur—he was their great Red Eagle.

And the child Attila, who from the moment of his tragic birth had been deprived of love, tenderness, and comfort, grew hard as steel in body and soul. He had learned not to cry when he was but a few days old. Crying did not help, crying only brought a voice colder than the winds chilling his small body, sharper than the pangs of hunger. The only lullabies he had ever known were rousing war songs, battlecries, and the whine of flying arrows. His only toys were sharp weapons and he soon learned not to cut himself, for if he did and whimpered with pain those icy eyes would freeze the whimpers in his throat.

He was hardly old enough to walk when he was strapped into the saddle and made to ride at the side of his father for long, weary hours. He had learned to handle bow and arrow before his speech had lost its childish lisp. His young muscles stretched, grew taut and strong, and if they sometimes ached almost unbearably no one ever knew it. The first words he learned were the thousand-times-repeated words of Bendeguz:

"Fear is sin. Weakness is sin." These words became his credo, a hard core around which he built his life.

Only after he had learned never to expect help or sympathy from anyone, did Bendeguz allow him to mingle with the men. Only then, listening to the tales and songs of the warriors, did he learn of the past of his people and of the future they believed in. And when he heard the story of that tragic night when he was born, a strange new feeling flooded his heart; love and compassion for this silent cold man who was his father. And a great determination surged up in him: to find that land, to find the sword of Hadur, to make the world kneel to its power.

From then on the child was a man, the Red Eagle who laughed at death. Death could not touch him, he had a promise to fulfill.

He was fifteen years old then. No one knew what had

changed boy into man almost overnight, least of all Bendeguz. He only saw that Attila was taking more and more of the burdens of leadership on his own shoulders, that he held the tremendous army in a grip far stronger than his own had ever been. The way of the serpent was not the Huns' way; they hated planned campaigns, feigned retreats, stealthy midnight attacks. Now, for Attila, they learned them all and scored more victories than ever before. They still loved the times best when Hun trumpets blared forth an open challenge to the enemy and Attila, clad in scarlet from head to foot, mounted on his coalblack steed, awesome like the god of war, led them into a whirlwind attack. Then indeed did they turn into demons tearing through the enemies' iron ranks as wind tears through a film of rain, demons roaring with laughter as the enemy scattered, scampering for the shelter of scrub and woods, a bloodspeckled dust-covered herd trying to escape the doom of trampling hoofs and swinging swords.

At night after these thundering attacks they flaunted their wounds, made light of their losses, and roared their exultation in triumphant songs.

One night, after one of these sweeping victories, old Bendeguz went to the tent of his son. Attila was asleep, his great body relaxed, a thin smile of triumph still lingering around his lips. Bendeguz stood for a long time looking down at him with a growing feeling of awe such as he had not known before. And then, for the night was cold, he removed his own cloak and laid it gently on his sleeping son. Attila stirred and Bendeguz left the tent quietly, puzzled at his own tender gesture.

He walked slowly to a near-by hill and up its gentle slope. The sleeping camp spread out below him and above stars trembled in the sky. He was alone in the misty night, seemingly in the center of the immense circle formed by starlit earth and star-spangled sky. Heaven and earth were silent, breathlessly, expectantly silent. And old Bendeguz, alone on the hill, alone with his God, sank slowly to his knees.

"Hadur," he sighed. "Mighty Hadur, I have kept my promise. I have made my son into the most dreadful weapon ever known to men. And now I am frightened at my own handiwork. Twenty years!" he cried, his voice suddenly loud. "Twenty years of war and millions of dead behind him . . . was it Thy will, Hadur? Will he ever wash himself clean of blood with the waters of the promised land?"

The cold stars trembled and the earth remained silent. But from above, from beyond the stars came a voice and at the sound of it the crust of ice suddenly melted from the heart of old Bendeguz. A voice sweet, soft, and so low that his ears did not hear it. He heard it with his heart.

> Lead me westward,
> White Eagle of the Moon, oh, lead me
> On silvery rays of the Moon—
> Westward I long to fly. . . .
> Westward . . . always westward.

The wild mountains of Altain-Ula were but a legend to the Huns, the years by the misty blue lake only a fading memory. The past lived in songs, the present in their flashing swords, and the future in their hearts. The future was "a land between two great rivers, surrounded by mountains."

Mountains. But they did not know what mountains were. Since the tribe had left the blue lake their path had led through deserts, plains, prairies—flat or gently rolling land where their eagle eyes could sweep the blue horizon, where they could see the ponderous iron-clad armies of the enemy advancing slowly, where they always had the advantage over them, mounted as they were on swift prairie-bred horses.

And then, after half a century of warfare, when Attila was

twenty-five years old, it seemed as if at last the great armies of Europe were exhausted. During the summer and fall of that year the Huns found less and less opposition. They were in eastern Dacia by late winter, having crossed the rivers Tyras (Dniester) and Pyretrus (Prut) at their lowest ebb.

Westward . . . thundering westward now like a wave lifting its crest. Warriors more than grains of sand or blades of grass on the plains. Under the hoofs of their horses the snow-covered frozen ground groaned and the icy air echoed with their shouts:

"Westward with Attila!"

Like a wave lifting its crest to hurl against a rock and fall back, its great power shattered into myriads of sparkling atoms, like a wave rushing on blindly, did they hurl themselves against a barrier, the great impassable sheer walls of the Carpathian Mountains.

Before them stretched the mountains in a tremendous arch, cliff after cliff, peak upon peak, icy, formidable, without a visible break anywhere. And behind them, closing in slowly, confidently, like the jaws of a steel trap sure of its prey, came the enemy.

Day after day Attila sent out scouts to find a pass across the mountains. The men went without a murmur into the icy wilderness so strange to them where wolves howled and treacherous chasms waited for the unwary and those who returned at all returned with the words:

"There is no way across."

And listening to the deep rumble of the ground, watching the ring of campfires across the white plains drawing closer and closer every night, Attila knew that there was no way back. That steel trap fashioned with cunning and hate and the lust for revenge was closing in on them; it was more inexorable than the icy walls of the mountains.

For days the weather had been growing steadily colder. The

sun was hiding behind leaden clouds heavy with snow. The Huns had no more wood for fires; the rocky cliffs around them were barren of trees. People huddled close together for a little warmth—silent, miserable, puzzled.

In the gray dusk of the seventh day Bendeguz and Attila were sitting alone in an icy tent. There was no need for words, there were no words to express what they felt. The impending doom of their people and their own helplessness tore at them with claws more vicious than the claws of the numbing cold. There was no hope in the heart of Attila, to him the future seemed darker than the thickening night.

Bendeguz was watching his son's face with a growing sense of apprehension. Those slanting amber-colored eagle eyes were mere slits now, slits through which he could see despair change into defiance and defiance into blazing fury. The sinewy hands of Attila were working, opening and clenching into terrible fists, and suddenly he was on his feet, his head thrown back, on his face a wretched semblance of a smile and his voice a tragic parody of laughter.

"The Red Eagle . . . look at me now, oh . . ."

"Attila!" snapped the voice of Bendeguz like the lash of a whip and his old eyes blazed again with an icy flame. "Attila, kill the snake of doubt in your soul, crush the worms of fear in your heart and mountains will move out of your way and your foes will become less than a handful of dust before your sword. Attila—pray, but do not challenge! Be strong, my son. Trust yourself and the god in your heart."

The tortured face of Attila relaxed. He laid his arm around the shoulders of Bendeguz.

"Forgive me, Father," he whispered. "Your faith is greater than mine."

"Yes, my son," sighed Bendeguz and his voice was heavy with memories, "it is, now." His steady gaze held the eyes of his

son and a great, understanding silence fell upon them both.

Outside snow hissed against the tent and the wind moaned mournfully. Attila lifted his head.

"Listen, Father, listen to that wind. No!" he cried. "It is not the wind—people are calling my name. Listen . . ."

"Attila . . . Attila . . ." came the cry of many voices. "Attila!"

He tore the tentflap open and the wind smote him with violence. Dark shapes of men were tumbling through the tearing flood of snow.

"Attila," gasped the first to reach him, "LOOK!"

For a moment he could see only the mad whirl of snowflakes and then he saw, luminously white against the white of the snow, standing still like a majestic statue, glowing with an unearthly light . . . the White Stag.

Attila whipped around and swept a bugle from the tent.

"To saddle! To saddle!" blared the bugle above the howls of the gale, and others took up the call in the distance.

"Follow the Stag!" cried Attila, leaping into the saddle.

"Follow the Stag!" echoed the mountains.

"Follow the Stag!" howled the wind.

The White Stag moved ahead of them, now slowly, now swiftly, like a shimmering will-o'-the-wisp, always just within sight but never letting them nearer, leading them safely over treacherous icy expanses, across deep drifts of snow. Attila and Bendeguz were in the van, behind them the tremendous cavalcade breaking a path wide and safe for the pack-horses and wagons to follow. No one knew whither the miraculous Stag was leading them—the White Stag of Hun legends—the Stag of Hunor and Magyar. Perhaps it was their own faith they were following now as always, faith in the guiding hand of Hadur the Powerful God. Faith smoothed the path under the stumbling feet of their horses, faith gave them strength to ride through the buffeting wind and whirlpools of stinging snow into the unknown.

Gradually the storm abated. Ahead of them was still night but in the east the sky grew gray with waking light. And then they saw that the Stag had led them into a winding defile between towering peaks, a deep secret gorge eaten through the rocks by a rivulet. To the left and right were the overhanging cliffs, leaning over the gorge curiously like giants leaning down to watch a procession of ants. A faint green light hovered above the cliffs, then the pale golden rays of the rising sun poured into the gorge. The pass widened, rocks and cliffs drew back and gave way to gentle wooded slopes.

The White Stag was hardly visible now, in the golden daylight it seemed to have lost all substance and become light against light. Attila and Bendeguz reined in their horses and watched that shining radiance until it was no more. Then they drew aside waiting for those behind them to pass. For hours the immense cavalcade poured forth from the gorge flooding the sunlit westerly slopes of the mountains, winding like a giant dragon amid trees and scrub. The slopes were a billowing sea of spears and the excited voices of the multitudes pulsed like the rushing of waves.

The sun reached its noonday height when the last heavy wagons arrived. After them the cavernous mouth of the gorge gaped empty; the Huns were across the barrier.

And on the other side of the Carpathians the blizzard raged for days. The east wind swept snow against the mountains like a gigantic broom, sweeping deep valleys in the snow on the ground, forming new ridges of drifts, covering the broken path of the Huns, and hiding, perhaps forever, the secret entrance to the pass.

"What enchanted land is this?" asked Attila of each golden dawn and every scarlet sunset as they advanced toward the west. The slim legs of his black steed fairly danced as he rode swiftly through the forest and field, his eyes scanning the ever-changing beauty of a land the like of which he had never seen before.

"What enchanted land is this," wondered old Bendeguz riding beside his son, "a land like an immense green bowl surrounded by mountains, warmed by the sun, sheltered from the cold?"

Behind them rolled the great army, their weapons and helmets glittering in the sunlight, in the moonlight.

"What enchanted land is this?" they thought as they rode through forests rich in game, across rivers alive with fish.

Spring had met them on the way and flung a glorious carpet of flowers under their feet as if spring were welcoming long-awaited friends. Winter and hostile armies were locked out by those gray rocky walls which had so miraculously opened to let them through. The few small tribes who inhabited this land showed no ill-will.

What enchanted land is this where new riches, new beauty, spread out before them every hour, riches and beauty cupped together under a laughing blue sky; where the joy of life and peace trembled in each opening bud; where the song of whispering breeze and gurgling brooks had the magic power to banish memories of bloodshed? Only seven days had passed since they had crossed the Carpathians and the despair of that stormy night seemed seven life-times away.

"A land, rich in game and green pastures, between two great rivers rich in fish, surrounded by mountains . . ." the legendary words of Nimrod chimed like bells of hope in the heart of Attila when, after crossing the river Pathissus, his swift-riding scouts returned and told him that within a day's journey to the west there was another wide river, the Danubius. He decided to let his people rest for a while.

All that day men and women worked joyously, happily, putting up tents, preparing for a great spring festival, a festival of thanksgiving to Hadur. They built an altar, the first altar to Hadur since they had left the Magyars. It was ready by sundown, a great altar carefully built; it stood like a monument of faith on the crest of a solitary hill above the rolling green plains.

Night fell, softly spreading its wings of silence over the sleeping camp. Sentry-fires glowed for a while then closed their eyes and only the stars, vigilant sentinels of the night, kept watch over the earth. They watched as the ghost-hour crept in among the tents trailing its mantle of dreams. They watched when, in the deep silence of the ghost-hour, a lone man, a tall majestic figure wrapped in a white cloak, walked slowly to the altar. The stars caught a glimpse of scarlet under the white cloak and they knew who the man was. They watched as the man before whose sword a continent trembled sank to his knees and touched his forehead to the cold stones. They listened and heard his prayers but the stars kept their silence, for it was not for them to answer.

Between the stars and the man, shadows passed on silent white wings; white herons returning from the south now that the long winter was over. They passed silently and when at last the man arose and lifted his eyes to the sky, the herons were gone. He only saw a single wispy white feather as it came drifting down, its edges pure silver in the starlight. It touched his upturned face and came to rest over his heart, and then he knew that his prayers had been heard and would be granted.

Before dawn people began to gather for the festival. They came afoot and on horseback from all directions, for the tribe was so numerous now that the forest of their tents stretched farther than eyes could see. Men, women, and children came bringing gifts to Hadur; single spring blossoms clutched in the tiny fists of babies, battleworn shields, jeweled swords and helmets, treasured possessions of old warriors. They came and laid their gifts around the altar, then joined the ever-growing crowd below the hill.

Old Bendeguz came, lighted the fire on the altar and stood waiting, his face turned toward the east where Attila's tent glowed like a giant red flower on the green grass. The dark sky behind the distant blue mountains grew luminous with the promise of sunrise. A murmur of admiration arose from the waiting crowd, for just as the first flaming arrow of the new day shot upward from the rising sun, they saw Attila riding toward them all red and gold against the glowing sky. His shining helmet caught the light behind him and it seemed as if he were wearing a golden crown. His ambercolored eyes looked straight ahead and the light in them matched the light of the sun.

There was no one among his people so silently watching his approach who would not have died a thousand deaths for him, their Red Eagle, greatest of all leaders. He was more than a leader, he was their king and he looked a god with the golden crown of the rising sun around his head.

A small girl tore her hand from her mother's fingers and ran toward Attila, toward all this shining glory, with outstretched arms. She ran, her little laughing face upturned, her small bare feet twinkling in the smooth grass. Attila dismounted and waited, smiling back at her, when the child stumbled and fell. She cried out and held up a bleeding hand to him and Attila, whose sword had dealt death to thousands, bent down to comfort the child.

Then, while he kneeled beside her, the sharp glint of metal caught his eyes, a curious, fiery glint. He reached for it, and his fingers closed on the hilt of a sword, deeply imbedded in the soil. It gave to the pull of his mighty arm and he looked at it with a growing sense of awe. It was a Hun sword, straight and slim, and on the smooth surface of its blade was the chased image of a flying eagle.

His face grew pale. Holding the sword on the palms of his hands, he walked slowly up to the altar, blind to the crowd thronging around him, his eyes never leaving the face of his father. He saw that face grow as white as his own, he saw the strong lips tremble and he heard the hoarse choked whisper.

"The sword of Hadur."

The words echoed from the lips of thousands.

"The sword of Hadur."

Slowly he turned and laid one arm around the bent old shoulders of Bendeguz. In his right hand he held the sword and lifted it high above his head, pointing straight to the morning sky. His eagle eyes gazed unflinchingly into the sun and his voice rose triumphant like a bugle cry of victory:

"Upon this altar of Hadur, our Powerful God, with His sword in my hand, I swear to Hadur above, to the Sun in the

east, to the Moon in the west, I swear to the stars in the north and the stars in the south, to protect and hold this land against all powers on earth, for my people."

Then he mounted to the highest step of the altar and slashed the air with the sword—to east, to west, to north, to south, and stood again facing the sun, the rising flames of the fire behind him like great flaming wings, the sword in his upraised arm pointing to the sky. He stood, King of the Promised Land, Attila the Conqueror.

Beowulf Conquers Grendel

by Zenuid A. Rogozim

adapted from *Seigfried and Beowulf*

Beowulf, one of the earliest of English heroes, had three main adventures. The first, the slaying of the monster Grendel, is told here. Following his battle with Grendel, Beowulf conquered Grendel's mother, and, later, paid with his life for a victory over an evil fire-dragon. The tale as we read it today comes from a ninth or a tenth century manuscript, carefully kept in the British Museum; but it was probably told as long ago as the fifth century.

As this story opens, Beowulf and his men are approaching the home of Hrothgar, King of Denmark, whose land Grendel has devastated. Beowulf has heard of the monster and has made a long journey to fight against him.

BEOWULF CONQUERS GRENDEL

Zenuid A. Rogozim

———◆•◆———

THE ROAD TO Hrothgar's hall was stone-paven, and so straight there was no need of a guide. Beowulf and his noble companions strode boldly forward, their burnished corslets shining, the iron rings of their mail shirt clanging as they marched. They glanced not to the right nor to the left until, at last, they reached the strong, sad walls of Heorot. There, before the entrance, they filled their eyes with all that lay about and waited in quiet dignity for a greeting from King Hrothgar.

Their coming had not gone unobserved, and soon an officer appeared.

"I am," he said in explanation, "Hrothgar's herald and esquire. Though I know not the reason for thy coming, never saw I foreigners of loftier mien. I think that ye must seek to visit Hrothgar not out of some desperate fortune, but bound on some high undertaking."

At this Beowulf arose and replied with gallant bearing:

"We are Hygelac's own table-fellows. My name is Beowulf. I will myself expound mine errand to thy lord, if he deign to admit us to his presence."

The officer, Wulfgar by name, hastened then to the place where Hrothgar sat, old and hoary, and bent with grief, amid his despondent warriors. Quickly did the trusted herald pour out the story of all that he had heard and seen, of the valiant guests who waited now without the hall. "Give them a friendly reception," he advised. "In the deep distress of these sorry times, any change must be for the better, and every stranger must bring hope."

The weary king brightened at the words, for he knew well the deeds of Beowulf. In truth he himself had been companion to the father of the young lord once in the long-gone days of youth. It pleased him now to recall the joy and the renown he once had known.

"This son," he said, "I mind him well. I knew him when he was a page; and now he hath grown into a campaigner of great reputation. It is said that he hath the strength of thirty men in the handgrip of one hand. Surely God of his grace hath sent him to us in our great need. Bid him and his men, one and all, into my presence straight, with every martial honor. Say to them moreover, that they are welcome."

Wulfgar, rejoicing in the word, took the royal message to the waiting guests and ushered them into the royal presence. In full warlike equipment they went, helm on head, sword on hip. Beowulf, tall and commanding, his corslet of cunningly-linked mail shining as a network of light, took his stand at once before the king. With firm eye and becoming assurance, he spoke at length of what was nearest to his heart and to the hearts of all the Danes.

"To Hrothgar hail! I am King Hygelac's cousin-thane. From Gothland have I come with these well-tried companions. All that ye suffer here from Grendel was of late revealed to us. As we sat by our own fireside, seafaring men told us how that this hall, this most princely of all strongholds, standeth useless and empty from dark to dawn, from the time the star of day is first hid from view until its light again breaks full upon the land.

Then did my people, the wisest and best among them, urge me to visit thee, O royal Hrothgar. They knew the strength of mine arm; time and again they had seen me return from the field battered by foes, but never beaten. Five monsters I have bound on land, and in the waves I have slain many a sea monster in the nighttime. And now I am bound to champion thy quarrel, O King, against Grendel, the evil giant.

"But one petition I have, which thou, O Shelter of the Danes, wilt not refuse to one who is come from far to serve thee; it is that I may have the task alone, I and my band of earls, to purge Heorot. And as I have learned that the terrible one, out of sheer boastfulness, despises the use of weapons, so I, too, will forego them. I will bear not sword, nor spear, nor broad shield to my battle with him; but with handgrip alone will I meet him, foe to foe, and him of the two whom the Lord doometh, let grim death take for his own.

"Should the doom fall upon me," Beowulf continued, "thou wilt not, O King, be put to the trouble of building a mound over my head. For if all the tales of Grendel be true, he will bear away the gory corpse, to feast on it in his lonely moor. But this do thou for love of me: send Hygelac the matchless armour that protecteth my breast——it is a work of Weland, cunningest of smiths, and such are not made nowadays; meet gift from a departing friend."

To this speech, manly and heroic, Hrothgar at once made long reply——for age is not sparing of its breath in words. He gave thanks to the God-sent young champion; he recollected the deeds of his youth, in company with his brothers and many brave comrades long dead; and he dwelt on the horrors of his latter years. Then, at length, bethinking himself that the wayfarers must be a-weary and ready for meat, he said:

"But now sit thee down to the banquet with thy fellows, and merrily share the feast as the spirit moves thee."

A table was promptly cleared for the Goths. Thither they went, and sat in the pride of their strength. A thane attended to their wants. At times a minstrel's voice rose in Heorot, ringing and clear, and there was right brave merriment and goodwill in the mixed company of Goths and Danes.

Yet was there one eye that gleamed not with merriment and good-will, one head that held no friendly thoughts, because the heart swelled with malice and envy. Unferth it was, the King's own story-teller, who sat always at the king's feet, ready to tell brave tales. He could not bear that another should come, bearing accounts both brave and true, and so he broached a most unwelcome theme.

"Art thou not," he began tauntingly, "that same Beowulf who strove with Breca on the open sea in a swimming match, in which ye both most foolishly exposed your lives. Is it not true that for a se'n-night ye twain toiled in the realm of the waters, and did he not in the end outdo thee in the swimming? Was not his the greater strength? This being so, I fear me much thou mayest meet with sorry luck if thou darest to bide here for Grendel for the space of a whole night."

Beowulf, though angered, controlled his temper and replied with great coolness:

"Big things are these, friend Unferth, which thou hast spoken. Yea, Breca and I talked much between ourselves when we were pages, and each spoke strongly of his prowess; until, being but youngsters, we made up the foolish match between us, and having made it, we stuck to it. Drawn sword in hand and clothed in heavy armour we set out into the deep. Five nights we kept together, and neither did outrun the other. Then came a dark night, freezing cold, with a fierce wind from the north dead against us and the waves running high. The mighty flood of those waves parted us, as nothing had before; but still we strove ahead, plunging on; not knowing that strange creatures of the very depths had been stirred from rest by waves and by our contest. We knew not this was so until a spotty monster seized and dragged me to the bottom. Then, though taken unaware, I did not lose grip upon my sword, and with calm dispatch I slew the mighty sea-brute. But the one great beast was not alone. I know not how many more I fought and killed: it was a grewsome night. When at last the welcome light broke in the east and the waves grew calmer so I could see the headlands, the sea cast me upon the shore. I escaped with my life, though worn and spent. Never heard I of harder fight or of man more sorely tried. Yet I considered it my good fortune that I had met and slain these many sea-beasts. Nevermore would they destroy unwary ships and seamen. Therefore, methinks I may rightly claim that I have proved more sea-prowess, endured more buffetings from waves, than any other man."

Thus Beowulf told of his youthful prank. Then turning upon Unferth with flashing eyes and clouded brow, he cried:

"Of a sooth, I say to thee, Unferth, that never would Grendel, the foul ruffian, have made this hall so much a horror, wrought such disgrace in Heorot, if thy spirit wert as high as thou wouldst claim for thyself. But he hath found too often that such mighty Danes as thou givest him not much to fear; and so he slaughters and makes feast whatever time he chooseth. It will take the Goth to show him another kind of spirit; and when the light of another day ariseth over the world, then shall all who choose, walk proudly into this hall, with head erect."

This speech, so brave and cheery, gladdened the old King's heart, and even the Danes applauded it, although it held a bitter sting: it seemed a worthy answer to the unmannered Unferth. So laughter greeted Beowulf's words, music sounded again, jolly songs filled the hall; and none seemed to remember —although at heart none forgot—that night was coming on and with it, mayhap, another kind of feast.

And then, behold! Hrothgar's royal consort, Queen Wealhtheow, well versed in ceremonies and courtly lore, entered the hall, resplendent in cloth of gold, to honor her husband's guests with a gracious word. Her stately greeting took in every man. Then around the hall she went, to elder and to younger, until she came to Beowulf, sitting among the ethelings. With befitting dignity she greeted the leader of the Goths as he stood before her, thanking God with wise choice of words that he had come. He, the hero of many battles, repeated his solemn pledge:

"When I went on board and sat in my ship, as she sped over the waters, with this my chosen band, I vowed I would work out the deliverance of your people. I am bound as an earl to fulfil my vow, or in this hall to meet my death tonight."

The noble lady inclined her diademed head, for his words were well to her liking. Then slowly, with trailing robes, she walked to the head of the hall, to sit by her lord.

For some time yet the banqueting went on as merrily as ever. Then as daylight began to wane, song and laughter died on the revellers' lips, and King Hrothgar knew that it was time for sleep and for whatever else the dark might bring. When shrouding night descended and the creatures of darkness began to stalk abroad, then would the monster come. In silence all the company arose.

Hrothgar in his parting spoke some solemn words:

"Never before, since my hand first felt a sword, have I entrusted the guard-house of the Danes to any man, never but now to thee. Have and hold the sacred house against the foe. Be watchful, valiant, and may victory wait on thee! No wish of thine shall go unfulfilled if thou dost perform the great work and livest to tell it."

Thus spoke Hrothgar the Skylding, and gravely departed from the hall, with his Queen, followed by his men.

Silently Beowulf looked after the Danes; and silently he laid aside his armour, mindful of his vow to fight the goblin with no weapon save his strength. He laid off his shining mail, his helmet, and his sword of choicest steel, and gave them to his esquire; then he stretched himself upon the floor and laid his cheek upon a pillow. For the hall had been promptly cleared of tables and of benches, now pushed against the walls, and couches of soft pelts and rugs had been spread upon the floor.

As the mighty leader laid himself to rest, his companions also sought to sleep. But rest came not easily to any; for not one thought in his heart that he should see again his native land or the place where he was born. Such thoughts as these keep sleep, but not for long from weary men; in time their limbs relaxed, their lids grew heavy, and—they slept. All slept, but one,—and he lay still, straining his ear to listen and his eye to peer through the dim night.

For minute after minute and hour after hour there came no sound. No form emerged from out the gloom-encrusted night. The waiting and the watching and the wondering seemed destined for no great reward. Then quietly it came at first—a distant thud, a heavy tramp of mighty foot, that louder grew, and louder yet. He was marching from the moor—Grendel, the night-sent scourge. Straight for the hall he bent his way; and well he knew the path, for this was not the first time he had come to Hrothgar's hall.

He came carelessly along, as one assured of his entertainment. The door, though fastened with bars of wrought iron, sprang open at his touch. Quickly he stepped across the flagged floor, his eyes ablaze; and when he perceived the troop of strange warriors, lying close together, asleep, he laughed aloud. He gloated as he stood over them, and thought that long before the light of day should see the hall, the life of each of them would be torn from out the body.

Beowulf, watchful all the while, held himself in quiet that he might first assess the strength of that foul ruffian. The delay was not long; Grendel quickly, at one grab, seized a sleeping warrior, tore him up, crunched the bony frame, drank the blood

from the veins, and swallowed the flesh in huge morsels. In a trice he had devoured the lifeless body, feet and hands and all. Beowulf, aghast at such a deed, was more than ever ready to do battle as the monster stepped forward to where the hero lay, and reached out a hand to seize him on his bed. Then met the foul fiend with a reception such as he had never known before; for his arm was held tight in such a grip as he had never felt from any man in all the world. He knew at once that he was in an evil plight; and since his courage did not match his strength, in mortal fear he strove to free himself and flee. But flee he could not; fight he must.

Now were all awake, within the hall and out. The sounds of heavy strife filled all the air. Furious were both the maddened champions; from wall to wall and end to end of that great hall they stove with feverish wrestling. It seemed surely that the mighty Heorot must that night be brought to endless ruin; only the strong iron stanchions inside and out, and the masterly skill of its builders, kept it whole. In this night of terror it made good the ancient boast that no mortal force short of fire could ever bring destruction there.

The noise rose high; the violence increased. The Danes who stood outside, though brave men all, were numb with horror at the unearthly shrieks and dismal howlings of the God-forsaken fiend. And still the fight went on. The whole earth shook; the waves dashed strong upon the shore; and even the heavens trembled.

Many an earl of Beowulf's unsheathed and plunged into the fight; they knew not that they could not help their leader, much as they desired it. No choicest blade on earth could touch that destroyer, because he had secured himself by spells and incantations against weapons of all kinds. But he was not proof against human courage and human might. These alone now brought upon him his meet end, the death wound he had never thought to see; for with one desperate grip and tug, Beowulf wrenched out a mighty arm from out a pain-drenched shoulder. With a terrific yell, which told to listening Danes that now the dire struggle had seen its end and victory had been won by him they trusted, Grendel fled to the coverts of the fen: well he knew that the number of his days was full.

Thus was the valiant champion's pledge redeemed; thus was Heorot purged. The leader of the Goths had made good his vaunt, and, in token thereof, he hung up Grendel's hand, arm, and shoulder under the gabled roof.

The Coming of Arthur

by Sir Thomas Malory

from *Boys' King Arthur* edited by Sidney Lanier

*Of all the old epic tales, the stories of King Arthur are per-
haps the best known.*

*The earliest of these legends came from Wales. They may
have begun as stories about a chieftain who really lived, about
the sixth century. But gradually, as the tales were told over and
over, other incidents were added. Geoffrey of Monmouth made
the first known written collection of the stories in the twelfth
century. The most famous is* Le Morte d'Arthur *written by Sir
Thomas Malory in the fifteenth century.*

*This excerpt is based on Sir Thomas Malory's book and
tells how Arthur became king, how he found his sword, and
how he received his famous roundtable. Through all of the
story, Merlin, the great magician who helped Arthur, works to
make sure that events come out as they should.*

THE COMING OF ARTHUR

Sir Thomas Malory

———◆◆———

I T befell in the days of the noble Uther Pendragon, when he was King of England, [that there was born to him a son who in after time was King Arthur. Howbeit the boy knew not he was the king's son. For when he was but a babe] the king commanded two knights and two ladies to take the child bound in rich cloth of gold, "and deliver him to what poor man you meet at the postern gate of the castle." So the child was delivered unto Merlin, and so he bare it forth unto Sir Ector, and made an holy man to christen him, and named him Arthur; and so Sir Ector's wife nourished him.

Then within two years King Uther fell sick of a great malady; [and thereof he died]. Then stood the realm in great [danger] a long while, for every lord made him strong, and many weened [*thought*] to have been king.

[And so at last, by Merlin's counsel, all the lords of England came together in the greatest church of London on Christmas morn before it was day, to see if God would not show by some miracle who should be king.] And when the first mass was done there was seen in the church-yard, against the high altar, a great stone four-square, like to a marble stone, and in the midst thereof was an anvil of steel, a foot of height, and therein stuck a fair sword naked by the point, and letters of gold were written about the sword that said thus: WHO SO PULLETH OUT THIS SWORD OF THIS STONE AND ANVIL, IS RIGHTWISE KING BORN OF ENGLAND.

So when all the masses were done, all the [lords] went for to behold the stone and the sword. And when they saw the scripture, some assayed [*tried*] such as would have been king. But none might stir the sword nor move it.

"He is not yet here," said the archbishop, "that shall achieve the sword, but doubt not God will make him to be known. But this is my counsel," said the archbishop, "that we let purvey [*provide*] ten knights, men of good fame, and they to keep this sword."

And upon New Year's day the barons let make a tournament for to keep the lords together, for the archbishop trusted that God would make him known that should win the sword. So upon New Year's day when the service was done the barons rode to the field.

And so it happened that Sir Ector rode to the jousts, and with him rode Sir Kay, his son, and young Arthur that was his nourished brother. [But Sir] Kay had lost his sword, for he had left it at his father's lodging, and so he prayed young Arthur to ride for his sword. "I will with a good will," said Arthur, and rode fast after the sword; and when he came home, the lady and all were gone out to see the jousting. Then was Arthur wroth, and said to himself, "I will ride to the church-yard and take the sword with me that sticketh in the stone, for my brother Sir Kay shall not be without a sword this day." And so when he came to the church-yard Arthur alighted, and tied his horse to the stile, and so went to the tent, and found no knights there, for they were all at the jousting; and so he handled the sword by the handles, and lightly and fiercely he pulled it out of the stone, and took his horse and rode his way till he came to his brother Sir Kay, and delivered him the sword. And as soon as

Sir Kay saw the sword, he wist [*knew*] well that it was the sword of the stone, and so he rode to his father, Sir Ector, and said: "Sir, lo here is the sword of the stone; wherefore I must be king of this land." When Sir Ector beheld the sword, he returned again and came to the church, and there they alighted, all three, and went into the church, and anon he made Sir Kay to swear upon a book how he came to that sword.

"Sir," said Sir Kay, "by my brother Arthur, for he brought it to me."

"How gate [*got*] you this sword?" said Sir Ector to Arthur.

"Sir, I will tell you . . . When I came home for my brother's sword, I found nobody at home for to deliver me his sword, and so I thought my brother Sir Kay should not be swordless, and so I came thither eagerly and pulled it out of the stone.

"Found ye any knights about this sword?" said Sir Ector.

"Nay," said Arthur.

"Now," said Sir Ector to Arthur, "I understand that you must be king of this land."

"Wherefore I?" said Arthur.

"Sir," said Ector, "for there should never man have drawn out this sword but he that shall be rightwise king of this land. Now let me see whether ye can put the sword there as it was and pull it out again."

"That is no mastery," said Arthur; and so he put it in the stone. Therewith Sir Ector assayed to pull out the sword, and failed.

"Now assay," said Sir Ector to Sir Kay. And anon he pulled at the sword with all his might but it would not be. "Now shall ye assay," said Sir Ector to Arthur.

"I will well," said Arthur, and pulled it out easily. And therewithal Sir Ector kneeled down to the earth, and Sir Kay.

"Alas," said Arthur, "mine own dear father and brother, why kneel ye to me?"

"Nay, nay, my lord Arthur, it is not so: I was never your father nor of your blood, but I wote [*know*] well ye are of an higher blood than I weened [*thought*] ye were." And then Sir Ector told him all. Then Arthur made great moan when he understood that Sir Ector was not his father.

"Sir," said Ector unto Arthur, "will ye be my good and gracious lord when ye are king?"

"Else were I to blame," said Arthur, "for ye are the man in the world that I am most beholding [*obliged*] to, and my good lady and mother, your wife, that as well as her own hath fostered and kept me. And if ever it be God's will that I be king, as ye say, ye shall desire of me what I may do, and I shall not fail you."

"Sir," said Sir Ector, "I will ask no more of you but that you will make my son, your fostered brother Sir Kay, seneschal of all your lands."

"That shall be done, sir," said Arthur, "and more by the faith of my body; and never man shall have that office but he while that he and I live."

Therewithal they went unto the archbishop, and told him how the sword was achieved, and by whom. And upon the twelfth day all the barons came thither for to assay to take the sword. But there afore them all, there might none take it out but only Arthur; wherefore there were many great lords wroth, and said, "It was great shame unto them all and the realm to be governed with a boy of no high blood born." And so they fell out at that time, that it was put off till Candlemas, and then all the barons should meet there again. But always the ten knights were ordained for to watch the sword both day and night; and so they set a pavilion over the stone and the sword, and five always watched. And at Candlemas many more great lords came thither for to have won the sword, but none of them might prevail. And right as Arthur did at Christmas he did at Candlemas, and pulled out the sword easily, whereof the barons were sore aggrieved, and put it in delay till the high feast of Easter. And as Arthur sped afore, so did he at Easter; and yet there were some of the great lords had indignation that Arthur should be their king, and put it off in delay till the feast of Pentecost.

And at the feast of Pentecost all manner of men assayed to pull at the sword that would assay, and none might prevail; but Arthur pulled it out afore all the lords and commons that were there, wherefore all the commons cried at once: "We will have Arthur unto our king; we will put him no more in delay; for we all see that it is God's will that he shall be our king, and who that holdeth against it we will slay him." And therewithal they kneeled down all at once, both rich and poor, and cried Arthur mercy, because they had delayed him so long. And Arthur forgave it them, and took the sword between both his hands, and offered it upon the altar where the archbishop was, and so was he made knight of [1] the best man that was there.

And so anon was the coronation made, and there was he sworn to the lords and commons for to be a true king, to stand with true justice from thenceforth all the days of this life. Also then he made all lords that held of the crown to come in, and to do service as they ought to do. And many complaints were made unto King Arthur of great wrongs that were done since the death of King Uther, of many lands that were bereaved of lords, knights, ladies and gentlemen. Wherefore King Arthur made the lands to be given again unto them that owned them.

[1] "Of" was often used for the modern *by* in Sir Thomas Malory's time, and is still so used upon occasion. "Made knight of the best man" thus means *made knight by the best man*.

When this was done that the king had established all the countries about London, then he let make Sir Kay seneschal of England; and Sir Baudwin of Britain was made constable; and Sir Ulfius was made chamberlain; and Sir Brastias was made warden to wait upon the north from Trent forwards, for it was that time for the most part enemy to the king.

Then on a day there came into the court a squire on horseback, leading a knight before him wounded to the death, and told him there was a knight in the forest that had reared up a pavilion by a well [*spring*] side, "and hath slain my master, a good knight, and his name was Miles; wherefore I beseech you that my master may be buried, and that some good knight may revenge my master's death." Then was in the court great noise of the knight's death, and every man said his advice. Then came Griflet, that was but a squire, and he was but young, of the age of King Arthur, so he besought the king, for all his service that he had done, to give him the order of knighthood.

"Thou art full young and tender of age," said King Arthur, "for to take so high an order upon thee."

"Sir," said Griflet, "I beseech you to make me a knight."

"Sir," said Merlin, "it were pity to leese [*lose*] Griflet, for he will be a passing good man when he cometh to age, abiding with you the terms of his life; and if he adventure his body with yonder knight at the fountain, he shall be in great peril if [2] ever he come again, for he is one of the best knights of the world, and the strongest man of arms."

"Well," said King Arthur. So, at the desire of Griflet, the king made him knight.

"Now," said King Arthur to Sir Griflet, "sithen [*since*]

---

[2] "If" here means *whether*. "In great peril if ever he come again," *in great danger of never getting back.*

that I have made thee knight, thou must grant me a gift."

"What ye will, my lord," said Sir Griflet.

"Thou shalt promise me, by the faith of thy body, that when thou has jousted with the knight at the fountain, whether it fall [happen] that ye be on foot or on horseback, that in the same manner ye shall come again unto me without any question or making any more debate."

"I will promise you," said Griflet, "as ye desire." Then Sir Griflet took his horse in great haste, and dressed his shield, and took a great spear in his hand, and so he rode a great gallop till he came to the fountain, and thereby he saw a rich pavilion, and thereby under a cloth stood a fair horse well saddled and bridled, and on a tree a shield of divers colors, and a great spear. Then Sir Griflet smote upon the shield with the end of his spear, that the shield fell down to the ground.

With that came the knight out of the pavilion, and said, "Fair knight, why smote ye down my shield?"

"For I will joust with you," said Sir Griflet.

"It were better ye did not," said the knight, "for ye are but young and late made knight, and your might is nothing to mine."

"As for that," said Sir Griflet, "I will joust with you."

"That is me loth," said the knight, "but sith [since] I must needs, I will dress me thereto; but of whence be ye?" said the knight.

"Sir, I am of King Arthur's court." So they ran together that Sir Griflet's spear all to-shivered [shivered all to pieces], and therewithal he smote Sir Griflet through the shield and the left side, and brake the spear, that the truncheon stuck in his body, that horse and knight fell down.

When the knight saw him lie so on the ground he alighted, and was passing heavy, for he wend [weened] he had slain him, and then he unlaced his helm and got him wind, and so with the truncheon he set him on his horse, and betook him to God, and said he had a mighty heart, and if he might live he would prove a passing good knight. And so Sir Griflet rode to the court, whereas great moan was made for him. But through good leeches [*surgeons*] he was healed and his life saved.

And King Arthur was passing wroth for the hurt of Sir Griflet. And by and by he commanded a man of his chamber that his best horse and armor "be without the city or [*before*] to-morrow day." Right so in the morning he met with his man and his horse, and so mounted up and dressed his shield, and took his spear, and bade his chamberlain tarry there till he came again. And so King Arthur rode but a soft pace till it was day, and then was he ware of three churls which chased Merlin, and would have slain him. Then King Arthur rode unto them a good pace, and cried to them: "Flee, churls." Then were they afraid when they saw a knight, and fled away. "O Merlin," said King Arthur, "here hadst thou been slain for[3] all thy craft, had I not been."

"Nay," said Merlin, "not so, for I could save myself if I would, and thou art more near thy death than I am, for thou goest towards thy death, and [4] God be not thy friend."

So as they went thus talking, they came to the fountain, and the rich pavilion by it. Then King Arthur was ware where a knight sat all armed in a chair. "Sir knight," said King Arthur, "for what cause abidest thou here? That there may no knight ride this way but if he do joust with thee?" said the king. "I rede [*advise*] thee leave that custom," said King Arthur.

"This custom," said the knight, "have I used and will use,

---

[3] "For" here means *in spite of;* as still used, in certain phrases.

[4] "And" means *if* here. In later times it becomes contracted into "an," when used in this sense.

maugre [*in spite of*] who saith nay; and who is grieved with my custom, let him amend it that will."

"I will amend it," said King Arthur.

"And I shall defend it," said the knight. Anon he took his horse, and dressed his shield, and took a spear, and they met so hard either on other's shield, that they all to-shivered [*shivered all to pieces*] their spears. Therewith King Arthur drew his sword. "Nay, not so," said the knight, "it is fairer that we twain run more together with sharp spears."

"I will well," said King Arthur, "and [*if*] I had any mo [*more*] spears."

"I have spears enough," said the knight. So there came a squire, and brought two good spears, and King Arthur took one and he another. So they spurred their horses, and came together with all their mights, that either brake their spears to their hands. Then Arthur set hand on his sword. "Nay," said the knight, "ye shall do better; ye are a passing good jouster as ever I met withal, and for the love of the high order of knighthood let us joust once again."

"I assent me," said King Arthur. Anon there were brought two great spears, and every knight gat a spear, and therewith they ran together that Arthur's spear all to-shivered. But the other knight hit him so hard in midst of the shield that horse and man fell to the earth, and therewith Arthur was eager, and pulled out his sword, and said, "I will assay thee, Sir Knight, on foot, for I have lost the honor on horseback."

"I will be on horseback," said the knight. Then was Arthur wroth, and dressed his shield towards him with his sword drawn. When the knight saw that, he alight, for him thought no worship to have a knight at such avail, he to be on horseback, and he on foot, and so he alight and dressed his shield unto Arthur. And there began a strong battle with many great strokes, and so hewed with their swords that the cantels [*pieces, of ar-*

mor or of flesh] flew in the fields, and much blood they bled both, that all the place there as they fought was over-bled with blood, and thus they fought long, and rested them, and then they went to the battle again, and so hurtled together like two rams that either fell to the earth. So at the last they smote together, that both their swords met even together. But the sword of the knight smote King Arthur's sword in two pieces, wherefore he was heavy. Then said the knight unto Arthur, "Thou art in my danger whether me list to save thee or slay thee, and but thou yield thee as overcome and recreant thou shalt die."

"As for death," said King Arthur, "welcome be it when it cometh, but as to yield me to thee as recreant, I had liever die than to be so shamed." And there withal the king leapt unto Pellinore, and took him by the middle, and threw him down, and raced [5] off his helm. When the knight felt that, he was adread, for he was a passing big man of might, and anon he brought King Arthur under him, and raced off his helm, and would have smitten off his head.

Therewithal came Merlin, and said: "Knight, hold thy hand, for and [*if*] thou slay that knight, thou puttest this realm in the greatest damage that ever realm was in, for this knight is a man of more worship than thou wottest of."

"Why, who is he?" said the knight.

"It is King Arthur."

Then would he have slain him for dread of his wrath, and heaved up his sword, and therewith Merlin cast an enchantment on the knight, that he fell to the earth in a great sleep. Then Merlin took up King Arthur, and rode forth upon the knight's horse. "Alas," said King Arthur, "what hast thou done, Merlin? hast thou slain this good knight by thy crafts? There lived not so worshipful a knight as he was; I had liever than the

---

[5] "Raced" off: *violently tore off.*

stint [*loss*] of my land a year, that he were on [6] live."

"Care ye not," said Merlin, "for he is wholer than ye, for he is but on[7] sleep, and will awake within three hours. I told you," said Merlin, "what a knight he was; here had ye been slain had I not been. Also, there liveth not a better knight than he is, and he shall do you hereafter right good service, and his name is Pellinore, and he shall have two sons, that shall be passing good men."

Right so the king and he departed, and went unto an hermit that was a good man and a great leech. So the hermit searched all his wounds and gave him good salves; and the king was there three days, and then were his wounds well amended that he might ride and go. So Merlin and he departed, and as they rode, Arthur said, "I have no sword."

"No force," [8] said Merlin, "hereby is a sword that shall be yours, and [if] I may." So they rode till they came to a lake, which was a fair water and a broad, and in the middest of the lake King Arthur was ware of an arm clothed in white samite, that held a fair sword in the hand. "Lo," said Merlin, "yonder is that sword that I spake of." With that they saw a damsel going upon the lake.

"What damsel is that?" said Arthur.

"That is the Lady of the Lake," said Merlin; "and this damsel will come to you anon, and then speak ye fair to her that she will give you that sword." Anon withal came the damsel unto Arthur and saluted him, and he her again.

"Damsel," said Arthur, "what sword is that, that yonder the arm holdeth above the water? I would it were mine, for I have no sword."

[6] "On live": old form of *alive*.
[7] "On sleep," *asleep;* as just above "on live," *alive.*
[8] "No force," *no matter.*

"Sir king," said the damsel, "that sword is mine, and if ye will
give me a gift when I ask it you, ye shall have it."

"By my faith," said Arthur, "I will give you what gift ye
will ask."

"Well," said the damsel, "go ye into yonder barge and
row yourself to the sword, and take it and the scabbard with
you, and I will ask my gift when I see my time."

So King Arthur and Merlin alighted and tied their horses to
two trees, and so they went into the ship, and when they came
to the sword that the hand held, King Arthur took it up by
the handles, and took it with him. And the arm and the hand
went under the water; and so they came unto the land and
rode forth. And then King Arthur saw a rich pavilion: "What
signifieth yonder pavilion?"

"It is the knight's pavilion," said Merlin, "that ye fought with last, Sir Pellinore, but he is out, he is not there; he hath ado with a knight of yours, that hight [*was named*] Egglame, and they have fought together, but at the last Egglame fled, and else he had been dead, and he hath chased him to Caerleon, and we shall anon meet with him in the high way."

"It is well said," quoth King Arthur, "now I have a sword, and now will I wage battle with him and be avenged on him."

"Sir, ye shall not do so," said Merlin, "for the knight is weary of fighting and chasing, so that ye shall have no worship to have ado with him; also he will not lightly be matched of one knight living; and therefore my counsel is that ye let him pass, for he shall do you good service in short time, and his sons after his days. Also ye shall see that day in short space, that ye shall be right glad to give him your sister to wife."

"When I see him," said King Arthur, "I will do as ye advise me."

Then King Arthur looked upon the sword and liked it passing well.

"Whether liketh you better," said Merlin, "the sword or the scabbard?"

"Me liketh better the sword," said King Arthur.

"Ye are more unwise," said Merlin, "for the scabbard is worth ten of the sword, for while ye have the scabbard upon you ye leese [*lose*] no blood be ye never so sore wounded, therefore keep well the scabbard alway with you."

So they rode on to Caerleon, and by the way they met with Sir Pellinore. But Merlin had done such a craft that Pellinore saw not Arthur, and so he passed by without any words.

"I marvel," said the king, "that the knight would not speak."

"Sir," said Merlin, "he saw you not, for and [*if*] he had seen you, he had not lightly departed."

So they came unto Caerleon, whereof the knights were passing glad; and when they heard of his adventures, they marvelled that he would jeopard his person so alone. But all men of worship said it was merry to be under such a chieftain that would put his person in adventure as other poor knights did.

It befell on a time that King Arthur said to Merlin: "My barons will let me have no rest, but needs they will have that I take a wife, and I will none take but by thy counsel and by thine advice."

"It is well done," said Merlin, "that ye take a wife, for a man of your bounty and nobleness should not be without a wife. Now is there any fair lady that ye love better than another?"

"Yes," said King Arthur, "I love Guenever, the king's daughter Leodegrance[9] of the land of Cameliard, which Leodegrance holdeth in his house the Table Round that ye told he had of my father Uther. And this damsel is the most gentlest and fairest lady that I know living, or yet that ever I could find."

And Merlin went forth to King Leodegrance of Cameliard, and told him of the desire of the king, that he would have to his wife Guenever his daughter.

"That is to me," said King Leodegrance, "the best tidings that ever I heard, that so worthy a king of prowess and of nobleness will wed my daughter. And as for my lands I will give him, wished I that it might please him, but he hath lands enough, he needeth none; but I shall send him a gift that shall please him much more, for I shall give him the Table Round, the which Uther Pendragon gave me; and when it is full complete, there is an hundred knights and fifty, and as for an hundred good knights I have myself, but I lack fifty, for so many have been slain in my days."

And so King Leodegrance delivered his daughter Guenever unto Merlin, and the Table Round with the hundred knights;

[9] "The king's daughter Leodegrance," *King Leodegrance's daughter.*

and so they rode freshly with great royalty, what by water and what by land, till they came that night unto London.

When King Arthur heard of the coming of Guenever and the hundred knights with the Table Round, he made great joy for their coming, and said openly, "This fair lady is passing welcome to me, for I loved her long, and therefore there is nothing so pleasing to me. And these knights with the Round Table please me more than right great riches."

Then in all haste the king did ordain for the marriage and the coronation in the most honorablest wise that could be devised.

"Now, Merlin," said King Arthur, "go thou and espy me in all this land fifty knights which be of most prowess and worship."

Within short time Merlin had found such knights that should fulfill twenty and eight knights, but no more he could find. Then the bishop of Canterbury was fetched, and he blessed the sieges [seats] with great royalty and devotion, and there set the eight and twenty knights in their sieges.

And when this was done Merlin said, "Fair sirs, ye must all arise and come to King Arthur for to do him homage; he will have the better will to maintain you."

And so they arose and did their homage. And when they were gone Merlin found in every siege letters of gold that told the knights' names that had sitten therein. But two sieges were void.

"What is the cause," said King Arthur, "that there be two places void in the sieges?"

"Sir," said Merlin, "there shall no man sit in those places but they that shall be of most worship. But in the Siege Perilous there shall no man sit therein but one, and if there be any so hardy to do it he shall be destroyed, and he that shall sit there shall have no fellow."

And therewith Merlin took King Pellinore by the hand, and, in the one hand next the two sieges and the Siege Perilous, he said in open audience, "This is your place, and best ye be worthy to sit therein of any that is here."

The Tournament in Ireland

by Howard Pyle

from *Story of the Champions of the Round Table*

Along with the stories of King Arthur, himself, there are many stories of the valiant deeds performed by the Knights of the Round Table. Some of these stories tell about Sir Tristram, who was knighted by King Mark of Cornwall.

In one adventure, Sir Tristram killed a Sir Marhaus in battle. Because he was grievously wounded, Sir Tristram sought the aid of the daughter of Angus, King of Ireland; for she, Belle Isoult, was marvelously skilled in the art of healing. Since he knew that Sir Marhaus was the brother of the Queen, Sir Tristram concealed his identity by calling himself Tramtris. The Lady Belle Isoult succeeded so well in restoring his strength that Tristram was able to attend a tournament held by Angus.

THE TOURNAMENT IN IRELAND

Howard Pyle

———◆•◆———

S
O CAME THE time for the tournament that King Angus
of Ireland had ordained; and that was a very famous
affairs of arms indeed. For it hath very rarely happened that so noble a gathering of knights hath ever come together as that company which there presented itself for that
occasion at the court of the King of Ireland.

For you may know how excellent was the court of chivalry
that foregathered thereat when you shall hear that there came to
that tournament, the King of an Hundred Knights and the
King of the Scots, and that there came several knights of the
Round Table, to wit: Sir Gawaine, Sir Gaheris and Sir Agravaine; and Sir Bagdemagus and Sir Kay and Sir Dodinas, and
Sir Sagramore le Desirous, and Sir Gumret the Less, and Sir
Griflet; and that there came besides these many other knights
of great renown. . . .

And on the day of the tournament there came great crowds
of people into the lists, so that all that place was alive with movement. For it was as though a sea of people had arisen to over-
flow the seats and stalls thereof.

Now that tournament was to last for three days, and upon
the third day there was to be a grand mêlée in which all these
knights contestant were to take stand upon this side or upon
that.

But upon the first two of those three days Sir Tristram sat in the stall of the King and looked down upon the jousting, for, because of the illness from which he had recovered, he was minded to save his body until the right time should come, that time he should be called upon to do his uttermost.

And in those two days, Sir Tristram beheld that Sir Palamydes did more wonderfully in battle than he would have believed it possible for any knight to do. For Sir Palamydes was aware that the eyes of the Lady Belle Isoult were gazing upon him, wherefore he felt himself uplifted to battle as with the strength of ten. Wherefore he raged about that field like a lion of battle, seeking whom he might overthrow and destroy. And upon the first day he challenged Sir Gawaine to joust with him, and then he challenged Sir Gaheris, and the King of an Hundred Knights, and Sir Griflet, and Sir Sagramore le Desirous and fourteen other knights, and all of these he met and many he overcame, and that without any mishap to himself. And upon the second day he met with great success Sir Agravaine and Sir Griflet and Sir Kay and Sir Dodinas and twelve other knights. Wherefore those who beheld how he did gave great shouts and outcries of applause and acclaim, saying: "Certes, there was never knight in all of the world so great as this knight. Yea; even Sir Launcelot himself could not do more than that knight doeth."

Then Belle Isoult was troubled in her mind, and she said: "Tramtris, yonder in very truth is a most fierce and terrible knight. Now somewhiles I have fear that you may not be able to overcome him."

Thereat Sir Tristram smiled very grimly, and said: "Lady, already I have overcome in battle a bigger knight than ever Sir Palamydes has been or is like to be." But the Lady Belle Isoult wist not that that knight of whom Sir Tristram spake was Sir Marhaus of Ireland. . . .

So came the third day of that very famous contest at arms, and when the morning was come there began to gather together in the two parties those who were to contest the one against the other. Of one of these parties, Sir Palamydes was the chiefest knight, and upon that side was also Sir Gawaine and several of the knights who were with him. For these said, "There shall certes be greater credit to be had with Sir Palamydes than against him," and so they joined them with his party. Of the other party the chiefest knights were the King of an Hundred Knights and the King of Scots, and both of these were very famous and well-approved champions, of high courage and remarkable achievements.

Now when the time was nigh ready for that tournament, Sir Tristram went to put on the armor that the Lady Belle Isoult had provided him, and when he was armed he mounted very lightly upon the horse which she had given him. And the armor of Sir Tristram was white, shining like to silver, and the horse was altogether white, and the furniture and trappings thereof were all white, so that Sir Tristram glistened with extraordinary splendor.

Now when he was armed and prepared in all ways, the Lady Belle Isoult came to where he was and she said, "Tramtris, are you ready?" And he answered "Yea." Therewith she took the horse of Sir Tristram by the bridle and she led him to the postern gate of the castle, and put him out that way into a fair field that lay beyond; and Sir Tristram abided in the fields for some while until the tournament should have begun.

But the Lady Belle Isoult went to the tournament with her father, the King, and her mother, the Queen, and took her station at that place assigned to her whence she might overlook the field.

So in a little while that friendly battle began. And again Sir Palamydes was filled with the vehement fury of contest,

wherefore he raged about the field, spreading terror whithersoever he came. For first he made at the King of an Hundred
Knights, and he struck that knight so direful a blow that
both horse and man fell to the ground with the force thereof.
Then in the same manner he struck the King of Scots with
his sword, and smote him straightway out of the saddle also.
Then he struck down one after another, seven other knights,
all of well-proved strength and prowess, so that all those who
looked thereon cried out, "Is he a man or is he a demon?" So,
because of the terror of Sir Palamydes, all those in that contest
bore away from him as they might do from a lion in anger.

At this time came Sir Tristram, riding at a free pace, shining
like to a figure of silver. Then many saw him and observed him
and said to one another: "Who is this knight, and what party
will he join with to do battle?" These had not long to wait to
know what side he would join, for immediately Sir Tristram
took stand with that party which was the party of the King of
an Hundred Knights and the King of Scots, and at that the one
party was very glad, and the other party was sorry; for they
deemed that Sir Tristram was certes some great champion.

Then straightway there came against Sir Tristram four
knights of the other party, and one of these was Sir Gaheris,
and another was Sir Griflet and another was Sir Bagdemagus
and another was Sir Kay. But Sir Tristram was possessed with
a great joy of battle, so that in a very short time he had struck
down or overthrown all those knights, beginning with Sir Gaheris, and ending with Sir Kay the seneschal.

This Sir Gawaine beheld, and said to Sir Sagramore: "Yonder is certes a knight of terrible strength; now let us go and
see of what mettle he be."

Therewith Sir Gawaine pushed against Sir Tristram from
the one side, and Sir Sagramore came against him on the
other side, and so they met him both at once. Then first

Sir Gawaine struck Sir Tristram such a buffet that the horse of Sir Tristram turned twice about with the force of that stroke; and therewith Sir Sagramore smote him a buffet upon the other side so that Sir Tristram wist not upon which side to defend himself.

Then, at those blows Sir Tristram waxed so exceedingly fierce that it was as though a fire of rage flamed up into his brains and set them into a blaze of rage. So with that he rose up in his stirrups and launched so dreadful a blow upon Sir Gawaine that I believe nothing could have withstood the force of that blow. For it clave through the shield of Sir Gawaine and it descended upon the crown of his helmet and it clave away a part of his helmet and a part of the épaulière of his shoulder; and with the force of that dreadful, terrible blow,

Sir Gawaine fell down upon the ground and lay there as though he were dead.

Then Sir Tristram wheeled upon Sir Sagramore (who sat wonder-struck at that blow he had beheld) and thereafter he smote him too, so that he fell down and lay upon the ground in a swoon from which he did not recover for more than two hours.

Now Sir Palamydes also had beheld those two strokes that Sir Tristram had given, wherefore he said: "Hah! Yonder is a very wonderful knight. Now if I do not presently meet him, and that to my credit, he will have more honor in this battle than I."

So therewith Sir Palamydes pushed straight against Sir Tristram, and when Sir Tristram beheld that he was very glad, for he said: "Now it will either be Sir Palamydes his day, or else it will be mine." So he upon his part pushed against Sir Palamydes with good intent to engage him in battle, and then they two met in the midst of the field.

Then immediately Sir Palamydes smote Sir Tristram such a buffet that Sir Tristram thought a bolt of lightning had burst upon him, and for a little while he was altogether bemazed and wist not where he was. But when he came to himself he was so filled with fury that his heart was like to break therewith.

Thereupon he rushed upon Sir Palamydes and smote him again and again and again with such fury and strength that Sir Palamydes was altogether stunned at the blows he received and bare back before them. Then Sir Tristram perceived how that Sir Palamydes bare his shield low because of the fierceness of that assault, and thereupon he rose up in his stirrups and struck Sir Palamydes upon the crown of the helmet so dreadful a buffet that the brains of Sir Palamydes swam like water, and he must needs catch the pommel of his saddle to save himself from falling. Then Sir Tristram smote him another buffet, and therewith darkness came upon the sight of Sir Palamydes and he rolled off from his horse into the dust beneath its feet.

Then all who beheld the encounter shouted very loud and with great vehemence, for it was the very best and most notable assault at arms that had been performed in all that battle. But most of those who beheld that assault cried out "The Silver Knight!" For at that time no one but the Lady Belle Isoult wist who that silver knight was. But she wist very well who he was, and was so filled with the glory of his prowess that she wept for joy thereof.

Then the King of Ireland said: "Who is yonder knight who hath so wonderfully overthrown Sir Palamydes? I had not thought there was any knight in the world so great as he; but this must be some great champion whom none of us know." Upon that the Lady Belle Isoult, still weeping for joy, could contain herself no longer, but cried out: "Sir, that is Tramtris, who came to us so nigh to death and who hath now done us so great honor being of our household! For I knew very well that he was no common knight but some mighty champion when I first beheld him."

At that the King of Ireland was very much astonished and overjoyed, and he said: "If that is indeed so, then it is a very great honor for us all."

Now after that assault Sir Tristram took no more part in that battle but withdrew to one side. But he perceived where the esquires attendant upon Sir Palamydes came to him and lifted him up and took him away. Then by and by he perceived that Sir Palamydes had mounted his horse again with intent to leave that meadow of battle, and in a little he saw Sir Palamydes ride away with his head bowed down like to one whose heart was broken.

All this Sir Tristram beheld and did not try to stay Sir Palamydes in his departure. But some while after Sir Palamydes had quitted that place, Sir Tristram also took his departure, going in that same direction that Sir Palamydes had gone. Then after he had come well away from the meadow of battle, Sir Tristram set spurs to his horse and rode at a hard gallop along that way that Sir Palamydes had taken.

So he rode at such a gait for a considerable pass until, by and by, he perceived Sir Palamydes upon the road before him; and Sir Palamydes was at that time come to the edge of a woods where there were several stone windmills with great sails swinging very slowly around before a strong wind that was blowing.

Now this was a lonely place, and one very fit to do battle in, wherefore Sir Tristram cried out to Sir Palamydes in a loud voice: "Sir Palamydes! Sir Palamydes! Turn you about! For here is the chance for you to recover the honor that you have lost to me."

Thereupon Sir Palamydes, hearing that loud voice, turned him about. But when he beheld that the knight who called was he who had just now wrought such shame upon him, he ground his teeth together with rage, and therewith drave his horse at Sir Tristram, drawing his sword so that it flashed like lightning in the bright sunlight. And when he came nigh to Sir Tristram, he stood up in his stirrups and lashed a blow at him with all his might and main; for he said to himself: "Maybe I shall now recover mine honor with one blow which I lost to this knight a while since."

But Sir Tristram put aside that blow of Sir Palamydes with his shield with very great skill and dexterity, and thereupon, recovering himself, he lashed at Sir Palamydes upon his part. And at the first stroke Sir Tristram smote down the shield of Sir Palamydes, and gave him such a blow upon the head that Sir Palamydes fell down off his horse upon the earth. Then Sir

Tristram voided his own horse very quickly, and running to Sir Palamydes where he lay he plucked off his helmet with great violence. Therewith he cried out very fiercely: "Sir Knight, yield thee to me, or I will slay thee." And therewithal he lifted up his sword as though to strike off the head of Sir Palamydes.

Then when Sir Palamydes saw Sir Tristram standing above him in that wise, he dreaded his buffets so that he said: "Sir Knight, I yield me to thee to do thy commands, if so be thou wilt spare my life."

Thereupon Sir Tristram said, "Arise," and at that Sir Palamydes got him up to his knees with some ado, and so remained kneeling before Sir Tristram.

"Well," said Sir Tristram. "I believe you have saved your life by thus yielding yourself to me. Now this shall be my commandment upon you. First of all, my commandment is that you forsake the Lady Belle Isoult, and that you do not come near her for the space of an entire year. And this is my second commandment; that from this day you do not assume the arms of knighthood for an entire year and a day."

"Alas!" said Sir Palamydes, "why do you not slay me instead of bringing me to such shame as this! Would that I had died instead of yielding myself to you as I did." And therewith he wept for shame and despite.

"Well," said Sir Tristram, "let that pass which was not done. For now you have yielded yourself to me and these are my commands." So with that Sir Tristram set his sword back again into its sheath, and he mounted his horse and rode away, leaving Sir Palamydes where he was. . . .

Now when Tristram came back to the castle of the King of Ireland once more, he thought to enter privily in by the postern-gate as he had gone out. But lo! instead of that he found a great party waiting for him before the castle and these gave him loud acclaim, crying, "Welcome, Sir Tramtris! Welcome Sir Tramtris!" And King Angus came forward and took the hand of Sir Tristram, and he also said: "Welcome, Sir Tramtris, for you have brought us great honor this day!"

But Sir Tristram looked at the Lady the Belle Isoult with great reproach and by and by when they were together he said: "Lady, why did you betray me who I was when you had promised me not to do so?" "Sir," she said, "I meant not to betray you, but in the joy of your victory I know not very well what I said." "Well," said Sir Tristram, "God grant that no harm come of it." She said, "What harm can come of it, Messire?" Sir Tristram said: "I may not tell you, Lady, but I fear that harm will come of it."

Anon the Queen of Ireland came and said: "Tramtris, one so nigh to death as you have been should not so soon have done battle as you have done. Now I will have a bain prepared and you shall bathe therein, for you are not yet hale and strong."

"Lady," said Tristram, "I do not need any bain. For I believe I am now strong and well in all wise."

"Nay," said the Queen, "you must have that bain so that no ill may come to you hereafter from this battle which you have fought."

So she had that bain prepared of tepid water, and it was very strong and potent with spices and powerful herbs of divers sorts. And when that bain was prepared, Sir Tristram undressed and entered the bath, and the Queen and the Lady Belle Isoult were in the adjoining chamber which was his bed-chamber.

Now whilst Sir Tristram was in that bath, the Queen and Belle Isoult looked all about his chamber. And they beheld the sword of Sir Tristram where it lay, for he had laid it upon the bed when he had unlatched the belt to make himself ready for that bath. Then the Queen said to the Lady Belle Isoult, "See what a great huge sword this is," and thereupon she lifted it and drew the blade out of its sheath, and she beheld what a fair, bright, glistering sword it was. Then in a little she saw where, within about a foot and a half from the point, there was a great piece in the shape of a half-moon broken out of the edge of the sword; and she looked at that place for a long while. Then of a sudden she felt a great terror, for she remembered how even such a piece of sword as that which had been broken off from that blade, she had found in the wound of Sir Marhaus of which he had died. So she stood for a while holding that sword of Sir Tristram in her hand and looking as she had been turned to stone. At this the Lady Belle Isoult was filled with a sort of fear, wherefore she said, "Lady, what ails you?" The Queen said, "Nothing that matters," and therewith she laid aside the sword of Sir Tristram and went very quickly to her own chamber. There she opened her cabinet and took thence the piece of sword-blade which she had drawn from the wound of Sir Marhaus, and which she had kept ever since. With this she hurried back to the chamber of Sir Tristram, and fitted that piece of the blade to the blade; and lo! it fitted exactly, and without flaw.

Upon that the Queen was seized as with a sudden madness; for she shrieked out in a very loud voice, "Traitor! Traitor! Traitor!" saying that word three times. Therewith she snatched up the sword of Sir Tristram and she ran with great fury into the room where he lay in his bath. And she beheld him where he was there all naked in his bath, and therewith she rushed at him and lashed at him with his sword. But Sir Tristram threw himself to one side and so that blow failed of its purpose. Then the Queen would have lashed at him again or have thrust him through with the weapon; but at that Gouvernail and Sir Helles ran to her and catched her and held her back, struggling and screaming very violently. So they took the sword away from her out of her hands, and all the while she shrieked like one gone entirely distracted.

Then as soon as Gouvernail and Sir Helles loosed her, she ran very violently out of that room with great outcry of screaming, and so to King Angus and flung herself upon her knees before him, crying out: "Justice! Justice! I have found that man who slew my brother! I beseech of you that you will deal justice upon him."

Then King Angus rose from where he sat, and he said: "Where is that man? Bring me to him." And the Queen said: "It is Tramtris, who hath come hither unknown unto this place."

King Angus said: "Lady, what is this you tell me? I cannot believe that what you say is true." Upon this the Queen cried out: "Go yourself, Lord, and inquire, and find out how true it is."

Then King Angus rose, and went forth from that place, and he went to the chamber of Sir Tristram. And there he found that Sir Tristram had very hastily dressed himself and had armed himself in such wise as he was able. Then King Angus came to Tristram, and he said: "How is this, that I find thee armed? Art thou an enemy to my house?" And Tristram wept, and said: "Nay, Lord, I am not your enemy, but your friend, for I have great love for you and for all that is yours, so that I would be very willing to do battle for you even unto death if so be I were called upon to do so."

Then King Angus said: "If that is so, how is it that I find thee here armed as if for battle, with thy sword in thy hand?" "Lord," said Sir Tristram, "although I be friends with you and yours, yet I know not whether you be friends or enemies unto me; wherefore I have prepared myself so that I may see what is your will with me, for I will not have you slay me without defence upon my part." Then King Angus said: "Thou speakest in a very foolish way, for how could a single knight hope to defend himself against my whole household? Now I bid thee tell me who thou art, and what is thy name, and why thou camest hither knowing that thou hadst slain my brother?"

Then Sir Tristram said, "Lord, I will tell thee all the truth." And therewith he confessed everything to King Angus, to wit: who was his father and his mother, and how he was born and reared; how he fought Sir Marhaus, and for what reason; and of how he came hither to be healed of his wound, from which else he must die in very grievous pain. And he said: "All this is truth, Lord, and it is truth that I had no ill-will against Sir Marhaus; for I only stood to do battle with him for the sake of mine uncle, King Mark of Cornwall, and to enhance mine own honor; and I took my fortune with him as he took his with me. Moreover, I fought with Sir Marhaus upon the same day that I was made knight, and that was the first battle which I fought, and in that battle I was wounded so sorely that I was like to die as you very well know. As for him, he was a knight well-tried and seasoned with many battles, and he suffered by no treachery but only with the fortune of war."

So King Angus listened to all that Sir Tristram said, and when he had ended, quoth he: "As God sees me, Tristram, I cannot deny that you did with Sir Marhaus as a true knight should. For it was certes your part to take the cause of your uncle upon you if you had the heart to do so, and it was truly a real knightly thing for you who were so young to seek honor at the hands of so famous a knight as Sir Marhaus. . . .

"But though all this is true, nevertheless it will not be possible for me to maintain you in this country, for if I keep you here I shall greatly displease not only the Queen and her kin, but many of those lords and knights who were kin to Sir Marhaus or who were united to him in pledges of friendship. So you must even save yourself as you can and leave here straightway, for I may not help or aid you in any way."

Then Sir Tristram said: "Lord, I thank you for your great kindness unto me, and I know not how I shall repay the great goodness that my Lady Belle Isoult hath showed to me. For I swear to you upon the pommel of my sword which I now hold up before me that I would lay down my life for her sake. Yes, and my honor too! for she hath the entire love of my heart, so that I would willingly die for her, or give up for her all that I have in the world." . . .

Then King Angus meditated upon this for a while, and he said: "Tristram, what thou sayest is very well said, but how shall I get you away from this place in safety?"

Sir Tristram said: "Lord, there is but one way to get me away with credit unto yourself. Now I beseech you of your grace that I may take leave of my lady your daughter, and that I may then take leave of all your knights and kinsmen as a right knight should. And if there be any among them who chooses to stop me or to challenge my going, then I must face that one at my peril, however great it may be."

"Well," said King Angus, "that is a very knightly way to behave, and so it shall be as you will have it."

So Sir Tristram went downstairs to a certain chamber where Belle Isoult was. And he went straight to her and took her by the hand; and he said: "Lady, I am to go away from this place, if I may do so with credit to my honor; but before I go I must tell you that I shall ever be your own true knight in all ways that a knight may serve a lady. For no other lady shall have my heart but you, so I shall ever be your true knight. Even though I shall haply never see your face again, yet I shall ever carry your face with me in my heart, and the thought of you shall always abide with me whithersoever I go."

At this the Lady Belle Isoult fell to weeping in great measure, and thereat the countenance of Sir Tristram also was all writhed with passion, and he said, "Lady, do not weep so!" She said, "Alas, I cannot help it!" Then he said: "Lady, you gave me my life when I thought I was to lose it, and you brought me back from pain unto ease, and from sorrow unto joy. Would God I were suffering all those pangs as aforetime, so that there might be no more tears upon your face." . . .

After that Sir Tristram went straight unto the hall of the castle, and there he found a great many of the lords of the castle and knights attendant upon the King. For the news of these things had flown fast, and many of them were angry and some were doubtful. But Tristram came in very boldly, clad all in full armor, and when he stood in the midst of them he spoke loud and with great courage, saying: "If there be any man here whom I have offended in any way, let him speak, and I will give him entire satisfaction whoever he may be. But let such speech be now or never, for here is my body to make good my knighthood against the body of any man, whomsoever he may be."

At this all those knights who were there stood still and held their peace, and no man said anything against Sir Tristram (although there were several knights and lords who were kin to the Queen), for the boldness of Tristram overawed them, and no one had the heart to answer him.

So after a little while Sir Tristram left that place, without turning his head to see if any man followed him.

So he left that castle and Gouvernail went with him, and no one stopped him in his going.

The Dream of Ronabbway

by Padraic Colum

from *The Island of the Mighty*

Not so well known as the other Arthurian legends are the Welsh stories about him recorded in a collection called The Red Book of Hergest. *Some of these stories were translated in 1838 and 1839 by Lady Charlotte Guest in a book she called the* Mabinogian. *In the* Mabinogian, *Arthur is an English king, but he is of pure Welsh blood, and he and his attendant warriors have strange and magical powers.*

"The Dream of Ronabbway" tells some of the wonderous things that happened to Arthur, and also tells something about his death.

THE DREAM OF RONABBWAY

Padraic Colum

———◆•◆———

THERE was once a party of men who went upon a quest
that need not be told of here. One of the men was called
Ronabbway. And Ronabbway and some others came
together to a house that they knew of. But when they came
near, they saw an old hall, very black and having an upright
gable, whence issued a great smoke; and on entering, they
found the floor full of puddles and mounds; and it was difficult
to stand thereon, so slippery was it with the mire of cattle. There
were boughs of holly spread over the floor, whereof the cattle
had browsed the sprigs. When the men came into the house,
they beheld an old hag making a fire. And whenever she felt
cold she cast a lapful of chaff upon the fire, and raised such a
smoke that it was scarcely to be borne, as it rose up to the nostrils. On the other side of the house there was a yellow calfskin
on the floor.

And when the men came within there arose a storm of wind
and rain, so that it was hardly possible to go forth with safety.
And being weary with their journey, they laid themselves down
and sought to sleep. When they looked at the couch, it seemed
to be made but of a little coarse straw full of dust and vermin,
with the stems of boughs sticking up therethrough, for the cattle
had eaten all the straw that was placed at the head and the foot.

And upon it was stretched an old russet-coloured rug, thread-bare and ragged; and a coarse sheet, full of slits, was upon the rug, and an ill-stuffed pillow, and a worn-out cover upon the sheet. And after much suffering from the vermin, and from the discomfort of their couch, a heavy sleep fell upon Ronabbway's companions. But Ronabbway, not being able either to sleep or to rest, thought he should suffer less if he went to lie upon the yellow calf-skin that was stretched out on the floor. And there he slept.

As soon as sleep came upon his eyes, it seemed to him that he was journeying with his companions across a plain, and he thought that he went towards the Severn. As he journeyed, he heard a mighty noise, the like whereof heard he never before; and looking behind him, he beheld a youth mounted on a chestnut horse, whereof the legs were grey from the top of the forelegs, and from the bend of the hindlegs downwards. The rider wore a coat of yellow satin sewn with green silk, and on his thigh was a gold-hilted sword, with a scabbard of new leather of Cordova, belted with the skin of a deer, and clasped with gold. And over this was a scarf of yellow satin wrought with green silk, the borders whereof were likewise green. The green of the caparison of the horse, and of his rider, was as green as the leaves of the fir-tree, and the yellow was as yellow as the blossom of the broom.

Now as this knight came toward them, his aspect was so fierce that fear seized upon Ronabbway and his companions, and they began to flee. The knight pursued them. And when his horse breathed forth, the men became distant from him, and when the horse drew in his breath, they were drawn near to him, even to the horse's chest. When the knight had overtaken Ronabbway and his companions, they besought his mercy. "You shall have it gladly," said he, "fear nought." "Ha, Chieftain, since thou hast mercy upon me, tell me also who thou art," said Ronabbway. "I am Iddog, yet not by my name, but by my nickname, am I best known." "And wilt thou tell me what thy nickname is?" "I will tell thee, but I will tell thee after this."

All this was in Ronabbway's dream. And he and his companions with the knight journeyed over the plain as far as a ford on the Severn. And for a mile around the ford on both sides of the road, they saw tents and encampments, and there was the clamour of a mighty host. And they came to the edge of the ford, and there they beheld King Arthur; he was on a flat island below the ford. And a tall, auburn-haired youth stood before him, with his sheathed sword in his hand, and clad in a coat and cap of jet-black satin. The youth's face was as white as ivory, and his eyebrows black as jet, and such part of his wrist as could be seen between his glove and his sleeve was whiter than the lily, and thicker than a warrior's ankle.

And in Ronabbway's dream, he and the knight and his companions stood before King Arthur and saluted him. "Heaven grant thee good," said Arthur to the knight, "and where didst thou find these little men?" said he, looking at Ronabbway and his companions. "I found them, Lord, up yonder on the road," said the knight. Then King Arthur smiled. "Lord," said the knight, "wherefore dost thou laugh?" "I laugh not," said Arthur; "but it pitieth me that men so small as these should have this Island in their keeping, after the men who guarded it in my time." Then said the knight to Ronabbway, "dost thou see the ring with the stone set in it, that is upon the King's hand?" "I see it," he answered. "It is one of the properties of that stone to enable thee to remember what thou seest here to-night, and hadst thou not seen the stone, thou wouldst never have been able to remember aught thereof."

Then they heard a call made for Arthur's servant, and a red, rough, ill-favoured man, upon a tall red horse with the mane parted on each side, came forward, and he brought with him a large and beautiful sumpter pack. He dismounted before Arthur, and he drew a golden chair out of the pack, and a carpet of diapered satin. And he spread the carpet before Arthur, and he placed the chair upon the carpet. And so large was the chair that three armed warriors might have sat therein.

Then Ronabbway saw Arthur sitting on the chair within the carpet, and he saw Owen standing before him. "Owen," said Arthur, "wilt thou play chess?" "I will, Lord," said Owen. And Arthur's servant brought the chess for Arthur and Owen; golden pieces and a board of silver. And they began to play.

And while they were playing, behold they saw a white tent with a red canopy, and the figure of a jet-black serpent on the top of the tent, and red, glaring, venomous eyes in the head of the serpent, and a red flaming tongue. Then there came a young page who bore a heavy, three-edged sword with a golden hilt, in a scabbard of black leather tipped with fine gold. And he came to the place where King Arthur and Owen were playing at chess.

The youth saluted Owen. And Owen marvelled that the youth should salute him, and should not have saluted the King. Arthur knew what was in Owen's thoughts, and he said, "Marvel not that the youth salutes thee now, for he saluted me erewhile; and it is unto thee that his errand is." Then said the youth to Owen, "Lord, is it with thy leave that the young pages and attendants of the King harass and torment and worry thy Ravens? And if it be not with thy leave, cause the King to forbid them." "Lord," said Owen to the King, "thou hearest what the youth says; if it seem good to thee, forbid them from my Ravens." "Play the game," said Arthur. They played, and the youth returned to the tent.

That game did they finish, and another they began, and when they were in the middle of the game, behold, a ruddy young man with auburn curling hair and large eyes, well-grown, and having his beard new-shorn, came forth from a bright yellow tent, upon the top of which was the figure of a bright red lion. In his hand there was a huge, heavy, three-edged sword with a scabbard of red deer-hide, tipped with gold. He came to the place where Arthur and Owen were playing at chess. He saluted Owen. And Owen was troubled at his salutation, but Arthur minded it no more than before. The youth said unto Owen, "Is it not against thy will that the attendants of the King harass thy Ravens, killing some and worrying others? If against thy will it be, beseech him to forbid them." "Lord," said Owen, "forbid thy men, if it seem good to thee." "Play thy game," said the King. And the youth returned to the tent.

And that game was ended and another begun. As they were beginning the first move of the game, they beheld at a small distance from them a tent speckled yellow, the largest ever seen, and the figure of an eagle of gold upon it, and a precious stone on the eagle's head. And coming out of the tent, they saw a youth with thick yellow hair upon his head, fair and comely, and a scarf of blue satin upon him, and a brooch of gold in the scarf upon his right shoulder as large as a warrior's middle finger. In the hand of the youth was a mighty lance, speckled yellow, with a newly sharpened head; and upon the lance a banner displayed.

Fiercely angry, and with rapid pace, came the youth to the place where Arthur was playing at chess with Owen. They perceived that he was wroth. And thereupon he saluted Owen, and told him that his Ravens had been killed, the chief part of them, and that such of them as were not slain were so wounded and bruised that not one of them could raise its wings a single fathom above the earth. "Lord," said Owen, "forbid thy men." "Play," said Arthur, "if it please thee." Then said Owen, speaking to the youth, "Go back, and wherever thou findest the strife at the thickest, there lift up the

banner, and let come what pleases Heaven."

So the youth returned back to the place where the strife bore hardest upon the Ravens, and he lifted up the banner; and as he did so they all rose up in the air, wrathful and fierce and high of spirit, clapping their wings in the wind, and shaking off the weariness that was upon them. And recovering their energy and courage, furiously and with exaltation did they, with one sweep, descend upon the heads of the men, who had erewhile caused them anger and pain and damage, and they seized some by the heads, and some by the ears, and others by the arms, and carried them up into the air; and in the air there was a mighty tumult with the flapping of the wings of the triumphant Ravens, and with their croaking; and there was another mighty tumult with the groaning of the men, who were being torn and wounded, and some of whom were slain.

And Arthur and Owen marvelled at the tumult as they played at chess; and, looking, they perceived a knight upon a dun-coloured horse coming towards them. Bright red was the horse's right shoulder, and from the top of his legs to the centre of his hoof was bright yellow. Both the knight and his horse were fully equipped with heavy foreign armour. A large gold-hilted one-edged sword had the knight upon his thigh. The belt of the sword was of dark green leather with golden slides and a clasp of ivory upon it, and a buckle of jet-black upon the clasp. A helmet of gold was upon the head of the knight, set with precious stones of great virtue, and at the top of the helmet was the image of a flame-coloured leopard with two ruby-red stones in its head, so that it was astounding for a warrior, however stout his heart, to look at the face of the leopard, much more at the face of the knight. He had in his hand a blue-shafted lance, but from the haft to the point it was stained crimson-red with the blood of the Ravens.

The knight came to the place where Arthur and Owen were seated at chess. And they perceived that he was harassed and vexed and weary as he came towards them. The youth saluted Arthur and told him that the Ravens of Owen were slaying his young men and attendants. And Arthur looked at Owen and said, "Forbid thy Ravens." "Lord," said Owen, "play thy game." They played. And the knight returned back towards the strife, and the Ravens were not forbidden any more than before.

When they had played a while, they heard a mighty tumult, and a wailing of men, and a croaking of Ravens, as they carried the men in their strength into the air, and, tearing them betwixt them, let them fall piecemeal to the earth. And during the tumult they saw a knight coming towards them, on a light gray horse, and the left foreleg of the horse was jet-black to the centre of his hoof. The knight and the horse were fully accoutred with huge, heavy blue armour. A robe of honour of yellow diapered satin was upon the knight, and the borders of the robe were blue. On the thigh of the knight was a sword, long, and three-edged, and heavy. The scabbard was of red cut leather, and the belt of new red deer-skin, having upon it many golden slides and a buckle of the bone of the sea-horse, the tongue of which was jet black. A golden helmet was upon the head of the knight, wherein were set sapphire-stones of great virtue. At the top of the helmet was the figure of a flame-colored lion, with a fiery-red tongue, issuing about a foot from his mouth, and with venomous eyes, crimson-red, in his head. And the knight came, bearing in his hand a thick ashen lance, the head whereof, which had been newly steeped in blood, was overlaid with silver.

The knight saluted King Arthur. "Lord," said he, "carest thou not for the slaying of thy pages, and thy young men, and the sons of the nobles of the Island of Britain, whereby it will be difficult to defend this island from henceforward for ever?" "Owen," said Arthur, "forbid thy Ravens." "Play this game, Lord," said Owen.

They finished the game and began another; and as they were finishing that game, lo, they heard a great tumult and a clamour of armed men, and a croaking of Ravens, and a flapping of wings in the air, as they flung down the armor entire to the ground, and the men and the horses piecemeal. Then they saw coming a knight on a lofty-headed piebald horse. The left shoulder of the horse was of bright red, and its right leg from the chest to the hollow of the hoof was pure white. The knight and horse were equipped with arms of speckled yellow. And there was a robe of honour upon him, and upon his horse, divided in two parts, white and black, and the borders of the robe of honour were of purple. He wore a sword three-edged and bright, with a golden hilt. And the belt of the sword was of yellow goldwork, having a clasp upon it of the eyelid of a black sea-horse, and a tongue of yellow gold to the clasp. Upon the head of the knight was a bright helmet of yellow laton, with sparkling stones of crystal in it, and at the crest of the helmet was the figure of a griffin, with a stone of many virtues in its head. He had an ashen spear in his hand, with a round shaft, colored with azure blue. And the head of the spear was newly stained with blood.

Wrathfully came the knight to the place where Arthur was, and he told him that the Ravens had slain his household and the sons of the chief men of the Island of Britain, and he besought him to cause Owen to forbid his Ravens. And Arthur besought Owen to forbid them. Then Arthur took the golden chess-men that were upon the board, and crushed them until they became as dust. But he spoke no more to Owen. Then Owen ordered the one he had sent to lower the banner. So it was lowered, and all was peace.

Then spake a tall and stately man, of noble and flowing speech, saying that it was a marvel that so vast a host should be assembled in so narrow a space, and that it was a still greater marvel that those should be there at that time when they had promised to be by mid-day in the battle. Thereupon they heard a call made for Arthur's sword-bearer, and behold he arose with the sword of Arthur in his hand. The similitude of two serpents was upon the sword in gold. And when the sword was drawn from its scabbard, it seemed as if two flames of fire burst forth from the jaws of the serpent, and then, so wonderful was the sword, that it was hard for anyone to look upon it. And the host became still, and the tumult ceased, and the sword-bearer returned to the tent.

"Iddog," said Ronabbway, "who is the man who bore the sword of Arthur?" "Kaddar, the Earl of Cornwall, whose duty it is to arm the King on the days of battle and warfare."

Then Iddog took Ronabbway behind him on his horse, and that mighty host moved forward, each troop in its order. And when they came to the middle of the ford of the Severn, Iddog turned his horse's head, and Ronabbway looked along the valley of the Severn. And he beheld two fair armies coming towards the ford. After they had dismounted he heard a great tumult and confusion amongst the host, and such as were then at the flanks turned to the centre, and such as had been in the centre moved to the flanks. And then, behold, he saw a knight coming, clad, both he and his horse, in mail, of which the rings were whiter than the whitest lily, and the rivets redder than the ruddiest blood. And this knight rode amongst the host.

"Iddog," said Ronabbway, "will yonder host flee?"

"King Arthur never fled, and if this discourse of thine were heard, thou wert a lost man. But as to the knight whom thou seest yonder, it is Kai. The fairest horseman is Kai in all Arthur's Court; and the men who are at the front of the army hasten to the rear to see Kai ride, and the men who are in the centre flee to the side, from the shock of his horse. And this is the cause of the confusion of the host."

Then Kai said: "Whoever will follow Arthur, let him be with him to-night in Cornwall, and whosoever will not, let him be opposed to Arthur. For now the battle comes on."

Then Ronabbway turned to Iddog and said: "Wilt thou tell me what thy nickname is?" "I will tell thee," his companion said, "it is Iddog, the Stirrer-up of Britain." "Ha, Chieftain," said Ronabbway, "why art thou called thus?" "I will tell thee," said his companion. "I was at the battle the opening of which has been shown to thee. I was one of the messengers between Arthur and Medraud, his nephew, at the battle of Camlan;

and I was then a reckless youth, and through my desire for battle, I kindled strife between them, and stirred up wrath, when I was sent by Arthur to reason with Medraud, and to show him that Arthur was his foster-father and his uncle, and to seek for peace, lest the sons of the nobles of the Island of Britain should be slain. And whereas Arthur charged me with the fairest sayings he could think of, I uttered unto Medraud the harshest I could devise. And from this did the battle of Camlan ensue. And the nobles of the Island of Britain and the great companions of Arthur were slain in that battle, and an end was made to the Court of Arthur. And a magic sleep fell upon Arthur, and he stays within a hill. But he will come forth again when the Island of Britain is in danger and he will deliver his people."

Then again Ronabbway heard the voice of Kai saying, "Whosoever will follow Arthur, let him be with him to-night in Cornwall, and whosoever will not, let him be opposed to Arthur." And through the greatness of the tumult that ensued, Ronabbway awoke. And when he awoke he was upon the yellow calf-skin, having slept three days and three nights.

Manawyddan Son of the Boundless

by Kenneth Morris

from *Book of the Three Dragons*

King Arthur is not the only hero of the Mabinogian. *Even more important are the great Welsh heroes Manawyddan and his son Pryderi. Manawyddan was born a man, but after many trials the gods lifted him up to be one of themselves. In this story Manawydden wins his name and begins his life of struggle and adventure.*

This great tale is from the early Celtic days in Wales, long before the coming of Christianity. The author based his re-telling on the Mabinogian *and other early sources. "The Cymry" are the Welsh people; "The Island of the Mighty" re-fers to ancient Britain; and "The Blessed Bran" was a Welsh hero who died in the attempt to avenge his sister's wrongs, and who was the son of Llyr, the sea god. His head was said to have been severed from his body and placed so that it could watch over the people of Wales and protect them.*

MANAWYDDAN SON OF THE BOUNDLESS

Kenneth Morris

———◆———

A T one time there was no Crowned King in London; and for lack of one, often there would be confusion and the failure of crops. So Six Chieftains of the Cymry consulted among themselves who should get the crown. Taliesin the Chief of Bards was at the head of them: his forehead shone like the Morning Star.

"If you will take advice of mine," said he, "the one to wear the crown will be the Blessed Bran."

"The best advice in the world," they agreed, "if there be any getting him." He had been crowned King of London none knew how many ages before; and there would be no finding him but in the Islands of the Blessed in the West of the World; and the journey thither they were for making.

"It would be beneath his dignity to have less than seven men come to him on an embassy," said Heilyn ab Gwyn Hen. (He was the most impatient of all warriors and horsemen.)

"That is true," said Taliesin Benbardd. "We shall meet the seventh in Mon as we go forward; he will be a son of the Boundless as Bran Fendigaid is; he will be at the head of us."

In Mon they met Manawyddan; and all could see that he was to be their leader. Now here is who this Manawyddan son of the Boundless was.

It happened of old that the Gods of the Island of the Mighty desired to raise auxiliar godhood from the ranks of the Cymry, the men of that island. So Hu the Mighty called them into council; and in the council they decided that Pwyll, Prince of Dyfed in Wales, should be the man they would make a god of, if he were capable of it. So first they sent him to reign in Annwn the Great Deep; and a year and a day he was king there, and undergoing the trials incident to the place, and nowise failing in them. They sent one of their own divine kindred, Rhianon Ren the daughter of Hefeydd, into Wales to become his wife; that she might help him towards godhood as only a goddess could.

But it was when his son Pryderi was born that they put the heaviest trial on him; and in that he failed. So they did what they had to do by him: took the memory from his mind, and himself from his kin and his kingdom; and cast him loose on Wales and the world. Whatever misfortune they could devise, they brought him deep into the midst of it, and poured it out over the head of him, and set it howling and fanged at his heels; and all for no reason but that bound they were to make a god of him, and to have him fighting in their ranks with them against Hell and Chaos along the borders of space.

He knew nothing, at that time, of his having been Pwyll Pen Annwn, Lord of Dyfed and the Great Deep; style or title he had none; the best name there was for him was Dienw'r Anffodion, the Nameless One with the Misfortunes; and to get a better he would have to come into Pair Dadeni, the Caldron of Ceridwen, the Mother of the World; but he knew nothing of that. In it the dead come by new life and the nameless by a name; and the Gods were guiding him towards it always, by the shortest path there was. For Hu Gadarn sent Gwydion ab Don, the God of Wisdom and Laughter, to guide him; and by reason of that, towards Pair Dadeni his face was set. Gwydion ab Don was beside him on all his wanderings: through Europe and through Africa and the Islands of Corsica, and through Sach and Salach, and Lotor and Ffotor, and India the Greater and India the Less, and Powys and Meirion and Arfon.

And there, one day, he was traversing the mountains towards Mon and Ireland; and it seemed to him he had never been anything but fortunate, compared to what he was then.

It was long since he had passed any habitation, or looked on the faces of men. The fields bore no mushrooms for him, nor the thorns blackberries, although it was the beginning of Autumn; and if there were eels or trout in the streams, he could get no news of them. Three days before he had shot an old lean rabbit; and had seen neither bird nor beast to shoot at since. Nothing was left of it but the right hind leg; and the best that could be said for that was that it was dry and tough and withered. He was shoeless and in rags; and lame with a wounded foot a sharp rock had torn the day before and that now was festering.

He had risen from the heather at dawn after a night of rain and fever; and thought that death could not be far from him. Now and again hunger tormented him; but he took no thought for the rabbit leg in his wallet. Through the morning he limped on, and the rain drove down on him; and the thoughts in his mind were either numb and silent or else fantastic and beyond control; and the one thing he hoped for in his heart was death.

And then suddenly he became aware of that which had already driven the clouds from the sky, and the rain from mid air, and now the grief and confusion from his mind. It was harping and song that filled the mountain world with wonder, and made the morning wholly beautiful, with sunlit raindrops sparkling everywhere on the fern. The rabbits came hurrying from their burrows to listen, and paid no heed to him as he passed. An old gray wolf, sauntering down the hillside, turned, and stood still with trembling ears. Three eagles came down out of the sky, and lighted on boulders, intent. Wild goats on the crags above stood motionless. Nothing living moved but himself; and he, as best he could, hurried forward to come to the heart of the enchantment.

A hundred paces brought him to it. A youth sat on a rock, his harp at his breast, floating out the music on the sunlight. A motion of his eyes bade Dienw be seated; and so he kept him until the song was sung. It was healing and happiness to listen to it. The singer was hardly more than a boy; yet had the blue robe of an Institutional Bard of that island on him.

He ended the song and set down the harp, and picked up his wand of alterwood studded with gold. "The greeting of the god and the man to you, pleasantly and kindly!" said he. It was the best greeting Dienw had had, so far as he knew, during the whole of his life.

"And better be it with you than it is with me—better and more copious!" he answered. "It would be a delight to me to remember, in after times, the name of the one who could so ingratiate these mountains with his harping and his vocal song."

"As to the name, it will be Goreu fab Ser," said the Bard; and clear it was he would be of starry lineage, and few his betters throughout the worlds. "It was foretold to me that I should meet here the man I desired to meet; and I made the music to attract him to me."

"It would be pleasant to know who that one might be," said Dienw.

"It is a Prince of the Cymry, a Son of the Boundless, to go with Taliesin Benbardd into the Western World. Is it you who are the man?"

"Dear, help me better!" said Dienw. "Is it the look of a Prince of the Cymry or a Son of the Boundless is with me?"

"Whether it is or not," said Goreu, "the fate is on any man

who heard the music, that he shall accompany me today until I find that man; if it is all Arfon and Mon itself I must travel."

"I will do that gladly," said Dienw.

"That is well," said Goreu fab Ser. "We will go forward."

They journeyed on; and what with Goreu's songs and his stories, and his laughter and diverting conversation, Dienw had no memory of his sorrows and pain; and was happy for the first time in his life, so far as he knew. As noon Goreu stopped, and said:

"The hunger of the world has overtaken me. Is there food with you in the wallet?"

Dienw remembered the rabbit's leg, and was overcome with shame. "Such food as it is," said he. He opened the wallet and brought out what it contained.

"Dear, a miserable provision is this, for such a one as I am," said Goreu. "In your deed, is there nothing better with you than this poor and dilapidated meat?"

"There is not," said Dienw, sighing.

"Detestable to me, truly, is loathsome hunger; abominable an insufficiency of food upon a journey. Mournful, I declare to you, is such a fate as this, to one of my lineage and nurture!"

"Well, well," said Dienw'r Anffodion, with the bitter hunger awaking in him again; "common with me is knowledge of famine. Take you the whole of the food, if you will."

"Yes," said Goreu; "that will be better." With that he ate the meat and gnawed the bone and flung it from him. "Now that I have partaken of food," said he, "I am refreshed, and grief and fatigue have forsaken me; and I am filled with a desire for music. Play you the harp for my diversion!"

Dienw took it, and played *The Little Mountain Bird* on it, singing the song as best he could. When he came to, "God fired with song his wild, prophetic tongue," Goreu fab Ser, groaning piteously snatched the harp from him.

"Music I desired, and not this soul-piercing cacophony!" he cried. "A poor return is this for my kindness! Listen you now, and be silent."

Then he struck chords from the harp and began singing; and hurried forward as he played and sang; and the harping was a ruthless torment, and the song, hideous screeching: the birds in the air hearing it fell dead, and the rabbits perished in their burrows; the wolves fled howling, and the winds of heaven moaned and mourned. And as for Dienw, his pains and sorrows came back to him a thousandfold, and there was nothing for him to do but mourn and follow: over the mountains and the wild places, by sharp crag and raging torrent: his legs jerked miserably into speed by the harping; his mind and body in anguish.

"Come!" cried Goreu fab Ser augustly; "I am refreshed with food and glorious music; I loathe this dawdling unenterprise; it is a poor return for my kindness to you, that you should delay me thus on the road!" Thus he dragged him on and never spared him; keeping neither to road nor path, rabbit run nor goat track; but to gorse-grown level and jagged steep; trailing the way with crimson from Dienw's wounds, but going weightless and dauntless himself: until they came to the shore of the Menai and the house of the ferryman.

"Soul," said Goru fab Ser; "is there food in the house with you, to appease the enormous hunger of the world that afflicts me?"

"Such as it is," said the ferryman; "and little enough of it." He brought out half an oatcake and a thumb's weight of cheese; and it was Goreu who took them from him.

"Better for one to be filled than for two to go hungry," said he to Dienw. "Is it grudge me the provisions you do?"

"Not I," said Dienw. "Hunger and famine I am familiar with."

"It will be the better for you," said Goreu; and compassion in his voice instead of mockery and merriment; if anyone had been listening for it.

The ferryman launched his coracle, and the three of them went into it and began the crossing. And now a mood of restlessness came on Goreu, and he became wilder and merrier than ever he had been; yet losing nothing of his augustness of mien and tone. Night was drifting westward at that time, and the deep gray of the twilight over the waters of Menai.

"Dear, help thee better!" he cried, leaping to his feet, "behold yonder!" What was there to be beheld, none was to know: for no man may leap to his feet in a coracle without overturning it. The three of them were in the water; the ferryman swimming back towards Arfon, and pushing his boat before him as he swam.

"Peace now to drown and forget," thought Dienw with the Misfortunes. But there was no peace for him. "On me is the sorrow of all my race!" cried Goreu son of the Stars. "Never have I feared anything so much as death by loathsome drowning—a watery and evil death, and to end my life beneath Menai waves. Were there one here better than a poltroon and a braggart, he would quit his extreme selfishness and save me from the fury of the deep sea!"

"I am here," gasped Dienw; "it is not fated that you should drown." He gathered what strength he had, and made the best use of it, and held Goreu up in the water, and began swimming with him towards Mon. Whilst he swam, Goreu struggled and encumbered his limbs, and made no end of his august lamentations and reproofs. "If I save him, it is as much as I shall do," thought Dienw. "As for me, there will be peace when the waves have closed over me." Night fell, and the stars shone fitfully through gaps in the clouds. "I will save him," thought Dienw; "in my deed to Heaven I will." Then he thought, "It is a hun-

dred miles between me and Mon"; and with that a wave lifted
the two of them, and cast them up upon the beach. Mind and
thought were gone from him, as if death had taken him.

Goreu son of the Stars arose, and lifted him beyond reach of
the tide, and laid him down in a hollow between the sand-hills;
and then the likeness of human flesh and bone departed from
Goreu, and he took fire-form and godform, and rose up flaming into mountain stature till the peak of the Wyddfa was less
lofty than he; and turned his face southward and east toward
that holy mountaintop; and he said:

"Lord Mighty One, he is ready; the breath is gone from
him; the Nameless One with the Misfortunes is ready; Pwyll
Pen Annwn is ready at last."

Out of the peak of the Wyddfa rose Hu Gadarn, who was appointed in those days to be Emperor of the Gods and the Cymry
of Ynys Wen. He too flamed skyward, his crest burning among
the stars of Capricorn, his eyes shining with wisdom and
beneficence, his White Shield better than seven moons in the
heavens.

"I commend you, Lord Gwydion ab Don," said he. "Let him
be brought now into the Caldron of Ceridwen my daughter;
let his body be laid in Pair Dadeni, that new life and name may
be his."

From the midst of Mon, light streamed up into the sky;
flame-flakes of rainbow hues; and thence came nine dragons
through the air, and lighted down among the sand dunes, and
became the Nine Faery Princes that watch the fires under
Ceridwen's Caldron. They picked up the body of the Nameless One, and bore it to the Caldron.

In the morning when Dienw awoke, not an ache nor wound
was in his body, nor any sorrow in his mind. One stood over
him of immortal beauty, whose forehead shone like the Morning Star; five others came up the beach toward them.

"The greeting of heaven and man to you, Manawyddan son of the Boundless!" said Taliesin the Chief of Bards.

"And better be it with you than with me, Lord Taliesin!" said he, arising from the sand. "And better be it with the other five Chief Chieftains that are approaching us. It is I who will go with you into the Western World."

"Yes, it is you," said Taliesin Benbardd. "Behold here, the seventh who will be at the head of us!" said he, "Son of the Boundless, as befits the Blessed One's dignity!"

He went with them towards the Malltraeth; remembering how he had come by the name Taliesin had called him by, in the Caldron of Ceridwen in the night. "Goreu fab Ser," said he; "the Beset One, the son of the Stars; and Gwydion ab Don he was, whatever. And I that was Pwyll Pen Annwn, am Manawyddan son of the Boundless."

How Cuchulain Wooed His Wife

by Eleanor Hull

from *Boys' Cuchulain*

Cuchulain, the hero of many Irish legends, is often thought to have been the nephew of King Conchubar mac Nessa, said to have ruled in Ireland in the first century A.D. and himself the hero of a whole cycle of legends. Cuchulain came to the court of Conchubar at the age of six and from that time on distinguished himself by great deeds of strength. While still very young, he killed the fierce watch dog of the smith Culann and acted as guard in its stead. It was from this that he received his name, Cu Chulainn, "the Hound of Culann."

When Cuchulain grew up, he was brave and handsome and daring and many were the stories told of his mighty prowess.

HOW CUCHULAIN WOOED HIS WIFE

Eleanor Hull

———••———

I T was on a day of the days of summer that Emer, daughter of Forgall the Wily, sat on a bench before her father's door, at his fort that is called Lusk to-day, but which in olden days men spoke of as the Gardens of the Sun-god Lugh. And Emer sat, a fair and noble maid, among her young companions, foster-sisters of her own, who came from all the farms and forts around to grow up with the daughters of the house, and learn from them high-bred and gentle ways, to fashion rich embroideries such as Irish women used to practice as an art, and weaving, and fine needlework, and all the ways of managing a house.

Of all maids in Erin, Emer was the best, for hers were the six gifts of womanhood, the gift of loveliness, the gift of song, the gift of sweet and pleasant speech, the gift of handiwork, the gifts of wisdom and of modesty.

And in his distant home in Ulster, Cuchulain heard of her. For he was young and brave, and women loved him for his nobleness, and all men wished that he should take a wife. But for a while he would not, for among the women whom he saw, not one of them came up to his desires. And when they urged him, wilfully he said, "Well, find for me a woman I could love, and I will marry her."

Then sent the King his heralds out through every part of
Ulster and the south to seek a wife whom Cuchulain would
care to woo. But still he said the same, "This one, and this,
has some bad temper or some want of grace, or she is vain or
she is weak, not fitted as a mate to such as I. She must be brave,
for she must suffer much; she must be gentle, lest I anger her;
she must be fair and noble, not alone to give me pleasure as her
spouse, but that all men may think of her with pride, saying,
'As Cuchulain is the first of Ulster's braves, the hero of her
many fighting-fields, so is his wife the noblest and the first of
Erin's women, a worthy mate for him.' "

So when the princely messengers returned, their search was
vain; among the daughters of the chiefs and noble lords not
one was found whom Cuchulain cared to woo. But one who
loved him told him of a night he spent in Forgall's fort, and of
the loveliness and noble spirit of Forgall's second girl, Emer, the
maiden of the waving hair, but just grown up to womanhood.
He told him of her noble mien and stately step, the soft and
liquid brightness of her eyes, the colour of her hair, that like
to ruddy gold fresh from the burnishing, was rolled around her
head. Her graceful form he praised, her skilfulness in song and
handiwork, her courage with her father, a harsh and wily man,
whom all within the house hated and feared but she.

He told him also that for any man to win the maiden for his
wife would be a troublesome and dangerous thing, for out of
all the world, her father Forgall loved and prized but her, and
he had made it known that none beneath a king or ruling
prince should marry her, and any man who dared to win her
love, but such as these, should meet a cruel death; and this he
laid upon his sons and made them swear to him upon their
swords, that any who should come to woo the girl should never
leave the fort alive again.

All that they said but made Cuchulain yet the more desire to

see the maid and talk with her. "This girl, so brave, so wise, so fair of face and form," he pondered with himself, "would be a fitting mate for any chief. I think she is the fitting mate for me."

So on the very day when Emer sat upon her playing fields, Cuchulain in the early morn set forth in all his festal garb in his chariot with his prancing steeds, with Laeg before him as his charioteer, and took the shortest route towards the plain of Bray, where lie the Gardens of the Sun-god Lugh. The way they went from Emain lay between the Mountains of the Wood, and thence along the High-road of the Plain, where once the sea had passed; across the marsh that bore the name the Whisper of the Secret of the Gods. Then driving on towards the River Boyne they passed the Ridge of the Great Sow, where not far off is seen the fairy haunt of Angus, God of Beauty and of Youth; and so they reached the ford of Washing of the Horses of the Gods, and the fair, flowering plains of Lugh, called Lusk to-day.

Now all the girls were busied with their work, when on the high-road leading to the fort they heard a sound like thunder from the north, that made them pause and listen in surprise.

Nearer and nearer yet it came as though at furious pace a band of warriors bore down towards the house. "Let one of you see from the ramparts of the fort," said Emer, "what is the sound that we hear coming towards us." Fiall, her sister, Forgall's eldest girl, ran to the top of the rath or earthen mound that circled round the playing-fields, and looked out towards the north, shading her eyes against the brilliant sun. "What do you see there?" asked they all, and eagerly she cried: "I see a splendid chariot-chief coming at furious pace along the road. Two steeds, like day and night, of equal size and beauty, come thundering beneath that chariot on the plain. Curling their manes and long, and as they come, one would think fire darted from their curbed jaws, so strain and bound they forward; high in the air the turf beneath their feet is thrown around them, as though a flock of birds were following as they go. On the right side the horse is grey, broad in the haunches, active, swift and wild; with head erect and breast expanded, madly he moves along the plain, bounding and prancing as he goes. The other horse jet-black, head firmly knit, feet broad-hoofed, firm, and slender; in all this land never had chariot-chief such steeds as these."

"Heed not the steeds," the girls replied, "tell us, for this concerns us most, who is the chariot-chief who rides within?"

"Worthy of the chariot in which he rides is he who sits within. Youthful he seems, as standing on the very borders of a noble manhood, and yet I think his face and form are older than his years. Gravely he looks, as though his mind revolved some serious thought, and yet a radiance as of the summer's day

enfolds him round. About his shoulders a rich five-folded mantle
hangs, caught by a brooch across the chest sparkling with precious gems, above his white and gold-embroidered shirt. His
massive sword rests on his thigh, and yet I think he comes not
here to fight. Before him stands his charioteer, the reins held
firmly in his hand, urging the horses onward with a goad."

"What like is he, the charioteer?" demand the girls again.

"A ruddy man and freckled," answered Fiall; "his hair is
very curly and bright-red, held by a bronze fillet across his
brow, and caught at either side his head in little cups of gold, to
keep the locks from falling on his face. A light cloak on his
shoulders, made with open sleeves, flies back in the wind, as
rapidly they course along the plain." But Emer heard not what
the maiden said, for to her mind there came the memory of a
wondrous youth whom Ulster loved and yet of whom all Erin
stood in awe. Great warriors spoke of him in whispers and with
shaking of the head. They told how when he was a little child,
he fought with full-grown warriors and mastered them; of a
huge hound that he had slain and many feats of courage he
had done. Into her mind there came a memory, that she had
heard of prophets who foretold for him a strange and perilous
career; a life of danger, and an early death. Full many a time
she longed to see this youth, foredoomed to peril, yet whose
praise should ring from age to age through Erin; and in her
mind, when all along she pondered on these things, she still
would end: "This were a worthy mate! This were a man to win
a woman's love!" And half aloud she uttered the old words:
"This were a man to win a woman's love!"

Now hardly had the words sprung to her lips, when the
chariot stood before the door, close to the place where all the
girls were gathered. And when she saw him Emer knew it was
the man of whom she dreamed. He wished a blessing to them,
and her lovely face she lifted in reply. "May God make smooth

the path before thy feet," she gently said. "And thou, mayest thou be safe from every harm," was his reply. "Whence comest thou?" she asked; for he had alighted from his seat and stood beside her, gazing on her face. "From Conor's court we come," he answered then; "from Emain, kingliest of Ulster's forts, and this the way we took. We drove between the Mountains of the Wood, along the High-road of the Plain, where once the sea had been; across the Marsh they call the Secret of the Gods, and to the Boyne's ford named of old the Washing of the Horses of the Gods. And now at last, O maiden, we have come to the bright flowery Garden-grounds of Lugh. This is the story of myself, O maid; let me now hear of thee."

Then Emer said: "Daughter am I to Forgall, whom men call the Wily Chief. Cunning his mind and strange his powers; for he is stronger than any labouring man, more learned than any Druid, more sharp and clever than any man of verse. Men say that thou art skilled in feats of war, but it will be more than all thy games to fight against Forgall himself; therefore be cautious what thou doest, for men cannot number the multitudes of his warlike deeds nor the cunning and craft with which he works. He has given me as a bodyguard twenty valiant men, their captain Con, son of Forgall, and my brother; therefore I am well protected, and no man can come near me, but that Forgall knows of it. To-day he is gone from home on a warrior expedition, and those men are gone with him; else, had he been within, I trow he would have asked thee of thy business here."

"Why, O maiden, dost thou talk thus to me? Dost thou not reckon me among the strong men, who know not fear?" "If thy deeds were known to me," she said, "I then might reckon them; but hitherto I have not heard of all thy exploits." "Truly, I swear, O maiden," said Cuchulain, "that I will make my deeds to be recounted among the glories of the warrior-feats of heroes." "How do men reckon thee?" she said again. "What then is thy strength?" "This is my strength," he said. "When my might in fight is weakest, I can defend myself alone against twenty. I fear not by my own might to fight with forty. Under my protection a hundred are secure. From dread of me, strong warriors avoid my path, and come not against me in the battle-field. Hosts and multitudes and armed men fly before my name."

"Thou seemest to boast," said Emer, "and truly for a tender boy those feats are very good; but they rank not with the deeds of chariot-chiefs. Who then were they who brought thee up in these deeds of which thou boastest?"

"Truly, O maiden, King Conor is himself my foster-father, and not as a churl or common man was I brought up by him. Among chariot-chiefs and champions, among poets and learned men, among the lords and nobles of Ulster, have I been reared, and they have taught me courage and skill and manly gifts. In birth and bravery I am a match for any chariot-chief; I direct the counsels of Ulster, and at my own fort at Dun Dalgan they come to me for entertainment. Not as one of the common herd do I stand before thee here to-day, but as the favourite of the King and the darling of all the warriors of Ulster. Moreover, the god Lugh the Longhanded is my protector, for I am of the race of the great gods, and his especial foster-child.

"And now, O maiden, tell me of thyself; how in the sunny plains of Lugh has thou been reared within thy father's fort?"

"That I will tell thee," said the girl. "I was brought up in noble behaviour as every queen is reared; in stateliness of form, in wise, calm speech, in comeliness of manner, so that to me is imputed every noble grace among the hosts of the women of Erin."

"Good, indeed, are those virtues," said the youth; "and yet I see one excellence thou has not noted in thy speech. Never before, until this day, among all women with whom I have at

times conversed, have I found one but thee to speak the mystic ancient language of the bards, which we are talking now for secrecy one with the other. And all these things are good, but one is best of all, and that is, that I love thee, and I think thou lovest me. What hinders, then, that we should be betrothed?"

But Emer would not hasten, but teasing him, she said, "Perhaps thou hast already found a wife?"

"Not so," said he, "and by my right-hand's valour here I vow, none but thyself shall ever be my wife."

"A pity it were, indeed, thou shouldst not have a wife," said Emer, playing with him still; "see, here is Fiall, my elder sister, a clever girl and excellent in needlework. Make her thy wife, for well is it known to thee, a younger sister in Ireland may not marry before an elder. Take her! I'll call her hither."

Then Cuchulain was vexed because she seemed to play with him. "Verily and indeed," he said, "not Fiall, but thee, it is with whom I am in love; and if thou weddest me not, never will I, Cuchulain, wed at all."

Then Emer saw that Cuchulain loved her, but she was not satisfied, because he had not yet done the deeds of prime heroes, and she desired that he should prove himself by champion feats and deeds of valour before he won her as his bride.

So she bade him go away and prove himself for a year by deeds of prowess to be indeed a worthy mate and spouse for her, and then, if he would come again she would go with him as his one and only wife. But she bade him beware of her father, for she knew that he would try to kill him, in order that he might not come again. And this was true, for every way he sought to kill Cuchulain, or to have him killed by his enemies, but he did not prevail.

When Cuchulain had taken farewell of Emer and gained her promise, he returned to Emain Macha. And that night the maidens of the fort told Forgall that Cuchulain had been there and that they thought he had come to woo Emer; but of this they were not sure, because he and Emer had talked together in the poet's mystic tongue, that was not known to them. For Emer and Cuchulain talked on this wise, that no one might repeat what they had said to Forgall.

And for a whole year Cuchulain was away, and Forgall guarded the fort so well that he could not come near Emer to speak with her; but at last, when the year was out, he could wait no longer, and he wrote a message to Emer on a piece of stick, telling her to be ready. And he came in his war-chariot with scythes upon its wheels, and he brought a band of hardy men with him, who entered the outer rampart of the fort and carried off Emer, striking down men on every side. And Forgall followed them to the earthen out-works, but he fell over the rath, and was taken up lifeless. And Cuchulain placed Emer and her foster-sister in his chariot, carrying with them their garments and ornaments of gold and silver, and they drove northward to Cuchulain's fort at Dun Dalgan, which is Dundalk today.

And they were pursued to the Boyne, and there Cuchulain placed Emer in a house of safety, and he turned and drove off his enemies who followed him, pursuing them along the banks and destroying them, so that the place, which had before been called the White Field, was called the Turf of Blood from that day. Then he and Emer reached their home in safety, nor were they henceforth parted until death.

Deirdre

by Alan Michael Buck

from *The Harper's Daughter*

Deirdre was the daughter of Feidlimid, son of Dall, the storyteller of King Conchubar. Before her birth, it was foretold that she would bring great evil to the house of the King and to the sons of Usnach, nephews of the king. Some men advised the king to have her killed the moment she was born. But instead he hid her away at his hunting lodge, under the care of a woman named Levorcam, and determined to marry her himself when she was of an age to be married.

Deirdre, however, grew up into a lovely young woman who had ideas of her own. Her dreams did not include marriage to Conchubar, now an old man. When he asked, she refused him. The following winter events took place that began to fulfill the old prophecy.

DEIRDRE

Alan Michael Buck

———◆•◆———

WINTER had set in. 'Twas a bitter winter that year—cold, and bleak and dismal. Gales blew in from the sea. Rain fell in torrents. Rivers overflowed their banks. The forests were a shambles of uprooted giants. The wind shrieked unceasingly. Then snow came and the first fall was heavy; it lay deep and in treacherous drifts all over the land and consequently Conchubar was for the time being unable to get provisions through to Deirdre and Levorcam. Fortunately, they had the calf he had sent them some time before, else might they have starved. Levorcam postponed killing the animal as long as possible but faced at length with the absolute necessity of so doing, she stifled her feelings and went about the task.

During the killing, Deirdre, a-quiver with pity, remained indoors. But so soon as Levorcam called out that the calf was dead, she regained her composure and, curiosity getting the better of her, went out to see it skinned. Blood lay over the snow and as she drew near a raven flew down from a near-by tree to drink it. Struck at once by the vividly contrasting colours thus assembled before her, she could not help crying out, "Levorcam, the only man I will ever love will have those three colours—his hair black like a raven; his cheeks red with blood, and his body as white as snow."

Whereupon Levorcam made a pitying noise with her tongue. "Ah, my pulse," she sighed, "there is only one man the like of that living and it is not for you he is."

"Who could he be?" asked Deirdre.

"Niasi of the sons of Usnech," revealed Levorcam, forgetting that she should not be speaking or putting ideas of any man in Deirdre's head, and particularly Niasi.

"The warrior the hunter spoke of," mused Deirdre. "Tell me about him, Levorcam."

But Levorcam suddenly, and she hoped in time, remembered her trust. "Let you not be deafening me with your nonsense and I up to my elbows in gore itself," she chided roughly.

Deirdre smiled sadly. "Niasi," softly she repeated the noble name to herself, the while silently vowing never to be happy again until she had seen him.

"Niasi," she whispered.

That night it fell out that Deirdre had a disturbing dream. She dreamed she saw three men hunting on a hill. Puissant they were, three combative heroes. Black shone their hair as a raven's wing. Rosy glowed their cheeks with blood and snow itself was no whiter than their skin. It was the sons of Usnech were in it and the head and shoulders of Niasi were above all the men of the land.

Yet more remarkable is the fact that on the following day Niasi and his brothers, Ainnle and Ardan, actually did come hunting in the vicinity of Slieve Fuad. From bright early morning a boar had led them a merry chase out of Emain. Up hill and down dale they pursued the angry beast till close on dusk they cornered and made an end of it. Then did they utter their musical warrior-cry of victory; enchanted was the warrior-cry of the sons of Usnech; two thirds more milk gave each cow that heard it and if it were a man heard it he did not feel the need of food that day. And after that they pointed their steps homeward again, little dreaming that it would be many years before they arrived there.

For on the way they wandered from the path and presently stumbled upon the king's hunting lodge. A wall about the place they saw and a grassy roof and a line of apple trees before the door and they did not know who lived there nor what place it might be at all.

"It is an out-of-the-way place," observed Ainnle.

"There is a rushlight burning in the window," Ardan pointed out.

"Let us go in," Niasi suggested. "If we can but get the sup of milk itself we will not be wasting our time for it is the way the chase has filled my throat with dust and I am dry near unto parching."

Whereupon they went up and knocked on the door.

"Who's in it?" Levorcam's voice rang out sharp and hostile.

"The sons of Usnech," Niasi made known. "We are headed for Emain but have strayed from the path and crave food and drink before continuing on our way."

The sons of Usnech! Levorcam was panic-stricken momentarily. She hoped that Deirdre had not heard, that they had not awakened her for she had retired early pleading a headache. The sons of Usnech, indeed! If they were to drop in their tracks and slowly starve before the door they were the last three people in the world to whom she would dare to give admittance. Think what Conchubar would say! Thinking, she trembled all over with fright. "There is no food in this poor place," she cried. "Let you be following the skirt of the forest till you come to a running brook and you will be on the path again to Emain and to home."

Niasi grunted his disappointment. "Faith now, it is the mean mouth you have on you, old woman," he grumbled, turning disconsolately away.

Levorcam almost swooned with relief to hear their fast retreating footsteps.

Yet nevertheless, and despite all her hopes, Deirdre had heard their voices and, peeping through the window of her sleeping room, saw Niasi and his brothers go by. Instantly recognizing them from her dream, her heart beat fastly and a shining joy arose in her soul. "It is Niasi is it," she cried. And hastily seizing a cloak she tossed it about her and, not minding Levorcam at all, ran out into the night.

Who shall attempt to say what madness possessed Deirdre that night? All she could think of was Niasi; of how she had actually seen him and, having seen him, lost her heart to him for all time. Here was a man she could love, the one man in all the world. This was no Conchubar, no aged and bearded king soon to be laying up his weapons. Niasi was young. And he was beautiful. He was everything she had dreamed he would be. In that one fleeting glimpse she had had of him she could have sworn that his soul cried out to her soul, wherefore she felt that their love had been preordained, that it had been from the beginning and would survive the grave itself.

"I must follow him," she told herself desperately. "I must follow after him."

Difficult though it was to see in the dark she began to run in the direction he had taken.

"Niasi," she cried out and she running, "Niasi are you going to leave me?"

On ahead Niasi heard her cry and stopped to listen. "Has the old woman changed her mind? Do I hear her calling after us?" he asked his brothers.

Impatient to get home now that they had been directed aright, Ainnle and Ardan pretended they had not heard anything. "There is no one calling," they replied. "It is the wind in the trees you hear. There is a storm blowing out of the north this night. We would do well to be lengthening our steps from here out. A forest is no place to be caught and lightning itself riding the sky like as not."

Taking them at their word, Niasi plunged ahead.

The night was now pitch black. Not a star was visible and the wind was beginning to shriek like a woman in pain. Any minute and the storm would break and rain come pelting down. Realizing all this and feeling herself out-distanced, Deirdre called out a second time.

"Niasi! Are you going to leave me, Niasi?"

"Someone *is* calling after us!"

Niasi halted dead in his tracks and turned and listened.

" 'Tis the owls you do be hearing and they screeching," scoffed Ainnle and Ardan, hastening on.

Whereupon Deirdre called out a third time and her voice was one despairing wail, rivalling the keen of the wind. "Niasi! Are you going to leave me, Niasi?"

Niasi stopped again. "By the venom of my sword that is a maiden calling out in her distress!" he exclaimed.

"Is it daft you are to be hearing things," scoffed Ainnle and Ardan. "That noise is the waters of the river you hear swelling and swirling to run wild in the teeth of the gale."

"Not so. Not so, my brothers."

Niasi was convinced.

"Not so at all," he reiterated. "That was the third cry of a maiden and I'll not go forward a step till I find her."

And back he strode through the night and he not minding the storm brewing nor the dark nor his brothers calling after him to know was it out of his mind he was.

To have seen Niasi that night was to have gazed on a man among men. Consider his regalia, his appearance generally! A haw-red cloak he had about him. A brooch of hammered gold sparkled at his throat. Under his cloak he had on a white linen

lena, interwoven purple with gold. In his hand he carried a
spear and against his thighs a gold-hilted sword hung brightly
suspended. His countenance was frank and fearless. His jet
black eyebrows slanted like little roofs over his keen blue eyes.
His lips were richly red and his hair streamed out behind him
on the wind. It is not to be wondered at the trees bowed down
before him as he went.

At length in his quest he came to the running brook by the
pathside to which Levorcam had previously directed them. He
was always to remember the spot and forever hold it dear, for
it was there by the light of a watery storm-clouded moon that he
first beheld Deirdre.

She stood with her back to him. Her head was bowed and
he heard her sobbing as if her heart would break.

"Why do you weep, O maiden?" he queried softly.

He startled her. She did not hear him approach. But as soon
as she saw who it was she was overjoyed and she smiled up at
him through her tears. "I thought you had left me behind,
Niasi," she whispered.

"Left you behind?"

Niasi seemed puzzled. Who was she? he asked himself.
Where did she come from at all? Was it mortal she was or the
fairy people? Such beauty he had never seen on earth. "Left
you behind, is it?" he repeated, accenting his words in such a
manner as to convey the impression that that was the last thing
he would ever dream of doing. "But tell me," he went on, "who
are you to be saying that to me?"

"I am Deirdre, Niasi."

"Deirdre!"

Niasi fell back a pace, a troubled look darkening his countenance.

"Feidlimid's child of woe, is it?" he asked.

"Even so, Niasi. Strange things are foretold concerning us."

"You know the prophecy then?"

"Levorcam has told me."

"Aye, strange the things foretold," muttered Niasi. Who should know that so well as he? Was it not Cathbad the Druid, his own grandfather, made the prophecy? By the gods but it would have been infinitely better, he thought, had he never laid eyes on the maiden. Now, having seen her how was he ever to put her from his mind? But she was speaking to him. He must listen.

"Because of her shall Usnech's sons, the three noble chiefs, be driven into banishment."

She was quoting from the prophecy.

"Aye," he groaned, "and worse than that would befall."

"Some people do be looking for ashes and the fire not yet lit," Deirdre observed pointedly.

It seemed to Niasi that she was mocking him, accusing him of cowardice of all things. "Banishment would be the small enough price could I have you," he vowed heatedly.

"Nor would I reck the cost, Niasi."

Deirdre blushed as she made the avowal.

Niasi could not credit his ears. He moved to take her in his arms only to be halted by his conscience. He had forgotten the king. To embrace her would have been to betray Conchubar to whom he had sworn an oath of fealty. "We have forgotten my uncle," he sighed.

"Your uncle?"

Deirdre did not understand.

"Conchubar. The king."

"Oh, you are his nephew, is it?"

"Aye."

"Well," and Deirdre stamped her foot, "I shall never be his queen. Never!"

"There is no going against him, little spit-fire," smiled Niasi.

"And I thinking Niasi a man," flashed Deirdre scornfully.

Niasi clenched his fists, stirred to anger. "If it were a man said that his head would be at my belt even now," he stormed.

"And because it is a woman it is her heart you would take, is it?" retorted Deirde.

Niasi turned aside, broodingly. What was he to do, say? He had never been faced with such a dilemma in all his life. To defy Conchubar was to invite death not alone for himself but for the maiden and his brothers to boot. What right, he asked himself, had he to place so many lives in jeopardy? Besides even if he did take Deirdre with him where could they go? Where hide from the wrath of the king who was sure to follow them to the four corners of Erin if need be? No, the thing was impossible in its every phase.

Sensing something of his inward anguish, Deirdre went up

to him and placed her rounded, very soft arms about his neck. "Do you love me, Niasi?" she whispered.

"Love you!" Wonderfully, Niasi realized that he did and to distraction. "Aye," he vowed, "with all my heart."

"Why then do you torment yourself?" reasoned Deirdre. "Is not love a cause for rejoicing?"

"Death would come of it"—gravely.

With trembling, loving fingers Deirdre stroked his brow. "Death," she said, "is a small pitiful thing."

"For me, yes," Niasi was quick to agree. "But you are a maiden. You are young. You are beautiful. All your years lie before you. Wouldn't it be the great pity you to be cut down and you not having tasted the joys of the world at all?"

"Hush, beloved."

Deirdre put her finger to his lips, silencing him. "You are all the joys of the world to me, Niasi," she said.

Wondering what he had done to deserve such happiness Niasi resisted no longer. Straining her to his breast, he embraced her fiercely.

"We must go now, my heart's darling, to Ainnle and Ardan for they will be wondering what is keeping me," Niasi remarked quite some time later.

"I am ready," said Deirdre simply, placing her hand in his.

Whereupon Niasi lifted her on his shoulder and carried her back the way he had come.

Half-way they were met by Ainnle and Ardan, come seeking them. In a very few words Niasi acquainted them with what had happened and introduced Deirdre whom, it must be confessed, they received very coldly at first. "Och, Niasi," they protested, "will you stir up strife between us and the men of Ulster?"

Niasi set Deirdre down. "We have sealed our troth," he announced. "There is no turning back now."

"But think what Conchubar will say, man," reasoned his brothers excitedly.

"I have thought on it," sighed Niasi to whom, despite the great love he had found, the thought of breaking his vow of fealty was still a sore spot and one which he wished to forget as rapidly as possible, that is if one could forget such things. "The thing is beyond me," he confessed wildly. "Beyond me, I tell you! And I'll not give her up."

"Nor will I forsake Niasi," declared Deirdre with no little show of heat.

Ainnle and Ardan stood abashed. Shyly, they examined this maiden who had in so short a space of time obtained such a hold on the affections of their brother. And each felt within himself that it would indeed be difficult to put Conchubar before such ravishing beauty.

Deirdre smiled on them. "I will be a sister to you," she proffered.

Ainnle and Ardan looked at one another. "And we will be your brothers," they agreed in unison.

Then to hide their embarrassment they turned to Niasi. "We must make plans," they said. "There is no time to be lost in fleeing the wrath of the king."

"Aye, let us do so."

Excited and fearless, they charted their course.

The Lordship of the Fianna

by Ella Young

from *The Tangle-Coated Horse and Other Tales*

Fionn, or Finn, is another of the ancient heroes of Ireland. He served Conn, a legendary king of Ireland, whose palace was known as Tara. Fionn's father, Uail, had been chief of the Fianna, the royal militia, but he had been killed by Goll his enemy, in a great battle. Fionn lived only for the day when he could avenge his father and assume for himself the lordship of the Fianna. It is said that Fionn was just ten years old when he succeeded in this task. The story of how he achieved this is only the first of the many tales of his adventures.

These stories may be based on the deeds of an Irish chieftain who lived in the second or third century. The tales of Fionn, however, are told not only in Ireland, but in Scotland as well, where he is known as Finn MacCool. All of the legends agree that Fionn did spend part of his life in Scotland.

THE LORDSHIP OF THE FIANNA

Ella Young

———◦———

FIONN, son of Uail, stood on a small eminence and let his eyes delight themselves with the palaces of Tara. They were spread multitudinously below him, with their silken banners and their carved roof-poles and their gaily colored walls, like a piece of rich broidery-work flung for a vaunt on the green slanting meadows. Fionn had dreamed of those palaces upon hearsay for many a long year. His childish mind had colored them and carved their roof-beams with incredible devices. Man-grown his desire had dwelt among them. He had toughened his sinews in many a fight, he had endured hardship, he had denied himself pleasure, for the sake of this moment—Tara beneath him, and his feet on the road to it! The sun was high in the heavens, he had no need to hasten his steps. The palaces of Conn, Son of Felimy, the king that his father had loved; the palaces where Goll could lord it now as chief of the Fianna of Ireland! Uail, while he lived had been chief of the Fianna: Goll had slain him.

"It is a goodly spectacle," said a voice beside him, "fill your eyes with it. To-morrow the sun will look on blackened ruins."

"Who are you," cried Fionn, "to prophesy such devastation?"

"I am Datho, one who has lands and thralls in this place. If you were not country-bred and a stranger you would know that on the Eve of Sowan, every three years, Allyn, son of Midna, burns Tara."

"One man burns Tara!"

"He is of the folk of Dahna: and those that are wise in such matters say even that he comes from the Mountain of the Smith, Slieve Cullion."

"The Mountain of Cullion! The Mountain of Mananaun?"

"That Mountain! And it is from Shee Finnacha where Lear himself dwells that he comes: the High Radiant Dwelling-Place on the crest of the Mountain that is crowned with Flames redder than carbuncle stones through the hours of the day; and crowned with White Fire at night, lest man or beast or smallest creeping thing set foot there."

"Have not the Gods their share of honor?" asked Fionn, "Have they not their fill of praise and sacrifice? Why does this one torment us?"

"If the ancient rocks know it they keep the secret: but men will never be without stories of any happenings; or deaf to prophecies and haphazard sayings."

"What stories have they of this happening?"

"They say it is for the sake of a spear. They say that Uail, he that was chief of Clann Bassna and Head of the Fianna once, took that spear out of a Faery Palace, the palace of Allyn, son of Midna."

"Where is that spear?" cried Fionn.

"Where is last year's snow?" said the man.

"Is it with Goll of the Clann Morna the spear is?"

"It is not with Goll, or with any man so far as is known. Goll sacked the strong dune of Uail and took many a treasure from it, but he did not take the spear."

"Has strength withered in the hand of every champion: is there no strength in the battalions of the Fianna to withstand the burning?"

"You can try your own strength on it for the matter of that," said Datho. "The king offers his choice of a reward, and the contentment of his heart-wish, to the man who will stay the burning."

"Has Goll made trial of it?"

"Aye, Goll has made trial of it; and Goll's brother Garra; and bald-headed Cunnaun: the king himself has made trial; and slept with the best of them!"

"Slept!"

"Even so—slept—for when Allyn, son of Midna, comes he brings such music with him that a man in the very extremity of torture would sleep at the sound of it. The hounds sleep, the very rats in the granaries sleep. Everything that draws the breath of life sleeps, till Allyn, son of Midna, makes an end of playing. It is music he brings instead of a sword."

"If Uail, son of Trenmor, were here there might be need of a sword."

"Uail did not keep his own head safe," said Datho, "upon his proud shoulders."

"Who are you to take lightly in your mouth the name of Uail, son of Trenmor, son of Bassna?"

"One that saw him in his magnificence a time or two: but if you would speak with a clansman that held him dear from boyhood, there limps your choice!"

A large-limbed man, whom age had bowed without taming, was walking heavily and lamely along the road.

"That man," said Datho, "is Fiacha, son of Conga, once a man of mark, a follower that wrecked his fortunes for Uail. Rather than submit to Goll he lives in a mean hut without even a hound to share his poverty."

"I will speak with him," said Fionn.

"Come hither, Fiacha, son of Conga," cried Datho, "here is one that would question you."

"I am beholden to no man," said Fiacha, "let him who would question me keep step for step with me on the road."

"Well-spoken!" cried Fionn, and crossing to the old man he kept step for step with him on the road.

"What name do you bear," asked Fiacha, "you who would question me?"

"I am Fionn, son of Uail, son of Trenmor, son of Bassna."

The old man stopped suddenly on the road: his hands began to tremble.

"Why do you say this thing to tempt me?" he cried.

"I say the truth to you: have I no semblance of my father?"

The old man peered closely into Fionn's face. "You have Uail's eyes," he said, "and if you be indeed his son, tell me what mark was on the Treasure-Wallet of Uail."

"The Treasure-Wallet came from the Brugh of Angus: the marks that are upon the threshold stone of the Brugh are upon the Treasure-Wallet."

"Oh, if your hands have touched it, tell me how is it marked within."

"It is marked within with the secret names of the Four Jewels that the Gods of Dahna brought from the Heaven-World."

"May the sun protect you, Fionn son of Uail: may the earth make safe the pathways for you. Have you, my lord, the Treasure-Wallet of Uail?"

"I have the Treasure-Wallet."

"Pulse of my Heart, and Chieftain of Clann Bassna, I have a gift for you," said Fiacha, "poor and broken though I am— I have a thing hidden away: a treasure that I never hoped to put in the hand of Uail's son."

"Good will be the gift of one who loved my father. Tell me of it."

"It is the Spear that Uail took from the Gods of Dahna. I snatched it away, wrapped in its cloak of darkness, even whilst Goll and his people sacked the dune. Wrapped in its cloak I buried it, and over the place of its sepulture I built my poor hut. To-night, if you will, your hands shall hold it."

"Fiacha, friend of my father, with that Spear tonight I may win back my heritage: for it is in my mind to try fortunes with Allyn son of Midna."

"Terrible is the Spear, son of Uail. I would not bribe you with it to your death. Who knows if Allyn can be slain!"

"My mind was hardened to encounter him ere I met you. With or without the Spear I will engage to guard Tara to-night."

"The word in your mouth is the word of a chief. Hasten to Tara. Say naught of the Spear. I will bring it to you secretly when you shall have chosen your vantage ground."

"Fiacha," said Fionn, "had my father lived he would have given me to a princely house to foster. I have a noble foster-mother though she fostered me without a roof. No man is my foster-father: if I win out to-night, I will be your foster-son."

"Win victory, son of Uail! I would say that to you though you should never waste a second word on me. Win victory for Uail that is dead, and for the broken men of the Clann Bassna."

"For Clann Bassna!" said Fionn, and he set forth swiftly on the road to Tara.

CONN THE HUNDRED-FIGHTER

Conn the Hundred-Fighter sat in his chair of state in the royal hall at Tara. A tower of strength was Conn the Hundred-Fighter, a flaming torch of valor, a candle of munificence. Gorgeously apparelled he made a brightness where he sat. The Chief Druid, Kith the Red, was on his right, his head bound with a golden fillet, his purple robe embroidered in seven colors: on his left was the Royal Poet wearing his ceremonial robe made of the bright feathers of birds. Huge waxen candles lit the hall, their reflections danced and flickered on the walls where thin sheets of beaten copper took the place of tapestry. Rivetted with studs and knobs of red bronze that copper was, and fashioned to the shapes of strange birds; birds such as druids summon with incantations. Upon the crests of these birds, jewels glittered, cunningly wrought: red carbuncles served them for eyes.

There was gloom on the face of Conn: his brows were drawn in a frown, his thoughts were on the burning of Tara. And even as he sat thus, the trumpets of his proclamation sounded without. Great trumpets of bronze, brazen-throated, of a bulk that scarce one man could carry; they made a roaring sound like the bellowing of unearthly bulls or like thunder shut in a cavern. Seven of them gave bellowing voice, and earth reverberated with the sound. Scarce had the air ceased to tremble when Conn seized the bell-branch, the branch of silver with little bells upon it like apples of gold. Conn shook it for silence within the hall; it made a high sweet ecstatic sound like the twittering of small birds in Springtime. The loud voice of the herald came resonant from without:

"The High King of Ireland, Conn the Hundred-Fighter, offers to whatsoever warrior; magician; son of learning; poet; or simple artificer, has power or skill to keep the flames this night from Tara, his own asking of reward: and the contentment of his heart's wish if it be in a king's power to grant it."

The trumpets bellowed again: and whilst they bellowed, Fionn entered the hall. His red-gold hair and his height would have drawn men's eyes in any assembly. Tall and lithe and strong he was and young and goodly to look upon: his hair was wound close about his head, braided like the locks of a champion ready for combat, but save for the short sword in his belt he had neither shield nor weapon.

"Greeting to the High King of Ireland," said Fionn, "may prosperity multiply itself upon him."

"Greeting and blessing to you, young warrior," replied Conn.

"High King of Ireland," said Fionn, "if it should please the gods that I shelter Tara from the flames tonight, will you indeed give me my own asking of a reward: my heart's desire?"

"I will give it indeed," said the King.

Fionn looked to where Goll sat, broad-shouldered and fierce-eyed under his thick brows.

"O King," said Fionn, "it may be that to some lords in this assembly the reward I have it in my mind to ask will prove unpleasing. I would have the King's word bound on sureties."

Conn laughed a great laugh and looked around his hall. Kings from the five provinces of Ireland were there; they had come to take part in the ceremonies of the Festival of Sowan; magicians and druids of note were there.

"You have a high and confident heart, my Champion," said Conn. "Will you bind the bond on the kings that are here; and on Red Kith, the chief magician; and the magicians that follow him?"

"I could ask no better sureties," said Fionn.

Then was the oath tied with magic knots and strength of earth and fire and water to the satisfaction of Fionn. It was an uplifting of heart to the assembly.

"Tell me, my Treasure," said Conn, "of what lineage are you, and what name had your father?"

"Royal King," said Fionn, "I have not uttered my father's name save in secret: let it still be secret if I perish to-night. If I win victory I will make known my father's name and his lineage when I ask my reward."

"Let it be so, my Hawk of Battle," said the King, "and if shield or spear be lacking to you, choose from the best of mine."

"I have proffer of a weapon," said Fionn, "it will suffice me."

"May the great Battle-Queen lend power to it," said the King, "and have now a bite of bread with me and with these kings and lords who wish you well."

The high servants of the king brought then a loaf of white bread. Fionn took it in his hand and ate.

"Win victory and blessing, O King," he said, "this hour, and in every hour that the Smith hammers out for you."

"Win victory and blessing, my Hawk of Battle," said the King.

Fionn turned himself to the gathering night.

THE SPEAR BIRGHA

Behind Fionn, ramparted Tara crouched in darkness. The King had ordered it so. No smallest glimmer of a rushlight showed in any place: if Tara flamed to-night it would be lit by Allyn, son of Midna. From the North the son of Midna would come: even now he might be approaching, and Fionn had not the Spear! Alert as a wolf, his eyes searched the gloom, his ears searched the stillness; and before he could see anything he knew by faint and scarce detected sounds that someone was coming with stealthy cautious steps.

"Son of Uail," a voice whispered, "it is I, Fiacha. I have the Spear."

"My blessing on you," said Fionn, "give it into my hands; it is my choice of a weapon to-night."

"Very terrible is the Spear," said Fiacha, "Birgha it is named: feel how the blade leaps and quivers, even though the cloak that is wound so tightly all the length of it binds and restrains it. A demon writhes there: only once did your father unhood it, and then—by a hazard leap from his hand—it drank the life-blood of a warrior that he loved!"

Fionn's eager fingers closed on the haft: his hand moved circumspectly on the muffled blade.

"It lives, of a truth," he said, "but this cloak that hoods it seems no more than a silken swathe."

"Do not unwind that swathe till you are ready to launch the Spear. It is a cloak of some outlandish stuff: so fine that you could draw it through your thumb-ring. It came from that same palace whence your father reft the Spear: the ardency of the blade has not worn it, nor the years of its hiding cankered it. I would you could see the colors it has. It is a cloak from Faery-land."

"My mother came thence; mayhap she had such cloaks."

"Do not tangle your mind with aught but the night's work," said Fiacha. "If sleep does not thicken my lids, my heart will watch with you."

"Your heart will watch," said Fionn, "and dead men that were comrades of yours may watch in company. Go safely!"

"Win victory and blessing, Son of Uail: and should this night thrust you from life, say to Uail that Fiacha, Conga's son, was faithful."

Fionn was alone. The Spear writhed and trembled in his grasp. The dark plain spread widely to the dark horizon. It was Sowan Eve: no one who could help it would be outdoors on Sowan Eve. Every palisaded dune, every wattled hut would be closed and barred to-night. But the dunes of the Folk of Dahna would be open. The mountain-palaces would be open. To-night the Folk of Dahna walked abroad. To-night they had power. To-night, if a man dared the hazard, he could question the gods! Fionn tightened his grasp on the Spear: he was glad to feel the demon life in it, glad to feel it writhe and twist in his hands, eager and venomous.

The night crawled dumbly by like a wounded cumbrous beast dragging its heavy length. Fionn's mind dragged wearily and heavily like the hours; his hands wrestled with the Spear. No sight—no sound—no faintest stirring! So the hours dragged: endlessly, listlessly. But of a sudden between his hands the Spear tensed. The earth stirred itself. The air took lightness. MUSIC! Yes, it was music, very far off: a faint music, yet shrill and of an unearthly sweetness.

Fionn never could say afterwards what instrument it was that played. It was like a high lilting voice, and at the sound of it something in himself gave a great leap for joy: he felt that he was towering above himself, towering as if to equal the surge of melody, the tumult that was suddenly everywhere: in the earth; in the air; in the low distant hills; in the nearby dark druid-hill of Thlacta. Voices cried in that mighty surge; exultantly, defiantly: voices that wavered like tongues of flame. Vast litanies intoned themselves with multitudinous responses as if every forest leaf had a tongue. Trumpets gave it urgency. There were clashings of cymbals; and sweet strings of viol; and timpaun; and harp. Voices more than mortal sang in exalted chorus: and through every maze of sound there ran and scintilated and glittered—like stars in the milky way, like sparks of fire from an anvil—a myriad silver tinklings of shaken bells.

Minute by minute the music changed. It was patterned, as reedy shallows are patterned by the feet of the wind: it gathered itself as a wave gathers, curving to fall: and like foam on the running eager crest of a wave—like the silvery flash of a salmon in swirling waters—the first unearthly melody, the high lilting sweetness, maintained itself. Ah, what was it that the son of Midna was playing? Why did Fionn take part with him against himself? He was playing the stars out of the sky; he was playing the earth to nothingness, and yet Fionn exulted and towered out of his body to listen! What was that thin sweet song! Sun moon and stars were dust upon the wind—small scattered dust —and yet the song persisted: how could so thin and fine a sweetness consume the heart?

It was Fionn's heart now that fed the song, it was his strength that shrivelled in the wind: almost fainting he leant his forehead on the spear-point. And then he knew a strange thing. The Spear Birgha had a song—a song like a shaft of white light! Birgha, the Spear, was singing of battles, and of hero-deeds; of hazards and ventures; and of hardship; of men that dared, and snatched a victory; of men that dared and lost: and recked not of loss. What vibrant strength was in the song! Fionn's heart grew red again and his feet took a firmer grip of the Earth.

But was it the Earth—any Earth that Fionn knew? The grass was taking color of greenness—burning with greenness such as never daylight gave it! Flowers of scarlet and vermilion and azure—flowers the sun had never looked upon—trembled in it. The great dome of the sky bent low and low, a burning insufferable sapphire.

And now he saw the son of Midna, as if he had stepped over the rim of the world. Every color flamed and flashed about him, every surge of melody pulsed and fell: the whiteness of his body in the midst of it was like the whiteness of flame.

Fionn thrust the point of the Spear savagely against his forehead. He was standing for the men of Clann Bassna: men who had watched and starved on the hills; who had died in waste places, fugitive and broken—men who had kept the will to thwart Destiny. Hunted, harassed, poverty-bitten, they were outcast for Uail his father; they had died—some of them—for Fionn. They were blood of his blood; bone of his bone. Did they not cry to him out of their anguish, out of their unvanquishable valor: "Stand fast. STAND FAST."

Fionn began to unswathe the Spear: with deliberation he unswathed it lest he should injure the cloak; and as he loosened it, Allyn son of Midna—blinding, terrible in his beauty—was close upon him. He stood for a moment like a bright unearthly bird. He did not seem to be aware of Fionn, his eyes looked through and beyond Fionn as though he looked into the nothingness that is beyond the world.

He blew a breath from between his lips towards the ramparted palaces of Tara.

The hissing fierceness of lightning was in that breath!

Fionn had but loosed the cloak: almost despairingly he held it spread against that vehemence of flame. The flame played upon the cloak, dazzling it to a thousand colors: then sped hissing into the earth.

Allyn son of Midna blew for the second time a breath from between his lips towards the ramparted palaces of Tara.

It had the white fierceness of lightning—that breath! Like lightning it shone and dazzled on the cloak; and sped hissing into the earth.

Allyn son of Midna cast a glance about him as a mighty antlered stag casts a glance when he is aware of some forest portent and scarce knows whether to fight or flee.

A third time he blew a breath towards the ramparted palaces of Tara.

A third time the vehement hissing flame descended into the earth!

Then Allyn son of Midna turned and fled.

With the naked Spear in his grasp Fionn son of Uail leaped after him: and still the music surged; and still the voices cried in it; still every instrument made riotous ecstacy while reeling earth and reeling heaven flamed together! Fionn could be sure of naught in this strange world save the beating of his heart and the pounding of his feet as he ran. Light as flame ran Allyn son of Midna; and behind him and about him and before him the earth blossomed in starry fire.

Northward they sped—northward towards the Mountain of the Smith, towards the Radiant Dwelling Place, Shee Finnacha.

Splashing through the shallows of the Boyne, Fionn lifted a handful of the silvery sacred water and dashed it in his face and eyes. "Hail, Goddess," he cried in a choking salutation, for the river was sacred to Dahna, the Mighty Mother. It may be that she helped him: it may be that the son of Midna felt the strangeness of Fionn's world clogging and interpenetrating his own, for he ran with less lightness. And Fionn, running like a wolf—the beast that brings down every other by sheer persistency—felt strength and toughness increasing in himself.

So they sped northward—always northward.

Allyn son of Midna was no longer aurioled. The music too was swooning to a stillness. Fionn heartened himself—and heartened himself again. The son of Midna was naught but a slender youth running wearily. Yet he could not come within spear-cast!

It was so till Slieve Cullion—the Mountain of the Smith, the Hammerer, the Shaper and Fashioner of the World—stood in their path. Fionn knew that mountain shouldering against the sky, steep and shaggy. Allyn son of Midna could not breast it, running so wearily. Fionn heartened himself once more—yet the son of Midna kept out of spear-cast! Then, of a sudden the mountain opened. It was not a mountain but a fortressed dune, a great palace whose roofs and pinnacles glittered to the stars and lost themselves amongst them!

Mountain-vast within, the palace glowed with a soft and changing radiance and from the deep recesses of its portal the folk of Dahna like bright-colored blossoms looked out. They cried encouragement to Allyn son of Midna: yet ever he ran more wearily, lagging step by step. Fionn—running as the wolf runs on the track of a hind—judged his distance. Suddenly with all his force he loosed the Spear Birgha. It struck the son of Midna between the shoulders and pierced him through. At that the folk of Dahna gave a great anguished cry: but the son of Midna by a mighty effort kept his feet. Lagging, fainting, he stumbled on.

"Win victory, O Blossomed Branch, win victory," cried the folk in the portal: but they did not leave the shelter of the dune; they did not stretch rescuing hands to the son of Midna. Almost as his feet gained the threshold Fionn seized him by the hair and drew him backward—drew him reeling to the earth!

With his fall there came a sound like a clap of thunder. The air was full of voices that cried: *"Aie," "Aie," "Aie,"* but there was no glimmer of radiance left, nor any pinnacle of all that heaven-scaling host. In a cold pallor of waning stars Slieve Cullion shouldered the sky blackly.

In the thin cold light of stars Fionn looked down upon his capture. Allyn son of Midna lay as one dead: yet his body— pallid and slender, white as the shadow of the moon in water—

showed no wound! Fionn's eyes searched for the Spear: keen as a hawk questing the ground, he searched for the Spear, Birgha. It was nowhere—nowhere! Fionn's gaze came back to the son of Midna: he was loath to draw weapon upon that fairness; his hands were loath to touch again hair that kept such brightness.

The son of Midna leaned upwards on one arm. He smiled wearily and mockingly at Fionn, his eyelids heavy on his eyes.

"My head is yours," he said, "for a night and part of a day. The Spear is mine till the end of time. I do not rue the bargain."

He let himself sink back upon the earth: he shuttered his eyes; and neither spoke word after that; nor drew breath.

Fionn took his head.

TARA

The nobles of Tara, at the palace gates, spread their cloaks for Fionn to tread upon; and cried:

"Let the Savior of Tara give battle-luck!"

And so he came proudly before the King.

"Conn, the Hundred-Fighter, son of Felimy, High King of Ireland," he said, "I bring you the head of Allyn son of Midna: grant to me my heart's desire, and my own asking of reward. It is Fionn, son of Uail, son of Trenmor, son of Bassna, who asks."

There was clash and rumor of voices in the hall: and chiefs got to their feet. "Fionn son of Uail! son of Trenmor!" Some whispered it in consternation; some doubtfully; some with open joy. "Son of Uail"—that name ran through the assembly—son of the great dead chief! "Fionn, the Savior of Tara!"

Conn the Hundred-Fighter shook the bell-branch till there was a great silence in the hall.

"Set the head of him that blackened Tara, pole-high upon the ramparts that the sun may look scornfully upon it; and the eyes of the people behold it," said the King, "and give ear to the Champion who has brought deliverance."

In all that assembly there was not one who did not turn his eyes upon Fionn.

"Son of Uail, what is your request," said Conn the Hundred-Fighter, "and what is the fulfillment of your heart's desire?"

"I ask the Lordship of the Fianna of Ireland," said Fionn, "and recompense and honor and the favor of the King's countenance for the broken men of Clann Bassna: that is my heart's desire."

"The Lordship of the Fianna, you have won," said the King, "and favor and recompense and honor for the men of Clann Bassna: and here before the kings and poets and royal druids shall the chiefs and leaders and champions of the Fianna swear faith to you. And if there is one who withholds service from you, let him take ship for Alba or for Scotland or whatever country seems good to him on the ridge of the world, and depart thence."

Goll, son of Morna—Lord, till that moment, of the Fianna of Ireland—got to his feet.

"Fionn, son of Uail," he said, "your battle-skill outbids mine. I put my hand in yours: I am your man."

Goll's brothers, Garra and Cunnaun and Art, and the chiefs next in rank to them, stood up and spoke as Goll had spoken: and with oaths and fitting ceremonies their fealty was bound to Fionn. But as they greeted him with joyous acclamation there arose a great clangor and clamor without, and one entered the hall crying:

"Behold a marvel—a marvel, O King! Scarce had we set the head of Allyn son of Midna high upon the rampart-pole—that all the folk might look on it—scarce had the sun beheld it, when a great bird swooped sudden out of the sky. Feathered with silver and crested with gold that bird was. He stooped upon the rampart-pole, he cherished and sheltered the head there with his feathers, and rising bore it away: making a sweet and lamentable crying."

"It is well known to us," said the King, "that Allyn son of Midna was of the Folk of Dahna. They care for their own."

But Fionn turned over in his mind the son of Midna's words:

"My head is yours for a night, and part of a day. The Spear is mine till the end of time. I do not rue the bargain."

The Squires Win Golden Spurs

by Mark Powell Hyde

from *The Singing Sword*

Ogier the Dane was reared in the court of Charlemagne, Emperor of France, for reasons explained in this story. His greatest friends were Oliver and Roland, nephews of the emperor. The three were all renowned in later years for their great skill in battle and for their knightly courage.

At the time this story opens the three young men have not yet been knighted. But they have traveled as squires with Charlemagne's forces that are to do battle with the Moors who are invading southern France. The three ask Charlemagne's permission to take part in the coming battle. Charlemagne is about to grant the request when his son, Prince Charlot, intervenes and the request is denied.

Ogier is reported to have really lived at the court of Charlemagne in the eighth century. Many of the deeds ascribed to him are said to be true, although other highly fanciful tales are also woven into the account of his life. Stories about him are still told in Denmark where he is a great national hero.

THE SQUIRES WIN GOLDEN SPURS

Mark Powell Hyde

———◦•◦———

FROM the moment of his birth Ogier had been unfortunate, for his coming into the world had spelled the death of his mother. Soon afterwards Duke Geoffroy took to himself another wife, an evil woman, to whom a son had been born. This son she plotted to make King of Denmark.

Now at that time Denmark, like many another outlying state within the Frankish empire, was only partly independent. The duke owed allegiance to King Charlemagne which must be acknowledged each year by a fixed sum of money sent to Paris as tribute. But inasmuch as the sum total of the tribute remained merely nominal in amount, it was an avowal of dependence rather than a burdensome tax. However, in addition to tribute, such vassal states as Denmark might, in times of national stress, be called upon for soldiers to swell the Frankish armies. In exchange the vassal received from Charlemagne assurance of protection against foreign invaders, that is, assurance that within his own domains he might rule unmolested.

The first step in the plan of Duke Geoffroy's second wife was to poison her husband's mind with suspicions concerning Ogier, his elder son and rightful heir. This accomplished, she induced the duke to revolt against the authority of Charlemagne.

Thereupon the king, though sorely angered, sent a peaceable embassy to Denmark to learn the cause of this unlooked for rebellion and with fair words to demand his lawful tribute. Duke Geoffroy, however, scouted all commands and even maltreated the Frankish ambassadors.

Then the king sent an army which so awed Geoffroy that he swore to remain loyal thereafter and offered, at the suggestion of his wife, as assurance of his good faith, his elder son, Ogier, to be held as hostage by the Franks. Thus was accomplished the second step in the plot of the Danish duchess.

With the departure of the French army, however, the duke forgot all promises and again became rebellious. Nor was he seemingly at all concerned by the fact that in doing so he threatened the life of his son; for in accordance with the custom of the times it was lawful to put hostages to death when those whose good faith they insured played false. Thus the stepmother believed she had brought to fulfilment the third and final step toward Ogier's destruction.

Fortunately Ogier had found a powerful protector who had managed to save him from the wrath of the king. This friend was Duke Naymes of Bavaria, the one adviser at the court who had the most influence over Charlemagne. More than once, however, Ogier's life had hung by a thread, so incensed had the King become at times because of the treacheries of Geoffroy.

To have escaped death was, of course, a cause for thankfulness, but at times Ogier's lot seemed so distressing to him that he wished he might never have been born. In Denmark he had endured the malice of his stepmother and later the harsh cruelty of a suspicious father who had surrounded him, not with well-wishers but with hard task-masters who treated him with cruel contempt. Again, at the court of the Franks, all men had looked askance at the son of Geoffroy of Denmark. Gradually he had grown to expect disdain and suspicion from every one—every one except his fellow squires and old Duke Naymes. Even in these good friends he confided but little. Rather, he sought solitude where he could dream of doing great deeds and thereby cause men to respect him despite his ignoble sire. Of such dreams had been born the idea of obtaining permission to fight in the coming battle with the Saracens. If he could but distinguish himself by performing some especially honorable feat of arms, perhaps his associates would become friendly. Perhaps he himself would become lighthearted like the other squires. Charlemagne's refusal had been a sad blow.

So for a time after leaving the King, Ogier hated Prince Charlot, but the hatred did not continue, for in his heart the young Dane believed that the prince, like the others, mocked him because of the treacheries of Duke Geoffroy. Had he been less modest, however, he would have realized that Charlot's animosity was due to another cause—to jealousy. For Charlot was a vain man, one who constantly desired praise. He therefore was envious of Ogier's beauty and strength which in all war-like games and manly sports gave the Dane preeminence among the youths at the French court. This distinction Charlot could not forgive.

"When the rest of ye came in to the presence of the King," now spoke up one of the younger squires, "I had been in attendance on him and thus heard his talk and that of his captains. Methinks never before have such heavy doubts assailed Charlemagne. Here on this field is gathered nigh all his power, and feeble enough it seems when confronted with the paynim host. King Corsuble hath boasted that he will join in wedlock Gloriande, his daughter, to Caraheu, the Indian Prince—and that Caraheu shall later, at Paris, reign as King of France."

"Get ye all to laboring on the defenses!" cried a knight, as he galloped up and brought his horse to a sharp halt.

Peevishly but none the less promptly, the boys found im-

plements for the work and began to dig.

"We asked for swords and armor," grumbled Roland, "and we are given shovels."

That night the warriors of Charlemagne slept soundly until morn, but the squires, blackguards, and all of those not of the regular fighting forces worked far into the night strengthening the position of the Franks. Scarcely had the weary lads lain themselves down to sleep when day broke. They rose sleepily, but soon all weariness was forgotten in the excitement caused by a rumor that Charlemagne willed to do battle, though he hoped to receive an attack rather than to sound it.

As closely as they dared the squires approached the mound whereon Charlemagne sat his horse. A stream of scouts and spies continued to pass to and from him while he gazed in the brightening light at the movements of the enemy.

"Methinks we shall straightway see the beginning," cried Oliver excitedly. "See! Sir Allory comes!" He pointed to a knight in flaming orange-red armor who bore aloft on a gilded lance a gold-red, many-pointed banner.

Sir Allory was he who that day was to carry the Oriflamme of France—the battle standard of Charlemange. He drew up to a stand a little behind the King. His presence there meant battle. Like a torch in the night he gleamed against the grim, brown armor of the iron men. Sir Allory purposely wore bright colors that he might be conspicuous—he and his Oriflamme.

A cheer followed up on the arrival of Sir Allory, although in the minds of the Franks and, perchance too, in the hearts of their Italian allies, reposed some doubts concerning the wisdom of the choice of Sir Allory as battle-standard bearer. A Lombard he was and the greatest nobleman among all those Italians who before the battle had begged of Charlemagne that one of them might be honored by being appointed to the post of greatest danger. This request the King had granted, whereupon Sir Allory had claimed the position by right of his high rank. To many he seemed somewhat untried for a place which on a day of battle was second in importance only to that of the King himself.

"Would I were Sir Allory!" cried Roland passionately. A flaming spirit burned in Roland, one that ever drove him to attempt exploits greater than other men's. As youth and man he never knew rest from that relentless spirit, but because of it as time went on he did deeds at which men still marvel.

And now arose the sharp cries of captains, for the Saracens were coming on in great array from their center where **King**

Corsuble commanded. Across the stream they foamed and now the iron men and the Italian knights thundered to meet them. On the plain, beside the river, the two hosts crashed and at first the paynims gave way a little. A great shout went up from the French. A second infidel line, however, came on and held. The conflict swayed doubtfully, and in the thick of it fought Charlemagne. Before him and his knights the foe gave back until the King and his immediate companions reached like a spearhead far into the enemy's ranks. There at last they came to a stand, for those on their flanks had not kept pace with them. Like a rocky headland standing out into a turbulent sea, fought the King and his knights.

Taut of muscle, Ogier sat his horse, watching the mighty spectacle. A strong hand gripped his arm. "See!" shouted Oliver. "The riders of Caraheu!"

Turning, Ogier saw what seemed to be the firm earth moving swiftly upon the left wing of the French—so countless and closely arrayed were the troops of the Indian Prince. Along its whole length they struck the French left, some even making way around its end. Into the defences they smashed and spread confusion among the Christians.

Aghast, the squires saw the gold and purple armor of Sir Caraheu resistlessly leading the way. He clove a path through the French warriors until his great Damascus blade dripped with red. At length he stood triumphantly on a French rampart. There he paused to look about and, seeing how successfully his followers were fighting, gathered about him a doughty band and pressed toward the position of Charlemagne.

Now in so doing Caraheu met with strong opposition from the Italians, yet slowly his terrific onslaught drove them back, although they retired in the manner of men who fight to the death. No aid now could the Italians offer to the hard pressed King, nor did the Franks on his right render him any succor.

A groan of despair suddenly rose from the squires, for they saw Sir Allory giving back as in flight. More and more swiftly he retreated and finally broke headlong to the rear. Yet the squires again found courage for Sir Allory once more plunged into the fray where the Italians fought. Again, however, despair gripped them. Sir Allory seemed to be shouting warnings to his countrymen. Once more he was retreating, now flying incontinently as if for his life. The Italians thereupon became confused and began to give way as dismayed men do.

Rigidly and speechlessly, Ogier the Dane had been watching from his saddle, but when at last he could no longer doubt that Sir Allory was truly fleeing, he lept from his horse, seized an iron bar which chanced to lie near him, vaulted back to his saddle, and spurred like the wind to intercept the fleeing bearer of the Oriflamme. His astonished fellow squires followed to see what he would do.

Nearer and nearer to Sir Allory drew the Danish squire until he rode by his side. Suddenly he smote the recreant knight with his iron bar. Like a dead man the Lombard fell, but he came to earth hardly sooner than Ogier, who lept down and began to tear from the fallen knight his red helm and hauberk. The wondering squires gathered round.

"Strip him and on me bind his armor!" commanded Ogier so fiercely that the youths promptly dismounted to help him arm.

In a marvellously short time Sir Allory's armor was laced and buckled on Ogier. The Dane sprang to horse, waving the Oriflamme. Battle-axe in hand, he spurred back whence Sir Allory had come, and with his appearance courage returned to the French who saw their standard breasting its way toward where the King fought.

Facing fearful odds the Paladins of France and the King had managed so far to stand their ground, but of a sudden two

Saracen knights ran simultaneously upon Charlemagne and tumbled him with their lances. Down beside him lept the Saracens to make him prisoner. And in this they surely would have succeeded, had not the axe of Ogier fallen twice and laid them low. Quickly the Dane caught a horse and mounted his King, who once more rallied his knights and boldly opposed the foe.

And now, there in the center, the tide of battle began to turn, for the iron men on both sides the King were pressing forward and wreaking havoc amongst the Moslems. Thereupon Ogier plowed his way into the ranks of the faltering Italians to whom the bravely waving Oriflamme gave heart and courage.

Then, after some time had passed, Ogier became aware of two knights steading him on left and right. Intrepidly had these two held to his sides, despite the fiercest onset of the foe. To them Ogier cried out thankfully, "More than once have you two saved this banner and me. Better thanks shall ye have when the day is done."

Silently the two knights bowed that they had heard and steadfastly fought on. They had now drawn near the spot where Caraheu was fighting. Striving his mightiest, Ogier sought to meet the Indian Prince axe to sword, and Caraheu nowise avoided him, but in the press of men they could not come face to face.

At last Caraheu paused and saw how the Mussulmans were giving way in the center. The French right wing, too, was pushing back the Moslem left; wherefore the Indian Prince, a wise man of war, ordered the straightening of his lines. For a time Frank and Italian strove against Indian on equal terms, till of a sudden the main body of Caraheu's fighters wheeled and rode back across the stream. Behind them remained a thin, valiant line to cover the retreat, until like a flash this thin line also turned and rode back, leaving a gap betwixt the two hosts.

Nevertheless before these last doughty Indians crossed the stream, some few of them turned and singled out for combat the first of the Christians who raced in pursuit. One of the Indians thus wheeled directly in front of Ogier who made for him. But two Italian knights, forestalling Ogier, set upon the bold paynim, yet he smote both of them from their horses. Then Ogier was upon him and disarmed him with a blow of his battle-axe. Once more rose the blood-stained axe.

"Will ye yield?" shouted the Dane.

"In sooth, why should I not?" replied the Saracen coolly. "I am disarmed; albeit had ye come alone another tale might have been told."

Ogier lowered his axe. The Indian's fearlessness pleased him. "I cannot deny that I took ye at a disadvantage—nathless thou shalt go to the rear and there await me."

"To whom," asked the Indian, "shall I say I have yielded."

"Ogier, the Dane, I am called—and thou, what is thy name?"

"Sadonne, a captain under Prince Caraheu and his kinsman."

"Sayest so?" exclaimed Ogier. "Then am I honored, since thy fame for valiancy is not unknown amongst us."

For a moment he reflected and then resumed, "I took thee unaware, following the onset of the knights thou didst succeed in o'ermatching, wherefore in disarming thee I have gained but little honor. Now, if thou wilt do my bidding, ye shall go free and ransomless."

"Say on," returned the Indian knight.

"Do thou thus. Seek the Prince Caraheu and bear to him my challenge to trial by single combat which I would have take place tomorrow on yonder islet which lies in the river in plain sight of the armies. Consents Caraheu to meet me, then art thou free. Refuses he battle, thou must return as my prisoner."

Loudly laughed Sir Sadonne. "Free I am, e'en now. Caraheu not meet thee? Yea, he will meet thee or any other man. And when he does, Sir Ogier the Dane, look to thyself."

"Prithee make known to Prince Caraheu that I send my gage because I believe him to be the mightiest warrior of all Corsuble's host; else I had sent it to some other."

Up reared the horse of Sir Sadonne in turning; his master waved a hand and dashed across the stream.

And now was heard all along the French lines those trumpet notes which call the soldiers back to their defenses. The enemy, though nowise routed, was retreating. Their losses had been great, but great, too, were the breaches in the French lines, whence Charlemagne dared not hazard his thinned ranks among the good defenses where the paynims had taken stand.

A courier dashed up to Ogier and bade him attend Charlemagne in the royal tent.

"Come ye also," said Ogier to those two knights who had so well sustained him during the battle. "And I see certain others who have this day manfully followed this banner I carry. Come we all to the king." Silently they all nodded assent.

Still maintaining silence the two knights and their companions followed and soon all were kneeling to the King, who with his own hands raised Ogier to his feet.

"Forgive me, noble Allory," spake Charlemagne with tears of gratitude in his eyes. "For a time I believed thee a coward. Rise now and ask of me any boon as reward for they priceless achievements."

Then at last the knight who had stoutly held to Ogier's right hand found his voice.

"Allory, Sire? Here stands no such craven!"

Then the bold knight who had ridden on Ogier's left cried out, "Allory! That Allory should be hanged as a recreant. Look you!"

Both together the two loosened the straps on Ogier's helmet and lifted it from his head. And now when all stood spell-bound with surprise, none were more amazed than Ogier himself for he had recognized the voices of those two knights. With a quick motion he lifted the visor of one of them and looked into the haughty face of Roland. And when he lifted the other visor, the brown eyes of Oliver smiled on him. Whereupon Roland and Oliver bared the faces of the other warriors who had come with them and each of them proved a squire. The boys glanced nervously about, wondering how their disobedience would be taken. But Charlemagne smiled away their uneasiness.

"The tide of battle changed by striplings!" laughed Duke Naymes.

When the laughter died away, the King turned to Ogier and addressed him in musing tones.

"Thou, Ogier the Dane. Thee have I more than once thought to put to death. Had I done so all Christendom would have suffered." He paused while his eyes grew kind. "To the craven Allory promised I any boon he might ask. I now retract that promise, but to thee, youth Ogier, make I a like one. Speak. What shall I confer upon thee?"

"Sire, dare I ask not one, but two?"

"Speak them."

"First, that the order of knighthood be bestowed on these my comrades and on me. Second, whereas I have been a hostage, I would be freed from that restraint and made your envoy to my father, Duke Geoffroy. Methinks I can so contrive as to smooth away the odds 'twixt you and him more cheaply than by trial of war, the which I know you must attempt except my father change his ways."

"Truly," replied the King, "ye ask but little. . . ."

The King's further words were stayed by the entrance into

his presence of a tall, olive-skinned Saracen whose steady eyes revealed to all beholders that here was one who feared no man. Proudly he entered, his robe of monkish shape but of purple satin, richly broidered in many hues. On his head lay the folds of a blue turban in which jewels sparkled; a jewel-encrusted scimitar, more for display perchance than battle, hung at his waist. His short, pointed mustachios gleamed with oil. He bowed low to Charlemagne.

"Mighty Emperor of Christendom, 'tis Caraheu of India now greets you. In peace I come, seeking one amongst ye called Ogier the Dane." He straightened and looked to the King confidently.

"Prince Caraheu," quoth Charlemagne, "thy name and fame are known to all men. None here but honors thee. In truth such good will do I bear thee that if thou wilt consent to become a Christian, ye shall be welcomed amongst my lords as second to none."

"Sire, for thy praise I thank thee and in reply may avouch that, did ye but worship the True Prophet, no more devoted servant would be thine than Caraheu."

The King smiled and pointing said, "There stands Ogier the Dane. First, however, may I not learn the nature of thine errand with him?"

" 'Tis soon said. Oft before, O King of the Franks, have I desired to see and converse with thee and thy lords in friendly manner. Whence, upon receiving from Ogier the Dane his gage of battle, I came in person to accept it."

At these last words the King turned disquietedly to the Dane saying, "Ogier, I say in this ye have done ill. Are not the hazards of battle enough but that ye must jeopardize thy young life 'gainst this Indian Prince—he who wields Courtain, the terrible sword; he who is one of the world's mightiest?"

"Sire, we two in this day's battle failed to meet face to face, despite we tried to do so; therefore I sent my challenge. I prithee now make me knight that I may not fail him on the morrow."

"Nay, Sire," spake Prince Charlot. "Permit not this stripling, Danish hostage to thus blunder into greater matters than he dreams of. To-day he chanced to gain some honor by a trick and now thinks to find fame by humbling this princely guest of ours. Some better knight must meet Prince Caraheu, some seasoned warrior. I might well take the combat upon myself."

For a moment Charlemagne remained thoughtful, while a wave of uneasiness and contempt passed through the French knights. Gladly would they have seen the malicious Charlot humbled at the hands of Caraheu, but they knew well enough that this would never come to pass, inasmuch as Charlot by some pretense would avoid actual combat and thus shame the Frankish arms. With downcast eyes the Franks awaited the King's reply.

"What say ye, Sire?" said Charlot.

"Sir," quoth Caraheu addressing Charlot comtemptuously, "I came hither to accept the gage of Ogier the Dane. Him shall I meet or none. Howbeit," he continued still addressing the Prince, "whereas ye be so bent on combat I would nothing balk ye. My cousin, Sir Sadonne, I can promise will be blithe to meet thee. We four shall meet on that islet in the river, if your King permits."

Spake the King, "Ogier, approach and kneel before me, ye and thy graceless companion squires. Disobedient have ye all been this day but valiant. Henceforward shall ye all wear spurs of gold."

So Ogier knelt and became a knight, and so, too, Roland, Oliver, and the other squires.

Charlemagne seldom held in check the daring of his knights; rather he encouraged knightly exploits. Thus when all the

squires had been knighted, he again courteously addressed Prince Caraheu.

"Sir Prince, if thy cousin, Sir Sadonne, would meet my son I shall not gainsay the encounter. On the morrow, if our armies do not engage, the two combats shall take place at the ninth hour in the sight of all."

Caraheu once again bowed low. "Great Christian king," said he, "I thank ye for thy courteous reception. And to-morrow, if ye and King Corsuble do not renew the conflict, then shall my cousin meet thy son and I, Sir Ogier. Farewell."

Turning the Indian prince made his way outside where Ogier joined him to offer the courtesy of holding his stirrup. Diffidently the Dane addressed the noble Indian.

"Sir Prince, to-morrow we shall meet as foes, but if neither the one nor the other be slain, I beg that nevermore may we meet save as friends."

Leaning downward in his saddle, Sir Caraheu held out his hand and replied, "Youth that ye be, Sir Ogier, on the morrow I shall need all my warrior's skill. But thereafter we shall live as friends."

Away then he galloped, Ogier watching admiringly until the Indian had splashed through the river.

A Roland for an Oliver

by James Baldwin

from *The Story of Roland*

When Roland, nephew of the Emperor Charlemagne of France, and Oliver were boys in Charlemagne's court, each called the other brother and made a vow to be true throughout life. In later years they were separated, but finally they came together again unexpectedly, as this story tells.

The friendship of the two courageous knights was lifelong, and they died together in the Battle of Roncesvalles, fighting against the Moors. The Battle of Roncesvalles is supposed to have been fought in 778. The story is told in the French epic, Chanson de Roland, first written down in the eleventh century. Although tradition says the fighting was against the Moors, some modern scholars think the French were fighting the ancestors of the modern Basques.

A ROLAND FOR AN OLIVER

James Baldwin

———•••———

CHARLEMAGNE held high festival at Paris. It was in thanksgiving for the victories with which his arms had everywhere been blessed. Once more the foes of Christendom had been driven from Christian soil; once more did peace and prosperity seem to smile upon France. And the king had summoned the worthiest barons and warriors of his realm to award to each some fitting recompense for his services and good faith.

Among the knights who had come to Paris was old Count Gerard, the grandfather of Oliver, and one of the most powerful barons of France. He had come to renew his homage for his ancient fief of Viana; and he hoped that the king, as a reward for his lifelong services would grant him now the vacant fief of Burgundy. But from some reason best known to himself, Charlemagne failed to invest him with the wished-for dukedom. Some say that it was all the result of an awkward accident. The count, they say, after doing homage for Viana, stooped, as was the custom in those times, to kiss the king's foot. But, greatly to his chagrin, he stumbled, and his lips touched the foot of the queen, who was sitting by the side of Charlemagne. The knights who stood around were much amused, and could not forbear laughing at the unlucky count; but the king, in

anger, told him that the fief of Burgundy had already been granted to a younger and more courageous knight, and that he must content himself with Viana until he had learned better manners. Count Gerard, boiling over with rage, turned upon his heel, and strode out of the palace. He called his men together, mounted his horse, and set out with all speed for Viana.

It matters not whether this story be true or not, we know that Count Gerard rebelled against the king, and declared, that, for the affront which Charlemagne had offered him, he would no longer be his man, nor pay him tribute. He shut himself up in the stronghold of Viana, which he victualled and strengthened with great care, and made ready for a long and a close siege. He sent also to his brother Miles of Apulia and to his son Rainier of Genoa, craving their help. Miles came with a thousand men bearing shields; and Rainier, with two thousand crossbow-men. With Rainier came also his son Oliver, boldest of warriors, and his daughter Alda, beautiful as a Persian peri, brave as a Saxon valkyrie.

Great indeed was the siege which Charlemagne placed around Viana: none ever saw the like before. And he vowed that he would never leave it, nor give up the contest, until the proud Gerard should be humbled in the dust before him. For nine weeks he besieged the stronghold, and allowed no one to come in or to go out; and yet so well supplied was the garrison with all things needful for life and comfort that they cared but little for the blockade. Neither besiegers nor besieged spared any pains to annoy one another. If Charlemagne's warriors dared approach too near the walls, they were driven back by a shower of arrows from the crossbows of the sharp-sighted Genoans. If the men of Viana ventured outside of the gates, or beyond the moat, a troop of fleet horsemen drove them back at the point of the lance. Sometimes the besieged would make a bold sally, and attack their foes in the open plain; sometimes the besiegers would try to take the stronghold by storm. But day after day went by, the summer passed, and autumn came, and the war seemed no nearer at an end.

Sometimes the Lady Alda stood upon the ramparts, and cheered the besieged, or helped to throw down stones and other missiles upon the heads of those who were trying to scale the walls. And once, dressed in full armor, she ventured out at the head of the Vianese and boldly charged upon the besiegers. One day, Roland, seeing the fair lady standing upon the wall, rode up within call, and asked her her name.

"My name is Alda," she answered, "and my grandfather is the Count Gerard."

"And my name is Roland," said the hero, "and my uncle is King Charlemagne. Never have I seen a warrior-maiden fairer or nobler than thou. Never will I cease to love and to woo thee, though it should be at the cost of my life."

Week after week passed by and still the wearisome siege continued. Some say that Charlemagne was encamped around Viana for seven years, but I think it could not have been more than seven months. Nevertheless, the whole country, for leagues on every side, was laid waste; and what had once been a blooming garden was now in a fair way to become a desert.

The king allowed neither wind nor rain to turn him aside from his purpose, or to make him forget his vow; and all winter long his men sat by their camp fires, and surlily guarded the approaches to Viana. At length, however, Eastertide drew on apace; and the woods began to grow green again, and the flowers sprang up in the meadows, and the birds sang soft and sweet. And many knights bethought them then how idly and vainly their time was being spent in this fruitless war against one of their own number; and they longed to ride away in quest of other and more worthy adventures. The king tried hard to press the siege and to bring it to a speedy close, but in vain. The watchful and valiant crossbow-men held the besiegers at bay, and obliged them to keep their accustomed goodly distance from the walls.

One day a party of strange knights rode into the camp, and asked to see the king without delay. They came from the mountain land which borders France on the south; and they brought stirring news,—news which aroused the zeal of every loyal Christian warrior. Marsilius, the Pagan king of Spain, they said, had crossed the Pyrenees with a great host of Saracens, and was carrying fire and sword and dire distress into the fairest provinces of Southern France. Unless Charlemagne should come quickly to the help of his people all Aquitaine and Gascony would be lost, and the Pagans would possess the richest portion of his kingdom.

The king was much troubled when he heard these tidings, and he called his peers together to ask their advice. All declared at once in favor of raising the siege of Viana, of making some sort of peace with Gerard, and marching without delay against the invaders. But Charlemagne remembered, that, before undertaking the siege of Viana, he had vowed not to desist until Count Gerard was humbled in the dust at his feet.

"I have an oath in heaven," said he, "and I must not break it. This traitor Gerard shall not be spared."

"Which were better," asked Duke Ganelon mildly,—"to forget a vow which was made too hastily, or to sit here helpless, and see all Christendom trodden under the feet of accursed Saracens?"

"It seems to me," said sage Duke Namon, "that the present business might be speedily ended by leaving it to the judgment of God. Count Gerard knows nothing of the straits that you are in: he cannot have heard of this invasion by the Saracens; and he will gladly agree to any arrangement that will bring your quarrel with him to an honorable end. Let two knights be chosen by lot, one from each party, and let the combat between them decide the question between you and Count Gerard."

Charlemagne and his peers were much pleased with this plan; and a messenger with a truce-flag was sent into the fortress to propose the same to Count Gerard. The men of Viana were not only heartily tired of fighting against the king, but they foresaw, that, if the siege were kept up much longer, they would be obliged to surrender for want of food; for their provisions were already beginning to run low. So they very gladly agreed to leave the whole matter to the decision of Heaven; and, as they numbered among them some of the bravest and most skillful swordsmen in Christendom, they had little doubt but that the judgment would be in their favor.

When the messenger came back to Charlemagne with Count Gerard's answer, the king and his peers at once drew lots in order to determine which one of their number should be their champion. The lot fell upon Roland; and to him was assigned the danger and the honor of maintaining the dignity and authority of the king, and of deciding a question which many months of warfare and siege had failed to settle.

Early the following morning Roland was ferried over to an island meadow in the Rhone, where the knight who had been chosen by the Vianese folk to oppose him was already waiting. Roland was well armed; but instead of his own shield he carried another, which the king had given him—one wide and thick, but new and untried; yet his good sword, Durandal the terror, slept in its sheath by his side, and with it alone he would have felt sure of victory. The Knight of the Red Plume (his opponent) had armed himself with the greatest care. His war coat had been wrought by the famed smith, the good Jew Joachim, and was said to be proof against the stroke of the best-tempered sword. The hauberk which he wore was the one which King Aeneas, ages before, had won from the Greeks on the plains of Troy. His buckler was of fish skin from the great salt sea, stretched on a frame of iron, and hard enough to turn the edge of any common sword.

On one bank of the river stood the friends of Roland anxious to see how the young hero would acquit himself, and yet not at all fearful of the result. On the other side were Count Gerard and Miles and Rainier, and the bravest knights and the fairest ladies of Viana. And among these last, the fairest of all was Alda, the daughter of Rainier, and the sister of Oliver.

The signal for the onset is given. The two knights put spurs to their steeds, and dash toward each other with the fury of tigers and the speed of the wind. The lances of both are shivered in pieces against the opposing shields, but neither is moved from his place in his saddle. Quickly, then, they dismount, and draw their swords. How Durandal flashes in the light of the morning sun! Now does the helmet which the good Jew Joachim made do service for the red-plumed knight. The fair Alda is overcome with fear. She hastens back to the castle. She goes to the chapel to pray, and falls fainting at the altar.

Never before has there been so equal a fight. For more than two hours the two knights thrust and parry, ward and strike; but neither gains the better of the other. At last, however, the sword of the red-plumed knight is broken by a too hasty blow upon Roland's helmet: his shield, too, is split from top to bottom. He has neither wherewith to fight, nor to defend himself, yet he has made up his mind to die rather than to be vanquished, and he stands ready to fight with his fists. Roland is pleased to see such pluck, and he scorns to take advantage of his foe's ill plight.

"Friend," said he right courteously, "full great is your pride, and I love you for it. You have lost your sword and your shield, while my good Durandal has neither notch nor blemish. Nephew am I to the king of France, and his champion I am to-day. Great shame would be upon me, were I to slay an unarmed man when he is in my power. Choose you now another sword—one to your liking—and a more trusty shield, and meet me again as my equal."

Roland sat down upon the grass and rested himself, while the red-plumed knight bade his squires bring him another sword from the castle. Three swords were sent over to him,—that of Count Gerard, that of Rainier the Genoese, and Haultclear, a blade which the Jew Joachim had made, and which in old times had been the sword of Closamont the emperor.

The knight chose Haultclear. Roland rose from the grass, and the fierce fight began again. Never were weapons wielded with greater skill; never was there a nobler combat. The sun rose high in the heavens, and the noontide hour came; and still each knight stood firmly in his place, thrusting and parrying, striking and warding, and gaining no vantage over his foe. After a time, however, the patience of the red-plumed knight gave out. He grew furious. He was anxious to bring the combat to an end. He struck savagely at Roland; but the stroke was skilfully warded, and Hautclear snapped short off near the handle. At the same time Durandal, coming down with the force of a thunder-bolt, buried itself so deeply in the shield of the red-plumed knight, that Roland could not withdraw it.

Both knights were thus made weaponless; but neither was vanquished. Wrathfully they rushed together to seize each other, to throw each other down. Moved by the same thought, each snatched the other's helmet, and lifted it from his head. Some say that a bright cloud and an angel came down between them, and bade them cease their strife; but I know not whether

this be true, for, as they stood there, bareheaded, and face to face, memories of their boyhood came back to them. Both were struck dumb with astonishment for a moment. Roland saw before him his loved brother-in-arms, Oliver. Oliver, now no longer the red-plumed knight, recognized his old friend Roland. Then they rushed into each other's arms.

"I yield me!" cried Roland.

"I yield me!" cried Oliver.

Great was the wonder of Charlemagne and his peers when

FRANCE

they saw their champion thus giving up the fight when victory seemed assured. Equally great was the astonishment of
the Vianese and of Oliver's kinsmen. Knights and warriors from
both sides of the river hastened to cross to the island. They were
eager to know the meaning of conduct seemingly so unknightly. But when they came nearer, and saw the men, who had
fought each other so long and so valiantly, now standing hand
in hand, and pledging anew their faith as brothers-in-arms,
every thing was made clear. And with one voice all joined in
declaring that both were equally deserving of the victory. And
Ogier the Dane stood up, and said, that, although the question
between Charlemagne and Gerard was still unsettled, yet Roland and Oliver had acquitted themselves in all things as became true knights.

"Let him who would gainsay it speak now, or forever hold
his tongue!" he cried.

But in all the host there was not one who wished to break
lances with Ogier, or to risk his displeasure by disputing his
word.

Then the folk of Viana went back to their castle prison, and
their foes returned to their tents; and each party began anew to
plan means by which this tiresome and unprofitable war might
be brought to an end.

Another week, and a fortnight, passed by, and every day
messengers came to Charlemagne, telling of the ravages of
Marsilius the Moor, and begging him to hasten to the aid of
his people. Very willingly would he have gone, and left Viana
in peace, had it not been for the remembrance of his vow.

"I cannot go," said he, "until this rebel Gerard is humbled
upon his knees before me."

One by one his knights, tired of inaction, and preferring to
wage war against unbelievers rather than against men of their
own faith and nation, stole quietly from the camp, and rode

away toward the Pyrenees. It seemed as if the king would be left, after a while, to carry on the siege of Viana alone; yet he never faltered in his determination to perform his vow to the very letter.

One day some huntsmen brought word to Charlemagne that a fierce wild boar had been seen in Claremont wood, and that he was now hiding in a thicket not far from Viana. Ever eager for the chase, the king at once mounted his horse, and, followed by his men and his hounds, he hastened to the wood. It was not long until the grim beast was driven from his lair; and the king, as was his wont, gave chase. Duke Gerard and his knights, watching from the towers of Viana that morning, had seen the kingly party ride out into the wood.

"Let us have a hand in this hunt," said Rainier of Genoa. "We might hunt for royal game; and, could we but take the king, we might end this war on our own terms."

Count Gerard and the other nobles were pleased.

"I know a secret underground passage," said the count, "which leads directly from the castle to the wood. Once there, we might lie in wait in the thickets, and waylay the king as he passes by."

The knights at once girded on their armor, hung their shields to their necks, and took their bows and arrows in hand. Then, led by two trusty squires, who lighted the way with torches, they filed through the long, dark tunnel, and came out in the midst of a briery thicket in the wood of Claremont. The sound of the baying hounds told them that the game was not far away; and soon, as good fortune would have it, the hunted beast, furious with rage, rushed past them. Very close behind him came Charlemagne, riding upon his favorite hunting-steed and so intent upon spearing the boar that he neither saw nor thought of any thing else. The huntsman and most of the hounds had been left far behind.

"Now is our time!" cried Rainier. And, quick as thought, five well-armed knights rushed out of the thicket, and seized the king's charger by the reins, and called upon him to surrender. Having only the weapons of the chase, and being set upon so unexpectedly, Charlemagne was no match for his stout assailants. Quickly he was seized, and dragged from the saddle: firmly but gently was he held by his captors. Then Aymery of Narbonne, bloodthirsty, and at heart a traitor, whispered to Count Gerard, and advised him to kill the king.

"With him out of our way," said he, "we shall be free; our fiefs shall be our own; and no man shall claim homage or tribute from us."

But the count pushed him aside with scorn.

"Shame on thee!" he answered. "May it not please God that ever king of France be killed by me: of him I will hold my castle and my lands!" And he knelt humbly before the captive king.

Charlemagne's heart was touched by the words of loyalty and good faith which fell from the lips of the count.

"Gerard of Viana," he cried, "all this trouble between thee and me is ended and forgotten. If thou hast harmed me, I freely forgive thee. No tribute shalt thou pay for land, or fief, or castle. Only for the sake of my vow, renew thy homage."

Then Gerard ungirt his sword from his side, and uncovered his head, and knelt again before the king; and he placed both his hands between those of the king, and said,—

"From this day forward I become your man of life and limb, and of all worldly worship; and unto you I will be loyal and true, and I will bear you faith for the lands and the castles and the houses that I claim of you. And to no other lord will I grant obedience, save at your behest."

Then the king raised him gently from the ground and kissed him, and answered,—

"Count of Viana, my man shalt thou be in life and limb and worldly worship; and to thee do I grant the lands, the fiefs, and the castles of Viana, to have and to hold without any payment of tribute, or any other service save that which is given in honorable war."

Then the other knights, in the order of their rank, came and knelt likewise before the king; and each in his turn promised to be his man,—first Rainier of Genoa, then Miles of Apulia, then Oliver, and lastly the headstrong Aymery of Narbonne. And the king forgave each one all the wrong that he had ever done him, and gave back to each all the lands and fiefs and tenements and all the honors that he had held before.

"And now," said Charlemagne to Count Gerard, "I will go with you, and sup with you to-night in your lordly castle of Viana."

Great was the wonder of the Vianese when they saw the king enter their halls, not as the prisoner, but as the friend and guest, of the count. And great, indeed, was the joy when it was known that peace had been made, and that the wearisome siege was at an end. In the broad feast hall, a rich banquet was spread, and the night was given up to feasting and music and merry-making. And among the knights who sat at the table there was none more noble or more handsome than Oliver. And among the ladies who added grace and beauty to the glad occasion not one was so fair as Oliver's sister, the matchless Alda.

But in the tents of the besiegers that night there was much disquietude and bewilderment. The huntsmen had sought in vain for Charlemagne in the wood; and, when they could not find him, they came back to the camp, thinking that he had become wearied of the chase and had returned. On their way they had found his horse grazing among the herbage, with the reins lying loose on his neck. Great now was their uneasiness. Roland put himself at the head of fifty horsemen, and scoured the country for miles around. But as the darkness of night began to settle over the earth, they were forced to return, sadder and more perplexed than ever, to the camp.

The next morning, what was the astonishment of the besiegers to see the gates of Viana thrown wide open, and the men, to the number of two thousand, march out with music playing, and banners flying, as if it were a gay holiday! But greater still was their wonder when they saw that the knight who rode so grandly in the van by the side of Count Gerard was their own loved king. Roland, who at first was fearful that the Vianese were plotting some treachery, had hastily drawn up his warriors in line of battle, ready to defend the camp. But Charlemagne, as soon as he had come near enough to be heard, explained that peace had been made, and that Count Gerard and the barons who were with him in Viana had renewed their homage, and that all past differences had been forgotten.

After this the king held his court for seven days in the castle of Viana; and the men who had so lately been foes stood together in the halls as sworn friends, loyal and true. And the days were given over to merry-making. And Roland and Oliver, the long separated brothers-in-arms, sat together in the hall and at the feast table, and talked of what had befallen them since the day when they plighted their faith to each other among the hills of Sutri. And, before the week had passed, Roland and Alda, the sister of Oliver, were betrothed.

The Wedding of the Cid's Daughters

by Merriam Sherwood

from Tales of the Warrior Lord; El Cantar de Mio Cid

*Don Rodrigo Díaz of Vivar enjoyed the favor of Don
Alfonso, King of León and Castile, until others spoke ill of him.
When he was banished from the kingdom, he set out forthwith
to do great deeds. So great were his victories in war that he was
given the name "Cid Campeador," which means "the Lord
Champion." At last he set out for the Spanish city of Valencia,
held by the Moors, and conquered and entered it. This was so
great an achievement that he was restored to the king's good
graces. Immediately after this the Moors, under the King of
Morocco, attacked the city, but the Cid routed them and earned
even greater renown for himself. He then proceeded to send
gifts to the king. His emissaries were his nephews Minaya
Alvar Fáñez and Pedro Vermúdez.*

*This great Spanish hero is reputed to be a real person who
lived in the eleventh century. The author of a twelfth century poem about him is unknown, but it is claimed that much
of it is reasonably true to fact. Since then many poets and
dramatists have told his story.*

THE WEDDING OF THE CID'S DAUGHTERS

Merriam Sherwood

———◦◦———

AFTER they had thus routed the King of Morocco, Alvar Fáñez was left to make a complete count. With one hundred knights the Cid entered Valencia, his coif folded on his head, which was without the helmet and the hood of mail. Thus he rode in, on Babieca, sword in hand. The ladies, who were expecting him, welcomed him. The Cid stopped before them, drawing his horse's rein:

"I bow before you, Ladies; I have won you great renown: while you were holding Valencia, I conquered the field. God and all His saints wished this, since they have given us such spoils at your coming. Behold my sword bloody and my horse sweating: thus are Moors vanquished in the field. Pray to the Creator that I may live for some time—you will win renown and have vassals to kiss your hands."

The Cid said this, dismounting from his horse. When they saw him on foot, the ladies and his daughters and his noble wife fell on their knees before the Campeador:

"Do with us what you will, and may you live many years!"

Together with him they went into the palace, and they all sat down on rich benches.

"How now, wife, Doña Jimena, did you not ask this of me? I wish to marry to some of my vassals these ladies whom you have brought and who serve you so well. I will give each of them two hundred silver marks, that those in Castile may know who it is these ladies have served so well! Of your daughters we shall speak later on."

They all rose and kissed his hands. Great was the joy throughout the palace. The orders of the Cid were obeyed.

Minaya Alvar Fáñez was outside in the field, among all the troops, writing and counting. What with tents and arms and fine clothes, they found so much that it was a mighty store. But I will say what is greater: they could not tell the number of the horses wandering with their trappings, and no one to catch them. The Moors of the country profited by that. In spite of all this, there fell to the famous Campeador one thousand horses in the division of the spoils. Since so many came to the Cid in his fifth, the others might well rest content. How many costly tents and carved tent poles the Cid and all his vassals won!

They went into Valencia with all those riches. The Bishop Don Jerome, the tonsured chief, when he had had his fill of fighting with his two hands, did not know the number of the Moors he had slain. His share of the spoils was mighty. The Cid Don Rodrigo, he who in lucky hour was born, sent him the tenth of his own fifth.

The good Cid did not idle:

"Where are you, Chief? Come hither Minaya. Do not give thanks for the part that is your share, but take whatever you wish of my fifth, and leave the rest. And tomorrow morning you will go with horses of the fifth that I have won, each with saddle and with bridle and with sword. For love of my wife and my two daughters, because he sent them to me in such wise as to please them, these two hundred horses shall go as gifts to King Alfonso, that he may not speak ill of him who rules Valencia."

He ordered Pedro Vermúdez to go with Minaya. The next morning they mounted quickly. They took two hundred men in their company, bearing greetings to the King from the Cid, who kissed his hands with this message: The Cid was sending him a present of two hundred horses from that battle he had won, saying: "I shall serve King Alfonso as long as I live."

They left Valencia and rode on. They took so much of the spoils that they had to guard them well. They went day and night, crossing the mountains that cut off the other lands. They crossed mountains and forests and rivers. They reached Valladolid, where the King was biding. Pedro Vermúdez and Minaya sent him a message: to be ready to receive their company, for the Cid of Valencia was making him a present.

The King was joyful—you never saw the like. He commanded all his nobles to mount at once. There, among the first, the King rode forth, to learn the message from him who in lucky hour was born. The Heirs of Carrión, you may be sure, were of the company, and the Count Don García, the Cid's evil enemy. Some were pleased and others were not. They beheld the vassals of him who in lucky hour was born. They thought it was an army, not men just bearing a message! King Alfonso crossed himself.

Minaya and Pedro Vermúdez came into his presence. They dismounted and fell on their knees before the King. They kissed the earth and both his feet:

"Your grace, King Alfonso, full of honor! We kiss you thus for the Cid Campeador. He calls you lord and holds himself your vassal. The Cid prizes greatly the honor you have done him. A few days ago, King, he won a battle. He put to flight the King of Morocco, Yúsuf by name, and fifty thousand men. Huge were the spoils he took. All his vassals have been made rich. He sends you two hundred horses and kisses your hands."

Said King Alfonso:

"Thanks be to the Creator, and to my Lord Saint Isidore of León, for these two hundred horses that the Cid has sent me. For the rest of my reign he will be able to serve me better. You, Minaya Alvar Fáñez, and Pedro Vermúdez here, I will order you honorably waited on and richly clothed and fitted out with all the arms you wish—that you may make a noble appearance before Ruy Díaz the Cid. And I give you three horses—here, take them. As it seems to me, and as my heart tells me, all these happenings are bound to come to good."

They kissed his hands and went into their lodgings for the night. The King commanded them to be well served with all they needed.

I will tell you of the Heirs of Carrión, who were laying their plans and talking together in secret:

"The fortunes of the Cid are marching ahead. Let us ask for his daughters in marriage. This will add to our honor and will profit us much."

They went to King Alfonso with this secret plan:

"We ask you a favor as our king and rightful lord. We beseech your help, that you ask the Campeador for his daughters for us. We wish to marry them, for their honor and our profit."

The King thought this over for a long hour:

"I exiled the good Campeador from the land, and, since I have done him ill and he has done me great good, I know not whether he will relish this marriage. But since you wish it, let us talk it over."

The King Don Alfonso now called Minaya Alvar Fáñez and Pedro Vermúdez. He led them aside into a room:

"Listen to me, Minaya, and you, Pedro Vermúdez. The Cid Campeador serves me. He deserves my pardon and he shall have it. If he wants to, let him come to parley with me. There are other happenings in my court: Diego and Fernando, the Heirs of Carrión, wish to marry his two daughters. Be good messengers and, I pray you, tell this to the worthy Campeador. It will add to his honor and his fiefs to take for sons-in-law the Heirs of Carrión."

Minaya spoke, and it was pleasing to Pedro Vermúdez:

"We shall ask what you wish. Afterward, let the Cid do as he likes."

"Tell Ruy Díaz, he who in lucky hour was born, that I will go to meet him at any fitting spot. Let the trysting-place be wherever he says. I wish to favor the Cid in every way."

They took leave of the King, and then turned about. With all their men they rode toward Valencia. When the good Campeador learned of their coming, he straightway mounted and went out to meet them. The Cid smiled and embraced them eagerly:

"Are you come, Minaya, and you, Pedro Vermúdez? In few lands are there two such barons! What greetings sends Alfonso my Lord? Is he satisfied, and did he accept the gift?"

Said Minaya: "He is well content and he sends you his royal love."

Said the Cid: "Thanks be to the Creator!"

After that they began to talk of what Alfonso of León asked of the Cid: to give his daughters to the Heirs of Carrión, for this would bring him honor and increase his lands; and the King advised him warmly to do it. When the Cid, the good Campeador, heard that he thought it over for a long hour:

"I thank Christ my Lord for this. I was driven from the land and my fief was taken from me. I won what I have with great travail. I thank God that I have the King's grace and that he asks my daughters for the Heirs of Carrión. They are very haughty and have favor at court. I should not care for this marriage; but, since he who is higher placed than we, advises it, let us consult about it privately, and may the God of Heaven counsel us for the best."

"Besides this, Alfonso said that he would come to see you where you like. He wishes to hold parley with you and take you back into his favor. After that you will settle things for the best."

Then said the Cid: "I am glad at heart for this."

Said Minaya: "Decide where you will hold this meeting."

"It would be no wonder if King Alfonso wanted us to go to seek him until we found him, to do him honor, as king of the country. But let his wish be ours: on the Tajo, which is a great river, let us hold the meeting, since my lord wishes it."

They wrote a letter. The Cid sealed it well, and sent it out by two knights. He said that he would do as the King wished.

They presented the letter to the honored King. When he saw it he was glad at heart:

"Greet the Cid for me—he who in lucky hour girded on his sword. Let the meeting be three weeks from now. If I am alive I shall go there without fail."

Forthwith they returned to the Cid. Both parties got ready for the meeting. Who ever saw in Castile so many mules of value and so many smooth-paced palfreys, and horses large and fleet; or so many fair pennons fixed on good lances, or so many shields with bosses of gold and of silver; or so many mantles and furred tunics and fine cendals of Alexandria? The King commanded ample supplies to be sent to the Tajo River, where the meeting had been set. With the King were many good companies. The Heirs of Carrión were very joyful: they ran into debt for some things and paid for others. They believed that their wealth was already increasing, that they would have as much gold and silver as they wanted.

In Valencia, the Cid Campeador was not idling, but was getting ready for the meeting. Many were the big mules and the seasoned palfreys; many the good arms and and the swift chargers; many the fine cloaks and mantles and furred tunics.

The Campeador commanded Alvar Salvadórez and Galindo García of Aragon to guard Valencia with good will, and that all the rest should be in their keeping. The gates of the castle were not to be opened day or night. Within were his wife and his two daughters—whom he loved with heart and soul—and the other ladies who served their wishes. Like a good baron, he gave orders that none of them should go out until he returned.

They left Valencia and spurred forward. A great many chargers, large and swift, the Cid had won—they had not been given to him. Now he was riding to the meeting that he had arranged with the King.

The King Don Alfonso got there a day before the Cid. When the King's party saw the good Campeador coming, they went out to meet him with great pomp. As soon as he who in lucky hour was born caught sight of the King, he ordered all his men to stay behind, except those knights whom he loved in his heart. He dismounted with fifteen, as he that in lucky hour was born had planned. He got down on his hands and knees on the ground and took the grass of the field in his teeth, weeping with his eyes, so great was his joy. In this way he humbled himself before Alfonso his Lord. Thus did he fall at his feet. This did not please King Alfonso at all:

"Rise up, O Cid Campeador! Kiss my hands, not my feet. Unless you do so, you will not win my love."

The Campeador stayed on his knees:

"I ask your grace, my rightful Lord. To me in this posture grant your love, so that all who are here may catch your words."

Said the King:

"I will do this with all my heart. Here in this spot I pardon you and give you my love, and welcome you into my kingdom henceforth from today."

The Cid spoke and this is what he said:

"Thanks! I accept your pardon, Alfonso my Lord! I thank

first the God of Heaven for it, and then you and those followers who are standing around you."

Kneeling, he kissed the King's hands.

The Cid spoke and uttered these words:

"I thank the Creator for this: that I have the grace of
Alfonso my Lord. God will protect me day and night. Be my
guest, if it please you, Lord."

Said the King:

"That would not be fitting today, for you have just arrived
and we came yesterday. You shall be my guest, Cid Campeador,
and tomorrow we shall do as you wish."

The Cid kissed his hand and granted what he asked. Then
the Heirs of Carrión bowed before him:

"We salute you, Cid—in lucky hour were you born! In every
way we can we shall stand by you."

The Cid answered:

"May the Creator will it so!"

The Cid Ruy Díaz, who in lucky hour was born, was the
guest of the King on that day. Alfonso could not have enough
of him, so warmly did he love him. He sat looking at the Cid's
beard, which had grown so fast. All who were there were mar-
veling at the Cid.

That day passed and night came. The next morning the
sun shone forth brightly. The Campeador ordered food to be
prepared for all who were there. The Cid Campeador pleased
them so well that they were very happy, and agreed on one
point: that they had not eaten better for three years past!

The day after that, when the sun came up, the Bishop Don
Jerome sang Mass. After Mass they all assembled. The King
spoke without delay:

"Hear me, Vassals, Counts and Lords! I wish to make a
proposal to the Cid Campeador. May Christ will that it be
for his good! Cid, I ask for your daughters, Doña Elvira and

Doña Sol, as brides for the Heirs of Carrión. The marriage seems to me honorable and very worth while. They ask them of you and it is my will that you consent. On the one side and the other, let all those who are here, mine and yours, be sponsors. Give your daughters to us, Cid, and may the Creator keep you!"

"I really have no daughters to marry," answered the Campeador, "for they have no great age but are very young. The Heirs of Carrión are high placed. They are suited to my daughters and even to better matches. I am their father and you their foster father. I and they are at your disposition. I place them in your hands—Doña Elvira and Doña Sol. Give them to whom you please, and I shall be content."

"Thanks," said the King, "to you and to all this court."

Then the Heirs of Carrión arose. They went to kiss the hands of him who in lucky hour was born, and they exchanged swords with him before the King Don Alfonso.

The King Don Alfonso spoke as a good lord should:

"Thanks to you, good Cid, but first to the Creator, for giving me your daughters for the Heirs of Carrión. From now on I take them into my hands—Doña Elvira and Doña Sol—and I give them as brides to the Heirs of Carrión. I marry them, your daughters, with your good pleasure. May it please the Creator that you have joy therein! Here are the Heirs of Carrión in your hands. Let them go with you, for I am returning now. I give them three hundred marks of silver for their expenses, to use for the weddings, or in any way you wish. When the brothers are in your keeping in Valencia the Great, sons-in-law and daughters will all be your children. Do what you please with them, Campeador."

The Cid received them. He kissed the King's hands:

"I thank you much for this, as my King and Lord! It is you who are giving my daughters in marriage, not I."

It was agreed that at sunrise the next morning everyone should go back whence he had come. Then the Cid Campeador made himself talked about: many a great mule and many a seasoned palfrey, many a fine and costly garment did the Cid give to all who would take his gifts. Each one had what he asked for, and no one said him nay. The Cid gave sixty of his horses as gifts. All who were there were pleased with the meeting. Then they separated, for night had come.

The King took the Heirs of Carrión by the hand. He placed them in the care of the Cid Campeador:

"These are your sons, since they are your sons-in-law. From today it is for you to decide what to do with them, Campeador."

"I thank you, King, and I accept your gift. May God, who is in Heaven, give you good reward for this! I ask a boon of you, my rightful King: since you are marrying my daughters, in such wise as pleases you, name someone in place of you to whom I may give them; for you are taking them over. I will not give them in marriage with my own hand, nor will they have that cause for joy."

The King answered:

"Here is Alvar Fáñez: do you take them into your hands and give them to the Heirs of Carrión—just as I do now, as if I were there. Act in their father's stead all through the wedding ceremony. When you come back to me, tell me truly what happened."

Said Alvar Fáñez: "Lord, I am pleased to do this."

Everything was arranged, you may know, with great forethought.

Then the Cid took his leave of his Lord Alfonso. He did not want the King to escort him, so he left at once.

They set out for Valencia, in a lucky moment won. The Cid commanded Pedro Vermúdez and Muño Gustioz—in his household there were no two better—to watch Fernando and

Diego, that they might learn the ways of the Heirs of Carrión. Great honor was due to the heirs of Carrión.

Lo, they are at Valencia, which the Cid had won! When they drew in sight of it they all rejoiced. Said the Cid to Don Pedro and to Muño Gustioz:

"Take the Heirs of Carrión to their lodgings, and do you stay with them, for that is my wish. When morning comes and the sun is up, they shall see their brides, Doña Elvira and Doña Sol."

That night they all went to their lodgings. The Cid Campeador entered the castle. Doña Jimena and both her daughters welcomed him:

"Are you come, Campeador? In lucky hour you girded on your sword! May we see you for many days with the eyes of our faces!"

"I come, honored wife, thanks to the Creator! I bring you sons-in-law from whom we shall have honor. Thank me, my daughters, for I have married you well!"

His wife and his daughters kissed his hands, and so did all the ladies who served them:

"Thanks be to the Creator, and to you, Cid, Beautiful Beard! All that you do is good. Your daughters will not be poor all the days of your life!"

"When you marry us we shall indeed be rich."

"Wife, Doña Jimena, thanks be to the Creator! I tell you, my daughters, Doña Elvira and Doña Sol, we shall increase in honor by this marriage. But you must know the truth: it is not I who proposed it. My Lord Don Alfonso begged me for you, asking so insistently and warmly that I knew not how to say him nay in anything. I placed you both in his hands, daughters. You may indeed believe me: it is he who is marrying you, and not I."

Then they began to get the palace ready. They covered the

floor and hung the walls with carpets, all of purple and samite
and costly fabrics. You would have liked to sit down and to eat
in the palace. All the Cid's knights had gathered quickly.

Then they sent for the Heirs of Carrión, who mounted and
set out for the palace, dressed in fine clothes and very richly
decked out. On foot and properly, my, how meekly they went
in! The Cid received them, with all his vassals. They bowed
before him and his wife, and went to sit on a costly bench. All
those of the Cid were very prudent: they were watching with
attention him who in lucky hour was born.

The Campeador rose to his feet:

"Since we have to do it, why do we delay? Come hither,

Alvar Fáñez, whom I cherish and love! Here are my two daughters, I place them in your hands. You know that I have the King's command for this. I do not wish to fail in anything to which I have agreed. With your hand give them to the Heirs of Carrión. Let them receive the benediction, and let us finish this."

Then said Minaya: "I shall do so gladly."

The daughters rose and the Cid gave them into Minaya's charge.

To the Heirs of Carrión Minaya said:

"Here you stand before Minaya. You are brothers. In the name of King Alfonso, who commanded me to do it, I give you these ladies—both of noble birth—for you to take to wife in honorable and legal marriage."

They received their brides with gladness and went to kiss the hands of the Cid and of his wife. When they had done this they left the palace, taking their way to Santa María. The Bishop Don Jerome put on his vestments very quickly. He was waiting for them at the door of the church. He gave them the benediction and sang the Mass.

On leaving the church, they rode swiftly out to the beach of Valencia. My! How well the Cid and his vassals showed their skill at arms! Three times did he who in lucky hour was born change horses. The Cid was much pleased with what he saw: the Heirs of Carrión rode well. They went back to Valencia with the ladies. Rich was the marriage feast in the noble castle. The next day the Cid had seven quintains set up. Before coming in to dinner they broke them all to pieces.

They stayed at the wedding a full fortnight. Towards the end of that time the nobles began to go. The Cid Don Rodrigo, he who in lucky hour was born, what with palfreys and mules and swift chargers, of beasts alone gave away a hundred; mantles and furred tunics and other garments abounded; while countless was the moneyed wealth bestowed. The vassals of the Cid had agreed that each one should make gifts for himself. Whoever wished to take something was well satisfied. Those who had come to the wedding went back to Castile rich. The guests were beginning to go. They took leave of Ruy Díaz, who in lucky hour was born, of all the ladies and of the noble- men. They went away content with the Cid and his vassals, speaking well of their hosts, for that was only fitting. Diego and Fernando, the sons of the Count Don Gonzalo, were very happy.

The guests reached Castile. The Cid and his sons-in-law stayed in Valencia. The Heirs of Carrión dwelt there very nearly two years, and the love that was shown them was very great. Joyful was the Cid, and so were all his vassals.

(The Heirs of Carrión later betrayed and almost killed the daughters of the Cid. But their plot was discovered in time and the two were suitably punished. The two girls married again, this time to the Kings of Aragon and Navarre)

A Young Prince Named Siegfried

by James Baldwin

from *The Story of Siegfried*

Many famous stories center around this hero. In the Norse and Icelandic stories, the Volsunga Saga, *he is Sigurd; in the Germanic epic, the* Nibelungenlied, *and in Wagner's opera, he is Siegfried. The stories told in both are much the same. He is said to come of a lofty race of great heroes, and he lived to become the greatest of them all. The sources of these tales are lost in antiquity for they were told for many centuries in the great halls of the north before they were gathered and written down in the twelfth through the fifteenth centuries.*

In this story Siegfried forges the sword that will later serve him well and catches a glimpse of what the future holds for him.

A YOUNG PRINCE NAMED SIEGFRIED

James Baldwin

———◆●◆———

T Santen, in the Lowlands, there once lived a young
prince named Siegfried. His father, Siegmund, was
king of the rich country through which the lazy Rhine
winds its way just before reaching the great North Sea; and
he was known, both far and near, for his good deeds and his
prudent thrift. And Siegfried's mother, the gentle Sigelind,
was loved by all for her goodness of heart and her kindly charity
to the poor.

Neither king nor queen left aught undone that might make
the young prince happy, or fit him for life's usefulness. Wise
men were brought from far-off lands to be his teachers; and
every day something was added to his store of knowledge or
his stock of happiness. And very skilful did he become in war-
like games and in manly feats of strength. No other youth
could throw the spear with so great force, or shoot the arrow
with surer aim. No other youth could run more swiftly, or ride
with more becoming ease. His gentle mother took delight in
adding to the beauty of his matchless form by clothing him in
costly garments decked with the rarest jewels.

The old, the young, the rich, the poor, the high, the low, all
praised the fearless Siegfried, and all vied in friendly strife to
win his favor. One would have thought that the life of the

young prince could never be aught but a holiday, and that the birds would sing, and the flowers would bloom, and the sun would shine forever for his sake.

But the business of man's life is not mere pastime; and none knew this truth better than the wise old king, Siegmund.

"All work is noble," said he to Siegfried; "and he who yearns to win fame must not shun toil. Even princes should know how to earn a livelihood by the labor of their hands."

And so, while Siegfried was still a young lad, his father sent him to live with a smith called Mimer, whose smithy was among the hills not far from the great forest. For in those early times the work of the smith was looked upon as the most worthy of all trades,—a trade which the gods themselves were not ashamed to follow. And this smith Mimer was a wonderful master,—the wisest and most cunning that the world had ever seen. Men said that he was akin to the dwarf-folk who had ruled the earth in the early days, and who were learned in every lore, and skilled in every craft; and they said that he was so exceeding old that no one could remember the day when he came to dwell in the land of Siegmund's fathers. And some said, too, that he was the keeper of a wonderful well, or flowering spring, the waters of which imparted wisdom and far-seeing knowledge to all who drank of them.

To Mimer's school, then, where he would be taught to work skilfully and to think wisely, Siegfried was sent, to be in all respects like the other pupils there. A coarse blue blouse, and heavy leggings, and a leathern apron, took the place of the costly clothing which he had worn in his father's dwelling. His feet were incased in awkward wooden shoes, and his head was covered with a wolfskin cap. The dainty bed, with its downy pillows, wherein every night his mother had been wont, with gentle care, to see him safely covered, was given up for a rude heap of straw in a corner of the smithy. And the rich food to which he had been used gave place to the coarsest and humblest fare. But the lad did not complain. The days which he passed in the smithy were mirthful and happy; and the sound of his hammer rang cheerfully, and the sparks from his forge flew briskly, from morning till night.

And a wonderful smith he became. No one could do more work than he, and none wrought with greater skill. The heaviest chains and the strongest bolts, for prison or for treasure-house, were but as toys in his stout hands, so easily and quickly did he beat them into shape. And he was alike cunning in work of the most delicate and brittle kind. Ornaments of gold and silver, studded with the rarest jewels, were fashioned into beautiful forms by his deft fingers. And among all of Mimer's apprentices none learned the master's lore so readily, or gained the master's favor more.

One morning the master, Mimer, came to the smithy with a troubled look upon his face. It was clear that something had gone amiss; and what it was the apprentices soon learned from the smith himself. Never, until lately, had any one questioned Mimer's right to be called the foremost smith in all the world; but now a rival had come forward. An unknown upstart—one Amilias, in Burgundyland—had made a suit of armor, which, he boasted, no stroke of sword could dint, and no blow of spear could scratch; and he had sent a challenge to all other smiths, both in the Rhine country and elsewhere, to equal that piece of workmanship, or else acknowledge themselves his under-lings and vassals. For many days had Mimer himself toiled, alone and vainly, trying to forge a sword whose edge the boasted armor of Amilias could not foil; and now, in despair, he came to ask the help of his pupils and apprentices.

"Who among you is skilful enough to forge such a sword?" he asked.

One after another, the pupils shook their heads. And Veliant, the foreman of the apprentices, said, "I have heard much about that wonderful armor, and its extreme hardness, and I doubt if any skill can make a sword with edge so sharp and true as to cut into it. The best that can be done is to try to make another war coat whose temper shall equal that of Amilias's armor.

Then the lad Siegfried quickly said, "I will make such a sword as you want,—a blade that no war coat can foil. Give me but leave to try!"

The other pupils laughed in scorn, but Mimer checked them. "You hear how this boy can talk: we will see what he can do. He is the king's son, and we know that he has uncommon talent. He shall make the sword; but if, upon trial, it fail, I will make him rue the day."

Then Siegfried went to his task. And for seven days and seven nights the sparks never stopped flying from his forge; and the ringing of his anvil, and the hissing of the hot metal as he tempered it, were heard continuously. On the eighth day the sword was fashioned, and Siegfried brought it to Mimer.

The smith felt the razor edge of the bright weapon, and said, "This seems, indeed, a fair fire edge. Let us make a trial of its keenness."

Then a thread of wool as light as thistle down was thrown upon water, and, as it floated there, Mimer struck it with the sword. The glittering blade cleft the slender thread in twain, and the pieces floated undisturbed upon the surface of the liquid.

"Well done!" cried the delighted smith. "Never have I seen a keener edge. If its temper is as true as its sharpness would lead us to believe, it will indeed serve me well."

But Siegfried took the sword again, and broke it into many pieces; and for three days he welded it in a white-hot fire, and tempered it with milk and oatmeal. Then, in sight of Mimer and the sneering apprentices, he cast a light ball of fine-spun wool upon the flowing water of the brook; and it was caught in the swift eddies of the stream, and whirled about until it met the bared blade of the sword, which was held in Mimer's hands. And it was parted as easily and clean as the rippling water, and not the smallest thread was moved out of its place.

Then back to the smithy Siegfried went again; and his forge glowed with a brighter fire, and his hammer rang upon the anvil with a cheerier sound, than ever before. But he suffered no one to come near, and no one ever knew what witchery he used. But some of his fellow pupils afterwards told how, in the dusky twilight, they had seen a one-eyed man, long-bearded, and clad in a cloud-gray kirtle, and wearing a sky-blue hood, talking with Siegfried at the smithy door. And they said that the stranger's face was at once pleasant and fearful to look upon, and that his one eye shone in the gloaming like the evening star, and that, when he had placed in Siegfried's hands bright shards, like pieces of a broken sword, he faded suddenly from their sight, and was seen no more.

For seven weeks the lad wrought day and night at his forge; and then, pale and haggard, but with a pleased smile upon his face, he stood before Mimer, with the gleaming sword in his hands. "It is finished," he said. "Behold the glittering terror!— the blade Balmung. Let us try its edge, and prove its temper once again, that so we may know whether you can place your trust in it."

And Mimer looked long at the ruddy hilt of the weapon, and at the mystic runes that were scored upon its sides, and at the keen edge, which gleamed like a ray of sunlight in the gathering gloom of the evening. But no word came from his lips, and his eyes were dim and dazed; and he seemed as one lost in thoughts of days long past and gone.

Siegfried raised the blade high over his head; and the gleam-

ing edge flashed hither and thither, like the lightning's play
when Thor rides over the storm clouds. Then suddenly it fell
upon the master's anvil, and the great block of iron was cleft
in two; but the bright blade was no whit dulled by the stroke,
and the line of light which marked the edge was brighter than
before.

Then to the flowing brook they went; and a great pack of
wool, the fleeces of ten sheep, was brought, and thrown upon
the swirling water. As the stream bore the bundle downwards,
Mimer held the sword in its way. And the whole was divided
as easily and as clean as the woollen ball or the slender woollen
thread had been cleft before.

"Now, indeed," cried Mimer, "I no longer fear to meet that upstart, Amilias. If his war coat can withstand the stroke of such a sword as Balmung, then I shall not be ashamed to be his underling. But, if this good blade is what it seems to be, it will not fail me; and I, Mimer the Old, shall still be called the wisest and greatest of smiths."

And he sent word at once to Amilias, in Burgundyland, to meet him on a day, and settle forever the question as to which of the two should be the master, and which the underling. And heralds proclaimed it in every town and dwelling. When the time which had been set drew near, Mimer, bearing the sword Balmung, and followed by all his pupils and apprentices, wended his way towards the place of meeting.

Through the forest they went, and then along the banks of the sluggish river, for many a league, to the height of land which marked the line between King Siegmund's country and the country of the Burgundians. It was in this place, midway between the shops of Mimer and Amilias, that the great trial of metal and of skill was to be made. And here were already gathered great numbers of people from the Lowlands and from Burgundy, anxiously waiting for the coming of the champions. On the one side were the wise old Siegmund and his gentle queen, and their train of knights and courtiers and fair ladies. On the other side the three Burgundian kings, Gunther, Gernot, and Giselher, and a mighty retinue of warriors, led by grim old Hagen, the uncle of the kings, and the wariest chief in all Rhineland.

When every thing was in readiness for the contest, Amilias, clad in his boasted war coat, went up to the top of the hill, and sat upon a great rock, and waited for Mimer's coming. As he sat there, he looked, to the people below, like some great castle tower; for he was almost a giant in size, and his coat of mail, so skilfully wrought, was so huge that twenty men of common mould might have found shelter, or hidden themselves, within it. As the smith Mimer, so dwarfish in stature, toiled up the steep hillside, Amilias smiled to see him; for he felt no fear of the slender, gleaming blade that was to try the metal of his war coat. And already a shout of expectant triumph went up from the throats of the Burgundian hosts, so sure were they of their champion's success.

But Mimer's friends waited in breathless silence, hoping, and yet fearing. Only King Siegmund whispered to his queen, and said, "Knowledge is stronger than brute force. The smallest dwarf who has drunk from the well of the Knowing One may safely meet the stoutest giant in battle."

When Mimer reached the top of the hill, Amilias folded his huge arms, and smiled again; for he felt that this contest was mere play for him, and that Mimer was already as good as beaten, and his thrall. The smith paused a moment to take breath, and as he stood by the side of his foe he looked to those below like a mere black speck close beside a steel-gray castle tower.

"Are you ready?" asked the smith.

"Ready," answered Amilias. "Strike!"

Mimer raised the beaming blade in the air, and for a moment the lightning seemed to play around his head. The muscles on his short, brawny arms stood out like great ropes; and then Balmung, descending, cleft the air from right to left. The waiting lookers-on in the plain below thought to hear the noise of clashing steel; but they listened in vain, for no sound came to their ears, save a sharp hiss like that which red hot iron gives when plunged into a tank of cold water. The huge Amilias sat unmoved, with his arms still folded upon his breast; but the smile had faded from his face.

"How do you feel now?" asked Mimer in a half-mocking tone.

"Rather strangely, as if cold iron had touched me," faintly answered the upstart.

"Shake thyself!" cried Mimer.

Amilias did so, and lo! he fell in two halves; for the sword had cut sheer through the vaunted war coat, and cleft in twain the great body incased within. Down tumbled the giant head and the still folded arms, and they rolled with thundering noise to the foot of the hill, and fell with a fearful splash into the deep waters of the river; and there, fathoms down, they may even now be seen, when the water is clear, lying like great gray rocks among the sand and gravel below. The rest of the body, with the armor which incased it, still sat upright in its place; and to this day travellers sailing down the river are shown on moonlit evenings the luckless armor of Amilias on the high hilltop. In the dim, uncertain light, one easily fancies it to be the ivy-covered ruins of some old castle of feudal times.

The master, Mimer, sheathed his sword, and walked slowly down the hillside to the plain, where his friends welcomed him with glad cheers and shouts of joy. But the Burgundians, baffled, and feeling vexed, turned silently homeward, nor cast a single look back to the scene of their disappointment and their ill-fated champion's defeat.

And Siegfried went again with the master and his fellows to the smoky smithy, to his roaring bellows and ringing anvil, and to his coarse fare, and rude, hard bed, and to a life of labor. And while all men praised Mimer and his knowing skill, and the fiery edge of the sunbeam blade, no one knew that it was the boy Siegfried who had wrought that piece of workmanship.

But after a while it was whispered around that not Mimer, but one of his pupils, had forged the sword. And, when the master was asked what truth there was in this story, his eyes twinkled, and the corners of his mouth twitched strangely, and he made no answer. But Veliant, the foreman of the smithy, and the greatest of boasters, said, "It was I who forged the fire-edge of the blade Balmung." And although none denied the truth of what he said, but few who knew what sort of a man he was believed his story. And this is the reason, my children, in the ancient songs and stories which tell of this wondrous sword, it is said by most that Mimer, and by a few that Veliant, forged its blade. But I prefer to believe that it was made by Siegfried, the hero who afterwards wielded it in so many adventures.

Be this as it may, however, blind hate and jealousy were from this time uppermost in the coarse and selfish mind of Veliant; and he sought how he might drive the lad away from the smithy in disgrace. "This boy has done what no one else could do," said he. "He may yet do greater deeds, and set himself up as the master smith of the world, and then we shall all have to humble ourselves as his underlings and thralls."

And he nursed this thought, and brooded over the hatred which he felt towards the blameless boy; but he did not dare to harm him, for fear of their master, Mimer. And Siegfried busied himself at his forge, where the sparks flew as briskly and as merrily as before, and his bellows roared from early morning till late at evening. Nor did the foreman's unkindness trouble him, for he knew the master's heart was warm.

Oftentimes, when the day's work was done, Siegfried sat with Mimer by the glowing light of the furnace fire, and listened to the sweet tales which the master told of the deeds of early days, when the world was young, and the dwarf-folk and the giants had a name and a place upon earth. And one night, as they thus sat, the master talked of Odin the All-Father, and of the gods who dwell with him in Asgard, and of the puny men folk whom they protect and befriend, until his words grew full of bitterness, and his soul of a fierce longing for something he dared not name. And the lad's heart was stirred with a strange uneasiness, and he said,—

"Tell me, I pray, dear master, something about my own kin, my father's fathers,—those mighty kings, who, I have heard said, were the bravest and best of men."

Then the smith seemed pleased again. And his eyes grew brighter, and lost their faraway look; and a smile played among the wrinkles of his swarthy face, as he told a tale of old King Volsung and of the deeds of the Volsung kings:—

"Long years ago, before the evil days had dawned, King Volsung ruled over all the land which lies between the sea and the country of the Goths. The days were golden; and the good Frey dropped peace and plenty everywhere, and men went in and out and feared no wrong. King Volsung had a dwelling in the midst of fertile fields and fruitful gardens. Fairer than any dream was that dwelling. The roof was thatched with gold, and red turrets and towers rose above. The great feast hall was long and high, and its walls were hung with sunbright shields; and the door nails were of silver. In the middle of the hall stood the pride of the Volsungs,—a tree whose blossoms filled the air with fragrance, and whose green branches, thrusting themselves through the ceiling, covered the roof with fair foliage. It was Odin's tree, and King Volsung had planted it there with his own hands.

"On a day in winter King Volsung held a great feast in his hall in honor of Siggeir, the King of the Goths, who was his guest. And the fires blazed bright in the broad chimneys, and music and mirth went round. But in the midst of the merry-making the guests were startled by a sudden peal of thunder, which seemed to come from the cloudless sky, and which made the shields upon the walls rattle and ring. In wonder they looked around. A strange man stood in the doorway, and laughed, but said not a word. And they noticed that he wore no shoes upon his feet, but that a cloud-gray cloak was thrown over his shoulders, and a blue hood was drawn down over his

head. His face was half hidden by a heavy beard; and he had
but one eye, which twinkled and glowed like a burning coal.
And all the guests sat moveless in their seats, so awed were they
in the presence of him who stood at the door; for they knew
that he was none other than Odin the All-Father, the king of
gods and men. He spoke not a word, but straight into the hall
he strode, and he paused not until he stood beneath the blossom-
ing branches of the tree. Then, forth from beneath his cloud-
gray cloak, he drew a gleaming sword, and struck the blade
deep into the wood,—so deep that nothing but the hilt was
left in sight. And, turning to the awe-struck guests, he said, 'A
blade of mighty worth have I hidden in this tree. Never have
the earth folk wrought better steel, nor has any man ever wielded
a more trusty sword. Whoever there is among you brave enough
and strong enough to draw it forth from the wood, he shall
have it as a gift from Odin.' Then slowly to the door he strode
again, and no one saw him any more.

"And after he had gone, the Volsungs and their guests sat
a long time silent, fearing to stir, lest the vision should prove
a dream. But at last the old king arose, and cried, 'Come, guests
and kinsmen, and set your hands to the ruddy hilt! Odin's gift
stays, waiting for its fated owner. Let us see which one of you
is the favored of the All-Father.' First Siggeir, the King of the
Goths, and his earls, the Volsungs' guests, tried their hands. But
the blade stuck fast; and the stoutest man among them failed
to move it. Then King Volsung, laughing, seized the hilt, and
drew with all his strength; but the sword held still in the wood
of Odin's tree. And one by one the nine sons of Volsung tugged
and strained in vain; and each was greeted with shouts and
laughter, as, ashamed and beaten, he wended to his seat
again. Then, at last, Sigmund, the youngest son, stood up, and
laid his hand upon the ruddy hilt, scarce thinking to try what
all had failed to do. When, lo! the blade came out of the tree as

if therein it had all along lain loose. And Sigmund raised it high over his head, and shook it, and the bright flame that leaped from its edge lit up the hall like the lightning's gleaming; and the Volsungs and their guests rent the air with cheers and shouts of gladness. For no one among all the men of the mid-world was more worthy of Odin's gift than young Sigmund the brave."

The rest of Mimer's story would be too long to tell you now; for he and his young apprentice sat for hours by the dying coals, and talked of Siegfried's kinsmen,—the Volsung kings of old. And he told how Siggeir, the Goth king, was wedded to Signy the fair, the only daughter of Volsung, and the pride of the old king's heart; and how he carried her with him to his home in the land of the Goths; and how he coveted Sigmund's sword, and plotted to gain it by guile; and how, through pretense of friendship, he invited the Volsung kings to visit him in Gothland, as the guests of himself and Signy; and how he betrayed and slew them, save Sigmund alone, who escaped, and for long years lived an outlaw in the land of his treacherous foe. And then he told how Sigmund afterwards came back to his own country of the Volsungs; and how his people welcomed him, and he became a mighty king, such as the world had never known before; and how, when he had grown old, and full of years and honors, he went out with his earls and fighting men to battle against the hosts of King Lyngi the Mighty; and how, in the midst of the fight, when his sword had hewn down numbers of the foe, and the end of the strife and victory seemed near, an old man, one-eyed and bearded, and wearing a cloud-gray cloak, stood up before him in the din, and his sword was broken in pieces, and he fell dead on the heap of the slain. And when Mimer had finished his tale, his dark face seemed to grow darker, and his twinkling eyes grew brighter, as he cried out in a tone of despair and hopeless yearning,—

"Oh, past are those days of old and the worthy deeds of the brave! And these are the days of the home-stayers,—of the wise, but feeble-hearted. Yet the Norns have spoken; and it must be that another hero shall arise of the Volsung blood and he shall restore the name and the fame of his kin of the early days. And he shall be my bane; and in him shall the race of heroes have an end."

Siegfried's heart was strangely stirred within him as he hearkened to this story of ancient times and to the fateful words of the master, and for a long time he sat in silent thought; and neither he nor Mimer moved, or spoke again, until the darkness of the night had begun to fade, and the gray light of morning to steal into the smithy. Then, as if moved by a sudden impulse, he turned to the master, and said,—

"You speak of the Norns, dear master, and of their fore-telling; but your words are vague, and their meaning very broad. When shall that hero come? and who shall he be? and what deeds shall be his doing?"

"Alas!" answered Mimer, "I know not, save that he shall be of the Volsung race, and that my fate is linked with his."

"And why do you not know?" returned Siegfried. "Are you not that old Mimer, in whom it is said the garnered wisdom of the world is stored? Is there not truth in the old story that even Odin pawned one of his eyes for a single draught from your fountain of knowledge? And is the possessor of so much wisdom unable to look into the future with clearness and certainty?"

"Alas!" answered Mimer again, and his words came hard and slow, "I am not that Mimer, of whom old stories tell, who gave wisdom to the All-Father in exchange for an eye. He is one of the giants, and he still watches his fountain in far-off Jotunheim. I claim kinship with the dwarfs, and am sometimes known as an elf, sometimes as a wood-sprite. Men have called me

Mimer because of my wisdom and skill, and the learning which I impart to my pupils. Could I but drink from the fountain of the real Mimer, then the wisdom of the world would in truth be mine, and the secrets of the future would be no longer hidden. But I must wait, as I have long waited, for the day and the deed and the doom that the Norns have foretold."

And the old strange look of longing came again into his eyes, and the wrinkles on his swarthy face seemed to deepen with agony, as he arose, and left the smithy. And Siegfried sat alone before the smouldering fire, and pondered upon what he had heard.

How Sigurd Awoke Brynhild

by Dorothy Hosford

from *Sons of the Volsungs*

After recording many deeds of courage and daring, the tale of Sigurd the Volsung reaches a climax as the hero discovers a sleeping woman, Brynhild, on a mighty mountain. Brynhild had once been the helper of Allfather Odin, mightiest of the gods, and had chosen for him the victors in battle. She had been placed upon the mountain, surrounded by a ring of fire, by Odin as a punishment for disobedience. Only the bravest of men could rescue her.

HOW SIGURD AWOKE BRYNHILD

Dorothy Hosford

———◦•◦———

WHEN Sigurd had passed beyond the Glittering Heath he found himself in a place of great crags and mountains. Greyfell went swift and light and Sigurd turned somewhat to the southward, for he longed to hear again the speech of men and to be with his own kind. But the desert still endured and he had ridden a long road when, early on a morning, he saw before him a mighty mountain. The clouds about its top were lit with flame as though a great torch burned there. Sigurd turned toward the mountain, for from thence he deemed that he might look over the world and see which way was best to take.

So he rode higher and higher, and a strange light shone about him from those flame-lit clouds on the mountain's crest. Toward noon the clouds grew darker and settled thickly, hiding the top of the mountain from Sigurd's sight, but he kept riding ever higher and higher toward it. In the late afternoon the winds blew up and the clouds were cleared away and again Sigurd saw the mountain. But the light that had seemed a torch from afar off was now a blazing river of fire, and the mountain was black above it and below it, and the head of Hindfell rose like an island in the sunset sky.

Night fell, but yet Sigurd rode on and on, and had no thought of rest, for he longed to climb that mighty rock and look forth over the world. As he came among the foot-hills he could see the light no more, but the stars were lovely and gleaming above him. He rode on through a dark pass in the mountain till the stars were dimmed and the world grew cold with the dawn. Then afar off he beheld a breach in the rock wall and forth from it poured a flood of light. Swiftly Sigurd rode thither and found the place. He drew up Greyfell and gazed in wonder on the marvel before him. For lo, the side of Hindfell was enwrapped by a fervent blaze and there was nought betwixt earth and heaven save a shifting world of flame. Sigurd cried to Greyfell and they hastened up and nearer, until he drew rein in the dawning on the steep side of Hindfell. But Sigurd heeded not the dawning, for before him the flames wove a great wavering wall. No wind could drive it back, nor could rain drench it, nor was there any opening or pause in it for the wayfarer to pass through. A mammoth wall of fire, it flamed before Sigurd. Sigurd trembled not, but smiled as the breath of it lifted up his hair, and his eyes shone bright with its image and his coat of mail gleamed white and fair. In his war helm the heavens and the waning stars behind him were reflected. But Greyfell stretched his neck to snuff at the flame wall and his cloudy flanks heaved.

Then turned Sigurd in his saddle and drew the girths tighter and shifted the hilt of his Wrath. Gathering up the reins, he cried aloud to Greyfell and rode straight at the wildfire's heart. But the flame wall wavered before him and parted and rose o'er his head, roaring wild above him. But he rode through its roaring as a warrior rides through a field of waving rye. The white flame licked his raiment and swept through Greyfell's mane. It covered Sigurd's hands and the hilt of his sword and wound about his helmet and his hair. But the fire hurt him not, neither was his raiment marred nor his war gear dimmed. Then of a sudden the flames failed and faded and darkened, and a heavy murkiness spread over the earth. Sigurd rode further till all was calm about him; then he turned his eyes backward. The side of Hindfell blazed no longer, but behind him on the scorched earth lay a ring of pale slaked ashes. And beyond it the waste world of crags and mountains lay hushed and grey in the early dawn.

Then before him Sigurd saw a Shield-burg, a wall of many shields wrought clear without a flaw. Silver shields gleamed beside those of gold and ruddy shields beside the white, and all were carved and blazoned brightly. The wall rose high to the heavens and o'er the topmost shield rim there hung, like a banner, a glorious golden buckler. It swayed in the morning breeze and rang against the staff that held it.

Sigurd leaped down from Greyfell and stood before the wall.

It rose above him as though 'twere the very dwelling of the Gods and he looked but little beneath it. He drew not his sword from its scabbard as he wended his way round the rampart. All was silent; 'twas only the wind and Sigurd that wakened any sound. Then lo, he came to the gate, and its doors were open wide. No warder withstood his way and no earls guarded the threshold. Sigurd stood a while and marveled at such strangeness. Then his Wrath gleamed bare in his hand as he wended his way inward, for he doubted some guile of the Gods, or some dwarf king's snare, or perchance a mock of the giant people that should fade before his eyes. But he took his way in and he saw the wall of shields, with the ruddy by the white and the silver by the gold, but within that wall no work of man was set. There was nought but the utmost head of Hindfell rising high. Then, as Sigurd gazed, he beheld below in the very midmost a giant-fashioned mound that was builded as high as the topmost rim of the shield wall. And there, on that mound of the giants, with nought but the wilderness about, a pale grey image lay and gleamed in the early morn.

So there was Sigurd alone in that desert of wonder; and he went forward with the Sword of the Branstock high in his hand. He set his face toward the earth mound and beheld the image, with the dawn growing light about it; and lo, he saw 'twas the shape of a man set forth in that desert place on the tower top of the world. So Sigurd climbed the mound to see if the man were living or dead, and who it was that lay there: some king of the days forgotten, or mayhap the frame of a God, or e'en some glorious heart beloved laid far from earthly strife. He stood over the body and saw that it was shapen fair and clad from head to foot-sole in pale grey-glittering mail as closely wrought as though it were grown to the flesh. A war helm, girt with a golden crown, hid the face from view. Sigurd stooped and knelt beside the figure, and he felt a breath as sweet as a summer wind come forth from the sleeping one. Then spake Sigurd to himself that he would look on the face and see whether it bore him love or hate and who it might be that so strangely rested here. So he drew the helm from the head, and lo, Sigurd beheld the snow-white brow, and the smooth unfurrowed cheeks, and the lightly breathing lips of a woman. A woman fair beyond all dreaming. And Sigurd looked, and he loved her sore, and longed to move her spirit and waken her heart to the world.

Gently he touched her and spake softly: "Awake! I am Sigurd." But she moved not.

Then looked Sigurd on the bare blade beside him. The pale blue edges burned brightly as the sun began to rise. The rims of the Shield-burg glittered and the east grew exceeding clear. Sigurd took the Sword of the Branstock and set the edge to the dwarf-wrought coat of mail where the ring-knit collar constrained the woman's throat. The sharp Wrath bit and rended the rings, and lo, white linen gleamed softly beneath the armor. Sigurd drove the blue steel onward through the coat and the skirt of mail, till nought but the rippling linen was wrapping her about. Then he deemed her breath came quicker, and he turned the Wrath and cut down either sleeve. Her arms lay white in her raiment and glorious sun-bright hair fell shining across her shoulders.

Then a flush came over her visage, a sigh stirred her breast, her eyelids quivered and opened, and slowly she awakened. Wide-eyed she gazed on the dawning, too glad to change or smile; nor did she speak, and moved but little. Motionless beside her Sigurd knelt, waiting her first words, while the soft waves of the daylight sped over the starless heavens. The gleaming rims of the Shield-burg grew bright and yet brighter in the rising sun, and the thin moon hung her horns dead-white in the golden glow.

Then she turned and gazed on Sigurd and her eyes met the Volsung's eyes, and mighty and measureless within him now swelled the tide of his love. Their longing met and mingled, and he knew in his heart that she loved, as she spake softly.

"O what is the thing so mighty that hath torn my sleep?"

Sigurd answered: "The hand of Sigurd and the sword of Sigmund's son, and the heart that the Volsungs fashioned have done this deed for thee."

But she said: "Where then is Odin who hath laid me here? O long is the grief of the world, and mankind's tangled woe!"

"Odin dwelleth above," said Sigurd, "but I dwell on the earth. And I came from the Glittering Heath to ride the waves of thy fire."

Even as he spake the sun rose upward and lightened all the earth, and the light flashed back to the heavens from the glorious gleaming shields. The twain uprose together, and as the risen sun bathed them in the light of the new day, she lifted her arms with palms outspread and cried:

"All hail, O Day and thy Sons, and thy kin of the coloured things!
Hail, following Night, and thy Daughter that leadeth thy wavering wings!
Look down with unangry eyes on us today alive,
And give us the hearts victorious, and the gain for which we strive!
All hail, ye Lords of God-home, and ye Queens of the House of Gold!
Hail, thou dear Earth that bearest, and thou Wealth of field and fold!
Give us, your noble children, the glory of wisdom and speech,
And the hearts and the hands of healing, and the mouths and the hands that teach!"

They turned then and embraced, and gladness and rejoicing
filled their hearts. Spake Sigurd:

"Thou art the fairest of the earth, and the wisest of the wise;
O who art thou? I am Sigurd, e'en as I told thee. I have slain the
Serpent Fafnir and gotten the ancient gold. Great indeed were

the gift of my days if I should gain thy love and we twain, through all of life, should never part. O who art thou that lovest, thou who art fairest of all things born? And what meaneth thy lonely slumber here?"

Said she: "I am she that loveth. I was born of earthly folk, but long ago Allfather took me from the home of the kings and he called me the Victory Wafter. I came and went and at Odin's will chose the victor on the battle field, and the slain for his war host; and my days were glorious and good. But the thoughts of my heart overcame me and pride in my wisdom and power, and I deemed that I alone could choose the slain, and scorned the will of Allfather. For that came my punishment. Allfather decreed that I should return again among men, to be one of them. But I cried: 'If I must live and wed in the world, and gather grief on the earth, then the fearless heart shall I wed. E'en there shall I fashion a tale brave and fair, that shall give hope to the Earth.'

"Allfather smiled somewhat, but he spake: 'So let it be! Still thy doom abideth. Fare forth, and forget and be weary 'neath the Sting of the Sleepful Thorn, and long shall the time pass over e'er the day of thy waking come.'

"So I came to the head of Hindfell and there the sleep thorn pierced me and the slumber fell on me, from which none might wake me save him who would not turn back from the waving flames of the wild fire. And that is the tale. Now I am she that loveth; and the day is near when I, who have ridden the sea realm and the regions of the land and dwelt in the measure-less mountains, shall live once more in the house of my fathers. There shall the days be joyous."

Grettir Becomes an Outlaw

by Allen French

from *Story of Grettir the Strong*

*Grettir was the "strongest man that ever lived in Iceland."
During the course of his adventures he overcame a huge ghost
named Glam, a troll, a giant, a witch, and, as this story tells,
some fierce robbers, called* baresarks *because they wore no coats
of mail. But strength did not bring Grettir happiness. Through
no fault of his own, he became an outlaw while still a young
man, and he was pursued by ill fortune all the rest of his life.*

*The Grettis Saga, as the whole tale is called, is one of
thirty-five family sagas written in Iceland in the twelfth, thir-
teenth, and fourteenth centuries. All of them tell of great misfortunes and end in tragedy. The authors of the sagas are unknown.*

GRETTIR BECOMES AN OUTLAW

Allen French

———◦•◦———

I N those days the news came to Iceland that Olaf Harald-
son, who later was called Olaf the Saint, was king in
Norway, and that many stout men were flocking to him,
for he received them well. When Grettir heard that he began
to weary of his life at home, where all was quiet, and made
ready to go to Norway to seek service with the king, who was of
his distant kin. So he left his father, who now was an old
man, and sailed to Norway. There he took passage in another
ship, and sailed northward along the coast, to meet the king.

The season was late, and the days were short and the nights
very cold. One night the sailors tried to reach a harbor, but
could not, and were forced to lay up under the lee of an
island. There was a wide channel between it and the mainland,
and the waves were very rough. On the island was no shelter at
all, and though there was wood, they had no fire, nor means to
make it. The wind was bitter cold, and the men were all wet,
and they feared they would freeze. Then at dark they saw
over on the mainland the lights of a hall.

Then the men questioned if they dared to launch the ship
and get across the sound, but the waves and the currents were
too dangerous. Yet they feared for their lives where they stayed,
and knew not what to do. Some of them asked if any one of

them was able to swim across dark, cold water and fetch fire.

"There have been men," said Grettir, "who would have done that."

"That is no help to us," said they. "But thou art called the bravest and hardiest of all Icelanders now living. Couldst thou do it?"

Grettir knew that would be a great feat, but remembering the words of Glam, that what he did should turn out against him, he said: "Do it I can, but I know not how ye will reward me for it."

"Of course we will reward thee well," answered they.

"That will be seen," said Grettir. "I will fetch fire for you, and do you bear in mind this promise of yours."

So he stripped off his outer clothing and swam the sound, and a hard swim it was on account of the tide-rips, and a difficult landing he found among the rocks. Then he walked to the hall and opened the door. Now the salt spray had frozen all over his hair and beard, and his clothes froze stiff as he walked, and when he walked in among those in the hall, they started from their seats, and stared at him, thinking him a troll.

Now those were Icelanders and men of spirit, and though they thought him a monster they took courage against him, and set on him with weapons before ever he had a chance to speak. But Grettir struck their weapons from their hands with his bare arms. Then seeing how they did nothing against him with their steel, they cried that evil spirits must yield to fire, and they snatched up burning brands and torches and struck at him with those, coming at him from all sides. Then Grettir, seeing that he would get nothing from them but blows, for in their shouting they did not hear his words, seized a torch from one of them, and with it he smote himself a way among them.

That was strange fighting, for with the swinging of the torches the fire leaped over all the hall, and set fire to the straw that lay there; and soon all was fire and smoke, with the sound of blows and the shouting of men. Then though they were so fierce against him, Grettir won the door and so got away; he ran down to the shore and leaped into the sea, and began his swim back to his shipmates.

And that was almost the hardest swim that ever man has made. For first he had to get clear of the breakers, and then he had to meet the currents and the adverse winds. The waves ran high, and the tides pulled him this way and that; it would have been a great enough task to make that swim without any burden. But all the time Grettir had to hold aloft his burning torch, and to take care that no splashing wave should put it out. So he had but one arm to swim with, and that made the work very hard, and all the time the cold was deadly. Sometimes he thought he would be cast back upon the rocks, and sometimes he thought he made no headway at all. But still he struggled, till at last he saw the islet before him, and so at last he came to land.

There his shipmates seized and welcomed him, and made a fire, and warmed him. He put on dry clothes, and made little of their thanks; and soon, in the safety of their fire, they were all asleep.

But across the sound, in the hall, those Icelanders who had fought Grettir made much of themselves when they saw that he had gone. Some peered after him from the door, and saw that he threw himself into the sea; thus they were sure that he was a troll. Then they set to and put out the fires among the straw, and talked it all over, and thought they had a great tale to tell of that night's affray. And so at length they lay down and went to sleep. Yet, as it happened, there was still fire smouldering in some straw that was heaped by the wall. The fire got into the wall, and burned there for a while, until at last it got into the thatch, and burst out all over the place. The men knew nothing of it until the timbers were falling upon their heads; by that time the place was so thick with smoke that they were half smothered and could see nothing. They had barred the door, and none of them got out, but all were burned there.

Then in the morning the gale had gone down, and when Grettir and his mates launched their ship they saw that across the sound there seemed to be the smoking embers of a great fire; and they wished to know who had been so uncourteous as to set on Grettir as those men had done. So they rowed across to the mainland, and when they came on shore they saw that the hall itself had burned down; and when they came to look they found the bones of men among the embers, and there was no one there to tell the tale.

Then some of the shipmen cried out on Grettir: "Thou hast burned those men!"

"How could I burn them?" he asked. "There was no fire seen from the islet even when we went to sleep, and that was long after I was here."

But they still looked upon him with suspicion.

"Now it is as I foreboded," said Grettir. "And this is how ye reward me for saving your lives."

But they had no shame, and feared only that suspicion might come upon them for burning those men. At the next harbor, when Grettir and others went on shore, they gave him the slip and sailed away northward without him, and wherever they stopped they told how Grettir had burned those men in their house. So that as Grettir also travelled northward he found men had turned against him. At last he came to Drontheim, where the king was; but the story had been told to the king, and Grettir found it hard to come before him until some days had passed. But at last he came before him where the king sat in his hall, with his men about him.

Said Grettir to the king: "An evil tale has been told against me, O king, and I wish to clear myself of it."

Then the king, who was saintly in all his ways and foresighted also, said to Grettir: "Well art thou called the Strong,
but I perceive that ill luck is ever ready to follow thee. Tell me
thy story."

So Grettir told his story, how those men had set on him with
firebrands, but that he had left them all alive in the hall, while
for a long while afterward no fire had sprung up in the building,
for it would have been seen from across the sound. Then Grettir
begged the king to help him clear himself before the law.

Then the king said: "Thou mayest clear thyself by bearing
hot iron in the church. And it is likely that the men were burnt
by evil fortune, but thy luck may not stay with thee to prove it
so."

Grettir thanked him and was pleased, for by the ordeal of bearing the glowing iron a man might clear himself from an accusation. So a day was set, and Grettir fasted until then, to make himself fit to prove his innocence. When the day came there was a great crowd by the church. The king and the bishop went inside, and Grettir came from his lodging to go to the church. The people gazed on him and wondered at his great size, and said that there was a man fit to do the things that were told of him.

So Grettir approached the church door, but before he came to it there started out from the crowd a lad of strange shape, large and with a huge head, with wild eyes and much hair. He wagged his head at Grettir and pointed at him, and he cried:—

"Fine mummery and mockery is this! And a great honor it is to Norway that this freebooter and man of violence shall thus escape from the penalty of his misdeeds! Any man is allowed to bear the iron who claims the right to do so, and so the greatest criminals escape punishment. And this man is the worst of all, for he burned helpless men, and for no cause. Now it is a great shame that he shall thus be allowed to get away scot-free."

And more words he said, standing in front of Grettir and pointing at him, and calling him evil names, such as sea-monster, and half-man—for no man, said he, could have such growth and strength. And so uncouth was he, and wild of look, that Grettir shuddered at him and hated him, and when the lad came near, Grettir struck him with his fist and felled him.

Then there was shouting and pressing of the people to see what had happened, and in the press the lad disappeared. Some say he vanished away suddenly, and the truth is that no one knows more of him. It is thought he was some troll, sent there by Glam to be Grettir's undoing, for if Grettir had come into the church the evil spirits could not reach him; and if he had borne the iron he would have broken the current of his ill-fortune.

But the word was brought to the king that Grettir was in a brawl, and Olaf came out of the church and found Grettir standing looking about him for the lad, and all amazed.

"Now," said the king, "by this violence thou hast put from thyself all the virtue gained by thy fasting, and hast broken in upon the solemn ordeal. After this it will not be possible to clear thee by means of the hot iron."

Then Grettir was much cast down, and spoke to the king of the kinship between them, and how he had made the long journey from Iceland in the hope of taking service with the king. He asked to be taken into the king's body-guard.

"Nay," answered Olaf. "None of my men is a match for thee in courage or in strength, but thy luck will bring trouble on all who are with thee, and that I cannot have."

"But how can I clear myself of this suspicion of the burning?" asked Grettir.

"In no way that I see," replied Olaf. "And because there will always be violence wherever thou art I must forbid thee to stay in this kingdom. Here mayest thou stay in peace this winter and no more; in the summer shalt thou go home to Iceland, for there thou shalt die. Many a man's hand will be against thee, for I see that an evil curse hangs over thee."

Then Grettir, much cast down, went away and saw the king no more. He thought of going to his friend Thorfinn, but it seemed as if he had brought on him trouble enough. Then he said to himself he would seek his brother in Tunsberg, and so set out by land to go there.

At Christmas time he came to the house of a farmer named Einar, who took Grettir in and treated him well. Einar was a rich man, and it was well-known that he had much goods with him in his house.

So it happened that two days after Christmas, when all Einar's Christmas guests had gone away, excepting only Grettir, that there came out of the woods a band of men, and before them a leader on a horse, who called Einar out to speak with him.

"Now heaven help us!" said Einar to Grettir, "here is the baresark Snaekol and his men, and they will rob me of all my goods."

"Let us hold the house against him," said Grettir.

But the house was large, and those two and the housecarles could not hold it against so many, who would not scruple at setting it afire above their heads. So Einar went out to speak with the baresark, and Grettir went with him, but without arms.

The baresark sat on his horse and shouted at Einar that he should give up all his goods and his household, or else fight with him for them. Einar was old, and was no fighting man; he whispered to Grettir, asking what he should do.

"Thou shalt do only that which is not shameful," answered Grettir.

Then the baresark rode nearer. "What art thou saying with that big fellow?" he asked. "Will he perhaps fight me?"

"I also have no skill in arms," said Grettir.

"You are both afraid of me," cried Snaekol.

"Thou art very terrible," answered Grettir.

But because he did not seem to be afraid the baresark grew angry, and thought to cow Grettir. So he rode closer still, gritted his teeth, and began to howl after the manner of baresarks, and to foam at the mouth. He opened his mouth and thrust his shield into it, bit the edge of the shield, and howled louder than before. Then Grettir took a step forward, and drove his foot up against the shield, so that it was dashed into the baresark's mouth, and tore out his teeth and broke his lower jaw. Then while the fellow tottered in his saddle Grettir seized him and dragged him from his horse, and drew the outlaw's short-sword, and cut off his head at a stroke.

At sight of that the baresark's followers, a mere rabble, were frightened and fled to the woods. Having lost their leader each man ran his own way, and that was the end of that band of evil-doers. This was another of Grettir's deeds in ridding lands of their pests, and he was thanked not by Einar alone, but also by all the men of that neighborhood.

Grettir went on and came to Tunsberg, where he was welcomed gladly by his brother Thorstein Dromund, and lived with him that winter. No more deeds are told of Grettir in that season. He stayed with his brother until summer, and then made ready to take ship again for Iceland.

In Iceland that summer, at the Althing, before Grettir came to land, a suit was brought against him by Thorir of Garth, the father of two of those who had been burned in that house from which Grettir fetched the fire. Now Grettir's kinsmen had heard nothing of this, and they were not ready for the suit. They tried to postpone it until he should come and defend himself; but Thorir pressed the case so hard, and had so many men of influence to back him, that he made Grettir an outlaw throughout Iceland. Many said it was done unlawfully, but it was done for all that.

When Grettir landed in Iceland he was met by bad news, for first he learned that his father was dead, and next that he was outlawed and that a price was set upon him. And last he was told that just before he landed his brother had been slain by a neighbor, who now was trying to get Grettir's mother from her farm.

This is the story of the slaying of Atli, the brother of Grettir. He was in no way like his brother, for he was slow and good-natured, gentle and peace-loving. But because he was prosperous and much loved, there were also some who envied him, and they sought to get the better of him. Atli had a neighbor, Thorbiorn, a man of great strength, and so called Oxmain. This man egged two of his kinsmen on to slay Atli; but Atli, although he had never fought before, slew them both with the sword which Grettir had given him, the sword of his great-grandfather.

Thorbiorn Oxmain brought suit against Atli for the slaying of his kinsmen, but got little satisfaction save small fines, and that only made him eager for vengeance. Now one winter a workman of his ran away and went to Atli, who took him in and gave him work. Then in his anger Thorbiorn went one day to the house of Atli, got him to the door by a trick, and stabbed him with a great spear. No vengeance was taken for that by Grettir's kinsmen, for they waited to see what Grettir would do when he came to land.

So Grettir was told all that news, which might have overwhelmed a common man. But it seemed to him no worse than other evil luck which had come upon him, so he laughed and sang:

> "Mournful is the news I hear:
> Dead are both my kinsmen dear;
> Outlaw have I just been made.
> I should therefore be afraid.
> —But there may be one or two
> Who shall soon my coming rue."

And that night, before his shipmates suspected, he stole away from them, and by various paths crossed the hills to his own homestead of Biarg, and so chose his time that he came there at night, when all folk were asleep. He went into the hall by a secret way, and came to his mother's locked bed, and waked her up by taking her hand.

"Who is there?" she asked.

"It is thy son Grettir," answered he.

Then she sat up and kissed him, but with tears; and she welcomed him, but sadly. "For thy life is in danger," she said, "and thy brother's enemy presses upon me to drive me from this house, and thy brother Illugi cannot help me for many years, since he is but three years old."

"Be of better heart," said Grettir. "For it may chance that my brother's enemy will not trouble thee much longer. Truly my luck is bad, but it may serve me so far as to get me to meet him, and after that his luck must be great indeed if he gets away from me. For he who is struck will strike in return, and that is known of me already."

Then Grettir stayed there a day or two in secret, and sent a man over the ridge to see whether Thorbiorn Oxmain was at home. The man came back and said that Thorbiorn was at home with few men, working at his haying. Then on a bright morning Grettir rode over the ridge to Thorbiorn's house, and came there at midday. The women came to the door at his knock, and did not know him. They said that the master had gone to his meadow for hay, and his son was with him. So Grettir rode along the way they showed him, and when he came to the meadow and saw Thorbiorn working on the hill-side above him, he came down from his horse, and looked to his weapons. He had his short-sword and his helmet, with a large spear, of which the head was inlaid with silver.

He saw how Thorbiorn and his son had stopped working and were looking at him. Their arms were close at hand: Thorbiorn had a shield and sword, and his son, Arnor, had a small axe. The lad was sixteen years old, but well grown. With them a woman had been working, raking the hay.

When Grettir saw how those two were armed, he sat down and knocked out of his spear the nail that held the head, so that, the spear once thrown, it would not be of use for Thorbiorn to throw it back.

"See what he is doing," said Thorbiorn to his son. "He comes against us to fight, and from his size he must be Grettir the Strong. But come," and he spoke to hearten the lad, "remember I am called Oxmain for my own strength, and we are two to one. This what we will do: I will undertake to hold my own against him for a while, and while I keep him busy do thou come at him from behind, and hew at his back. Be not afraid; he will have his hands so full with me that he will not harm thee."

So they took up their arms and made ready, although neither of them had a helmet. Grettir came up the slope against them, having knocked the nail out of his spear. When he was near enough, he cast the spear at Thorbiorn, but the head was so loose that it came off, and the spear turned aside and did no harm. Then Thorbiorn and his son separated, so that Arnor could come at Grettir from behind.

Grettir, when he saw their plan, did not let Thorbiorn come to close fighting, as he wished, but fought away from him, and scarcely kept within reach, while he watched to see what Arnor was doing. But when the lad thought he had a good chance, then he ran in against Grettir, with his axe lifted with both hands, to hew Grettir's backbone in two. Then Grettir swung round upon him with a back-handed blow, and cleft his skull at a stroke.

Just as he stood still to do that, Thorbiorn ran at him from in front, and struck mightily. But Grettir turned the blow with his shield, and having his arm already drawn back by the blow at Arnor, now he slashed forward with such a stroke that he split Thorbiorn's shield, and the sword passed on into Thorbiorn's head and killed him at once. So with those two strokes Grettir got full vengeance for his brother.

The woman who was there ran home shrieking, and told of the deed. Those at the house gathered men, but when they came to the meadow Grettir had gone. He stayed long enough to look for his spear-head, but could not find it. (Now it was found in the time of Sturla the Lawman, after more than two hundred years, in the field called Spearmead.) Grettir rode to the nearest house, and told of the slayings; then he rode home and told his mother.

"Well," said she, "now all may see how safe it is to anger thee. But soon they will be here with all their men, and because thou art an outlaw it is against the law for anyone to defend thee, so thou must away."

Grettir went away, therefore, but first he told his kinsmen of his deed, and they promised to help him in whatever way they might. After he had gone came the relatives of Thorbiorn Oxmain, his brother at their head. They asked if Grettir were hidden away there.

"Thou shouldest know by what has just happened," answered Grettir's mother, "if he is a man to hide. Now thou canst do thy best against him, but he is not here."

They went home with only their journey for their pains, and in the meantime Grettir went west, to Snorri the Priest. He was the wisest man in all Iceland in matters of craft, and was bound to Grettir's family by old ties of friendship, but he was well on in years. Grettir laid his case before Snorri, and begged advice, and asked him to take him under his care.

"I cannot take thee in," said Snorri, "for I care not to go against the law. But when thy case comes up before the Althing again, then I will go with thy family to help them, for I think I see a flaw in the suit against thee which may help thee out of thine outlawry."

So Grettir went away, but when those cases came before the courts at the next Althing, then Snorri the Priest was there to listen. There were two suits that were brought forward, one for the slaying of Atli, in which Grettir was made the suitor for the death of his brother; and one for the slaying of Thorbiorn Oxmain. Then the judges were about to set the cases off against each other, so that there should be nothing to pay on either side. Then the lawman asked (and he was of Grettir's kin) how it was possible to do that.

The judges said, because Atli and Thorbiorn were men of equal standing.

"But," answered the lawman, Skapti Thorod's son, "Grettir can come into neither of these suits, for at the time of both slayings he was an outlaw, and no outlaw can come into a suit at law. Thorbiorn's kinsmen cannot sue Grettir for the slaying, but Atli's kinsmen can sue against the kin of Thorbiorn,"—and so all saw that Atli's nephews could sue for payment for his slaying; while in the case of Thorbiorn it was as if no one had slain him, Grettir being an outlaw, with no one accountable for his deeds. So Thorbiorn's kin would have to pay a fine, but Atli's kin would not.

Then Snorri the Priest came forward, and he said: "Will not Grettir's kin drop their suit for the slaying of Atli, if only Grettir can be thus got out of his outlawry?"

Both sides agreed to that, and so it was all arranged, except for one thing, the consent of Thorir of Garth, at whose suit for the burning of his sons Grettir had been made outlaw. So Thorir of Garth was sent for, and his consent was asked.

But Thorir turned away in bitter anger, and said that Grettir should never be brought out of his outlawry, save only by death.

"This will be a heavy thing for Iceland, to keep Grettir in his outlawry for a deed that has never been proved against him," said Snorri the Priest. "And many a man will rue it."

But Thorir of Garth was not to be moved, and so the whole

matter fell to the ground. Thorir raised the price on Grettir's head to three marks of silver; and the kinsmen of Thorbiorn Oxmain, in wrath that they had to pay a fine for Atli's slaying, set another three marks on Grettir's head. And this was considered very wonderful, for never before had more than three marks been set on any outlaw.

So Grettir remained an outlawed man, and it was long before it was again tried to get him free from the ban. But because of the injustice of his outlawry he refused to leave Iceland, and never went abroad again.

Njal the Lawyer

by Allen French

from *Heroes of Iceland*

The following story is the first chapter of a book called
Gunnar of Lithend. *But this book is only one part of a longer
book called* The Story of Burnt Njal. *In all of the stories, the
wisdom of Njal helps to settle great problems of law. The
stories were written from seven to nine centuries ago at a time
when revenge was still a virtue. But Njal did not think that
revenge was good. "With law," he said, "shall our land be
built up and settled and with lawlessness wasted and spoiled."*

*The Njal Saga is the most elaborate and most famous of the
Icelandic family sagas.*

NJAL, THE LAWYER

Allen French

———•◦•———

THERE lived in Iceland two half-brothers, Hauskuld and Hrut, and they dwelt in Laxriverdale. Hrut was handsome, tall, and strong, well skilled in arms and mild of temper; he was one of the wisest of men,—stern toward his foes, but a good counsellor on great matters.

Now Hrut took a wife from the east, Unna the daughter of Fiddle Mord, but because of a spell that was laid upon Hrut she was unhappy with him, and separated herself from him and went back to her father. Mord was a great lawyer, but when he sued Hrut for his daughter's dower, then Hrut challenged the old man to fight for it, and Mord gave up the suit, for Hrut was a famous swordsman.

When Mord died his wealth came to Unna; she was so lavish and unthrifty that at last she had little left. She thought of her dower, and for aid in getting it back she turned to the best of her kinsmen. He was Gunnar of Lithend.

Gunnar was a tall man in growth, and a strong man,—best skilled in arms of all men. He could cut or thrust or shoot as well with his left as with his right hand, and he smote so swiftly with his sword that three seemed to flash through the air at once. He was the best shot with the bow, and never missed his mark. He could leap more than his own height with all his

war-gear, and as far backwards as forwards. He could swim
like a seal, and there was no game in which it was any good
for anyone to strive with him, and so it has been said that no
man was his match. He was handsome of feature and fair-
skinned. His nose was straight, and a little turned up at the
end. He was blue-eyed, and bright-eyed, and ruddy cheeked;
his hair was thick and of good hue, hanging down in comely
curls. The most courteous of men was he, of sturdy frame and
strong will, bountiful and gentle, a fast friend, but slow at
first to give his trust.

Unna told Gunnar her need, and said that he was the only
one of her kinsmen with the daring to undertake the suit, for
Hrut must be summoned in his own house.

"I have courage enough," said Gunnar, "but I do not know
how to begin the suit."

"Well!" she answered, "go and see Njal of Bergthorsknoll;
he will give thee advice." So Gunnar undertook her cause, and
rode to see Njal.

Njal dwelt at Bergthorsknoll; he was wealthy in goods and
handsome of face, but no beard grew on his chin. He was so
great a lawyer that his match was not to be found; wise too he
was, and foreknowing and foresighted. Of good counsel, and
ready to give it, and all that he advised men was sure to be the
best for them to do. Gentle and generous, he unravelled every
man's knotty points who came to see him about them.

Njal said he would give Gunnar his help. "And the end will
be good if thou breakest none of the rules I lay down; if thou
dost, thy life is in danger."

"I will break none of them," said Gunnar.

Then Njal held his peace for a little while, and after that
he spoke as follows:

"Thou shalt ride from home with two men at thy back, and
each of you must have two horses, one fat and the other lean;

ye shall load the fat ones with hardware and smith's work. Over thy good clothes thou shalt wear a cheap russet kirtle, and over that a great rough cloak. Thou shalt ride to the west, and when ye come into the Broadfirth dales, mind and slouch thy hat well over thy brows. Then men will ask who is this tall man, and thy mates shall say, 'Here is Huckster Hedinn the Big, with smith's work for sale.' This Hedinn is ill-tempered and a boaster; very often he snatches back his wares, and flies at men if everything is not done as he wishes. Be sure often to break off thy bargains, so that it shall be noised abroad that Huckster Hedinn is the worst of men to deal with. So thou shalt ride till thou comest to Hauskuld's house; there thou must stay a night, and sit in the lowest place, and act surlily. Hauskuld will tell them all not to meddle nor make with Huckster Hedinn, saying he is a rude, unfriendly fellow.

"Next morning thou must be off early and go to the farm

nearest Hrut's house. There thou must offer wares for sale, praising up the faults of thy goods, and when the master of the house differs with thee, thou shalt fly at him; but mind and spare thy strength, lest thou be found out. Then a man will be sent to tell Hrut to come and part you, and when he comes and asks thee to his house, thou shalt accept his offer. A place will be given thee on the lower bench over against Hrut's high-seat. He will ask thee if thou hast journeyed much, to which thou must answer: 'I know all Iceland by heart.'

"Then when he asks thee what champions live here or there, thou shalt belittle everyone, saying that in one place are shabby fellows enough and to spare, and in another are only thieves and scoundrels. Hrut will smile and think it sport to listen to thy scolding. But when he asks of this quarter, thou shalt say there is small choice of men left here since Fiddle Mord died; and thou shalt praise Mord as so wise a man and so good a lawyer that he never made a false step.

"Then Hrut will ask: 'Dost thou know how matters went between me and him?'

" 'I know all about it,' thou must reply. 'He took thy wife from thee, and thou hadst never a word to say.'

"Then Hrut will say: 'But there was some disgrace in losing his suit for the dower.'

" 'He was old,' thou shalt say, 'and his friends advised him not to fight with thee. But still I think the suit might be taken up again.'

"Then he will ask: 'Dost thou know anything about the law?'

" 'A little,' thou shalt say, 'and though it does not concern me, I should like to know how one should begin a suit against thee for Unna's dower.'

"Hrut will say: 'I must be summoned so that I can hear the summons, or else here in my lawful house.'

" 'Recite the summons, then,' thou must say, 'and let me see if I can say it after thee.'

"Then Hrut will recite the summons, so mind and pay great heed to every word he says. After that Hrut will bid thee repeat the summons, and thou must do so, and say it all wrong.

"Then he will smile and not mistrust thee, but say that scarce a word is right. Thou must throw the blame on thy companions, and say they put thee out; then thou must ask him to say the summons again, word by word, and let thee repeat the words after him. He will give thee leave, and will summon himself in the suit; thou shalt summon after him, and this time say every word right. When it is done, ask Hrut if that is rightly summoned, and he will answer: 'There is no flaw to be found in it.' Then thou shalt say in such a voice that thy companions may hear:

" 'I summon thee in the suit which Unna, Mord's daughter, has made over to me with her plighted hand.' And mind and say this as if thou art only silly and boastful.

"But when men are sound asleep, ye three shall rise and tread softly, and go out of the house, and saddle your fat horses and ride off on them, leaving the others behind. Ye must ride up into the hills away from the pastures and stay there three nights, for about so long will they seek you. After that ride home, riding always by night and resting by day. Then this summer, at the Althing, I will help thee in thy suit."

So Gunnar thanked Njal and went to do as he had bid. He rode with two companions to the west, doing everything as Njal had laid it down for him; and when he came to Hauskuld's house he stayed there the night, and thence he went on down the dale till he came to the house next to Hrut's. There he offered his wares for sale, and soon fell foul of the farmer, and Hrut was sent for to separate them; so the huckster was bidden to Hrut's house.

There Hrut seated Gunnar opposite himself, and their talk
went pretty much as Njal had guessed, till it came to the summoning, and Gunnar repeated it all wrong. Hrut burst out
laughing, and had no mistrust, and said the summons again;
this time Gunnar repeated it right, and called his companions
to witness the summons, but he so acted that Hrut thought it
sport to listen. At night they went to bed like other men; but
in the night all three took their clothes and arms, and went out
and took their horses and rode up among the hills to a spot
where they could not be found except by chance.

Hauskuld waked up that night at his house, and roused all
his household. "I have dreamed," said he "that I saw a great
bear and two cubs go from this house to Hrut's. Now tell me
if any of you saw aught strange about Huckster Hedinn."

One man answered: "I saw how a golden fringe and a bit of scarlet cloth peeped out at his arm, and on his right arm he had a ring of gold."

Hauskuld said: "The bear can mean no man save Gunnar of Lithend, and now methinks I see all about it. Up! let us ride to Hrut's." They did so, and Hauskuld roused Hrut and asked what guests were there.

"Only Huckster Hedinn," says Hrut.

"A broader man across the back it will be, I fear," says Hauskuld. "I guess here must have been Gunnar of Lithend."

"Then here has been a pretty trial of cunning," says Hrut, and tells all about the summoning.

"There has, indeed, been a great falling-off of wit on one side," says Hauskuld, "and Gunnar cannot have planned it all by himself. Njal must be at the bottom of this plot, for there is not his match for wit in all the land."

Now they looked for Gunnar, but he was off and away; they gathered folk and looked for him three days, but could not find him. Then Gunnar rode home safely.

Now all men ride to the Althing to bring suits and to plead causes before the Judges, and to make the laws. Hrut and Hauskuld rode there with a very large following, and when Gunnar opened his case they wished to make an onslaught on him, but mistrusted their strength. Gunnar took his oath, and declared his case, and brought forward his witnesses, though as yet Njal was not at the court. Hrut answered Gunnar, and showed flaws in the pleading. Then Njal came into the court.

He learned what had been done, and said that if they chose to strive by quibbles the suit would drag a long time. Gunnar said he would not have that, but he would do to Hrut as Hrut had done to Mord, and he asked if those brothers were so near that they could hear his voice.

"Hear it we can," answered Hrut. "What dost thou wish?"

"Now all men here present be ear-witnesses," says Gunnar, "that I challenge thee, Hrut, to single combat. But if thou wilt not fight, then pay up the money this very day."

Then both parties went away from the courts, and the suit was never pursued nor defended from that day forth. When the brothers were in their booth, Hrut said: "I have never yet shunned single combat."

"Thou shalt not fight if I have my way," said Hauskuld, "for no man is a match for Gunnar." And he persuaded Hrut to pay down the money; but when all was settled, then Hauskuld was more vexed than his brother, for Hrut had an even temper.

Said Hauskuld, "Will no vengeance come upon Gunnar?"

"Vengeance will reach him," said Hrut, "but not from us, and after all it is most likely that he will turn to us for friends." And as time passed by they laid aside their grudge against him.

Gunnar handed the dowry over to Unna, and would take no pay, but said he should look to her and her kin for help if ever he needed it. Yet when a man came to woo her, Valgard the Guileful, a cross-grained man who had few friends, Unna gave herself away to him without the advice of any of her kinsfolk. Gunnar thought ill of that. Unna and Valgard had a son named Mord, who comes much into this story; he was crafty in temper, and spiteful. When he was grown he worked ill to his kinsfolk, and worst of all to Gunnar.

Frithiof's Journey to the Orkneys

by Alice Hatch

from *Bag o' Tales*

In the ancient days when Vikings ruled the seas, there lived in the Northland a noble king named Bele. His daughter, Fair Ingeborg, was loved by Frithiof, son of Bele's friend Thorsten.

When the time came for the king to die, he admonished his two sons, who were to reign in his stead, to cherish forever the family friendship with Frithiof. But the sons did not obey. Instead they rejected Frithiof's suit for their sister's hand, bidding him serve them as a friend but never as a relative.

In spite of this, the love of Frithiof for Ingeborg was so great that he sought her out in Balder's Grove, where man and maid were forbidden to speak together, and there they exchanged betrothal rings. To punish Frithiof for this sin, Helga, eldest son of Bele, laid upon him the task of going to the Orkney Island to demand tribute money from Yarl Angantyr. So Frithiof bade Ingeborg farewell and set forth in his dragon ship, Ellida, with his foster brother, Bjorn, and twelve staunch seamen.

Frithiof is an eighth century hero, but his story was first recorded in Iceland in the fourteenth century. In 1825, Tegner, a Swede, used the old epic as a basis for his poem Frithiof's Saga, *from which most modern retellings of the story are made.*

FRITHIOF'S JOURNEY TO THE ORKNEYS

Alice Hatch

———•●•———

KING HELGA stood on the shore and watched the striped sails of Frithiof's vessel sink behind the horizon, while his sullen anger grew apace.

"Too easily hast thou escaped my wrath, cursed Frithiof. Thou of unkingly blood who has dared to sue for my sister; thou, not descended of gods, who hast dared profane Balder's temple. Nay, never again shall the keel of thy boat grate on the sands of thy country. Rise, storm fiends, out of the ocean's depths and drag him down to destruction."

Scarcely had Helga spoken when the sky grew dark and gloomy, and darker still grew the waters around the dragon ship. An icy breath bore down from the north and froze the sea spray on the sail ropes. From all directions swept the winds, shrieking and screaming. Great waves lifted the brave boat skyward, then plunged it headlong, quivering, into the hollows. Hailstones fell from the heavens like an onslaught of arrows, and in the boat's hold the water rose even higher.

Now Frithiof, pitting his might against might, felt the exultant joy of battle, as with steadying hand he grasped the helm and sang aloud, undaunted,

> "Storm is coming, comrades,
> Its angry winds I hear

Flapping in the distance
But fearless we may be.
Sit tranquil in the grove,
And fondly think on me,
Lovely in thy sorrow,
Beauteous Ingeborg."

Yet ever ahead of the ship, unseen in the fog and the tempest, rode the storm fiends, Ham and Heyde, urging the waves to madness and the winds to greater destruction, when out of the sea, in the path of the boat, rose an island, under whose sheltering rocks the water lay smooth as a mirror. Shall the hero escape from the storm, guiding his boat into this harbor? Nay, when ever did a Northman, like a trembling coward, turn from his course in the teeth of a tempest? Better far to go to one's death, than to lay down one's arms and surrender.

Now they were driven abreast of the isle; then it sank in the ocean behind them, and again they were fighting the merciless gale while the ship flew westward. Planks creaked and groaned as the waves tore over the decks, stripping the cordage loose and flinging it into the sea; the sails hung in useless tatters from the masts, and all of Frithiof's mighty strength was needed to keep the course as he steadied the cracking rudder, while his voice rose over the storm,

"Yet longer do I find it sweet
To battle with the breeze,
Thunderstorm and Northmen meet,
Exulting on the seas.
For shame might Ingeborg blush,
If her osprey flew
Frightened by a storm stroke
Heavy winged to land."

Now darkness shrouded the ship so that the prow was lost to the stern, and out of the night rose the shrieks of Ham and Heyde, shrill above the tumult of the waves that swept over the bare deck till the pumps could no longer check the incoming torrents of water. Then Frithiof, foreseeing the end at hand, stripped from his arm his treasured betrothal ring of gold, cunningly wrought by the pygmies, and, with his magic sword, Angurvadel, he cleft it in pieces, giving a share to each man that none might start on the hazardous journey to the land of the Dead, empty-handed.

At last the storm grew so violent that Frithiof could not believe it the work of the gods alone and, calling his friend to his side, he said,

> "Bjorn, come to the rudder,
> Hold it tight as a bear's hug;
> Valhall's power sendeth
> No such storm as this.
> Now at work is magic:
> Coward Helga singeth
> Spells above the ocean:
> I will mount and see."

While Bjorn bore down on the rudder, checking the boat in its wavering course, Frithiof climbed to the top of the mast and, looking far out over the sea, he saw in front of his boat, rising on the frothy waves, a whale, on whose back sat the storm demons; Heyde in the snow garb of an icy bear, and Ham like a great storm bird, flapping loud his wings.

Now had come the time to test the magic strength of the vessel in whose frame lay hidden the power to hear and obey the master's bidding.

> "Now Ellida let us see
> If in truth thou bearest
> Valor in thin iron-fastened
> Breast of bended oak.
> Hearken to my calling

If thou be heaven's daughter.
Up! and with thy keel of copper
Sting this magic whale."

Scarcely had Frithiof spoken when the good ship bounded forward and smote the mighty monster so that his blood spurted skyward and stained the waters red, as deep-wounded, he sank, bellowing, to die, while the storm fiends, tasting the bitterness of blue steel hurled by a Northman's arm, received Frithiof's spears in their breasts and ceased from their shrieking incantations forever.

No sooner had the three spirits of evil sunk beneath the waves than their magic spell was broken; the winds receded to the four corners of the earth; a calm spread over the waters, and the sun, breaking through the darkness, disclosed the grassy shores of the Orkneys, whither the storm-shattered boat crawled wearily till at last her keel was checked on the sandy beach.

But the twelve valiant sailors were too weak from their battling with the gale to creep ashore. Not even the strength of their sword blades could support them, so that they lay exhausted on the deck till the sturdy Bjorn ferried four to the land on his back, while great Frithiof brought eight in safety to the green slopes of the isle.

Now it chanced that on that day Yarl Angantyr sat feasting in his banquet hall, surrounded by valiant Vikings, while his faithful old guard, Halvar, stood without the window, one watchful eye, as was his wont, turned toward the sea—the other on his plate from which he constantly ate and passed through the window to be replenished. Suddenly he checked the hand that returned the empty plate and, letting it fall unheeded, cried out:

"A ship upon the sea is borne,
Full heavily she goes;

Now she seemeth to tarry.
Now reacheth she the land;
Two mighty giants carry
The pale crew to the land."

The Yarl rose from his throne at the head of the banquet
table and, following the pointing finger with his eye, spake,

"Those are Ellida's pinions,
That, too, must Frithiof be.
In all the north such bearing
Belongs to him alone."

At this the Viking, Atle, sprang up in furious mood. With
flashing eyes, he drew his sword and shouted,

"Now, now my hand shall show
If Frithiof, as they say,
A spell o'er steel itself can throw
And ne'er for quarter pray."

Followed by twelve warriors, swinging their clubs and eager
for battle, he rushed out of the hall and down to the grassy
slope where the weary crew rested while Frithiof stood guard
over them.

"Now," shouted the jealous Atle, "I have thee at my will,
and will cleave thee with my broad sword, unless thou'lt rather
sue for peace, or flee."

"Nay," said Frithiof, "weak I be from stress of storm, but
rather than seek a craven peace, I'll prove thy mighty sword."

With that the two Vikings rushed at one another. The sword
blows fell like a hail of death strokes upon their shields, till,
shattered and useless, these were cast aside and the champions
stood berserk, sword biting sword, yet neither moving one step
from his place until, by happy trick, Frithiof's magic blade,
Angurvadel—the runes on its hilt gleaming blood red—sprang
up, caught Atle's blade midway, and broke it short at the hilt
leaving him defenseless.

" 'Gainst swordless man," bold Frithiof cried, "My sword I'll never use. Let's try another fight." Then throwing his good blade on the grass beside Atle's useless hilt, the mighty heroes sprang into each other's arms, breast plate clashing against breast plate, and they wrestled as two bears of the snowy north, each bent on the other's destruction. Full many a rock has tottered from its place into the sea, many an oak has been laid low in the forest by lesser shock; yet long and hard they fought, neither bending, till great drops of sweat fell from their brows, and their breath came cold and hard; till the shrubs and stones were scattered afar by the might of their wrestling.

But Frithiof felled his foe at last and, placing his knee on the vanquished one's chest, he spake in tones of wrath,

"Oh, had I but my broadsword true,
Black-bearded, Berserk, I
Should drive its point triumphant through
Your entrails, as you lie."

"Let that be no care of thine," quoth Atle. "Go get thee thy sword and slay me now. I shall not try escape. Sometime we both must pass to Valhall's joys, and if I wander there today, tomorrow may fetch thee."

Seizing his sword, Frithiof raised it high above his head to strike, but Atle watched him with calm eyes and unafraid, till anger against one so noble left the victor's heart and happily he staid the falling blade, giving instead his other hand to raise the vanquished chief.

Then old Halvar, cutting the air with his white staff, shouted, "Come, heroes, let's make all haste to Angantyr and tell this mighty tale. There, on the banquet table a feast is cooling, and for me, I die of thirst."

So, reconciled, the heroes ascended the hill arm-in-arm and passed through the portals of Angantyr's hall. Here the visitors paused in amaze. Never had they seen a place so fair. Instead of bare oaken beams, the walls were hung with gilded leather; a marble hearth leaned against the wall and glass gleamed in the windows. The noble Angantyr sat at the head of his board on a throne of silver, and down either side were ranged his warriors, each served by a maid as fair as a star gleaming behind an angry cloud.

As Frithiof stood on the threshold the Yarl rose and came three paces forward to meet him and taking his hand, led him to a seat by his side on the throne, saying,

"Since here full many a groaning board,
    With Thorsten emptied we,
His son whose fame so far is borne,
    Shall not sit far from me."

Thus they sat feasting, while old Angantyr plied Frithiof with many a question concerning the land of Bele and Thorsten. And, this tale being ended, Frithiof next recounted the hazards of his journey till the table rocked with the roars of laughter and shouts of approval as he told how his dragon ship sent the whale of evil to his grave; but their mirth was stilled and the maidens sighed when he spoke of Ingeborg, so noble in her grief and care. And when at last he came to his errand hither and the cause of his coming, then indeed did Yarl Angantyr's brow darken. "I owe nothing to the sons of Bele. If they would demand tribute let them come themselves, like men, insisting with bared sword in hand, and I shall answer them with mine."

Then, calling his daughter to him, he sent her to the women's room with a whispered message and soon she returned bringing a purse of green, on which were embroidered rivers, wooded hills and moonlit seas, and having a clasp of rubies and tassels of gold. Angantyr took the purse and filled it with golden coins from many a foreign land and gave it to Frithiof, saying,

"This gift of welcome, take, oh guest,
    To do as thou mayst will,

But for the winter stay and rest
With us in friendship still.
Though valor never should be scorned
Yet now the storm rules wide;
By now again to life returned,
I'll wager Ham and Heyde.
Ellida may not always leap
So luckily again;
And whales are plenty in the deep
Though one she may have slain."

So it was that in merry mood Frithiof and his valiant crew
lingered in Angantyr's safe harbor through the winter, and
many a brave tale was sung in the mighty hall to pass the
time till spring should bring calm seas for the journey home—
and to Ingeborg.

Wainamoinen Finds the Lost-Words

translated by John Martin Crawford

¹from *The Kalwala, The Epic Poem of Finland*

*Early in the 1800's a young Finnish doctor named Elias
Lonnröt became interested in the old heroic tales and songs
sung by Finnish people everywhere. He traveled all over Finland collecting them, and when he had as many as he could find,
he put them in what he decided was the proper order and
published them. The story these old songs told is the story of
Wainamoinen, a great Finnish hero; and the meter of the
poetry was chosen by Longfellow for his epic poem, Hiawatha.*

*Wainamoinen, in the beginning of the story, falls in love
with a lovely young woman, the Fair Maid of Pohya, whose
mother is a witch. Before either the mother or the daughter
will consent to a marriage, certain tasks must be performed.
One of the tasks Wainamoinen undertakes is the building of
a magic boat. He must build the boat "using not the hand to
touch it, using not the foot to move it, using not the knee to
turn it, using nothing to propel it." Wainamoinen almost
finishes the boat, using only magic words to build it; but,
nearing the end, he finds he needs three words he does not
have. He searches long and hard, in many lands and many
kingdoms and even in the realm of the dead, but does not find
the magic words. As this story tells, Wainamoinen does find
the words he needs and finishes the boat.*

WAINAMOINEN FINDS THE LOST-WORDS

John Martin Crawford

———◁●▷———

WAINAMOINEN, old and truthful,
Did not learn the words of magic
In Tuoni's gloomy regions,
In the kingdom of Manala.
Thereupon he long debated,
Well considered, long reflected,
Where to find the magic sayings.

Then a shepherd came to meet him,
Speaking thus to Wainamoinen:
"Thou canst find of words a hundred,
Find a thousand wisdom-sayings,
In the mouth of wise Wipunen,
In the body of the hero;
To the spot I know the foot-path,
To his tomb the magic highway,
Trodden by a host of heroes.
Long the distance thou must travel,
On the sharpened points of needles;
Then a long way thou must journey
On the edges of the broadswords;
Thirdly thou must travel farther

On the edges of the hatchets."

Wainamoinen, old and trustful,
First considered all these journeys,
Traveled then to forge and smithy,
And addressed the metal-worker:

"Ilmarinen, worthy blacksmith,
Make a shoe for me of iron,
Forge me gloves of burnished copper,
Mold a staff of strongest metal,
Lay the steel upon the inside,
Forge within the might of magic.
I am going on a journey
To procure the magic sayings,
Find the lost-words of the Master,
From the mouth of the magician,
From the tongue of wise Wipunen."

Spake the artist, Ilmarinen:
"Long ago died wise Wipunen.
He is gone these many ages,
Lays no more his snares of copper,
Sets no longer traps of iron.
None can learn from him the wisdom,
None can find in him the lost-words."

Wainamoinen, old and hopeful,
Little heeding, not discouraged,
In his metal shoes and armor,
Hastened forward on his journey:
Ran the first day fleetly onward,

On the sharpened points of needles;
Sleepily he strode the second
On the edges of the broadswords;
Swung himself the third day forward
On the edges of the hatchets.

Then Wipunen, wisdom-singer,
Ancient bard, and great magician,
With his magic songs lay yonder.
Stretched beside him, lay his sayings;
On his shoulder grew an aspen;
On each temple grew a birch tree;
On his mighty chin an alder;
From his beard grew willow-bushes;
From his mouth a dark green fir-tree,
And an oak tree from his forehead.

Wainamoinen, coming closer,
Drew his sword, lay bare his hatchet
From his magic leathern scabbard.
Fell'd he aspen from the shoulder;
Fell'd the birch-trees from the temples;
From the chin he fell'd the alder,
From the beard, the branching willows,
From the mouth the dark-green fir tree;
Fell'd the oak tree from the forehead.
Next he thrust his staff of iron
Through the mouth of wise Wipunen,
Pried the mighty jaws asunder,
Spoke these words of master-magic;
"Rise, thou master of magicians,
From the sleep of Tuonela,
From thine everlasting slumber!"

Wise Wipunen, ancient singer,
Quickly waking from his sleeping,
Keenly felt the pangs of torture,
From the cruel staff of iron;
Bit with mighty force the metal,
Bit in twain the softer iron;
But when steel flew not asunder,
Open'd wide his mouth in anguish

Wainamoinen of Wainola,
In his iron-shoes and armor,

Careless walking, headlong stumbled,
Fell into the mouth thus opened
Of the Magic Bard, Wipunen.
Wise Wipunen, full of song-charms,
Closed his open mouth and swallowed
Wainamoinen and his magic,
Shoes, and staff, and iron armor.
Then, outspoke the wise Wipunen:
"Many things before I've eaten,
Dined on goat, and sheep, and reindeer,

Bear, and ox, and wolf, and wild-boar,
But in all my recollection
This must be the sweetest morsel!"

Wainamoinen soon decided
How to live and how to prosper,
How to conquer this condition.
In his belt he wore a poniard,
With a handle hewn from birch-wood,
And this handle soon through magic
Was a boat of large proportions.
In this vessel rowed he swiftly
Through the entrails of the hero,
Rowed through every gland and vessel
Of the wisest of magicians.
But Wipunen, master-singer,
Barely felt the hero's presence,
Gave no heed to Wainamoinen.

Then the artist of Wainola
Straightway set himself to forging,
Set at work to hammer metals.
Of his armor made he smithy,
Of his sleeves contrived the bellows;
Made the air-valve from his fur-coat;
From his stockings, made the muzzle;
Used his knees for sturdy anvil;
Made a hammer of his fore-arm.
Like the storm-wind roared the bellows,
Like the thunder rang the anvil.
For one day, and then a second,
And a third the forging pounded
In the body of Wipunen,

In the sorcerer's abdomen.

Then at last the Old Wipunen,
Spoke these words in wonder, guessing:
"Who art thou of ancient heroes,
Who of all the host of heroes?
Although many I have eaten,
And of men a countless number,
Never was there such as thou art.
Smoke arises from my nostrils,
From my mouth the fire is streaming,
In my throat are iron-clinkers.

    "Go, thou monster, hence to wander.
Flee this place, thou plague of Northland,
Ere I go to seek thy mother,
Tell the ancient dame thy mischief;
She shall bear thine evil conduct,
Great the burden she shall carry;
Great a mother's pain and anguish,
When her child runs wild and lawless.

    "Why thou camest here, O monster,
Camest here to give me torture?
Art thou Hisi sent from heaven,
Some calamity from Ukko?
Art, perchance, some new creation,
Ordered here to do me evil?
If thou art some evil genius,
Some calamity from Ukko,
Sent to me by my Creator,
Then am I resigned to suffer;
God does not forsake the worthy,
Does not ruin those that trust him,
Never are the good forsaken.

"If by man thou wert created,
If some hero sent thee hither,
I shall learn thy race of evil,
Shall destroy thy wicked tribe-folk.
If some scourge the winds have sent me,
Sent me on the air of spring-tide,
Brought me by the frosts of winter,
Quickly journey whence thou camest,
On the air-path of the heavens,
Perching not upon some aspen,
Resting not upon the birch-tree;
Fly away to copper mountains,
That the copper-winds may nurse thee,
Waves of ether, thy protection.

"Didst thou come from high Junala,
From the hems of ragged snow-clouds,
Quick ascend beyond the cloud-space,
Quickly journey whence thou camest,
To the snow-clouds, crystal-sprinkled,
To the twinkling stars of heaven;
There thy fire may burn forever;
There may flash thy forked lightnings,
In the Sun's undying furnace.

"Wert thou sent here by the spring-floods,
Driven here by river-torrents?
Quickly journey whence thou camest,
Quickly hasten to the waters,
To the borders of the rivers,
To the ancient water-mountain,
That the floods again may rock thee,
And thy water-mother nurse thee.

"Didst thou come from Kalma's kingdom,
From the castles of the death-land?

Haste thou back to thine own country,
To the Kalma-halls and castles,
To the fields with envy swollen,
Where contending armies perish.
  "Art thou from the Hisi-woodlands,
From ravines in Lempo's forest,
From the thickets of the pine-wood,
From the dwellings of the fir-glen?
Quick retrace thine evil footsteps
To the dwellings of thy master,
To the thickets of thine kindred;
There thou mayest dwell in pleasure,
Till thy house decays about thee,
Till thy walls shall mould and crumble.
  "Evil genius, thee I banish,
Get thee hence, thou horried monster,
To the caverns of the white-bear,
To the deep abysm of serpents,
To the vales, and swamps, and fenlands,
To the ever-silent waters,
To the hot-springs of the mountains,
To the dead-seas of the Northland,
To the lifeless lakes and rivers,
To the sacred stream and whirlpool.
  "Should thou ask for steeds for saddle,
Shouldst thou need a fleet-foot courser,
I will give thee worthy racers,
I will give thee saddle-horses;
Evil Hisi has a charger,
Crimson mane, and tail, and foretop,
Fire emitting from his nostrils,
As he prances through his pastures;
His hoofs that are of strongest iron

And his legs of steel and copper,
Quickly scale the highest mountains,
Dart like lightning through the valleys,
When a skilful master rides him.
  "Should this steed be insufficient,
I will give thee Lempo's snow-shoes,
Give thee Hisi's shoes of elm-wood,
Give to thee the staff of Piru,
That with these thou mayest journey
Into Hisi's courts and castles,
To the woods and fields of Juntas.
  "Hasten, hence, thou thing of evil,
Heinous monster, leave my body,
Ere the breaking of the morning,
Ere the Sun awakes from slumber;
Haste away, thou plague of Northland,
Haste along the track of moonbeams,
Wander hence, forever wander,
To the darksome fields of Pohya.
  "If at once thou dost not leave me,
I will send the eagle's talons,
Send to thee the beaks of vultures,
To devour thine evil body,
Hurl thy skeleton to Hisi.
Much more quickly cruel Lempo
Left my vitals when commanded,
When I called the aid of Ukko,
Called the help of my Creator.
Flee, thou motherless offendant,
Flee, thou fiend of Sariola,
Flee, thou hound without a master,
Ere the morning sun arises,
Ere the Moon withdraws to slumber!"

Wainamoinen, ancient hero,
Spoke at last to old Wipunen;
"Satisfied am I to linger
In these old and spacious caverns.
Pleasant here my home and dwelling;
For my meat I have thy tissues,
Have thy heart, and spleen, and liver;
For my drink, the blood of ages.
Goodly home for Wainamoinen.
    "I shall set my forge and bellows
Deeper, deeper in thy vitals;
I shall swing my heavy hammer,

Swing it with a greater power
On thy heart, and lungs, and liver.
I shall never, never leave thee
Till I learn thine incantations,
Learn thy many wisdom-sayings,
Learn the lost-words of the Master.
Never must these words be hidden;
Earth must never lose this wisdom,
Though the wisdom-singers perish."

Old Wipunen, wise magician,
Ancient prophet, filled with power,
Opened then his store of knowledge,
Lifted covers from his cases
Filled with old-time incantations,
Filled with songs of time primeval,
Filled with ancient wit and wisdom.
Sang he then the oldest folk-songs,
Sang the origin of witchcraft,
Sang of earth and its beginnings,
Sang the first of all creations,
Sang the source of good and evil,
Sung alas! by youth no longer.
Sang he orders of enchantment,
How, upon the will of Ukko,
By command of the Creator,
How the air was first divided,
How the water came from ether,
How the earth arose from water,
How from earth came vegetation,
Fish, and fowl, and man, and hero.
Sang again the wise Wipunen,
How the Moon was first created,

How the Sun was set in heaven,
Whence were made the rainbow's colors
Whence the ether's crystal pillars,
How the skies with stars were sprinkled.
    Then again sang wise Wipunen,
Sang in miracles of concord,
Sang in magic tones of wisdom.
Never was there heard such singing:
Songs he sang in countless numbers.
Sang he one day, then a second,
Sang a third from dawn till evening,
Sang from evening till the morning.
Listening were the stars of heaven,
And the Moon stood still to listen;
Stop'd the waves upon the sea-deep,
In the bay the tides stopped rising,
Stop'd the rivers in their courses,
Stop'd the waterfall of Rutya,
Even Jordan ceased its flowing
And Wuoksen stopped and listened.

When the ancient Wainamoinen
Well had learned the magic sayings,
Learned the ancient songs and legends,
Learned the words of ancient wisdom,
Learned the lost-words of the Master,
He prepared to leave the body
Of the wisdom-bard, Wipunen;
And he spoke to the enchanter,
"O thou Antero Wipunen,
Open wide thy mouth, and wider,
I have found the magic lost-words,
I will leave thee now forever,

Leave thee and thy wonderous singing,
Will return to Kalevala,
To Wainola's fields and firesides."

Then Wipunen spake in answer:
"Many are the things I've eaten,
Eaten bear, and elk, and reindeer,
Eaten ox, and wolf, and wild-boar,
Eaten man, and eaten hero;
But, O never have I eaten
Such a thing as Wainamoinen.
Thou hast found what thou desirest.
Found the three words of the Master;
Go in peace, and ne'er returning,
Take my blessing on thy going."

Thereupon the bard Wipunen
Open'd wide his mouth, and wider;
And the good, old Wainamoinen
Straightway left the wise enchanter,
Left Wipunen's great abdomen.
From the mouth he made his journey
O'er the hills and vales of Northland,
Swift as red-deer of the forest,
Swift as yellow-breasted marten,
To the fires of Wainola,
To the plains of Kalevala.
Straightway went he to the smithy
Of his brother, Ilmarinen.

There the iron-artist asked him,
"Hast thou found the long-lost wisdom,
Hast thou heard the secret doctrine,

Hast thou learned the master magic,
How to fasten in the ledges,
How the stern should be completed,
How to make the ship's forecastle?"

Wainamoinen thus made answer;
"I have learned of words a hundred,
Learned a thousand incantations,
Hidden deep for many ages;
Learned the words of ancient wisdom,
Found the keys of secret doctrine,
Found the lost-words of the Master."

Wainamoinen, magic-builder,
Straightway journeyed to his vessel,
To the spot of magic labor.
Quickly fastened he the ledges,
Firmly bound the stern together
And completed the forecastle.
Thus the ancient Wainamoinen
Built the boat with magic only,
And with magic launched his vessel,
Using not the hand to touch it,
Using not the foot to move it,
Using not the knee to turn it,
Using nothing to propel it.
Thus the third task was completed,
For the hostess of Pohyola,
Dowry for the Maid of Beauty
Sitting on the arch of heaven,
On the bow of many colors.

Antar the Hero

by Eunice Tietjens

from *Romance of Antar*

Antar is one of the greatest and most popular heroes of Arabia. He lived in the days before the coming of Mohammed and Islam. Antar was a great warrior and none could equal him in battle. But he was also a poet, and the songs he sang may still be read. This is the story of his boyhood and youth.

Antar lived and wrote in the sixth century A.D., but his writings and the stories that grew up about him were not collected until two hundred years later. Then al-Asma'll, a court poet, filled forty five volumes with the story, interspersed with other legends. Some of this material was translated into English in 1819 by an Englishman named Terrick Hamilton. There are also two French translations of the work.

ANTAR, THE HERO

Eunice Tietjens

———◦•◦———

T HE story of the hero Antar, warrior, lover, poet, whom none might conquer in battle, whom none might equal in love, and whom none might surpass in song. . . . The echo of his terrible war-cry still sighs in the gusty desert.

For long ago Antar lived, in the great simple days of the world, when the deeds of man were as the deeds of nature herself, terrible, ruthless and beautiful, and when great winds of passion blew across the earth. And even now, when the camp-fires of the Arabs gleam like golden stars on the arid immensity of the desert, stories are told of Antar, his songs are sung, and the hearts of men leap and cry out that such a man once moved under the canopy of the stars.

Now this is the manner of the hero's birth.

His father was an Arab, a noble and a warrior, great of stature, fearless of heart. Shaddad was his name, though he was often called "The Warrior of Jirwet" because of the horse he rode, the mare Jirwet, whose feet were swift on the sands of the desert, and whose fame had spread through all the countryside. Shaddad was of the Tribe of Abs, a noble tribe famed for the bravery of its men and the beauty of its women.

Now the Tribe of Abs was a wandering people, a people of the Bedouins, as were all the tribes of Arabia in that day, save only two or three who had settled in cities. There was enmity between the tribes, and each man's hand was against the stranger, for these were rough days and the clash of swords rang daily beneath the wide sky. Plunder was to the strong and no tribe might hope to keep its property—its women, its slaves, its flocks and its tents—save by endless vigilance and perpetual combat.

It happened then that the flocks of the Tribe of Abs had been depleted by marauders and a way was sought to replenish them. Therefore ten warriors, ten men strong of arm and ready in battle, set out across the desert in search of plunder that the loss might be made good. Among them was Shaddad.

By night the men traveled, and by day they lay concealed, that none might get wind of their coming. After some days they came at dusk to a place where there was a valley between hills, and certain tracks in the sand led them to believe that men were encamped here. So the Absians turned to the left up a hill, and when they reached the summit, looked down into the valley. And they saw many camp fires and the dim forms of tents. Fearing to attack what seemed like too numerous a party, they lay up in the hills till the light should come and they could see with whom they were met.

With the first light they saw that the valley was filled with the tents and flocks of a powerful tribe, too numerous and well armed for ten men to attack. But even as they looked, in the first gray glimmer of dawn, when the bitter cold of night in the desert was still unabated, and the faintly shimmering light gave a veil of unreality to everything that moved, a large herd of camels detached themselves from the valley and clambered slowly over the cup of the hills. They passed close beside the hidden men of Abs. And following them came a woman, with two children running at her side. For an instant she stood dark against the sky of dawn, and the men saw that she was a tall woman, of fine proportions, who walked with a lithe yet firm step and whose gestures were graceful. And the heart of Shaddad was moved by the woman.

The men of Abs turned aside, and circling among the rough country, followed the herd from a distance. When they had gone some way and were well removed from the camp, they swooped down upon the herd and turned the camels towards their own camp. And with the beasts they carried away also the slave woman and her two children.

It was not long however before the men of the tribe to whom the camels belonged missed the herd and rode in pursuit. They overtook the Absians and a savage combat took place. But Shaddad and his friends, though outnumbered, fought so fiercely that they beat off the others and remained in undisputed possession of the booty.

Later, in the confines of their own country, they came to a stream-bed where at this season a trickle of water ran. Here they watered the animals and sat down to divide the plunder. And they questioned the slave woman.

Now the woman was dusky of skin, darker than the Arabs, but of extraordinary beauty and well shaped. Her form was delicate, her features clearcut and fine, and her appearance elegant and striking. Her eyes inspired Shaddad with desire for her.

Her name, she said, was Zabeebah and she was an Abyssinian princess, whose father was a great chieftain in his own country. She had been carried off by the tribe from whom the men of Abs had taken her, and her two children Shiboob and Jereer had been born to her in captivity.

The men set her apart from themselves and fell to portioning the plunder. And Shaddad said, "Do you divide the camels between you. As for me, I ask nothing but the slave woman and her two children."

Then the men laughed and mocked at Shaddad, for the value of the camels was greater by far than that of a dusky slave. So they divided the camels and continued on their way.

When they arrived at their own quarters Shaddad established the woman and her children in a tent apart from the others. And he visited her often.

In the fullness of time Zabeebah brought forth a son. And the child was like no other child born of the desert. Already at birth he was a being apart, of great size, dark and swarthy as an elephant cub. He was harsh-featured and shaggy-haired, with blear eyes whose inner corners grew red as fire when he was angry, and from which sparks of fire seemed to flash. Strong-boned, long-footed, with ears immensely long, he was

like a fragment of a thunder-cloud. The shape of his body and
the form of his limbs resembled Shaddad, and his father was
overjoyed at seeing him and called him Antar. And for many
days Shaddad continued to gaze on him with delight.

Now this strange and savage child grew apace, and scarcely
was he walking on firm legs than it became apparent that he
would be a man of unparalleled physical strength and prowess.
Then the men of Abs who had been with Shaddad on the foray
in which they had captured his mother began to regret their
bargain. For now those camels which remained to them seemed
of less worth than this slave son of Shaddad's.

So they complained and went with their complaint to the
head of the tribe, the Chieftain Zoheir, saying: "We also assisted
in the capture of the child's mother. We should have a share
in the child."

The Chieftain said, "What manner of child is this that you
dispute concerning him? The matter concerns the Cadi, yet
bring him to me that I may see him."

So they brought Antar to the Chieftain as he sat before the
door of his tent, eating. And when Zoheir saw the child he
was filled with surprise, and he cried out loudly, "Ho, there!"
and flung a piece of meat to the boy.

But before Antar could seize it, one of the snarling and savage
dogs that follow the tents of the Arabs, and are practically wild
beasts, was there before him, snatched up the meat like a hawk
and ran. But Antar ran after it till he came up with it. He was
greatly enraged and the corners of his eyes glowed like fire.
He seized hold of the dog, wrenched open its jaws and tore
them in twain even to the shoulders, and snatched the meat out
of its mouth. Then he calmly ate it.

The Chieftain was amazed, and he said: "This matter is

not for me to decide. Take him to the Cadi." So the men took him to the Cadi, who is head of all matters of law. And the Cadi, after having heard and pondered the matter, awarded Antar to his father Shaddad.

Now Antar throve and grew. And he was more like the cub of a lion, fierce and untamable, than like any child known to the Bedouins. He knew not the meaning of fear.

When he was four years old he began to leave the camp on long expeditions of his own, for like a lion he loved solitude, the great free sweep of the desert under the blazing sun by day, and the freezing and terrible cold by night under the stars. He loved the ragged mountainsides also, and clambered like the wild antelope upon them. Of animals too, no matter how savage, he had not the slightest fear. He slew wolves. He would seize the fierce dogs and ride upon them. And his boldness increased day by day.

In the camp he was a great bully. He would eat nothing that he did not like. He would do nothing that did not please him. He tyrannized over the other slave boys, beating them savagely with a stick when they offended him. His half-brothers Shiboob and Jereer he also beat unmercifully, so that the camp was filled with his brawling. He would brook no authority save from his father Shaddad. As for his mother Zabeebah, he loved her as a cub loves, and though she could not command him, yet by love she ruled him.

When he was a little older it became his duty to go into the hills with the herds of camels and the flocks of scrawny brown sheep with their fat tails. At first he went with Zabeebah, but later he went alone with the animals. And this pleased him.

But he was no herdsman by nature, and with him the flocks fared ill. He would drive them before him, urging them on by a shower of small stones which he had learned to throw with unerring skill. When the animals had strayed away, even at a long distance, he would hit them with a stone from the sling he carried, and he would run after them so swiftly, with such raucous cries, that the beasts were terrified. They grew lean from much driving and little feeding, and ulcers grew upon their feet where they were cut by the sharp stones over which they were thus driven.

At other times he would forget the flocks altogether, and lie for long hours on his face in the sun, lost in far thoughts of his own. Then the flocks strayed away and were lost, or broke their legs in steep places—for the legs of camels break easily—or were eaten by wild beasts.

Now all these things marked Antar as a being apart, who fitted ill with the slaves of the tribe, and who seemed destined to make trouble as he grew older. His father Shaddad, though he took pride in the boy's strength and courage, yet was troubled concerning him. He beat him for injuring the flocks and knew not what to make of him.

"What will be the end of this strange son of mine?" thought Shaddad.

Yet for all the savagery of the boy, already there were stirring in him, underneath his uncouth deeds, two forces which were to mold him into what he became at last, and though they never weakened him, yet they set boundaries to the fierceness of his deeds and the insolence of his heart. These forces were tenderness and chivalry towards women, and the power of song. But as yet the forces were dormant in him.

When Antar was fifteen one of these forces woke him to a deed which was to be the pivot of his life, though as yet the force was but half the motive for the deed.

Now the manner of it was this.

The head of the tribe, the Chieftain Zoheir, had ten sons, and their characters differed among themselves. But with only two of them was the story of Antar concerned. The first was the eldest son, Prince Shas, who was heir to the possessions of Zoheir, a proud and restless man, who brooked interference ill. The other was a younger son, Prince Malik, a brave man also, yet just and generous, beloved by all the tribe for the gentle kindness of his disposition. And these men now took cognizance of the slave Antar, and as they saw him first so they continued throughout their lives towards him.

The Chieftain had two hundred slaves who tended his herds of he and she camels, and each of his sons had the same; for a powerful tribe was the Tribe of Abs. Now the leader of the slaves of Prince Shas was a man named Daji, a powerful man and a great bully, whom the prince valued highly because of his vast bodily strength. There was not a slave in the camp but feared him and trembled before him, save only the boy Antar who made no account of him, and disliked him, so that there was enmity between them, which as yet however had never broken into flame, since Daji disdained the boy and thought him beneath his notice.

One day the poor men, the widows and orphans of the tribe met together to drive their flocks to water. And this occurred when the tribe was encamped at a spot which was the furthermost point of the land of Hejaz and the first of the land of Yemen. There was water here, yet it was none too plentiful, and care must be taken that all might drink.

The poor people therefore drove their flocks some distance from the camp to a place where there was a pool of water. But the pool was shallow and filled slowly, and only once a day might it be used, for what water the herds did not drink was so muddied as to be useless.

Just as they had reached the spot however this Daji rode up and stopped them, driving them insolently from the water and taking possession of it for his master's cattle. Therefore an old man of the tribe came up to him and accosted him in a suppliant manner, saying,

"Be so good, master Daji, as to let my cattle drink. They are all the property I possess, and I live by their milk. Pity my flock; have compassion on me and grant my request, and let them drink." But Daji paid no attention to his demand and abused him.

Then came an old woman, shriveled and worn with the hard life of the desert, and addressed him:

"O master Daji," she implored him, "I am a poor weak old woman, as you see. Time has dealt hardly with me—it has aimed its arrows at me, and its daily and nightly calamities have destroyed all my men. I have lost my husband and my children, and am in great distress. These few sheep are all I possess and without them I shall perish. Pity my forlorn state, and be so good as to let them drink."

But when Daji heard these words, and perceived the crowd of women and men, his pride increased and his obstinacy was not to be moved. Bully that he was, he struck the old woman on the stomach, so that she fell over on her back, and her nakedness was uncovered. And all the slaves that were with Daji laughed at her distress.

Now Antar also was in that spot, and when he saw what had occurred, pity for the woman fanned into sudden flame his hatred of Daji, and a great rage played throughout all his limbs. He ran to Daji and cried out:

"You thing of ill omen! What mean you by this disgusting action? Do you dare so to insult an Arab woman? May God destroy your limbs, and all that consented to this act!"

When Daji saw himself thus confronted he was overcome

by surprise and indignation. He raised his hand and struck Antar a blow over the face that nearly knocked out his eyes. And Antar could scarcely see, for the blow and the rage that was in him. But he waited till he had recovered from the blow, and his senses had returned to him.

Then he rushed at the slave and, seizing him by one of his legs, he threw him on his back. He thrust one hand under Daji's thighs, and with the other he grasped his neck, and raising him by a terrible effort above his head he dashed him against the ground. So great was his force that the slave's length and his breadth were all one mass.

But Antar stood above the body, filled with a boundless fury, his eyes red as fire, and roared aloud, even as a lion roars.

When the slaves who were with Daji perceived the fate of their leader they cried out to Antar:

"You have slain the slave of Prince Shas! What man on earth can now protect you?" And they attacked him and fell upon him with staves and stones. But he resisted them all, and laid about him with his stick as a warrior with his sword.

Nevertheless, in spite of Antar's courage, since they were so many they might have overcome him and slain him, had not good fortune sent the gentle Prince Malik riding that way, who when he saw the unequal contest, ended it. And when he had questioned those standing by and learned the cause of the trouble, he promised Antar his protection.

So Prince Malik took the boy back to camp with him and presented him before the Chieftain Zoheir, with an account of what he had done. And Prince Shas came also to his father and demanded Antar's death in return for the slave he had killed.

But the Chieftain was a just man, and justice has always been highly esteemed among the Arabs. When he had heard the whole story he applauded the conduct of Antar, saying:

"This is a valiant fellow, who has defended the honor of women. He will shine a noble warrior, and destroy his enemies."

That day, upon Antar's return home, all the women crowded round him, praising him for his gallant behavior. And among them was Abla, the daughter of Milik, his father Shaddad's brother.

But though, following the Chieftain's lead, most of the tribe now praised Antar as a promising youth, yet by this deed he had made certain enemies. He had incurred the hatred of Prince Shas, a hatred which was to follow him throughout many years. His two uncles also, Shaddad's brothers Milik and Jewad, came to hate him with a feeling founded upon fear.

That evening these uncles met together and took counsel. And Milik said, "O my brother, I know not what will be the consequence of the actions of this swarthy slave of our family. This time no ill has come to us because of him, but he that has done one such deed will assuredly do others. I fear that to-morrow he will destroy some one of rank and power. Then a disturbance will arise throughout the tribe, our blood will be demanded, and our persons may pay the forfeit."

"Brother," answered Jewad, "you have hit the mark. After what has happened it will no longer be safe for Shaddad to let him take the family camels and cattle to the pasture. He is therefore of no further use to us, and he is certain in time to endanger our lives and that of Shaddad. Let us therefore take measures to put him to death."

"You are right," said Milik. "Let us do as you say. But it must be done in secret, or the Chieftain will be angry, and Shaddad also. Let us therefore waylay him and kill him in the meadows in some secret spot."

So a few days later Milik and Jewad followed Antar's steps

as he led the cattle forth to graze, for Shaddad had made no change in his employment.

Now on that day the boy was riding about in the wide plains and deserts, galloping at random over the wastes. At last he came to a valley called "The Valley of Lions" because many ferocious wild animals haunted it. And here Antar let the cattle graze.

"Perhaps," said he to himself, "I shall now find a lion, and I will slay him!" This he thought because the blood was hot in his veins. So he went up on a mound from which he could see all about him, and waited. Presently, while the cattle were grazing, behold! a lion appeared in the valley even as he thought. The lion stalked about and roared aloud. Vast was his strength and his force dreadful. His nostrils were wide and fire flashed from his eyes so that the whole valley trembled at every gnash of his fangs. He was a calamity. As soon as he appeared the cattle scented him and fled in terror and the camels were dispersed to the right and left.

No sooner did Antar observe this commotion than he ran down into the valley, brandishing his club. There he saw the lion, terrible in his strength, lashing his sides with his tail. Antar cried out to him, and the mountains re-echoed to his cry.

"Welcome, O father of lions, foul beast of the plains! Come now! Put forth your power and your might and pride yourself on your roar, for no doubt you are the monarch of the brute creation and all tremble before you. But do you think, foul-mouthed beast about to die, that you can frighten Antar with your roar or alarm him with your bellow? I will not condescend to slay you with an arrow or a weapon, but I will make you drink of the cup of death with these hands alone!"

So shouting the youth flung away his club, and rushed upon the lion.

Now it happened that Antar's uncles Milik and Jewad came

up to kill him at the moment when he descended into the valley. They saw him shout defiance to the lion and heard what he threatened. And Antar was but little less terrible than the lion to behold, his eyes red as fire, his every gesture fierce as an eagle's.

He sprang forward and fell on the lion like a hailstorm, and hissed at him like a black serpent. He met the lion as he sprang and outroared his bellow. Then he seized hold of the beast's mouth with his hands and wrenched it open to his shoulders. And he shouted aloud till the valley and the country round echoed at his roaring. He stuck to the lion till it was dead, then dragged him by the legs out of the valley.

Here he built a fire and waited till it blazed. Then he ripped up the lion, took out the entrails and cut off his four legs, which he threw into the flames. When he saw that they were roasted, he took them out and ate thereof till he had finished his meal.

Now his uncles had been watching all this with amazement and terror. When they had somewhat recovered themselves, Jewad said:

"Verily this slave has not his equal. No one in his senses would engage him!"

Milik also trembled. "What shall we do with the wretch?" he asked. "Great indeed has been the deed he has done. None of us can harm him. He would soon destroy us, and tear out our entrails, or do as he has done with the lion."

"Let us return home," said Jewad. "We must find some other means to kill him and accomplish our wishes." So they stole away in secret and told no one of what they had seen.

But Antar came swaggering into camp, his swarthy face lit with pride, the corners of his eyes still red from his rage against the lion, and his hands and his clothing rusty with blood. He threw down the lion's skin, with the head still gory upon it, before the feet of Zabeebah his mother, and he cried:

"This have I brought you in sign of my prowess. Had ever mother such a son?"

Now these were the early years of Antar, and of such stuff was the hero made.

Rustem and His Rose-Coloured Steed

by Helen Zimmern

from *The Epic of Kings; Hero Tales of Ancient Persia*
(*retold from* The Shah Nameh *by Firdusi*)

The three sons of Feridoun the Glorious, who ruled the world, were: Silim, the prudent; Tur, the courageous; and Irij, both prudent and brave. When the land of Feridoun was divided after his death, Irij was given Iran. He and his heirs ruled with great power; but the power of the grandson of Irij, Minuchihr, was greatest of all because the captain of his army was Saum.

In due time a child, called Zal, was born to Saum and his wife. Because Zal was born with white hair, he was thought to be a child of ill omen. Saum dared not let him live and had him placed on a lonely mountaintop to die of exposure. There a great bird called the Simurgh rescued him and reared him. When Zal became a man he was reunited with his father, married a woman named Rudabeh, and became the father of Rustem.

The stories of these great Persian heroes were passed on by storytellers for many years, although some are said to have been written down as they happened in the sixth and seventh centuries. The oft-repeated legends and the written records were collected in about 1000 by a man named Firdusi in a book he called The Shah Nameh, The Book of Kings.

RUSTEM AND HIS ROSE-COLORED STEED

Helen Zimmern

———————◆•◆———————

Now ere the son of Zal was born, Rudabeh was sore afflicted, and neither by day nor night could she find rest. Then Zal in his trouble bethought him of the Simurgh, his nurse, and how she had given unto him a feather that he might use it in the hour of his need. And he cast the feather into the fire as she had commanded, and straightway a sound of rushing wings filled the air, and the sky was darkened and the bird of God stood before Zal. And she said unto him—

"O my son, wherefore art thou troubled, and why are the eyes of this lion wet with tears?"

Then he told her of his sorrow, and she bade him be of good cheer, "For verily thy nurse who shielded thee, and reared thee when thy father cast thee out, is come yet again to succour thee."

And she told him how he should act, and when she had done speaking she turned her once more towards her nest. But Zal did as she had commanded, and there was born to him a son comely of limb. And when Rudabeh beheld the babe, she smiled and said—

"Verily he shall be called Rustem (which, being interpreted, meaneth delivered), for I am delivered of my pains."

And all the land was glad that a son was come unto Zal the hero, and the sounds of feasting and joy were heard throughout its breadth.

Then fleet messengers brought the sweet tidings unto Saum. And they bare with them an image of Rustem sewn of silk, whereon were traced the features of this lion's whelp, and a club was put into its hands, and it was mounted upon a dromedary. Now when Saum beheld the image his heart leaped up within him. He poured mountains of gold before the messengers, and gave thanks unto Ormuzd that he had suffered his eyes to look upon this child.

And when eight summers had rolled above their heads, Saum learned that Rustem was mighty of stature and fair of mien, and his heart yearned towards him. He therefore made ready a mighty host and passed unto Zaboulistan, that he might look upon his son. And Rustem rode forth to meet his sire, mounted upon an elephant of war, and when he beheld Saum he fell upon his face and craved his blessing. And Saum blessed Rustem, the son of Zal.

Then Rustem spake unto Saum and said, "O Pehliva, I rejoice in that I am sprung from thee, for my desires are not after the feast, neither do I covet sleep or rest. My heart is fixed upon valour, a horse do I crave and a saddle, a coat of mail and a helmet, and my delight is in the arrow. Thine enemies will I vanquish, and may my courage be like unto thine."

And Saum, when he had heard these words, was astonished, and blessed Rustem yet again. And his eyes could not cease from gazing upon the face of the boy, and he lingered in the land until a moon had run her course.

Now it befell that when yet two springs had passed, Rustem was awakened from his slumber by a mighty roaring that shook the walls of the house, even unto the foundation, and a cry went forth that the white elephant of the King had broken its chain in fury, and that the housemates were in danger. And Rustem, when he learned it, sprang from his bed, and desired of the guards that they should suffer him to pass into the court that he might conquer the beast. But the guards barred the way from him, saying—

"How can we answer for it before the King if thou run into danger?"

But Rustem would not listen to their voice. He forced a passage for himself with his mighty arms, with his strong fists he broke down the barriers of the door. And when he was without he beheld how that all the warriors were sore afraid of the elephant, because that he was mad with rage. And Rustem was ashamed for them in his soul, and he ran towards the beast with a loud cry. Then the elephant, when he saw him, raised his trunk to strike him, but Rustem beat him upon the head with his club, and smote him that he died. And when he had done this deed, he returned unto his bed and slept until the morning. But the news of his prowess spread throughout the house of the King and far into the land, even unto the realms of Saum. And Zal, and all men with him, rejoiced because a hero was arisen in Iran.

Now, while these things were passing in the house of Zal, in the land of Zaboulistan, Minuchihr made him ready to pass from the world, for he had reached twice sixty years. He called before him Nauder his son, and gave him wise counsels, and exhorted him that he should ever walk in the paths of wisdom. And he bade him rest his throne upon the strength of Saum and Zal, and the child that was sprung from their loins. Then when he had spoken, Minuchihr closed his eyes and sighed, and there remained of him only a memory in the world.

But Nauder forgot the counsels of his father. He vexed the land and reigned in anger, and cruel deeds were committed in his name, so that the people rose up and cried against the

King. And men of might came unto Saum and laid before him their plaints, and the petitions of the people, and they prayed that he would wrest the crown from the head of Nauder, and place it upon his own. But Saum was sore grieved when he had heard these words, and he spake, saying—

"Not so, for it beseemeth me not to put out my hand after the crown, for Nauder is of the race of the Kaianides, and unto them is given majesty and might."

Then he girt his sword about his loins, and took with him a host, and rode before the face of the Shah. And when he was come unto him, Saum exhorted him with prayers and tears that he would turn him from the paths of evil. And Nauder listened unto the voice of Saum the Pehliva, and joy was abroad once more.

But the tidings spread, even into Turan, that Minuchihr the just was departed, and that the hand of Nauder was heavy upon the land. And Poshang, who was of the race of Tur, heard the news thereof with gladness, for he deemed that the time was ripe to remember the vengeance that was due unto the blood of his sire. Therefore he called about him his warriors, and bade them go forth to war against Iran, saying the time was come to avenge his father and draw unto himself the heritage. And while his son Afrasiyab made ready the host to fulfil the desire of his father, there spread the news that Saum the Pehliva had been gathered unto the dust, and that Zal tarried in his house to build him a tomb. And the news gave courage unto Afrasiyab and his men, and they made haste to gain the frontier.

But the grandson of Feridoun had learned of their coming, and he prepared him to meet the foes of his land. Then he sent forth an army that overshadowed the earth in its progress. But the army of Afrasiyab was great also, and it covered the ground like unto ants and locusts. And both hosts pitched their tents

in the plains of Dehstan, and made them ready for the fight.
And the horses neighed aloud, and the pawing of their hoofs
shook the deep places of the earth, and the dust of their trampling uprose even unto heaven. Then when they had put their
men into array, they fell upon each other, and for two days did
they rage in fierce combat, neither did the victory lean to either
side. And the clamour and confusion were mighty, and earth
and sky seemed blended into one. And the carnage was great,
and blood flowed like water, and heads fell from their trunks
like unto autumn leaves that are withered. But on the third day
it came about that the upper hand was given unto the men of
Turan, and Nauder the King, and the flower of his army with
him, fell into the hands of the foe.

Then Afrasiyab cut off the head of Nauder the Shah, and sat himself down upon the throne of light. And he proclaimed himself lord of Iran, and required of all men that they should do him homage, and pour gifts before his face. But the people would not listen unto his voice, and they sent messengers into Seistan, and craved counsel of the Pehliva in their distress. And Zal, when he heard their tidings, cast aside the sorrow for Saum his father, and girded his loins in enmity against the son of Tur. And he bade the Iranians choose out Zew, the son of Thamasp, of the blood of Feridoun, of wisdom in speech, that he should rule over them on the throne of the Kaianides. And the people did as Zal commanded.

Now the throne of Feridoun grew young again under the sway of Zew. With power did he beat back the host of Turan, a covenant of peace did he wring from their hands. And it was written that the Jihun should divide the lands, and that the power of Zal the Pehliva should end where men take up their abode in tents. And Zew ruled rightly in the sight of Ormuzd, and God gave unto the land the key of abundance. Yet few were the years that he commanded with equity, and Garshasp his son reigned in his stead. But neither to him was it given to reign long with glory, and bitter fruit sprouted yet again from the tree of misfortune. For the throne of the Kaianides was empty, and Afrasiyab, when he learned thereof, followed of Poshang his father, and hurried him unto the land of Iran, that he might place himself upon the seat of power. And all the men of Iran, when they learned thereof, were sore afraid, and they turned them once again unto the son of Saum. And they spake unto him hard words, and heaped reproaches upon him that he had not averted these dangers from their heads. And Zal in his heart smiled at their ingratitude and lip-wisdom, but he also sorrowed with them and with his land. And he spake, saying—

"I have ever done for you what was fitting and right, and all my life have I feared no enemy save only old age. But that enemy is now upon me, therefore I charge you that ye look unto Rustem to deliver you. Howbeit he shall be backed by the counsels of his father."

Then he called before him his son, who was yet of tender age, and he said unto him—

"O my son, thy lips still smell of milk, and thy heart should go out to pleasure. But the days are grave, and Iran looketh unto thee in its danger. I must send thee forth to cope with heroes."

And Rustem answered and said, "Thou knowest, O my father, that my desires are rather after war than pleasures. Give unto me, therefore, a steed of strength and the mace of Saum thy father, and suffer that I go out to meet the hosts of Ahriman."

Then Zal's heart laughed within him when he heard these words of manhood. And he commanded that all the flocks of horses, both from Zaboulistan and Cabul, be brought before his son, that he might choose from their midst his steed of battle. And they were passed in order before Rustem, and he laid upon the backs of each his hand of might to test them if they could bear his weight of valour. And the horses shuddered as they bent beneath his grasp, and sank upon their haunches in weakness. And thus did he do with them all in turn, until he came unto the flocks of Cabul. Then he perceived in their midst a mare mighty and strong, and there followed after her a colt like to its mother, with the chest and shoulders of a lion. And in strength it seemed like an elephant, and in colour it was as rose leaves that have been scattered upon a saffron ground. Now Rustem, when he had tested the colt with his eyes, made a running knot in his cord and threw it about the breast. And he caught the colt in the snare, though the mare defended it mightily. Then the keeper of the flock came before Rustem and said—

"O youth puissant and tall, take not, I counsel thee, the horse of another."

And Rustem answered him and asked, "To whom then pertaineth this steed? I see no mark upon its flanks."

And the keeper said, "We know not its master, but rumours are rife anent it throughout the land, and men name it the Rakush of Rustem. And I warn thee, the mother will never permit thee to ride on it. Three years has it been ready for the saddle, but none would she suffer to mount thereon."

Then Rustem, when he heard these words, swung himself upon the colt with a great bound. And the mare, when she saw it, ran at him and would have pulled him down, but when she had heard his voice she suffered it. And the rose-coloured steed bore Rustem along the plains like unto the wind. Then when he was returned, the son of Zal spake and said to the keeper—

"I pray thee, tell unto me what is the price of this dragon?"

But the keeper replied, "If thou be Rustem, mount him, and retrieve the sorrows of Iran. For his price is the land of Iran, and seated upon him thou wilt save the world."

And Rustem rejoiced in Rakush (whose name, being interpreted, meaneth the lightning), and Zal rejoiced with him, and they made them ready to stand against Afrasiyab.

Now it was in the time of roses, and the meadows smiled with verdure, when Zal led forth his hosts against the offspring of Tur. And the standard of Kawah streamed upon the breeze, and Mihrab marched on the left, and Gustahem marched on the right, and Zal went in the midst of the men, but Rustem went at the head of all. And there followed after him a number like to the sands of the sea, and the sounds of cymbals made a noise throughout the land like unto the day of judgment, when the earth shall cry unto the dead, "Arise." And they marched in order even unto the shores of the river Rai, and the two armies were but some farsangs apart. Albeit, when Afrasiyab heard that Rustem and Zal were come out against him, he was in nowise dismayed, for he said, "The son is but a boy, and the father is old; it will not, therefore, be hard for me to keep my power in Iran." And he made ready his warriors with gladness of heart.

But Zal, when he had drawn up his army in battle array, spake unto them, saying—

"O men valiant in fight, we are great in number, but there is wanting to us a chief, for we are without the counsels of a Shah, and verily no labour succeedeth when the head is lacking. But rejoice, and be not downcast in your hearts, for a Mubid hath revealed unto me that there yet liveth one of the race of Feridoun to whom pertaineth the throne, and that he is a youth wise and brave."

And when he had thus spoken, he turned him to Rustem and said—

"I charge thee, O my son, depart in haste for the Mount Albertz, neither tarry by the way. And wend thee unto Kai Kobad, and say unto him that his army awaiteth him, and that the throne of the Kaianides is empty."

And Rustem, when he had heard his father's command, touched with his eyelashes the ground before his feet, and straightway departed. In his hand he bare a mace of might, and under him was Rakush the swift of foot. And he rode till he came within sight of the Mount Alberz, whereon had stood the cradle of his father. Then he beheld at its foot a house beauteous like unto that of a king. And around it was spread a garden whence came the sounds of running waters, and trees of tall stature uprose therein, and under their shade, by a gurgling rill, there stood a throne, and a youth, fair like to the moon, was

seated thereon. And round about him leaned knights girt with
red sashes of power, and you would have said it was a paradise
for perfume and beauty.

Now when those within the garden beheld the son of Zal
ride by, they came out unto him and said—

"O Pehliva, it behooveth us not to let thee go farther before
thou hast permitted us to greet thee as our guest. We pray
thee, therefore, descend from off thy horse and drink the cup
of friendship in our house."

But Rustem said, "Not so, I thank you, but suffer that I may
pass unto the mountain with an errand that brooketh no delay.
For the borders of Iran are encircled by the enemy, and
the throne is empty of a king. Wherefore I may not stay."

Then they answered him, "If thou goest unto the mount, tell
us, we pray thee, thy mission, for unto us is it given to guard its
sides."

And Rustem replied, "I seek there a king of the seed of
Feridoun, who cleansed the world of the abominations of
Zohak, a youth who reareth high his head. I pray ye, therefore,
if ye know aught of Kai Kobad, that ye give me tidings where
I may find him."

Then the youth that sat upon the throne opened his mouth
and said, "Kai Kobad is known to me, and if thou wilt enter
this garden and rejoice my soul with thy presence I will give
thee tidings concerning him."

When Rustem heard these words he sprang from off his
horse and came within the gates. And the youth took his hand
and led him unto the steps of the throne. Then he mounted it
yet again, and when he had seated himself upon it, he pledged
the guest within his gates. Then he gave a look unto Rustem,
and questioned him wherefore he sought for Kai Kobad, and
at whose desire he was come forth to find him. And Rustem
told him of the Mubids, and how that his father had sent him

with all speed to pray the young King that he would be their Shah, and lead the host against the enemies of Iran. Then the youth, when he had listened to an end, smiled and said—

"O Pehliva, behold me, for verily I am Kai Kobad of the race of Feridoun!"

And Rustem, when he had heard these words, fell on the ground before his feet, and saluted him Shah. Then the King raised him, . . .

"May the Shah live for ever!"

Then instruments of music rent the air, and joy spread over all the assembly. But when silence was fallen yet again, Kai Kobad opened his mouth and said—

"Hearken, O my knights, unto the dream that I had dreamed, and ye will know wherefore I called upon you this day to stand in majesty about my throne. For in my sleep I beheld two falcons white of wing, and they came out unto me from Iran, and in their beaks they bare a sunny crown. And the crown they placed upon my head. And behold now is Rustem come out unto me like to a white bird, and his father, the nursling of a bird, hath sent him, and they have given unto me the crown of Iran."

And Rustem, when he had heard this dream, said, "Surely thy vision was given unto thee of God! But now, I pray thee, up and tarry no longer, for the land of Iran groaneth sore and awaiteth thee with much travail."

So Kai Kobad listened to the desires of Rustem, and swung him upon his steed of war; and they rode day and night, until they came down from the hills unto the green plains that are watered by murmuring streams. And Rustem brought the King safely through the outposts of the enemy; and when the night was fallen, he led him within the tents of Zal, and none knew that he was come save only the Mubids. For seven days did they hold counsel together, and on the eighth the message of the

stars was received with joy. And Zal made ready a throne of
ivory and a banquet, and the crown of Iran was placed upon
the head of the young Shah. Then the nobles came and did
homage before him, and they revelled in praise till the night
was far spent. And they prayed him that he would make him
ready to lead them against the Turks. And Kai Kobad mustered
the army and did as they desired.

And soon the battle raged hot and strong many days, and
deeds of valour were done on either side; but the men of Turan
could not stand up against the men of Iran, neither could the
strength of Rustem be broken. For he put forth the power of
a lion, and his shadow extended for miles. And from that day
men named him Tehemten (which being interpreted, meaneth the stronglimbed), for he did deeds of prowess in the sight
of men. And Afrasiyab was discomfited, and fled before him,
and his army followed after, and their hearts were bruised and
full of care.

But the Iranians, when they beheld that their foes had vanished before them, turned them unto Kai Kobad and did homage before his throne. And Kai Kobad celebrated the victory
with much pomp, as is the manner of kings; and he placed
Rustem upon his right hand and Zal upon his left, and they
feasted and made them merry.

This Hound Hath Loved Me

by Mabel Ashe Beling

from *The Wicked Goldsmith*

This Hound Hath Loved Me *is a story taken from the* Mahabharata, *the oldest epic story of India. The work deals basically with the great wars between the two branches of the Bharata family, the Pandavs and the Kurus. Woven into the accounts of the lives and wars of these people of north India, however, is much material that is sacred to the Hindus of India today. Some of the greatest pieces of Hindu religious and devotional literature are found in the* Mahabharata. *This* Hound Hath Loved Me *tells a part of this great story and also shows some of the religious beliefs of the people. The events of the story took place many centuries before the birth of Christ but they still influence Indian people and Indian life.*

THIS HOUND HATH LOVED ME

Mabel Ashe Beling

————◦•◦————

AGES and ages ago there was a war in India, as fiercely fought, as nobly sung, as that war which Homer made immortal. It was the war between the five Pandav princes and their hundred cousins, the Kurus, and this is the way it came to pass.

King Pandu lay dying. Beside his couch knelt his blind brother, and the King whispered feebly, "I leave this world before my sons are old enough to take my place. Rule the land so long as you live, brother, and see to it that my sons are trained as kings should be. To you I trust them, my kingdom and my sons."

So a blind king came to the throne, and faithfully he bore the trust laid on him. He ruled justly, he had the five Pandav princes instructed in all that warrior princes should know.

Yudhisthir was eldest. Over his birth, the god of Justice presided—Yudhisthir was just and generous in heart. Bhima, the second, was godchild of the Wind, swift to think and swift to act. Arjun, the third, born under the sign of Indra, was a mighty archer like the god who speeds the arrows of the rain and the bolts of thunder. The youngest two were twins, godsons of the starry Aswin Twins who shine together in the night sky.

The blind King did not fail in the upbringing of his nephews, but he had a blind spot to the faults of his own sons—they were as bad as sons could be. Perhaps the King failed because there were so many of them. One hundred sons he had—and all were evil.

Eldest, proudest, cruelist was Duryodhan. By right of age and force he led the clan of Kuru princes and fostered in them a bitter jealousy of the five Pandavs, their cousins.

When Yudhisthir came of age, he shone in all the qualities his father had desired his sons to have. The five Pandav princes all were brave, wise, noble in spirit, but Yudhisthir was noblest of them all. Proudly the good blind King proclaimed him heir-apparent to the throne.

His own sons raged. Never, the Kurus vowed, would they submit to be ruled by a Pandav prince. But they raged in secret. Duryodhan counseled them to hide their hate, he had a plan to be rid of these rivals forever. The Kurus took the oath of fealty with smiling lips, while they waited a chance to slay their cousins.

The chance came soon. There was a festival in a town far distant from the capital city. The King was old and feeble, so he sent the Pandav princes with their mother to take his place at the festivities. As if to honor their visit, a special dwelling was built for them. Duryodhan ordered its building—every piece of wood which went into it was dry as tinder and soaked in oil.

As soon as the princes and their mother slept on the night of their arrival, one of the Kurus set fire to the house, and the Pandavs woke to the roar of flames about them.

But they were not to die. Workmen who built the house—perhaps they knew the plot and wished to save their rightful lords—had made an underground passage which led from the building to the jungle just behind it. Through this secret way the brothers escaped, carrying their old mother to safety.

Once in the jungle they considered what was best for them to do. They had no doubt the Kurus had planned their death, and the oath of fealty had been but a trick to lull suspicion. The Pandavs knew no fear for themselves, they feared for their mother. The Kurus had not scrupled to include her in the death they planned. What were five against one hundred? Five who would stoop to no shameful deed, against one hundred who had no honor, who felt no shame!

Only in the jungles and the forests, and only so long as the Kurus thought them dead in the flames, were they and their mother safe. They built in the forest a little house, well thatched against the weather. Then they joined an order of Brahmins near by and gave up the life of warrior princes to put on the robes of humble mendicants. Day by day, along the dusty roads, they begged their bread according to the rule of the order, and each night they took food home to their mother.

One day they met on the road a group of strangers, Brahmin mendicants like themselves, who hailed them with a great piece of news.

"Come along with us, brothers!" the Brahmins urged. "We are on our way to Panchala. The King has proclaimed 'Bride's Choice.' He will give his fair daughter as prize in the test of the bow. Any man not baseborn may try his skill. All the kings and princes of India will be there."

Arjun's heart leaped at thought of drawing bow again, but he shook his head. "We cannot go. We are five poor brothers with a mother to care for, we must stay here."

"Bring your mother with you. We travel but slowly, begging as we go. There are aged women and holy sisters among our number. Come, there will be feasts for all and gifts for all. There will be dancers and wrestlers, actors and storytellers. You will see all the chieftains and kings try their mightiest for the hand of fair Draupadi."

"Who knows? You are all handsome as princes—the princess may lose her heart to one of you; perhaps to this tall youth with arms stout as a bowman's," and they pointed to stalwart Arjun, standing with his arm about his old mother. "At least he may contend in some of the feats of valor, and perhaps win one of the thousand prizes."

So the five brothers and their mother joined the band of Brahmins, and slowly, on foot and begging their food along the way, they came after many days to the noble city of Panchala. It seemed all India had moved to the same place, humble folk a-foot, great ones on horseback, in chariot, or swaying in howdahs on the broad back of an elephant. No place was to be found in the crowded city for the Pandavs and their mother, but a kindly porter offered them room in his cottage outside the city gates, and they were grateful.

Every morning they left their mother to rest in this humble shelter and went forth to beg food and to see the wonders of the festive city. Beyond the wall and moat, a level field had been enclosed for the festivities. Around it, for the royal guests, were new-built mansions which shone in the sunshine white as silver swans.

Minstrels and dancers, strolling players and famous story-tellers swarmed thick as honey bees, and plied their arts to entertain the multitude.

Music, feasting, contests at sport and arms, gaity for fifteen days, and at last came the great day of "Bride's Choice." The people surged about the field of contest, thousands upon thousands of them. Under red canopies sat kings, queens, nobles, to watch the proudest youths of India contend for the hand of its fairest princess.

She came, Draupadi, in bridal dress, with the golden garland of bridal on her arm. That garland she would hang around the neck of the victor, and him she would wed. The Prince, her brother, led her to the altar where an aged priest kindled the holy fire and spoke the holy mantras.

Then brother and sister turned to face the multitude, and the Prince made proclamation, saluting first his aged father, King Drupad, sitting on a throne high above them. The Prince held aloft for all to see the huge war bow of the King.

"Behold the bow of Drupad, my father. By the ancient custom of our fathers, today we celebrate Bride's Choice. Far down the field shines the high-hung target. Mark well the ring of brass which whirls before it. Whoever, born of Arya blood, be he rich or be he poor, shall send five arrows from this bow through that whirling ring and hit the target, may stand forth and claim for his bride my sister, the Princess Draupadi."

A roar of applause went up from the throng. The Prince held up his hand for silence. He turned to the Princess and named aloud the roll call of her suitors. Like a herald he proclaimed the lineage and name of each, and the famous deeds he had done.

"Behold, my sister, these monarchs and princes who come to seek thy hand. Here are brave Duryodhan and his brothers, of the house of Kuru. Here are Kalinga and Tamra from the eastern ocean. Here is Pattan who rules the western shore. . . ." On he went down the long list of jewel-decked monarchs from north, east, south and west—and each, as his name and fame were spoken, sought a look from the lovely Draupadi.

"And now, my sister," he ended, "these suitors abide thy choice! Whoso hits the target, choose him for thy husband, Draupadi, if he please thy heart, and if he be of noble blood!"

The crowd cheered. One by one the noble suitors stepped forward to the test. In haughtiness and pride, they stepped forth. In shame, they slunk back. Most of them had not strength to bend the mighty bow, one was challenged as baseborn, the three whose arms were strong enough to nock the arrow and bend the bow, saw each his arrow strike the whirling ring, rebound, and fall to earth. Not a single shaft reached the target shining far down the field.

From under the red canopies, women's laughter rang at each defeat. The populace roared and jeered.

The defeated suitors stormed angrily to each other, "We have been tricked! The test is impossible. Indra himself could not bend that bow, nor strike that target with his thunderbolts! Drupad has shamed us before great queens, and made us a laughingstock for the populace!"

The five brothers, standing among the Brahmins, watched trials and failures. Arjun trembled like a hunting leopard held on leash, and looked to Yudhisthir. At last the older brother nodded, and Arjun, tall, calm now as a god, strode from the rank of mendicants and walked to the dais where the great bow lay. All eyes followed as he lifted it and took five arrows in his hand.

He bent his head to the fair Draupadi, then he nocked the arrow, and his mighty arm drew the bow full arc. With a long hiss, the arrow sped its way. Another, another, another—five arrows in air at the same time, like wild geese following their leader—flew through the whirling ring and struck the target with a clang! It fell to earth with a sound of thunder, and a roar like thunder echoed from the multitude. Draupadi looked deep into Arjun's eyes, then she stepped toward him, flung the golden garland of Bride's Choice round his neck, and stood beside him before the multitude.

The people went mad with delight, the Brahmins screamed and shook their deerskins, the heralds blew their trumpets.

But the suitors, stung by defeat, shouted a battle cry. This was the last insult, not to be borne. To have a beggar outdo them! To see the fairest princess in India won by a ragged mendicant!

They leaped to attack the old King, his son, and Draupadi herself! They yelled she was a shameless woman, she scorned kings and warriors for a beggar. Let her be burned on a blazing pyre to wipe out this insult she had put upon them!

But the Pandav brothers were ready to meet the maddened monarchs. At the first sign of attack, they dashed from their place and stood before old Drupad and his children, a mighty guard. Bhima was weaponless, but he snatched a living tree from its roots and wielded it before him like a mace.

There was a battle, but it was brief. The suitors could not pass that barrier of brothers who stood like a wall before the old King. At last the King was able to make his voice heard, and calm the tumult.

"Hear me, ye monarchs!" Drupad called. "Calm your rage

and hear me. You have naught to vex your pride. This lad whom you think a beggar is one of yourselves! I knew him the moment he drew bow. He is Arjun, son of Pandu, and these are his four brothers. How they came here in this guise I know not, but warriors they are and princes, not priests nor baseborn. I am proud to give my daughter to any son of the house of Pandu."

There was nothing for the suitors then but to make the best of their disappointment and withdraw with what grace they could. The Kuru princes were confounded. To them it was as if the dead had risen to face their murderers. They slunk quietly away, lest the brothers accuse them to King Drupad.

But the brothers had no thought of vengeance on this day of their triumph. Like good sons, they thought first of their mother. She would rejoice that the weary exile was over. With Drupad to support the Pandav cause, the Kurus would not dare withhold their rightful kingdom.

And Draupadi! Their mother would welcome the lovely princess to her heart. They must take Draupadi to her now, in the very moment of victory.

In triumph the five brothers led Draupadi to the humble cottage outside the gates where their mother awaited them. Joyously, they called out to her before entering. "Mother, Mother! Come see! We have won a noble prize this day!"

And the mother, answering from within, called back, "Share it as brothers should!" Seeing Draupadi, she trembled lest her words cause dissension among her sons. One princess-bride to be disputed among five princes! Yet the words of a mother cannot be recalled, nor disobeyed.

Arjun spoke. It was he who had won Draupadi, and he loved her, but nothing must come between him and his brothers, nothing must prevent obedience to a mother's command.

"Yudhisthir is eldest," Arjun said, "and he is to be king. He shall wed Draupadi, and yet she shall be queen to all of us. When the time comes for us to wed, each shall choose a bride, yet hold Draupadi always his First Queen."

Thus was the command obeyed, and thus it came about that Draupadi was wife to one brother, and queen to five.

With King Drupad his ally and father-in-law, Yudhisthir might have stripped his wicked cousins of their power and driven them into exile. But it was not in his heart to take revenge, and he loved the old blind King, his uncle. Never would he take his uncle's throne. Instead he made a division of the land. The blind King was left to rule the city and the rich lands on the Ganges, with Duryodhan to succeed him. The noble Pandavs took over the western part of the kingdom, watered by the Jumna, all jungle and forest.

By this generous division the brothers thought all cause of strife between Pandavs and Kurus was ended. They set their minds to clear the jungle and bring prosperity to the wild lands. Year by year saw fame and fortune grow. They built a noble city and lived at peace with neighbors, in harmony with each others.

But there was one who watched the Pandavs with a jealous eye. Duryodhan's hatred grew as the Pandavs prospered. He had failed to kill them—ceaselessly he pondered how to ruin them, ever he looked for a weak spot in the armor of their goodness and bravery.

At last Duryodhan hit upon a way to trap Yudhisthir. The noble Pandav had one weakness—a love of gambling. He knew the danger and tried to avoid all occasion to yield to his one vice. It was a point of honor among the monarchs and nobles of India never to refuse a challenge to a gambling match. Yudhisthir was as much bound to accept such a challenge as to honor his mother, feed the poor, and obey the priests.

He was a poor player. When luck ran in his favor he hated

to despoil an opponent, and always found some excuse to end the game. But when the dice ran against him, a sort of madness seized Yudhisthir, he thought each new throw would turn the tide, and he would not, could not stop.

Duryodhan was too venomous to trust to their play, even against an unlucky adversary. He bribed a chief who was master of false dice to teach him all his trickery and skill. Then he issued an invitation and a challenge. Let the Pandavs show their friendship by a visit to the Kuru court, and let Yudhisthir meet Duryodhan over the gaming table. Yudhisthir accepted the challenge, he could do no other.

It was a fatal meeting. Game after game Yudhisthir lost, but he would not rise from the board. Madness burned in his blood. The gold and gems of his treasury he lost, then his lands, his city, his people. Every possession was stripped from him, but the gambling fever in his blood was not quenched. He wagered then his faithful brothers, then himself—and lost! The Pandavs were no longer free men, but slaves to Duryodhan. In a frenzy of despair Yudhisthir staked on one last throw his fair wife— to win back all, or lose Draupadi. He lost! And now he owned nothing in all the world, not even his wife or himself.

"Bring me my slave, my pretty serving wench," Duryodhan shouted to one of his brothers. "Draupadi shall pass the food among my guests!"

But Draupadi was no biddable baseborn slave. She refused to dishonor herself or her husband by appearing in the banquet hall where triumphant Kurus roared.

"I will not come." She lifted her head proudly. "I am no slave woman. I am Drupad's daughter and Yudhisthir's wife. Princess and queen am I!"

"You will not! You will not! Ho, ho," laughed the Kuru prince. "Are you to say yes, or say no? Once you were a queen, but no more. You are but a slave wench, you will do what your master tells you. Yudhisthir set you up as a gambling stake, after he had lost his kingdom, his brothers and himself. Duryodhan is your master now, and you shall serve him!"

Draupadi tried to flee for protection to the good old queen in the women's rooms, but the Kuru prince seized her long black locks and dragged her, half fainting with shame and terror, to the banquet hall.

Draupadi was daughter of a warrior race. Anger drove out her fear. She saw her husband, broken with shame, the madness gone from him, despair on his white face. She saw his brothers, bound by duty to the eldest, helpless to help her. Arjun's eyes burned with contempt of Duryodhan, Bhima's red glance of hate was like a licking flame. She, helpless, knew she must fight for those she loved. Draupadi looked about her.

Not all the assembly were lost to honor. Among them were elders, brave in war and pure in conduct. She knew they wanted no share in this deed of shame—to them Draupadi turned.

"Are there no Kurus who remember their knightly vows? Is there never a chieftain among you who will lift a hand to save a wife and mother from shame?" Her voice rang with scorn.

One frowned, one tugged at his beard, one bit his tongue, one cursed Duryodhan under his breath—but only Karna spoke, and he a bitter enemy.

"No blame to you, fair Draupadi. A woman has only one duty—to obey. The wife falls with the husband. Yudhisthir has lost you. Turn your fancy to a husband who will not hold you so light as to stake your honor on a turn of the dice."

"My husband did not stake me," Draupadi denied.

A hundred voices shouted, "He did, he did. We heard the wager!"

But she spoke firmly. "My husband did not stake me. Has a slave a wife? Never! A slave owns neither wife nor child.

Yudhisthir was a slave and had no wife to wager, on that last throw!"

There was a tumult of voices, agreeing, denying, quarreling. Into the uproar, walked the old blind King, Duryodhan's father, leaning on the arm of a priest. To Draupadi they came, and the old King put a hand on her shoulder.

"My daughter, have no fear," he quavered, "forgive the evil my house has done you. This morning at the time of sacrifice, a jackal wailed, a raven croaked. We know those omens! Forgive us, lay no curse upon our house! I cannot undo the sin of my son, but ask of me what thou wilt, and I will give it."

Draupadi looked into his blind eyes with pity. "I have no curse for thee, nor for thy house, nor would I bring ruin here. The curse is to have sons who forsake the teaching of a good father. Grant my boon, and I will leave thee not a curse, but a blessing. Release my husband from his bondage—let it not be said that our son is the son of a slave!"

"Have thy wish, Draupadi," the old King cried eagerly, "have thy wish and ask another!"

"Another boon? Then I ask that all the brothers shall be free. Our wealth and kingdom are lost, but let us have our freedom."

"Granted, my daughter, gladly granted. But ask again. Ask back thy kingdom and thy wealth and I will freely give them."

Draupadi shook her head. "Nay, father, I can ask but two boons. Thou knowest it is forbid our race of warriors to ask more then two. Only unto the race of priests is it given to ask evermore. We are free, we do not fear to go into the world to seek our fortunes again."

So the Pandavs went forth, free men, and armed, but stripped of all their wealth. It is too long a tale to tell how they won back all they lost, and more. Too long a tale to tell how the hate of Duryodhan followed them always, and how at last, against their will, they had to wage war against their cousins. How the

Kurus all were slain, and Duryodhan reaped the bitter fruit of his evil deeds. It was many a year before peace came to the land.

Yudhisthir, with his four truehearted brothers and Draupadi, queen of them all, were enthroned at last, and reigned over a happy people. Sons grew up about them, tall and good, worthy to carry on the name and the labor. Wherever the Pandav brothers looked they saw their work done, their earthly duty ended. The time had come for them to seek a higher conquest.

Queen Draupadi laid aside her silken robes, the five brothers their kingly state, they bade farewell to sons and daughters and loyal subjects. These six, who had suffered together and conquered together, undertook the hardest quest of all. They set out to cross the burning deserts and find the City of the Gods.

And after them, unnoticed, there trailed a dog—Yudhisthir's faithful hound.

Now where this City of the Gods lay, and how far distant, they were not sure. They knew its general direction—a glimmer of its light had shone out to them once in a while on the far horizon of the desert. This was enough to set their course by.

Over the frightful distances they looked and were not afraid. The sands burned their feet by day, the winds chilled them to the bone by night. Yudhisthir tried in vain to order the old hound home—to leave his master was the only command to which he was deaf. In the daytime the dog followed humbly in the rear, when night came he crept close and warmed his master's body with his own. Yudhisthir shared his scanty food with the poor creature.

Daily the way grew harder, the travelers weaker. One day, at dawn, when they rose, the Queen lay wan and smiling. Bhima bent over her and looked at Yudhisthir with tears in his eyes. "She is dead. Why should our dear queen, who never did a wrong in all her life, why should she fail to reach the City of the Gods with us?"

Yudhisthir, with anguished lips, answered him. "Because she was too true she dies. She could rule her deeds, but not her inner heart. It was our brother Arjun she loved from the day his arrows won her—better than heaven itself she loved him."

And the brothers left their lady to the burial of the sands, and strode on, the hound trailing after their weary feet.

Then Bhima passed, Arjun, the twins, one by one they died, each for some fault so generous that it was near to a virtue—some fault borne lightly on the roadways of the world, but too heavy a weight to bear on one's shoulders in the desert.

Only Yudhisthir was left—Yudhisthir and the hound. Toiling onward, the King wondered why he, and not the others, had endured so long. Had he not a more grievous fault to weigh him down? Had not he sinned worse than they, and caused them all to suffer for his sin? In a timeless dream, the King strode on—and on, and on . . . alone, yet not alone, for always the dog was at his heels.

And on the horizon, the light shone clearer, and the horizon seemed not so far away.

The deadly sands were passed, a mountain rose before the King. He felt new strength in his limbs as he set foot to the rising slope. Then came a sudden thunder of chariot wheels, and lo, at Yudhisthir's side, Lord Indra appeared in a blaze of light. The hound, trembling, pressed close to his master's knee.

"Mount the chariot," the Lord said, smiling. "I have come to take you the rest of the way."

But Yudhisthir answered with a sick heart. "What is the City of the Gods to me now? My brothers have fallen by the way. My wife, too, my kind and faithful love—what is heaven without her?"

"They are there. Yudhisthir, they are there before you. What was earthly of them has been stripped away. But you alone of all men shall enter heaven in your own flesh!"

Still the King delayed. "There is one more I must have with me, Lord. This hound has followed me. I cannot leave him here."

Indra's face darkened, as the sun is darkened by a cloud passing over.

"You are a man no more. You have become as we, the gods. What need have you of this beast here?"

Yudhisthir groaned. "I cannot leave him, this hound has eaten my food, has shared my hardships, has loved me . . ."

"He is unclean!" Indra's voice was stern. "Angels sweep away the prayers of one whom a dog has touched while praying. Why did you leave your queen on the way, and all your brothers? And yet you will not leave this brute. Have you conquered your faults and reached the mount of heaven to yield to a foolish fondness for this unclean beast? Will you turn back on the very threshold of heaven for a dog?"

The King lifted his face. "When I was king on earth, men called me true and just. I never turned a suppliant away. Look at this hound of mine, shall I be less faithful to him? Shall I turn away and leave him to die alone, who has no friend but me? I left my brothers and my queen—I could do nothing for the dead. But not for heaven itself will I leave a living thing that looks to me for love."

And the King turned his face back again toward the desert.

A great light shone as Indra smiled. "Mount the chariot, my son, and bring with you the hound. True king are you, Yudhisthir, who would not enter heaven, and fail one humble soul who trusted you. You have met the last test. You have not failed even a poor dog who loved you."

And Yudhisthir, in his worn human flesh, the hound in his own shaggy hide, mounted the car of Indra and ascended with him into life immortal.

The Search for Sita

by Dhan Gopal Mukerji

from *Rama, the Hero of India*

Rama, his wife, Sita, and his brother Lakshmana are exiles from their home and wanderers in a great wilderness. Rama has been cheated out of his throne and his rightful inheritance by a trick and dares not go home or seek aid for himself or his wife or brother from his people.

As the story here begins, Rama and Lakshmana return from a journey to the cottage where they have been staying and where Sita has been told to remain. But Sita is gone. Earlier she had been angry with Lakshmana because he did not go to Rama's aid when it seemed necessary. Now the men fear that her anger has led her into great danger.

This tale of Rama and Sita is taken from the best known epic of ancient India, the Ramayana, *the deeds of Rama. Rama and Sita are now regarded as god and goddess by the Hindu people. Ravana who appears in the story was a ten-headed demon, a Rakshasa monster. Lanka, his home, is the island of Ceylon.*

THE SEARCH FOR SITA

Dhan Gopal Mukerji

———————•◦•———————

WHEN at last they reached the cottage an hour before sundown they found no Sita there. They shouted, clapped hands and made signs of other kinds but fate vouchsafed no response though their hearts were breaking. On the river-bank there was no sign of her. Near the lotus pool there was no sign of her. In the nearby Kadamba bower no mark of her coming! "Where, where are thou, Janaka's daughter?" wailed the two youths. "Nowhere, nowhere, nowhere," the air seemed to whisper in reply. "Nowhere, nowhere, nowhere," the trees and the creepers whispered.

"Is she kidnapped?" Rama asked.

"How could she be?" answered Lakshmana, "I put a spell around our cottage. Nothing could come within thirty feet of it. Unless Sita went beyond it none could penetrate the enchanted circle and put hand on her."

"Sita, speak. Where art thou! Speak, my beloved." To Rama's continued cry only silence answered, even the echoes were weary with grief, and night, unable to bear their cries and hopeless searchings, put forth the moon. In thick clusters she hung the sky with stars. With silver softness the world was hung. At last worn and exhausted the two brothers fell asleep.

But Rama almost insane with grief slept most restlessly. He

moaned and sobbed as he lay on the floor of the hut. At each
rustle of the wind he jumped to his feet. He listened intently
saying, "There she returns. Listen, brother, listen." Soon his
mind became so engrossed in hearing sounds that the stealthy
step of a panther, or a stag's wild dash for life—each he con-
strued as Sita's coming. And a buffalo's death-bellow under the
tiger's deafening roar he thought was Sita calling for help.
Lakshmana had to hold him by force in order to prevent him
from rushing into certain death at night. All night long the
elder prince acted like one out of his mind which tortured the
younger brother's patience.

At last the day broke and both of them set out to search for
Sita. The blow of calamity that had dazed their minds suddenly
made them keen-eyed like eagles, and alert as the very self of
cunning. Beyond Lakshmana's ring of charm, they noticed there
were marks of violence on the ground as if someone had dragged
Sita by her hair. They followed the marks wherever they led.
After a few feet there were no signs on the earth save the print
of a giant's foot. That puzzled the princes exceedingly. "How
can a man's foot suddenly change into that of a giant?" asked
Lakshmana.

"Follow the foot-prints, brother," begged Rama, "no matter
where."

Even so they ended soon at a place where were marks of
horses' hoofs and the track of a chariot. Suddenly the traces of
both hoofs and wheels disappeared. Only a sinister stillness lay
about that spot. Lo, there was not the sigh of the wind, not the
lifting of a twig to point the way whither the horses and chariot
had taken Rama's beloved.

In his wandering Rama came upon a cleared spot on whose
green grass lay Sita's bracelet. "Behold, Sita's ornament! Where
is she? . . . Thus far we have traced her, brother Lakshmana,
let us push on farther yet."

Hardly had they gone a thousand paces when they heard the piercing call of a being in great distress. They hurried through thorn bushes whose thorns were large as spears. Now and then cutting down creepers thick as an elephant's waist they pushed in the direction of that voice. At last after leaping over innumerable crags and rivulets, bleeding and bruised, they stumbled upon a giant bird wallowing in a pool of blood. It was repeating "Mara-Rama, Rama-Mara," in a heart-rending wail.

"Why dost thou take my name? demanded Rama.

"I am Jatayu, thy father's friend," answered the bird.

"A friend of my father's shall have the protection of my arm and the love of my heart." Rama said further, "What brought thee to such a pass? Why dost thou suffer so?"

"I sought to save Sita from the demon, Ravana."

"Sita, didst thou say?" screamed Rama. "Speak, thou overlord of the sky."

"Sita was carried off on his aerial chariot by the Rakshasa King Ravana. She called for help. I who knew thy father in our youth have never denied succour to any woman in trouble. So I came down, wings outspread like naked swords, and beak grim as the jaws of death. In an instant I smote Ravana so hard that his bow fell from his hand with his quiver. And as I smote him I heard thy wife say 'Tell Rama, Ravana has taken me. Fly to him, O compeller of speed.' Then Ravana shouted 'I am Ravana the King of Lanka; if there is skill in me thou shalt fall here dead as a viper killed. Thou shalt never fly to Rama to tell him anything.' Then he drew his sword. I flew far above him. His two winged beasts caught up with me. I wheeled away, afar. But his horses followed. Again they caught up to me as an eagle catches a dove. I swooped down under them like a fox between a tiger's feet, but those horses turned about as I was vaulting up and away. Now suddenly Ravana's sword cut my wing. Still I fought with my talons. With my beak I caught this pearl necklace from Sita which she gave me for thee. Now, Rama, go southwards, reach the Indian Ocean, cross it and rescue thy bride from Lanka's fiends. Take this pearl necklace as an earnest of the truth that I am telling thee." Then kissing Rama's feet as a sacramental act the wounded vulture breathed his last. Now his spirit rose from his body in a straight line to the abode of the gods. He who dies fighting for the weak, defeated or victorious, goes to Heaven be he bird, man, or beast.

The Ratnamala, the pearl garland from Sita's neck, gave the princes certainty. But with certainty came a desperate sense of haste. They were tortured by their fancies. They imagined many horrors that Sita might be enduring as the task of cremating Jatayu's body engaged their hands and minds for a while. It delayed them since the funeral had to be done properly. Now in order to do it with every just rite the princes banished all thoughts of Sita from their minds and concentrated themselves upon the prayers, hymns and right thoughts without which no good accrues to the soul of the dead. This change of thought, though very brief, refreshed the two princes. They felt completely relieved in mind and body when they resumed their search after Sita.

****

Acting according to the late Jatayu's advice the royal youths pushed southwards. But wherever they went they could find no further trace of Sita. No more ornaments or other tokens had she left behind anywhere. Rama made a superhuman effort to control his grief for he could not afford to indulge it now that he knew of Sita's fate. He must work and not grieve.

After scaling the southern mountains they reached Kishkindha—border of modern Mysore. Its peaks rose like spears of sapphire, its flanks were drenched with rainbows, while around it clamoured and danced thousand-throated cataracts. Behind it set the sun, a desolation of amber, purple and topaz. Against the sunset sky leaping from peak to peak like a tawny eagle an enormous monkey came down towards the two princes. Seeing that near-man approach them they held themselves ready to hurl an arrow or offer friendliness, depending on the tree-dweller's own intention. Fortunately it was a noble one. He had come to them as helper.

"I am Hanuman, nick-named Pavananandan," said he, "son of the wind-god. I caught this azure veil flung by a woman from an aerial chariot. She screamed out a prayer 'I beg you to show it to the two royal youths.' Since your bearing indicates to my monkey's eyes your lineage, I present you with the veil."

"Sita's scarf!" exclaimed the two brothers in one voice. Rama taking it tenderly from the monkey thanked the latter. With tears in his eyes said, "It is to thee I owe a mountain-heavy debt of gratitude. For days we have wandered looking for some sign of my wife. A Rakshasa named Ravana has stolen her and flown away on an aerial chariot."

"Now I understand why she screamed. If we had only known we could have leaped up and stopped that chariot in mid-air and carried out an act of rescue worthy of our mettle," announced Hanuman.

"Who are you? What do ye here? Tell us of your errand," asked Lakshmana.

"Besides myself there are two monkeys, Sugriva, known as the son of the sun-god, and Jambuban, the master of wisdom and all learning. Crownless Sugriva is our leader. But we two, Jambuban and I, have remained faithful to our chief. We have accompanied him in his exile in these woods. Though robbed of his dominion by his brother, King Sugriva has not lost his sense of hospitality and his excellent elegance. Through me he asks you to be his guests for the night, that is my errand."

Lakshmana accepted the monkey king's offer. With courtesy and reserve Hanuman led them. Accompanied by him they reached Sugriva's presence ere the beacon of day had been blown out by the blackness of night.

****

The princes now stayed for a while with Sugriva and the other monkeys, who decided to form themselves into four armies to seek for Sita in four directions. In the end one army found Jatayu's brother, Sampati, who gave them further news of Sita before he died, directing them to the sea and to the island Lanka (Ceylon) beyond.

After Sampati's funeral when the apes beheld Rama Giri's shore they could not believe their eyes. All of them save Hanuman had beheld no water save only the tawny rivers and blue lakes.

Now, behold, suddenly before them rose the emerald ramparts of the sea. Battlement upon battlement, foam-created parapets, distances flagged with opal spindrift smote their souls with wonder. As the green waves hammered the ivory beach the monkeys trembled like children in fright. Awe and terror pierced them as they descended onto the sand and scanned the simple line of the horizon against which the ocean charged. None spoke for a whole day in the presence of that majesty.

After they had become used to the ocean the apes held a council of war on the edge of Rama Giri. Each one quailed before the thought of crossing it. All monkeys fear the water, not that they cannot learn to swim but because the Indian Ocean is full of sharks, makars, and dragons who find monkeys a most toothsome diet. Fear entered every soul at the thought. Day and night they held council without deciding anything. In the meantime they beheld the July cloud raising its head in

the south. That was a signal—the season of rain was at hand. Something must be done before the heavens drew sheets of water like walls of impregnable moonstone between India and Ceylon. Seeing the monkeys wavering, at the first flush of dawn Angada announced, "O citizens of Kishkindha, I beg permission to leap over the ocean. I wish to vindicate the honour of our tribe."

Hanuman who had been silent all the time said, "No, prince, thou are the future ruler and may not risk thy dedicated life. If anyone is to go across it is I."

Angada answered, "I have yet to prove my prowess. Let me scale this fence of jade, I insist."

"Then," said Hanuman, "let us decide it thus." Hanuman
explained his plan. "I go first. If I do not return in a week come
thou after me. Rama gave me his signet ring, which shows that
he intended me to cross the Indian Sea. But I know if those
Rakshasas see me they will prevent my return. Thou, prince,
may come to rescue me, and I promise to keep alive at least a
week. In this manner shalt thou have thy coveted chance and
prove thyself brave beyond any doubting. Let me leap across
on the morrow."

Ere the Sun's wheels had churned the waters and his fire
had smitten the sea into myriad iridescences the ape, sired of
the Storm, leaped into the sky. The shore fell under him until

it looked flat as an ivory blade. The crags and cliffs that had appeared as the tousled heads of giants now were dwarfed to the size of tasseled larch. At last even the summits of Rama Giri flattened under him into huts of yellow thatch in the dawning light. Still higher rose Hanuman and looked about him. Nothing, nothing before him but the terrible wilderness of water, savage with heads of sharks and dragons that had seen him from afar. They bared their teeth large as swords and smacked their scaly lips. At such a sight shivers ran through the storm-god's son. He swiftly inclined his line of flight to the south, then closed his eyes.

"Land, land, land at any cost," he said to himself, "where I shall not have to see those devouring sea beasts." Before the short morning twilight was over he had gone so far that his comrades could see him no more. When he opened his eyes again he saw the Sun rise on his left like a mountain of gold on whose throat and chest hung the sea, an ornament of scorching beauty.

Hour after hour he flew yet there was no sight of Ravana's ravishing city. Alas, his strength was failing him and the sea seemed to draw him as it sprang to the horizon and licked from the sky the red of sunset. Against that terrible witchery he struggled as a bird ere the serpent's eyes hypnotizes it. Once he almost fell to the sea, but the chattering teeth of sharks below steadied him. He shut his eyes and flung upward. At last, after what seemed like a night of blindness he drew his eyelids back into his head and lo, before him rose the diamond towers of Lanka high as Himalaya where day still lingered too reluctant to yield the world to night. With a shout of "Rama, Rama," he plunged forward and as an eagle lands in his eyrie under the shadow of a high hill he softly descended on the sand under the diamond tower, while far away the sea echoed like the sound of a receding dream.

With a shiver of pleasure at the thought of his safe arrival Hanuman scrutinized the capital of the monster kingdom. Under a long wall hung the branches of sky-soaring cocopalms whose green, gemmed with the sunset colours, spread like a forest of peacock fans. Above them stretched the walls of Lanka piercing with their turrets and towers the purple clouds in the sky. There between them crouched well-armed Rakshasa sentries as lions crouching between tall reeds.

Before such a sight Hanuman's heart quailed. "How can I reach Sita beyond those sky-piercing walls?" Fortunately he stood in shadow and the watchmen of Ravana saw him not from those great heights whence they looked afar. Soon the short tropical twilight passed and all the world was wrapped in the black silence of night.

Hanuman was so fatigued that he slept through the entire night without being disturbed by the surge and thunder of the seas. When he woke in the morning he saw the Sun like a red bull charge through the sapphire forest of water and thrust his horns into the sky. The heavens shed red glory for a while: then all the world was white. But today the glory of the sunrise could not charm him, for Hanuman was hungry, and he, the storm-born, felt as if ten thousand wolves were howling for food within him. "Food, food, food," he heard himself say. He looked up at the coconut trees. Lo, there was food! No sooner seen than done, in one spring he was on the treetop splitting coconuts open with his knuckles and eating their meat. In half an hour Ravana's city woke up and his sentries hurled spears at Hanuman, but he dodged each sharp weapon as if they were feathers falling slowly.

That enraged the sentries so that they flung at him other weapons besides—arrows, bolts, discs and maces. Instead of taking them seriously the son of Storm leaped about briskly and ate coconuts as if he were at a picnic. Now in order to dodge a flying harpoon named serpent-mouth he leaped higher than before and as the fiend's weapon hissed and flashed beneath him, that titanic monkey beheld over the walls of Lanka Amra Kanan—a mango grove, bent down under the weight of ripe mangoes. The sight drew him like a magnet. Instead of coming down on the coconut tree he swung up and over the walls of Lanka, his tail knocking off a star from the sky which no human eye could see. That mammoth heavenly body fell half way between India and Lanka and made an island in the ocean. But Hanuman never saw the star fall and the seas churn and foam like a vat of boiling water as they received it. He beheld only mangoes. In an instant he had landed in the midst of them and was lost to the Rakshasa watcher's view. Unaware of every danger he sat down to finish his breakfast with the red, yellow, purple and saffron fruits. He ate as a forest fire devours trees. In an hour's time half the mangoes were reposing within him, while all the Rakshasa gardeners were chasing him from tree to tree.

Now that his hunger was appeased Hanuman recalled that he had come to Lanka not to play hide and seek with gardeners but to find Sita. Loath to give up annoying the Rakshasas he leaped out of sight.

"Where can I find her, where shall I seek?" He repeated these words the greater part of the morning. Palaces, grottoes, and pleasure-gardens, everywhere he looked but found no trace of Sita. In Ravana's own vast halls he saw all kinds of monster females but no human soul. On the roofs in the late afternoon where the ladies of Lanka had come to take the air he spied not one that resembled Rama's bride. "Where is Sita? How to seek her? Where to find Rama's queen?" He spoke to himself without receiving a response from within. At sundown he gave up all hope and decided to spend the night on the steepest tower of the royal palace where no sentry prowled.

Though he was worried and anxious he fell asleep like a child.

On the morrow, when he opened his eyes, the vision of dawn-swept Lanka ravished him. Ravana's abode was all gold, the fountains about it were fashioned from crystal and their blue waters fell like the voices of thrushes. Deodars (cedars) fanned the air above the singing fountains. In the courtyards and halls of gold, gods still captive dressed in celestial vestures toiled, sweeping and polishing pillars and floors.

Looking away from Ravana's palace he saw the Crown Prince Indrajit's house of amethyst. Its ivory walls were ornamented with topaz and onyx. No matter where he looked, opulent beauty choked his senses. No man nor monkey had ever seen anything like Lanka save in dreams. But even such enchantment could not dull his desire for food. He was hungry again and in a moment's time he was eating the rest of the mangoes of Amra Kanan.

****

A few of his divine powers Pavana, the wind-god, was allowed to retain when he was born as Hanuman the monkey. He could still increase or decrease the size of his body. At will he could grow small as a squirrel or big as a mountain. Now while he was feasting in the mango grove he decided to make himself as inconspicuous as possible in order to continue his hitherto unsuccessful search for Sita, and so he shrank into the size of a very small monkey. Thus he was hidden by the prodigious foliage of Lanka's many trees and had an opportunity to look and listen. At night he crawled soft as a python to palace windows and heard what the Rakshasas said to one another. In the daytime he stayed near the royal household hidden in a tree and listened to the gossip that went on there. High and low he searched but alas, could not find any sign of Sita. She was not in Ravana's palace, nor could he locate her in one of the many palaces of the demon-king. He sought to find her in the state prison so he crawled thither small as a mouse, but no Sita could he discover. Where then was Rama's beloved wife? Was she still alive?

That question filled his heart with gnawing misgiving. "Has Ravana killed her because she refused to be his wife?" asked Hanuman of himself. "Woe, woe unto me for arriving in Lanka too late," he wailed to himself. "If she be indeed dead I must have certain proof of it." This thought quickened his flagging will and mind. He sat awhile in his fortress of leaves on a tree and meditated. Since all clear conclusions come from meditation Hanuman arrived at a lucid plan soon. "Suppose Sita is alive, the only person to know of her whereabouts is Ravana." He thought further, "I shall therefore follow that monster wherever he goes day and night for some time; eventually I am positive he will wend his way to Sita's dwelling place and I shall thus discover her." He thought as monkeys do, stumbling upon the truth. But monkeys being more prone to action than men he acted swiftly and followed Ravana two days and two nights without food or sleep. As if the privations that he had suffered were the just price, fate now granted him what he was searching. The third day he followed Ravana to the Asoka forest. Ravana drove in his chariot of gold that glided into the emerald woods like the setting Sun into the green wilderness of the sea. In order to keep up to the vehicle drawn by demon horses who were faster than the wind, Hanuman leapt from trees and towers with great haste. Sometimes he coursed on the ground like a squirrel limbed with the lightning. Ravana drove alone, unaccompanied by his vigilant guard, and so by no art of his own Hanuman escaped detection, since Ravana's ten pairs of eyes were fixed upon his steeds. Thus he failed to notice his pursuer. Soon they reached the heart of the Asoka forest where, guarded by grotesque female demons, the captive Sita

dwelt. After tying his horses to a tree Ravana passed through cohorts of terrible grotesques and gained the presence of Sita. Hanuman who had climbed to the top of an Asoka tree at last beheld her. "The very moon fallen from heaven," he said to himself as her beauty charmed his eyes. The ugly guardians who held her captive were as ugly as she was beautiful. Though she was pale, too pale even for pity, the light of purity that shone on her face shamed the Sun. One glance at her human form told the monkey messenger from Rama that he was in the presence of a divine being. Even had his eyes been deceived his ears now heard the truth, for Ravana was speaking through his ten sets of teeth to Sita!

"Sita, if you do not love me, and will not marry me on the morrow I will have thine eyes plucked from thy head." Though he waited for an answer the queen of Rama disdained to reply. "Thy face shall be scratched into the very image of ugliness and then I will send thee back to thy husband Rama. Blind, ugly and terrifying, thou wilt be ruined in his eyes. Take my warning! Renounce Rama. Love me and be my queen."

"I can love you on one condition only," slowly spoke Sita. Those words pierced Hanuman's heart like the swiftest poisoned blades. He repressed a cry of horror with great difficulty. Alert as a tiger for its prey he listened for further words from Sita.

"My condition is that you in your own person become Rama whom alone I worship. In my heart is engraved Rama, in my soul is engraved Rama, in my bones is Rama. In my veins Rama runs. He is my blood, in my brain, in my soul. I can love only that which is within me. Therefore only if you become Rama can you win my love."

Ravana howled with anger. His ten mouths shouted all at once like a tenfold thunderclap. "I am a wizard, I could easily take on the form of Rama, but such tricks I utterly despise. I want to be loved as Ravana."

"Even if the Sun is plucked by a child, even if a lunatic empties the ocean into a cup, even if a rabbit's whimper slays a lion instantly, even if the sky grows like grass under our feet, Sita will not love Ravana. Begone from my presence. Plague me no more. O Rama, where art thou, O Rama, come to my rescue!" Sita wailed, repeating the name of her lord.

Though her words flowed out of a heart in torture they sent pangs of gladness through Hanuman's spirit. "I have at last found her. My journey to Lanka has not been in vain," he said within himself.

Ravana now gave some orders to his grotesques and drove off in anger and shame.

With the coming of noon all of Sita's guards went to their dinner and for a long siesta which was the custom of the Rakshasas, as of all peoples who dwell in the south. Slowly through a path between the Asoka trees came a young woman of great beauty bringing Sita her dinner on a platter of gold. She saluted Sita with great humility, "Thou must eat, dear friend, just to keep alive. Thou must not die of starvation before the news of thee reaches Rama."

"O Sarama, my only friend in this serpent's nest. Were it not for thy kindness I would have died long ago. But how can I eat such delicacies when I know not if Rama lives at all."

"Try, beloved lady. Eat a little of the rice with coconut curry, a little of the baked bread if it please thee and the Luddoo (a sweet made out of cheese and almonds). Nourish thyself to give me pleasure, dear friend."

Thus coaxed and cajoled by Sarama, the noble wife of Vivisana, Ravana's righteous brother, the wife of Rama ate. But what she ate was so little that Hanuman who was watching her from above was alarmed. He said to himself, "She can not live long if she pecks at her food like an absent-minded sparrow."

Soon came Sarama's maids to escort her back to her palace. Instead of letting one of them carry the plate that she had brought with her Sarama bore it away herself. This she did as a mark of her esteem for Sita. After seeing that no one was guarding Sita and making sure that he himself was not being spied upon, Hanuman came down from his perch, bowed very low before the bride of Rama and said, "Rejoice, Mother," paying her the same homage that men give to God, "I bring you news of your husband."

"Who art thou?" Sita cried in dismay. "Art thou another monster in disguise sent to torture me with tales of Rama?"

"Hush," whispered the monkey, "I am no Rakshasa in disguise. I bring you news of Rama. Fear naught, O pinnacle of purity; do put your trust in me and I will aid you."

"Though thou art no Rakshasa," whispered Sita, "how do I know that thou truly hast brought news of Rama?"

"Look, O incomparable one. Behold, I wear Rama's ring on my hand. Bring thy scrutiny to bear upon it. O Mother, I am but thy son, a slave of Rama, the backbone of truth. Is not that his ring?" Sita took the signet and put it on her finger. The very touch and fit of it unlocked tears from her eyes, blotting out all sight. "Rama, Rama, Rama," that is all that she could say. Hanuman, the bravest of the monkeys, shared her sorrow and wept with her. Soon the grotesque guardians of Sita were heard yawning into wakefulness like palm-fronds in the wind. Hanuman swiftly disappeared into a tree. Now that he had found the Asoka forest he decided to dwell there for several days in order to learn from Sita's lips how she was kidnapped and how she could be taken back to her husband.

Every day at the appointed hour he beheld Ravana's golden chariot. Every day Ravana came to plead with Sita to give up all thought of Rama. Videha's daughter seldom made reply, but when the monster irritated her most by praising himself to the skies she would answer him thus, indignant and unafraid:

"The bridge of right, the wearer of the garment of truth, Rama—his shoulders are set like mountain sides, his arms are stronger than a thousand tigers' limbs. He will fall and tear thee as the eagle swoops to catch a viper and makes ribbons of its slimy body. Rama's arms like the talons of the thunderbolt would seize and destroy many fiends like thee. Begone, thou ten-headed creeping beast."

"How can Rama slay me when the weapon that destroys Ravana is in the Creator's keeping?" Ravana set to bragging anew.

But Sita cut him short: "Though neither God nor fiend has power to smite thee down, yet from Rama's hands will leap the weapon that will end thy life of vice and sin. Begone, thou loathing's very soul!" Thus each day Ravana the compeller of the deities was spurned by a woman.

Yoro Reveals Himself as Gessar Khan

by Ida Zeitlin

from *Gessar Khan*

The story of Gessar Khan, or Gesar of Ling, as it is told here comes from north India or possibly Mongolia, but the earliest tales told of him were told in the wild lands of eastern Tibet, the country of the Khans. The first episodes were probably chanted by bards at campfires, ten to twelve centuries ago and may have been based on the deeds of some warrior chief who lived in the seventh or eighth century, the great days of Tibetian military glory. The stories spread through all of northeastern Asia, and the first translation into a European language was made in 1839, by a German from the Mongolian version. Since then other visitors to the region have translated other versions as well. The stories are still told in Tibet today, as they have been for centuries, and they are sometimes thought to have a protective power. Travelers sing the songs of Gessar as they go, feeling that they are then protected from bandits.

Gessar Khan was born because the gods felt a leader was needed to bring order to earth and surpress injustice and violence. Miraculous signs attended the birth of the baby whose father was a god. The king of the region recognized the signs and feared the baby who would one day become king. When all attempts to kill the child failed, the king drove Gessar and his mother into the wilderness. Life there was hard and poor, but when the proper time arrived, Gessar, posing as Yoro, claimed the heritage to which he had been born.

YORO REVEALS HIMSELF AS GESSAR KHAN

Ida Zeitlin

———◦•◦———

Now there dwelt in a pleasant land that bordered on Tibet the Lady Rogmo, and she was daughter to Sengeslu Khan, and so radiant was her beauty that of all the princes of her father's tribe, none was deemed worthy to be her mate.

And she sought audience of Sengeslu Khan and said to him: "I will journey to the land of Tibet and seek me there a mate, for men say it is a land peopled by heroes and the sons of gods."

And she journeyed to the land of Tibet, and a wise lama rode at her right hand, and a princely retinue followed after her, and at her left hand rode three peerless archers and three valiant knights that were her champions.

And in Tibet ten thousand chieftains were gathered to welcome her, and she rode into their midst and cried: "Lords of Tibet! I am come to choose a husband from among you, for men say your land is peopled by heroes and the sons of gods. And that ye may know me worthy to wed with the noblest, I will reveal to you the wonders that marked my birth. Though the skies grew black and with clouds, the sun shone brightly among them, yet when they vanished and the heavens cleared, out of the clear heavens the rains poured down. A unicorn and a blue elephant paced round and round about my father's dwelling, and a cuckoo sang above my mother's head, while on her right hand perched a parakeet and on her left a bird without a name. These are the signs of wonder that marked my birth, and therefore am I come among you to seek the hero destined to wed with the Lady Rogmo.

"Six champions bear me company—three warriors whom the mightiest princes of our tribe have sought in vain to overthrow, three bowmen whose skill is such that when they have shot their arrows from the bow, a man may thrice brew tea to slake his thirst ere they return again. Moreover, so truly do they aim that each one marks the spot where the arrow should return by laying his head upon it, and only when the arrow plunges earthward does he turn his ahead aside to make place for it. Such marksmanship as this do my champions boast, and he that would wed with me must still excel it."

And having spoken, Rogmo galloped to the crest of a high hill that overlooked the field, and saw how the lords and princes of Tibet strove with her archers and her warriors and strove in vain. And she cried in scorn: "Though ye be heroes and the sons of gods, yet ye are powerless to overthrow my champions!"

Then Yoro plucked the sleeve of the wise lama that rode at her right hand, and he cried: "I too would strive with Rogmo's champions, for though I be unseemly, my strength is as great as another's."

And the wise lama answered: "Beware, my son, nor venture thy tender bones where mighty warriors have striven in vain."

"Nay, though my bones be shattered into dust, still would I venture, father."

"Then have thy way and may Buddha be thy shield!"

And Yoro's blessèd sisters, seeing his need, lifted him from the earth and set one foot upon a mountain top and one on the

shore of the sea. And stooping, Yoro seized the strongest of
Lady Rogmo's warriors and hurled him over his head. And
the distance that he hurled him was a thousand leagues. And
the second he hurled two thousand leagues behind him, and
the third and weakest, three thousand. And the people gazed
in wonder upon Yoro who had wrought this deed.

And now he stood beside the archers of the Lady Rogmo.
And when she gave the signal, each one let fly his arrow, then
flung himself upon the ground to await its coming. And at
midday three arrows returned from their flight and plunged
themselves where lately the heads of the three archers had
lain. But the dart of Yoro returned not, for his sisters held it
on Sumeru, decking the shaft with gaily plumaged birds to be
a sign to Yoro of their love.

And when at length they hurled it earthward, the birds
spread wide their wings and hid the sun, so that darkness fell
upon the face of the earth and men cried out: "The gods are
wroth! Disaster is upon us!" and would have fled in terror.

But Shikeer lifted up his voice above the clamor and cried:
"Peace, foolish ones! It is the dart of Yoro that returns from
its far flight!"

And the singing shaft plunged itself into the earth where
Yoro's head had rested, and the gaily plumaged birds hovered
above him, then soared, still singing, into the blue heavens.

And the tribesmen shouted: "Hail to thee, Yoro, defender of
the valor of Tibet!"

And Chotong and the great ones that had been vanquished
murmured one to another: "Yes, though he be a stripling and
ill-favored, with eyes that look askance, yet he hath won the
Lady Rogmo for his bride."

And Rogmo descended from the crest of the high hill and
looked upon the ill-favored one that claimed her hand. And she
would have turned away in displeasure, but Shikeer held her

fast. And he spoke, saying: "Thou art fair, Rogmo, but thou art a woman. And though he be ill-favored as any goat, yet Yoro is a man. Therefore, submit thyself as woman should. Nor be so soon forgetful of thy pledge to wed with him that should encounter thy champions and vanquish them!"

And Rogmo could not choose but yield her hand to Yoro. And with a blade he pricked his finger, and through her red lips Rogmo drew the blood forth from his wound. Then plucking from the tail of a steed three hairs, he wove them together and clasped them about her throat, crying aloud: "Thus do I plight my troth with thee, I, Yoro, with thee, the daughter of Sengeslu Khan!" And they were plighted in the eyes of men.

But when night fell and the encampment slept, Rogmo stole forth from her tent and roused her retinue, and they took horse and galloped swiftly toward her father's realm. And as they sped away, Rogmo cried out: "Who follows after us?"

And the lama turned and viewed the plain and answered: "Naught save the wind!"

And they journeyed farther and again the Lady Rogmo cried: "Who follows after us?"

And the lama turned again and answered: "Naught save the silver shadow of the moon!"

And they journeyed farther, and the Lady Rogmo cried: "Nay, it is neither the wind's breath nor the shadow of the moon that lies upon my cheek! I pray thee, look again!"

And the lama looked and saw that Yoro, cloaked in darkness, sat behind her and clasped her in his arms. And he cried: "He that hath won thee for his wife sits behind thee now and clasps thee in his arms!"

And Rogmo wept and beat her breast, crying: "How shall I hide my shame? I that have spurned great lords and noble khans, how shall I bring my father this offspring of a camel to be

his son? Alas, alas, I am lost beyond all hope!" And thus lamenting, she continued on her way, and Yoro sat behind her, but spoke no word.

And when they were come within a hundred leagues of her father's kingdom, he caused a cloud of dust to rise before them as from the hoofbeats of ten thousand steeds, and the great Sengeslu Khan, watching from afar, turned to his councillors and cried: "It must be that our daughter is fallen to the lot of China's glorious Khan!"

And now the cloud of dust grew less, as though a thousand chargers, fleet of foot, drove it before them. And the joy of Sengeslu Khan was abated and he cried: "Though she hath missed the mightiest, yet she returns the bride of some great lord whose name will be to us a crown of glory."

And ever the cloud of dust grew less, till it was grown so small that it might be the herald of scarce a hundred swiftly flying steeds. And the brow of Sengeslu Khan grew black with foreboding, but he took heart again, crying: "Chotong, a prince of fair repute, hath won my daughter."

And now, surrounded by his chieftains, he made ready to welcome the Lady Rogmo and him that she had chosen from all the world to be her worthy mate. And the cavalcade approached his yurta, and his daughter alighted from her steed and bowed before him, weeping. Yoro followed after her.

And her father looked upon him and cried: "Is this the hero thou hast sought through the broad earth? Is this the god that hath subdued thine arrogance? Truly, my daughter, thou hast chosen a strange husband, and there is none that will dispute thy choice with thee. Only beware lest the hounds howling at night mistake him not for an abandoned carcass and so devour him!" And turning his back upon them, he entered into his yurta, but his knights encircled Yoro and taunted him, prodding him with their spears.

Now in Tibet, Chotong arose at dawn, and saw that Yoro was vanished from among them, neither could he discover trace of Rogmo nor her princely retinue. And he was filled with spleen, and summoned the great ones of the tribe and said to them: "Kinsmen and brothers! Dishonor and shame shall be your portion, if ye sit idly by and suffer a beggar to enjoy the prize that should have been a prince's. Through guile and treachery hath Yoro won the Lady Rogmo, and not in equal combat. Wherefore let us go forth and succor her from an unworthy mate!"

And he gave spurs to his steed, and galloped over the plain, and all the nobles of his tribe galloped behind him until at length they reached the kingdom of Sengeslu Khan.

And they halted before his abode, and he came forth amid his councillors and spoke to them, saying: "Whence do ye come, men of an alien land, and what is your will with me?"

And they answered: "We come from far Tibet, where Yoro strove against thy daughter's champions and overthrew them. And we would have thee yield her up to us, for Yoro is unworthy to be her mate."

"And though he be unworthy, how shall I take her from him, since he hath met her challenge and overthrown her champions?"

"We are not come to reason with thee, old man, but to hear thy yea or nay. If thou deem Yoro too poor a thing to wed with thy daughter, then yield her up to us. But if thou art fain to cling to this treasure thou has won, know that the princes of Tibet have wrought destruction upon heads nobler than thine."

And Sengeslu Khan, being a just monarch and a righteous, yet fearful of the loud-tongued strangers that menaced him, knew not how he should reply to them. He went apart with his ministers, and they took council together. Presently he returned to the princes of Tibet and his answer was in his mouth.

"Fierce words have ye spoken, warriors from afar, and patiently have I heard you. Hear ye now me. In marksmanship and in the art of single combat Yoro hath shown himself your master. Yet he is graceless and mean of stature and ill-fitted to wed with the Lady Rogmo. Therefore do I decree a match among you, and he whose steed shall first bear him to the appointed goal, shall take the Lady Rogmo to wife. But if my decree offend you, then let us wage war upon one another, for none shall persuade me from this course."

And Chotong answered: "Let it be as thou hast decreed."

And the edict went forth, and thirty thousand men gathered to contend for the hand of Lady Rogmo. And Yoro scattered incense and offered up a sacrifice to Kormuzda, crying: "My father and father of the gods! Let the brown wonder-steed descend, for I have need of him!"

And Kormuzda answered: "He will descend, my son, yet not in splendor as thou hast known him, but as a shrunken foal of two years' growth. For it is not meet that thou shouldst ride a godlike steed till thou have revealed thyself as Gessar Khan!"

And when he had spoken, a whirlwind descended out of the heavens, invisible to all save Yoro, and when it touched the earth a shrunken foal of two years' growth stepped forth, and circled round and round, seeking his master. And when he espied Yoro, he bowed before him and stood quietly.

And Yoro clambered upon his back and rode into the company of heroes, and when they beheld him astride his shrunken steed, they flung back their heads and mighty laughter shook them.

But Sengeslu Khan spoke sternly to Yoro, saying: "Dost thou hope with this beast, unsightly as thyself, to overtake the proud steeds of thy rivals? Or is it thy purpose to affront my daughter, unhappy that she is? Go take a stallion from my herds, swift-paced and ardent, and leave this stunted foal, lest thou shame me beyond all measure in the sight of men."

And Yoro answered: "I will not take thy stallion, swift-paced and ardent, but on my stunted foal I will run this match and abide the issue."

And Sengeslu Khan raised his hand aloft, signalling the departure, and thirty thousand riders leaped forward and vanished from sight. But Yoro, restraining his heavenly steed, was left behind till presently he loosed his hold upon him, and the brown wonder-steed in a single bound overtook ten thousand horsemen. And again he curbed him and again he set him free, and with a single bound he overtook again ten thousand horsemen. And yet a third time Yoro held him in check, then let him go his way, and now he had overtaken all save the blue-black steed of Chotong.

And Yoro said to him: "My little wonder-steed of two years' growth that in three bounds hath overtaken the glory of Tibet, when thou art come close to the blue-black steed of Chotong, do thou smite him with thy forefeet and tumble steed and rider into the dust."

And the foal did as Yoro bade him, and with his forefeet smote the blue-black steed of Chotong and overthrew him. And Chotong rolled in the dust, crying: "Alas, Yoro, what hast thou done to me?"

And Yoro answered: "Alas, uncle, I know not, for I seek but to safeguard my treasure from thieves that would despoil me, and thy blue-black steed hath barred my way." So saying, he galloped past him and reached the goal.

And Sengeslu Khan proclaimed: "Yoro hath won my daughter a second time."

But the princes of Tibet murmured together and they went before Sengeslu Khan and said: "Truly Yoro hath reached the goal before us all, and therefore he may be accounted a skilful horseman. But he that shall slay the Wild Boar of the Wilderness and bring thee for a sign his tail fashioned of thirteen strands, him shalt thou know as a hero, marked of the gods and worthy to wed with Lady Rogmo."

And Sengeslu Khan decreed that he who slew the Wild Boar of the Wilderness should wed with the Lady Rogmo. And thirty thousand chieftains sallied forth to hunt him, but Yoro was the first to come upon him where he bellowed in the forest, lashing his mighty tail and felling a hundred oaks at every blow. And he took aim and sped his shining arrow swiftly to the Wild Boar's heart and slew him. And as he was about to sever the tail, fashioned of thirteen strands, Chotong espied him and hailed him with honeyed words, crying: "Now is the maiden thine, good nephew, beyond gainsaying, and none shall take her from thee. Therefore, I pray thee, give me the Wild Boar's tail and I will bind it upon the bridle of my steed, and as the herald of thy valor will I bear it before the people, crying: "Yoro, my kinsman, hath slain the Wild Boar of the Wilderness!" Thus shall I share thy glory, and nevermore will I chide thee or use thee ill, but I will cherish thee more tenderly than the children of my loins."

"Take thou the tail, good uncle, for it is naught to me!" And Yoro severed the tail from the Wild Boar's body and gave it to Chotong, yet gave him not the whole, having thrust secretly into his bosom three strands thereof.

And Chotong galloped joyfully to the meeting-place, crying: "Comrades and heroes! Leave ye the hunt and pursue the chase no longer! For I, Chotong of Lik, have slain the Wild Board of the Wilderness. I have bound his tail, fashioned of thirteen strands, to the bridle of my stallion, and I claim the Lady Rogmo for my wife."

But Yoro who followed behind him cried: "Alack, **thou** faithless one, didst thou not come to me when **I had slain the**

Boar and pray that I might give thee the tail? Didst thou not say: 'I will proclaim thee victor and share thy glory'?"

"What villainy is this, thou wry-eyed knave? Dost thou think with railing and false oaths to wrest from me again what I have taken?"

"Sayest thou so, Chotong? Then show me this tail, fashioned of thirteen strands, that thou didst take from the Wild Boar to be a sign of thy victory."

And Chotong drew forth the tail and held it aloft in triumph, but soon his joy was turned to dismay, for he saw that the tail, fashioned of thirteen strands, bore only ten and that three strands were lacking.

And Yoro cried: "Did I not know thee for a shameless liar, and did I not therefore withhold from thee three strands of the mighty tail when in the forest thou didst entreat me to give it thee?" And with these words Yoro drew from his bosom the strands that had been lacking. And Chotong was shamed before the multitude and, turning his steed, galloped in haste away.

But now there rode out of the wilderness a horseman whose steed was flecked with foam, and his eyes shown like the eyes of one that hath looked on a god, and his lips bore tidings of wonder. And he cried out: "My lords and princes, following through the wilderness the Wild Boar's track, I heard the song of the Garuda Bird. And gazing upward, I beheld her where she sat in a tall pine, preening her golden plumage."

And Sengeslu Khan commanded his soothsayer to come before him and cried: "Read me this omen!"

And the soothsayer read the omen and answered: "It is the voice of heaven that bids thee give thy daughter to him that shall pluck from the tail of the magic bird her golden plumage, for none may pluck it forth save by the will of the high gods."

And Sengeslu Khan made known the word of the soothsayer to the heroes assembled before him, and they rode into the wilderness to try if they might pluck from the tail of the Garuda Bird her golden plumage.

And Yoro remained behind for a brief space, then followed after them, and when he came upon them, they were gathered together at the foot of a tall pine, and their arrows beat about the head of the Garuda Bird like silver rain. But she sat upon the topmost branch, unheeding of their darts, and uttered her strange cry and preened the golden plumage of her tail.

And Yoro spoke unto her soft words of praise, saying: "Proud bird! How sweetly soars thy voice above all others in this wilderness! Even so I ween, does thy bright plumage outshine the plumage of thy lesser brethren! Would we might gaze upon thee in thy glory!"

And the breast of the Garuda Bird grew big with pride, and she walked forth upon the branch that all might gaze on her, and she lifted her mighty pinions and let them fall again, and turned her stately head now to this side and now to that, flaunting her beauty.

And Yoro cried: "In truth, thy radiance is as the sun breaking through storm-clouds. But what of thy flight, O gracious bird of heaven, for surely when thy pinions bear thee above the earth, thou art like some god descended from Sumeru to dazzle with his splendor the eyes of men."

And hearing these words, the magic bird spread wide her wings and floated above the trees serenely as a cloud in a clear sky. But Yoro cried: "Draw nearer, thou blessèd one, that we may bow before thy majesty!" And she drew nearer, and all the multitude were blinded by her beauty and veiled their eyes in dread before her, but Yoro put forth his hand and plucked two golden feathers from her tail. And the Garuda Bird uttered a piercing cry and soared aloft and vanished.

And now Yoro, giving no heed to those that pressed about him, rode to the meeting-place, and the chieftains of Tibet

rode hard behind him. And when he was come to where the Lady Rogmo sat among her maidens, he bade her rise, and into her headdress he bound the golden plumes of the Garuda Bird.

And as he did so, the heavens darkened, and the gods, arching their bows, sped shafts of flame to the four corners of the sky, and the voices of their dragon-steeds thundered across the blackness, and from the everlasting streams the waters of life were loosed upon the multitude, beating them to the earth. And loud above the din a cry rang forth: "The gods have triumphed! Evil is put to rout!"

And when the darkness lifted and the floods ceased, a wonder stood revealed. For there where Yoro had sat astride his shrunken foal, a warrior, mounted on a lordly steed, towered above them. And his countenance was as the countenance of one beloved of Buddha, and his breast was as the breast of the mountain gods, and his thighs were as the thighs of the dragon-princes that dwell beneath the sea. And his armor was fashioned of seven jewels that sparkled like the dew at dawn, and a helmet, wrought of the woven light of the sun and moon, decked his noble head. And by his side he bore a lightning-sword three fathoms long, and an ebon bow was girded about his shoulders, and from his quiver thirty silver arrows, turquoise-notched, raised their bright heads.

And Shikeer, arrayed in splendor, was mounted beside him, and thirty shining heroes surrounded him.

And the warrior lifted up his voice and cried: "Ye heedless ones! Ye men of little worth! Know me for Gessar Khan, the son of heaven, sent by almighty Buddha to be your lord, that the tenfold evil may be uprooted and gladness restored to the hearts of men! Full fifteen years have I dwelt among you in Yoro's guise, for thus hath it been decreed. Yet when I journeyed into the country of the seven alwins and drove them beneath the sea, did I not reveal myself as a doer of mighty deeds? And when I seized in my hand the soul of Chotong and was like to destroy him, could ye not see in me one that had been marked of the gods? And when, with one foot on the mountaintop and one on the shore of the sea, I hurled the warriors of the Lady Rogmo over my head; and when I vanquished her archers and my arrow returned from the skies decked with birds of gay plumage; and when on a stunted foal of two years' growth I overtook the chargers of thrice ten thousand men, reaching the goal before them; and when I slew the Wild Boar of the Wilderness and plucked two golden feathers from the tail of the Garuda Bird, ye blind, ye sinful ones, though I was graceless and mean of stature, with eyes that looked askance, were these wondrous signs and portents no more to you than snowfall in winter or the braying of a wild ass on the mountainside?

"Bow down before me, for I am Kormuzda's son!

"Bow down before me, for I am the servant of Buddha!

"Bow down before me, ye princes and tribesmen and beggars, for I am the light of your darkness, the food of your hunger and the scourge of your evildoing! I wield the sword of righteousness in one hand! Let my foes beware of its edge! I bear the balm of peace in the other! Let my friends savor its sweetness! The lama of lamas is come to judge among you! Bow down before him! The prince of warriors is come to lead you to battle! Bow down before him! The all-conquering, all-healing Gessar Khan is come to dwell in your midst! Bow down before him, ye men of earth, and pay him homage!"

And all the people bowed down before him in awe and wonder.

And the Lady Rogmo was first to raise her head. And when she beheld the glory of Gessar Khan, she laughed aloud and then wept for joy.

The Empty City

by Louise Crane

from The Magic Spear

Wit and cleverness are two qualities greatly admired in China. The hero of The Empty City, Chuko Liang, was the greatest military strategist ever known in China and the only one who was never outwitted. His heroism is not like that of many who win fame with strength and weapons, his is a heroism of wit and courage.

This story and others about Chuko Liang belong to a group of tales that are the most popular and widely known accounts of early Chinese life. The actual events on which the legends are based occured in the period of 168-265 A. D. In the twelfth century the stories were woven into a series of historical dramas called the San Kuo Chih Yen I by Lo Kuan-ching, a court poet. Very little of this material has been made available in English, and this is one of the few retellings of this old story.

THE EMPTY CITY

Louise Crane

———◆●◆———

Y ou will laugh when you hear this story—and you may
not quite believe it. But I assure you it is true, quite
true. It is a story that tells of a great commander who
once set out to capture a certain city. And indeed, with less
than half the splendid army at his back, he might easily have
taken it. But instead, the great commander merely rode up to
the city gates, and then—now what do you suppose he
did then? You may not quite believe it, but I assure you it is
true that the great commander, with a splendid army at his
back, merely rode up to the city gates, and then, without striking a single blow, turned right round and rode away again!

This amazing thing happened with the great Empire of the
Hans was being divided into three parts, and the parts were
calling themselves the Kingdoms of Wei, Wu and Shu. They
ranked just so. Wei was the strongest, Wu came next, while,
by comparison, Shu was weak. Every now and again, this one
and that one would form an alliance against the third. But
mostly they were fighting against one another for the leading
place; and at the time of our story, the armies of Wei were
marching on Shu with (as they thought) great secrecy, and
every expectation of easy victory. But now, there is something
that must be said about Shu. Though it was not strong in itself,

it was, nevertheless, a place to be reckoned with at that particular time. For there had recently come into the service of its King that great Master of Strategy, Chuko Liang. It was a point that balanced the weakness of Shu. Just how weighty a point, the armies of Wei, approaching from the north, were very soon to discover for themselves.

Chuko Liang was Commander-in-Chief of the Shu armies, and he was a man of many parts. He was a great man, and a truly great general. He was also the Premier of Shu. Indeed, for wisdom and knowledge and resourcefulness, there was not another man in all the Three Kingdoms to be compared with Chuko Liang, except one, in Wei. There, in Wei, was Ssu Ma I. And it was Ssu Ma I, the great commander, who led the invading forces that were moving in the direction of the pass, at Chieh Ting, on the boundary.

Chuko Liang knew that the invaders were approaching the pass. No one else knew—not even the Intelligence Horsemen who roamed the kingdom night and day. But Chuko Liang was like that. Some said he was a wizard, that he foretold coming events so accurately because Kuei Sing, the Star God, had endowed him with six senses, instead of five, like ordinary folk. Others claimed he used magic. Still others put it all down to the queer instruments he used for measuring the planets and the heavens. Certainly, the instruments were always spread out on a table, wherever Chuko Liang happened to be; and certainly, one of the theories must have been right. Else how could he have known what was transpiring on the other side of those huge mountain ranges that stood between Shu and Wei?

Chuko Liang did not stop to explain how he came by the knowledge that the enemy were approaching the pass. There was no time for that. What he did was to send Ma Su to defend it.

Now Ma Su was a distinguished general, a man of robust courage, a daring leader—with one very serious fault. He thought himself the cleverest general in the whole kingdom of Shu, and so listened with but half a mind while the commander-in-Chief issued instructions.

"Pitch your camp here. . . ." Chuko Liang was saying, sketching rapidly as he spoke. "Be prepared to deploy your forces—bowmen, so—cavalry, so—chariots, thus and so. Make a map, and send me a copy, that I may know the exact position of the units. Be off!" he finished. Off they went—Ma Su, the brilliant, and Wang Ping, the not so brilliant, second in command. And it was well, as things turned out, that Wang Ping went, for Ma Su, who had been ordered to dispose his men thus and so, did nothing of the sort.

By the time he, and they, had reached the pass, Ma Su had formed his own opinion; and, of all the treasures of gold and jade and jewels in the Three Kingdoms, there was none that Ma Su valued as he did his own opinion. So, to Wang Ping's horror, and against his repeated advice and protest, Ma Su encamped his forces on the summit of a hill beside the Chieh Ting Pass.

And the map? Well, as to that, Ma Su considered—quite rightly—that a map, showing the encampment of the Shu forces on the top of a mountain, would have annoyed Chuko Liang. So he refrained from making it. But Wang Ping made one, quickly and secretly, and bade a mounted messenger ride off with it as if every one of the Ten Thousand Devils, each with a face more horrific than the next one's, were following close behind!

Meantime, while the messenger was on his way to headquarters, Ssu Ma I took the Chieh Ting Pass, very easily and with great dispatch, by besieging the mountain and cutting off the water supply of the Ma Su forces. Then, having captured

Chieh Ting, the Wei forces drove on in the direction of Hsi Cheng, West City, with a still greater victory in view.

Of course, Chuko Liang knew what had happenued, even before the messenger had brought him the map. Chuko Liang was like that. He knew, too, that the enemy was advancing on Hsi Cheng. But he said nothing whatever about Hsi Cheng, and only began rapidly dividing up his remaining forces. Detachments were sent to strategic positions here and there, some to guard against further invasions, some to pave the way for the Shu army, in case it was obliged to retreat. Then, with only the civil officials and a handful of soldiers, he proceeded to Hsi Cheng, West City.

Hardly had they entered the city, when an Intelligence Horseman rode up, panting with the bad news that Ssu Ma I, with 150,000 soldiers, was approaching at full speed! People rushed from their houses to see what the excitement was all about—and such a wailing and moaning as rose, when they heard!

"Aiya!" and *"Aiya!"* they cried. "Alas, for our beautiful city!"

"And alas, for us!" lamented the officials. "For us nothing is left but flight or death!"

Palefaced, the handful of soldiers regarded each other, then Chuko Liang. The people went rigid with fright.

Chuko Liang said nothing, but went calmly and ascended the steps of the watch tower on the city wall. And there he stood, for a time, looking out in the direction of a sound and a great cloud of dust that even the dullest *jen tun*, with wooden spectacles on his stupid nose, would have recognized without stopping to stammer *"kan pu t'o*—I can't see through." Every moment the roar and the rattle and the clanking drew nearer and nearer.

Chuko Liang calmly descended again. And now, if you try, you can perhaps imagine how the pale officials, the frightened

soldiers and the terror-stricken people felt when he began giving orders for the defense of Hsi Cheng. For these, very nearly,
were his exact words!

"Let all flags and banners and pennants be taken down, from
buildings, houses, shops, and temples. Conceal them well,
then conceal yourselves even better. When the enemy appears,
whatever he may do, let no man make the slightest noise, or
show himself, or venture outside the city wall. The penalty is
death!"

So much for the civilians.

As for the soldiers—the twenty he had saved out to defend
the city—they were ordered to exchange military dress for
civilian garb, after which they were to *open* the four gates of
the city! (They turned sick with horror as they heard.) They
were to open the gates as wide as ever they would go, so that
the divinities, and others who might be interested, might have
an unobstructed view of Hsi Cheng, from east to west, or, if
they preferred, from north to south!

As a matter of fact, it was precisely this view of the city that
the Wei Intelligence Horsemen reported to their chief, first
of all. Ssu Ma I could not credit the report, and sent an officer,
with a small company of soldiers, to investigate.

It was true, they found. Not a soldier was to be seen in Hsi
Cheng! The Wei scouts rode round the walls. Still no soldiers—
only a few street coolies—were to be seen. (There were twenty
in all, but perhaps the Wei soldiers did not stop to count them.)
And the street coolies went calmly about their business of
brushing up leaves and trash in and around the gateways, without even troubling to glance at the intruders!

But, look! Up there! Yonder, in the watchtower! What in
the name of all the wonders within the Four Seas—what was
that? An old man, dressed in a robe embroidered all over with
flying cranes! A hermit-scholar? To be sure. For there, on his

head, was the soft, silken *jun-chin*, the hermit's hat!

And was that a boy, on either side of him? Of course! They were *chin* boys, and that long, wooden board they were arranging in front of the hermit, was a *chin* of seven strings! Now, could the Wei soldiers—for the matter of that, could any living creature—be blamed for waiting to hear the soft, sweet music of the *chin*? Ah! . . . there it was! Like the brushing of swallows' wings against the willows—sweet, sweet music! And not a sound from the city to spoil the effect! Yes, and what a musician! Scarce as peonies in winter were *chin* players such as this one! Reluctantly, the Wei scouts rode away.

When they told him, Ssu Ma I laughed and laughed, long and loud. A hermit playing the *chin* in the watch-tower of a threatened city?

"You are all bewitched!" laughed Ssu Ma I—and went, himself, to see. With him rode his son, Ssu Ma Chao, a youth who was filled with the zest for battle, ambitious to become as great as his noble father. Perhaps, who knows, even greater. After all, why not, one would ask? Did not Ssu Ma Chao live to see his son ascend the Dragon Throne, to rule the land as the first Emperor of the Tsin dynasty?

But all this has nothing whatever to do with what the astonished pair, Ssu Ma I and Ssu Ma Chao, saw when they reached Hsi Cheng. What they saw was just what the officers had seen. And more. Ssu Ma I discerned instantly that the hermit was Chuko Liang! Chuko Liang, in scholars' robes, was sitting with an air of boundless leisure, on the wall of a threatened city! A placid smile was on his face, while his fingers glided smoothly over the strings of the *chin!*

A boy, clad in silk, was on one side of him, his hand resting negligently on the hilt of a jewelled sword. On the other, was a boy gently waving a fly whip made from a white yak's tail. Directly in front of the hermit, an incense-burner was weaving soft, grey spirals of scented smoke that rose languidly in the quiet air. It was a charming scene, so peaceful, so serene!

Ssu Ma I looked away from it to where a group of coolies were plying their brooms—with no great vim, to be sure. (Most of the leaves must have been swept up by this time.) Still, they showed no interest in anything else. Perhaps because there *was* nothing, not a sign of life, showing anywhere.

Ssu Ma I did not stop to listen to the music. Perhaps he did not even hear it, though that would be difficult to believe, as ever so many historians and novelists have spoken of the superb manner in which Chuko Liang played on that particular occasion. But, whether or not he heard the music, Ssu Ma I did nothing but turn about face, and ride back to his troops. And now, try to imagine, if you can, what Ssu Ma, the younger, must have felt when, all running over as he was with the zest for battle, he heard his illustrious father order "Retreat!"

As a matter of fact, Ssu Ma Chao was so taken aback, so bewildered, so overpowered with indignation, that he was led into doing a thing which simply is not done! He actually burst into an exclamation of protest!

"Father!" he exclaimed. "But *why*? Why should we *retreat?*"

Such a breach! A double breach, in fact! For, to say nothing of the respect due from a junior officer to his senior, that senior was also his father. And if there were any excuse to be found for the one, there was none for the other, since, as everybody knows, a son may not contradict his father.

Possibly Ssu Ma Chao even allowed his voice to rise, especially on that word "Retreat!" Possibly, again, he managed to avoid this offence, as historians and novelists have never spoken of it. In any case, it was a bad enough business without that; and what the father answered to it was, quite simply, "Hush! Be quiet, my son! What can you, a young man, know of such a situation as this?"

With that, Ssu Ma I, from his long experience and great wisdom, explained. He reminded his son and the other officers (who looked no less astonished by the move) of the disasters that had befallen those who had underestimated the tactical genius of Chuko Liang.

"He is the most artful and crafty of antagonists. *But,* stop and think a moment! He has never been known to take a chance, or incur a risk. The city gates were opened—why? To tempt us to rush in, to be overtaken by hidden troops, perhaps, or by some other trick that would have caught us in a trap."

The Wei armies retreated, with finish and speed.

When they had gone, Chuko Liang gave up playing the *chin,* and the *chin* boys carried it away. He clapped his hands, now that they were free, and he laughed and laughed. The officials and the handful of soldiers in coolie dress gathered round him; and, little by little, the people of the city began creeping from their hiding-places. All looked stupefied as if unable to believe their own eyes. No man understood what had happened; but they all knelt down before Chuko Liang, and at last one of the officials found his voice.

"Your Excellency," said he, humbly, "enlighten us. We do not understand. Ssu Ma I, the veteran commander, with a strong and numerous army behind him, has run away from an empty city. What does it mean?"

"It means," answered Chuko Liang, chuckling softly, and bidding them rise, "that Ssu Ma I, the veteran commander, has made a slight miscalculation. He could not bring himself to believe that I would take such a dangerous chance, and decided that the empty city was a ruse to tempt him to advance. So, instead, he retreated. And now, by this time," his tone grew musing, while he calculated rapidly in his mind.

"Ah, yes," he continued. "By this time he has realized that Hsi Cheng really *was* empty—at least of soldiers. Yes, at this

very moment—you must have heard them moving in the direction of the Pei Shan Pass—at this very moment the Wei forces are meeting a surprise attack which our army was waiting to deliver in case the ruse succeeded."

"Ahh! Mmmm!" the officials' voices hummed in deep admiration, while the people exclaimed more excitedly. *"Hai yu!* Hurrah! Your Excellency's wisdom is beyond our poor comprehension. And to think! Had you not been with us, we should have fled the city."

"And been captured as surely as the falcon catches the chicken! No, it was our only chance. A dangerous trick, true! But . . ." Chuko Liang's voice trailed off.

Now what a spirit of mirth and rejoicing possessed the people of Hsi Cheng, West City! Wu Lung Hsien Shen, the Honorable Mr. Sleeping Dragon, as the people called Chuko Liang, had not only saved their beautiful city, but provided them with a merry tale that would be told and retold as long as there were sons and grandsons, and *their* sons and grandsons, to listen and laugh and repeat the story of how a great commander had run away from an empty city. It was a treat to tell it, and, best of all, it was true!

No less true was it that, in the course of time, and by the genius of the Honorable Mr. Sleeping Dragon, Shu became strong instead of weak, so that, for a while, it stood on a level with Wei and Wu. But then, gradually, the Three Kingdoms were dissolved, a new dynasty rose, and the Empire was knit together again to be ruled over by the grandson of Ssu Ma I.

Shizuka's Dance

by May McNeer and Lynd Ward

from *Prince Bantam*

Yoshitsune, and his half-brother Yoritomo, Minnemoto princes of Japan, were deprived of their rightful inheritance because their father, the king, died when they were small children. As they grew up in the home of their foster father, a bitter enmity developed between the two princes. Finally Yoritomo by force and evil means attained great power, but Yoshitsune, called Prince Bantam, preferred to seek his fortune in better ways.

As this part of the story opens, Yoshitsune learns that Yoritomo seeks his life, and flees with his wife, the lovely Shizuka; his faithful companion, the giant Benkei; and some of the men who are loyal to him.

All of this is said to have occured in the last half of the twelfth century when two great military classes were warring with each other in Japan. Although the story of Yoshitsune does not end happily and he is killed in battle despite his great military prowess and wisdom, no other epic hero is so popular in Japan. This is one of the few English versions of the story.

SHIZUKA'S DANCE

May McNeer and Lynd Ward

———◆•◆———

THE little fisher sailboats bobbed about on the waves, tossed forward by a freshening wind. Yoshitsune sat sadly in the forward boat trying to keep his spirits up for the sake of his lady who was pale and quiet by his side.

"Where are we, Benkei?" asked the chief, looking around him with sudden recognition. "This place looks familiar."

"It should be," grinned the giant. "This is not far from the spot where the Dragon King took the Taira clan into his arms."

"Are we almost at Dan-no-ura?" questioned Yoshitsune in surprise.

"Yes, master, but," with a little frown crossing his huge forehead, "it looks like trouble ahead. There is a storm coming."

Benkei turned to warn the men, as Yoshitsune strained his eyes forward. Yes, there was a reddish cloud on the horizon, and the sky was already growing black. Shizuka's hands fluttered like frightened birds as she saw the anxious expression on the face of her lord.

The wind was rising to a moan, which changed in a trice to a shriek of dying souls. Benkei shivered. The waves, obedient to their master, the wind, were tumbling in frothy dispute, and the red cloud came nearer. It was so dark that Yoshitsune could not see the other boat now. Benkei stood up as well as

he was able in the little tossing craft and looked into the distance where the crimson cloud was approaching. The wind moaned and shrieked until the hairs of the giant's neck stood up in ridges. He dropped so suddenly into the boat that it careened violently and shipped water from one side.

"Benkei! What do you mean?" shouted Yoshitsune, "do you want to sink us?"

"No, master," said the giant, his teeth chattering. "But there is something coming toward us, and—may the Lord Buddha protect us—it looks to me as if there are red banners floating in the wind!"

"Red banners!" Yoshitsune sprang to his feet while Shizuka held his legs to steady him. Then he sat down again, pale as death.

"You are right, Benkei. That cloud surely is a host of crimson

banners waving like cherry blossoms toward us. But it cannot be. The Taira are dead; it has been a year since they drowned at Dan-no-ura. There is no reason to be frightened. None of the Taira live."

"However, I prefer such things farther off," answered the big priest, feeling for his rosary.

The storm came down, wiping out words as they left the lips, and the little boat, no more than a cockleshell now, struggled for life. Shizuka lay in the bottom of the craft, hands over agonized eyes, with her long black hair flung out in a pennant by the wind.

Like an angry ox the gale raged and the ship quivered like a willow leaf in a breeze. Yoshitsune drew his long sword and stood, braced against the side, waiting for the ghostly figures of the slain Taira army. Years seemed to pass him by as he stood there maintaining his balance by a supreme effort. The cloud was close enough now to see dim gray shapes, murderous, with red emblems floating, writhing fiercely above ghostly sails and phantom ships.

The fishermen could no longer look, but lay in huddled lumps on the planking of the boat. Benkei threw out the anchor, but hardly had it plunged into the water when its chain snapped as if it had been cut with a knife. There was a far-away din of halberds, of whirling arrows, and of shouting from the throats of a thousand men, but no arrows came near the struggling ships.

Masts on the little vessels of the Minemotos snapped like twigs before the passing of a crazed boar, and the Taira wraiths drew in closer. Now Yoshitsune's staring eyes could see bloodstained clothes and weapons glinting suddenly in the flashes of lightning, searing his eyes. The young general, afraid of no man but sure now that his end had come, stood erect, sword out to strike at a phantom warrior close beside the boat, extending vaporous arms to draw him from the ship. Yoshitsune plunged in his sword swiftly, and almost fell from his craft, for the weapon had shot through the figure and left no mark. The arms drew in toward him.

Benkei grasped his sword and turned suddenly as he heard the voice of the helmsman flung to him by the wind:

"When this happens men believe that the ancestral hall of Minemoto is quaking."

"I'll show you what is quaking," growled the giant as he tried to make his way to the fellow. But just then Benkei had a thought which made him drop his sword in its scabbard and lift his bow, which he began to string frantically. Raising the bow, which five men could not bend, the big priest shot three arrows into the cloud of blood-red spirits, with a prayer accompanying each on its singing flight. As he watched, his bulging eyes saw those arrows slide through the figures of the ghostly warriors as through a mist and disappear. The dread Taira soldiers remained, closer now. Benkei's teeth chattered and he dropped on his knees, with his hands fumbling for his rosary.

"Sacred God Hachiman," he prayed, "was not the Taira clan insolent to you and to yours for many years? For a million days they trod down the poor, insulted the shrines of the Great Gods, mistreated your holy priests. For a thousand nights they reviled your prayers and bled your loyal worshipers of their gold. They were not fit to serve the little Emperor, Child of Heaven. They deserved death for their misdeeds. Oh, may the Lord Buddha receive them into Paradise and let them rest in peace!"

Benkei looked up into the face of a gaunt Taira warrior, who was reaching clammy hands out slowly toward him. He bowed his head and shouted, in an agony of fervor:

"Gods of the Sea and Kwannan of a Thousand Hands! As divinities of mercy and benevolence, prove your claims and deliver us from this trouble."

"Sa-a-a Benkei, we are saved!"

The giant jumped up to see his master and the men shouting with joy. The winds were shifting and calming, and no wraiths were upon the waves. They had faded back into the waters whence they came.

Yoshitsune faced him, tears of relief in his eyes.

"Once again you deliver us out of the hands of the enemy, my Benkei."

"Yes," said the giant, "dirty work!"

Yoshitsune looked for his other boat, and when the mists had cleared away he saw it bobbing behind them. He drew a thankful breath as a cry came from the helmsman of "Land ahead."

Benkei landed the small company without difficulty, although he had to carry Shizuka through the surf on his back.

"But," said the giant, laughing, "you are no heavier than a butterfly up there on my shoulders."

Shizuka smiled at him although her heart fell as she saw the ground covered with snow, fallen during the night. Like driftwood cast ashore she sank down under a pine tree. She did not weep but tried to comfort her lord.

When the other boat had reached the shore Yoshitsune welcomed his men and then walked away a little in thought. Shizuka could never stand this trip and an indefinite period of hiding, in the cold, which was probably to tax all of a man's endurance to the utmost. She was too delicate and fragile in spite of her indomitable spirit. He could not let her go on, especially since she could live in Kyoto with her mother in safety. He would come back to her, he thought, before long, if his brother was not too far in the hands of Kaji-wari. He had yielded to her entreaties to come, but for her sake he could not yield again.

Coming back to the fire around which the friends and servants had gathered to warm their blue knuckles, Yoshitsune told them at once of his decision. Shizuka must go back to her mother in Kyoto, where she would very likely not be molested, and at the first opportunity he would come for her there. Meanwhile he must go at once into hiding, probably wandering from place to place. Shizuka paled, but bowed her head in submission. She knew well that she could not take that difficult march in the snow.

"Time was," said the young chief sadly, "when I sailed in a large ship with sails of finest Chinese cotton, with oars of sandalwood, and a helm of laurel polished as a mirror. Now I am miserable and unfortunate. With my six faithful servants Shizuka shall return by land. Benkei and all of the retainers who do not wish to leave me shall accompany me into my exile."

He gave the servants money and placed them in charge of

Shizuka, then the young leader took his farewell of his wife. Half up the steep mountain trail Shizuka stood, eyes wet with tears and long sleeves wet with mountain snow. This mountain which the northward party must cross was the property of priests and was forbidden to women. Shizuka did not dare go farther with her lord.

"You must go now," said Yoshitsune with pain in his eyes.

"Be it so," answered his wife, "but let me touch your hands once more in farewell." Yoshitsune gave her tenderly his family treasures to care for. He placed in her hands a mirror and a sandalwood drum called "Hatsune."

But Shizuka wept, saying, "The more I gaze into the mirror the more will my sorrow be, for I shall not see there the face of my beloved. At your command I obey you, but let not your love change, and so we shall meet again, I hope, under a happier star."

When the young prince said good-by and turned to go, Shizuka clung to his sleeve, and when she, in turn, said farewell and started away, Yoshitsune could not bear the sight but held her little fluttering hands.

"Ah, master," said Benkei woefully, "we must go at once. These priests may be in the pay of Yoritomo, as I strongly suspect."

Yoshitsune turned without a word and led the way up the mountain's snowy path.

The six servants gathered their belongings and told Shizuka that it would be dangerous for her to be found there by the priests, and more dangerous for Yoshitsune. She folded her sleeves over her precious gifts and walked as fast as her small sandals could carry her along the trail which led below the base of the mountain.

It was just on the other side that a band of priests, armed and resolute, was waiting, on the lookout for strangers. Shizuka stood with staring eyes as her bodyguard was bound and led away. The priests looked at her in her sorry plight and some of them laughed, but one old man, who seemed to be the leader, lingered to whisper to her:

"Our order forbids us to care for women, but if you walk along this path until you reach a crooked tree growing sidewise, in it you will see a small temple where you may get aid." He turned and hurried off.

"Alas!" cried one of the servants who loved Yoshitsune, "how we have failed in our duty to our lord! To leave his beloved lady alone in the snow! Aiaai, we can only hope for death."

Shizuka was standing, a tiny figure in the immense waste of snow, on the lonely trail. The mountainside echoed her wails as tears ran down her cheeks in rivulets. She walked and walked until her breath came in gasps and still she did not see the crooked tree growing sidewise. Her sandals were in pieces and her delicate feet were cut by ice. Her sleeves were wet with tears and lined with ice and her trailing skirts were weighted down with snow. She held up her mirror but tears dimmed her sight. Then she stopped at a rise in the path and rested a little in a crook of a tree root. But it was cold and she must go on in order to live for her lord.

Shizuka stood up trembling and saw below her a feeble light flickering in the gloom of approaching night. She stumbled and crept along the small path, hardly visible now, until she came to a torii with a temple light burning inside. The young wife fell on her knees, veiling her face with a dripping sleeve, and prayed there outside of the gate. So the priests found her.

These priests, who wondered at her beauty, knew, as all of the country knew, that Yoshitsune had fled with his wife and a few retainers into hiding, so it was not difficult for them to discover who the court lady was. They decided immediately to send her to Yoritomo at Kamakura, his capital not far away.

Yoritomo ruled with an iron hand, but it was well known that this hand could be turned from its purpose, or to a new purpose, by a more powerful will than the Minemoto prince possessed. Kaji-wari, the badger, had his way with the weak prince, but Yoritomo's wife occasionally told her husband exactly what he should do. This lady was known as Masaka, the Nun Ruler, so quiet and restrained was her bearing and so determined was she that Yoritomo should not fail.

When Yoritomo heard that Shizuka was being brought to him, he smiled, for never had there been a dancer more favored by the Gods than this one. He recalled the story of her dance which brought rain to the suffering crops, and he straightway planned an occasion when Shizuka should dance for him and for his court. Masaka looked a little anxious but said nothing.

Quietly arrangements were made for the entertainment in a large room of the palace, but when Yoritomo discussed his plans with an attendant he did not know that a friend of Yoshitsune, called Yori, was kneeling behind a bamboo screen in the room. This friend, slipping out, went to warn the dancer.

So Shizuka, after she had been allowed a rest of several weeks in a small house in Kamakura, knew when she was summoned to see Yoritomo that she was to be asked to dance. And she knew that she would not.

Yoritomo knelt in state, surrounded by his armed retainers, with Masaka just a little way behind him. Shizuka bowed deeply and said:

"Ah, most honorable ruler, there is no need to ask me where my lord is for I do not know. Alas! He is gone from me, and I know not where he wanders in the cold. I beg of you in the name of innocence to let him go free. He has done nothing unloyal against your lordship, but always did he love and protect your interests."

Kaji-wari scowled and whispered to Yoritomo, whose face

grew hard with jealousy as he thought of his popular younger brother who had so much more grace and beauty, and military skill, than he.

"Come, we will not discuss these things. But you will dance for us, Shizuka, to let us see of what the world talks."

Shizuka bent herself to the floor, but refused to dance.

"What!" growled Yoritomo. "Then you shall be a prisoner until you consent to let us see what kind of dancing the Gods approve."

Shizuka was taken away, pale but resolute, to her house, where a guard of women servants was placed around her.

It was spring, and purple wisteria was hanging pendent in the gardens of Hachiman Temple not far from the little house where the wife of Yoshitsune sat and grieved for her lord. She spent her nights wondering where he was wandering, and her days trying to think of some way in which she could help him. There seemed no way but prayer. So every day the dancer went to Hachiman Temple accompanied by several of her jailer servants and prayed fervently for Yoshitsune's success, and his vindication.

Once as she knelt there in the dim interior of the temple, a lady of the court came and bowed beside her. When Shizuka rose to go the lady walked just a little behind, but in front of the servants who always followed their mistress. Shizuka looked around as she passed through one of the stone gates, and the lady smiled at her, at the same time hurrying to her side.

"What do you want of me?" asked Shizuka anxiously. "Why do you follow me?"

"Ah," the court lady said softly, "I cannot say much, for you know what ears these women have," and she glanced fearfully back at the chattering servants, "but I feel sympathy for you in your misfortune. I want to help you."

Shizuka looked at first suspiciously at the pitying expression on the lady's face, then she thought that she could trust her.

"Tell me," she asked, "how I can help the cause of my innocent lord at the court of his brother?"

"Alas," said the lady sadly, "there is no way when Kaji-wari has the ear of Yoritomo. There is but one way, through the God Hachiman. He is displeased because you have not danced a prayer for him."

"Then," answered Shizuka, "I will dance in the Temple of Hachiman, for my husband.

"A bright day for my dance to the God," prayed Shizuka as she knelt in reverence in the temple, and a bright day was given her. The holy place with its green and red paintings and its finely tinted carvings was but newly built in honor of Hachiman, War God of the Minemoto family. And ancestor of Yoshitsune, outcast though he was, thought Shizuka proudly, as she prepared her finest garments for this dance of prayer. She would spare no honor to the God that he might bring to safety her lord.

Up the long road went the little dancer, heavily veiled and covered, but none the less peasants stopped work in the rice fields, where they stood to the knees in water, and shaded their eyes to stare at this beautiful woman who walked so hurriedly to the temple. Up the long lane between big pine trees she almost ran, eager to do this for her husband. Shizuka had found little difficulty escaping her jailers with the aid of her good friend, so now she came with but one maid pattering behind her.

Long before she reached the stone bridge, proudly arched, she could distinguish its soft red glow between the trees. At the temple she paused to get her breath beneath the first of three stone gates which led to a flight of steps.

"Mistress," gasped the little maid, hurrying up to her, "do you not think that the temple grounds look unusually crowded to-day? Do you not think there is some air of excitement about?"

Shizuka looked into the grounds where a group of people, some in rags, some in decent cotton, and some in rich brocade, walked slowly around or knelt in prayer.

"No, Aya," she said, "it seems to me as usual. We have chosen a crowded day, that is all." But nevertheless Shizuka, as she climbed the steps and bowed her body in prayer, glanced around the courtyard nervously before she prepared to enter the temple itself. As she rose from her knees the dancer looked at a covered gallery around the court and started in fright. Who were those handsome people there and why were two places marked off by golden screens? The pillars of this porch were wound with thin colored silk, and damask curtains hung behind fine floor mats, on which a large company dwelt.

"Come, Aya," she whispered, "we must go at once." But it was already too late, for a high priest was bowing before her, saying, "Most beautiful and illustrious lady, the God Hachiman is pleased with your intention. We have received word that you will dance before our temple."

Shizuka trembled from head to foot, but was mute when she saw among the people in that gallery the court lady who had persuaded her to fall into this trap. She found herself bowing before the golden screen but could say nothing, so overcome with sorrow was she.

A voice spoke: "Take away the screens and let us see this dancer, who so pleased the high priest of the Emperor that he gave her the finest kimono ever made in the land."

As the golden screens were drawn aside Shizuka saw through her downcast lashes a weak smile on the face of Yoritomo— weak but triumphant. Masaka was biting her lip; the Nun Ruler looked sad and infinitely pitying.

"My lordship," murmured Shizuka very low, "I cannot dance because there is no music fit for me."

Yoritomo looked in rage at the company of musicians, all country fellows unused to court tunes.

"Ah," he cried, lifting a long hand, "I have it. Some of our friends of the court are talented musicians. Let us see. Here are three who can play to the lady's satisfaction."

"But, worshipful lord," whispered Masaka in alarm, "you would not ask noblemen to play for a temple dance, like low-born musicians."

"Ah, Masaka, I would and I do. Make ready to play. I shall send a messenger to get your instruments while this lady makes her preparations for the dance."

Shizuka wept, but turned away to obey the chief. She only prayed silently that the God Hachiman would take this dance not as entertainment for the ruler but as a prayer to free her lord.

When the little dancer heard the music of drum and flute and cymbal she advanced slowly to the platform before the roofed porch of the temple, where the noble company knelt. Three men of high birth made music for her dance. Their costumes glowed brilliantly before the rich and gay assembly. A young samurai, whose sandalwood drumbeats echoed along the ceiling of the corridor, was dressed in a yellow robe above a blue skirt, while the blue kimono of another was beneath a gray robe. His cymbals of Chinese copper decorated with a gold and chrysanthemum pattern clashed like the sweet song of a night insect. The third was a giant in size, clad in a white skirt and white court dress, and the music which he drew from a chinese bamboo flute charmed the birds in the branches of the trees.

Shizuka, thin from her sorrowful trip and her anxiety, but graceful as a bending willow bow, advanced with tiny steps to the front of the red platform, which was used only for sacred dances to the God. The company gasped in astonishment.

White silk trousers showed beneath a crimson skirt, while the kimono above was of apple green edged with embroidery. High on her head was piled her black hair in an elaborate headdress above penciled brows, and her face, already pale, was powdered. In one small hand she carried a red-tipped fan. She was a goddess descended to earth from some heavenly court.

For a moment the dancer stood, swaying gently, her fan in supple, slow motion with her hands and her body, then as the music fell into the "Song of Inexhaustible Happiness," her voice rose clear and sweet above the temple. Gracefully she shook out her long sleeves with one arm, then with the other, and faintly she swayed to the song of cymbal, drum, and flute.

Slowly, so slowly she moved, until her swaying figure seemed no more than the gentle drifting of clouds on a summer day. Softly, so softly her fan waved to the delicate tones, until her wrist became a blossom palely bending on a bough, until her fan became a butterfly hovering over the sweetness of the flower.

Now the music quickened, and her posturing moved her as a freshening breeze bows an iris bloom on the edge of a pool. She was a dream of beauty. Back and forth she wove an imaginary pattern in a brilliant tapestry. As she fluttered her scarlet fan, so light was her dancing that she seemed a bird on the wing.

The musicians glanced at each other and struck up the first notes of the second part of the song, when voice and movement must unite in compliment to the lord Yoritomo. That the second half of a song must change to complimentary stanzas about the lord who listened, was a rule never to be ignored. But Shizuka, without ceasing to sway her delicate body and move her dipping hands, ended the "Song of Inexhaustible Happiness," and did not begin the complimentary stanzas. The musicians, looking at each other in dismay, continued their plaintive music.

Shizuka raised her head and with an upward look of inexpressible sorrow she began to sing again:

"On the peak of Yoshino-yama.
Falls the white snow, hiding all;
On this scene the wanderer enters
Seeking trace of him she loves.
The winding, winding of a trifling ball of yarn,
Thus feeble are my lowly wishes for his one-time fortune."

Her voice soared up as lightly as moving dust in the sunshine, and for a moment Yoritomo and all his court were spell-bound. Such an insult had never been offered him in all of his existence. He jumped to his feet with a cry of rage.

"You shall die for this insult to your master! Yoritomo, son of the Minemotos, cannot be insulted as one insults a slave. You die!" His face was purple; the veins stood out on his neck like cords.

Masaka touched his sleeve. "My lord," she implored, "my honorable lord, how can this dancer hurt you? What insult has she offered but to pray for her lord, who is beyond injuring Yoritomo, the great ruler. Wait and consider."

Yoritomo dropped his arm and his color went down, but he scowled like an angry God as he walked swiftly to his carriage and was gone. Shizuka wept, for she knew not what might befall her now. But the Gods must smile on Yoshitsune for this.

Next day, Aya, bowing and smiling, ushered in two servants of the court who were laden with gifts of embroidery, fish, and sweets, sent with a message from Masaka, the Nun Ruler, who bade the little dancer not to fear, for her life would be spared. She had permission, said the wife of Yoritomo, to return to her mother in Kyoto.

Scarface

by George Bird Grinnell

from *Blackfoot Lodge Tales*

This is a tale told by the Blackfoot Indians who lived in the great plains area of the United States and Southern Canada. It is translated from their language just as it was told by them to the author. The story can be interpreted as the Indian's journey across the plains and western mountains to the home of the Great Spirit, the sun.

SCARFACE

George Bird Grinnell

———————•◦•———————

I N the earliest times there was no war. All the tribes were
at peace. In those days there was a man who had a
daughter, a very beautiful girl. Many young men wanted
to marry her, but every time she was asked, she only shook her
head and said she did not want a husband.

"How is this?" asked her father. "Some of these young men
are rich, handsome, and brave."

"Why should I marry?" replied the girl. "I have a rich father
and mother. Our lodge is good. The parfleches are never empty.
There are plenty of tanned robes and soft furs for winter. Why
worry me, then?"

The Raven Bearers held a dance; they all dressed carefully
and wore their ornaments, and each one tried to dance the best.
Afterwards some of them asked for this girl, but still she said no.
Then the Bulls, the Kit-foxes, and others of the *I-kun-uh'-kah-
tsi* held their dances, and all those who were rich, many great
warriors, asked this man for his daughter, but to every one of
them she said no. Then her father was angry, and said: "Why,
now, this way? All the best men have asked for you, and still
you say no. I believe you have a secret lover."

"Father! mother!" replied the girl, "Pity me. I have no secret
lover, but now hear the truth. That Above Person, the Sun,

told me, 'Do not marry any of those men, for you are mine; thus you shall be happy, and live to great age'; and again he said, 'Take heed. You must not marry. You are mine.' "

"Ah!" replied her father. "It must always be as he says." And they talked no more about it.

There was a poor young man, very poor. His father, mother, all his relations, had gone to the Sand Hills. He had no lodge, no wife to tan his robes or sew his moccasins. He stopped in one lodge to-day, and to-morrow he ate and slept in another; thus he lived. He was a good-looking young man, except that on his cheek he had a scar, and his clothes were always old and poor.

After those dances some of the young men met this poor Scarface, and they laughed at him, and said: "Why don't you ask that girl to marry you? You are so rich and handsome!" Scarface did not laugh; he replied: "Ah! I will do as you say. I will go and ask her." All the young men thought this was funny. They laughed a great deal. But Scarface went down by the river. He waited by the river, where the women came to get water, and by and by the girl came along. "Girl," he said, "wait. I want to speak with you. Not as a designing person do I ask you, but openly where the Sun looks down, and all may see."

"Speak then," said the girl.

"I have seen the days," continued the young man. "You have refused those who are young, and rich, and brave. Now, to-day, they laughed and said to me, 'Why do you not ask her?' I am poor, very poor. I have no lodge, no food, no clothes, no robes and warm furs. I have no relations; all have gone to the Sand Hills; yet, now, to-day, I ask you, take pity, be my wife."

The girl hid her face in her robe and brushed the ground with the point of her moccasin, back and forth, back and forth; for she was thinking. After a time she said: "True. I have refused all those rich young men, yet now the poor one asks me, and I am glad. I will be your wife, and my people will be happy. You are poor, but it does not matter. My father will give you dogs. My mother will make us a lodge. My people will give us robes and furs. You will be poor no longer."

Then the young man was happy, and he started to kiss her, but she held him back, and said: "Wait! The Sun has spoken to me. He says I may not marry; that I belong to him. He says if I listen to him, I shall live to great age. But now I say: Go to the Sun. Tell him, 'She whom you spoke with heeds your words. She has never done wrong, but now she wants to marry. I want her for my wife.' Ask him to take that scar from your face. That will be his sign. I will know he is pleased. But if he refuses, or if you fail to find his lodge, then do not return to me."

"Oh!" cried the young man, "at first your words were good. I was glad. But now it is dark. My heart is dead. Where is that far-off lodge? Where the trail, which no one yet has travelled?"

"Take courage, take courage!" said the girl; and she went to her lodge.

Scarface was very sad. He sat down and covered his head with his robe and tried to think what to do. After a while he got up, and went to an old woman who had been kind to him. "Pity me," he said. "I am very poor. I am going away now on a long journey. Make me some moccasins."

"Where are you going?" asked the old woman. "There is no war; we are very peaceful here."

"I do not know where I shall go," replied Scarface. "I am in trouble, but I cannot tell you now what it is."

So the old woman made him some moccasins, seven pairs, with parfleche soles, and also she gave him a sack of food, pemmican of berries, pounded meat, and dried back fat; for this old woman had a good heart. She liked the young man.

All alone, and with a sad heart, he climbed the bluffs and stopped to take a last look at the camp. He wondered if he would ever see his sweetheart and the people again. *"Hai'-yu!* Pity me, O Sun," he prayed, and turning, he started to find the trail.

For many days he travelled on, over great prairies, along timbered rivers and among the mountains, and every day his sack of food grew lighter; but he saved it as much as he could, and ate berries, and roots, and sometimes he killed an animal of some kind. One night he stopped by the home of a wolf. *"Hai-yah!"* said that one; "what is my brother doing so far from home?"

"Ah!" replied Scarface, "I seek the place where the Sun lives; I am sent to speak with him."

"I have travelled far," said the wolf. "I know all the prairies, the valleys, and the mountains, but I have never seen the Sun's home. Wait; I know one who is very wise. Ask the bear. He may tell you."

The next day the man travelled on again, stopping now and then to pick a few berries, and when night came he arrived at the bear's lodge.

"Where is your home?" asked the bear. "Why are you travelling alone, my brother?"

"Help me! Pity me!" replied the young man; "because of her words[1] I seek the Sun. I go to ask him for her."

"I know not where he stops," replied the bear. "I have travelled by many rivers, and I know the mountains, yet I have never seen his lodge. There is some one beyond, that striped-face, who is very smart. Go and ask him."

The badger was in his hole. Stooping over, the young man

---

[1] A Blackfoot often talks of what this or that person said, without mentioning names.

shouted: "Oh, cunning striped-face! Oh, generous animal! I wish to speak with you."

"What do you want?" said the badger, poking his head out of the hole.

"I want to find the Sun's home," replied Scarface. "I want to speak with him."

"I do not know where he lives," replied the badger. "I never travel very far. Over there in the timber is a wolverine. He is always travelling around, and is of much knowledge. Maybe he can tell you."

Then Scarface went to the woods and looked all around for the wolverine, but could not find him. So he sat down to rest. "*Hai'-yu; Hai'-yu!*" he cried. "Wolverine, take pity on me. My food is gone, my moccasins are worn out. Now I must die."

"What is it, my brother?" he heard, and looking around, he saw the animal sitting near.

"She whom I would marry," said Scarface, "belongs to the Sun; I am trying to find where he lives, to ask him for her."

"Ah!" said the wolverine. "I know where he lives. Wait; it is nearly night. To-morrow I will show you the trail to the big water. He lives on the other side of it."

Early in the morning, the wolverine showed him the trail, and Scarface followed it until he came to the water's edge. He looked out over it, and his heart almost stopped. Never before had any one seen such a big water. The other side could not be seen, and there was no end to it. Scarface sat down on the shore. His food was all gone, his moccasins worn out. His heart was sick. "I cannot cross this big water," he said. "I cannot return to the people. Here, by this water, I shall die."

Not so. His helpers were there. Two swans came swimming up to the shore. "Why have you come here?" they asked him. "What are you doing? It is very far to the place where your people live."

"I am here," replied Scarface, "to die. Far away, in my country, is a beautiful girl. I want to marry her, but she belongs to the Sun. So I started to find him and ask for her. I have travelled many days. My food is gone. I cannot go back. I cannot cross this big water, so I am going to die."

"No," said the swans; "it shall not be so. Across this water is the home of that Above Person. Get on our backs, and we will take you there."

Scarface quickly arose. He felt strong again. He waded out into the water and lay down on the swans' backs, and they started off. Very deep and black is that fearful water. Strange people live there, mighty animals which often seize and drown a person. The swans carried him safely, and took him to the other side. Here was a broad hard trail leading back from the water's edge.

"*Kyi*," said the swans. "You are now close to the Sun's lodge. Follow that trail, and you will soon see it."

Scarface started up the trail, and pretty soon he came to some beautiful things, lying in it. There was a war shirt, a shield, and a bow and arrows. He had never seen such pretty weapons; but he did not touch them. He walked carefully around them, and travelled on. A little way further on, he met a young man, the handsomest person he had even seen. His hair was very long, and he wore clothing made of strange skins. His moccasins were sewn with bright colored feathers. The young man said to him, "Did you see some weapons lying on the trail?"

"Yes," replied Scarface; "I saw them."

"But did you not touch them?" asked the young man.

"No; I thought some one had left them there, so I did not take them."

"You are not a thief," said the young man. "What is your name?"

"Scarface."

"Where are you going?"

"To the Sun."

"My name," said the young man, "is A-pi-su-ahts.[2] The Sun is my father; come, I will take you to our lodge. My father is not now at home, but he will come in at night."

Soon they came to the lodge. It was very large and handsome; strange medicine animals were painted on it. Behind, on a tripod, were strange weapons and beautiful clothes—the Sun's. Scarface was ashamed to go in, but Morning Star said, "Do not be afraid, my friend; we are glad you have come."

They entered. One person was sitting there, Ko-ko-mik'-e-is,[3]

[2] Early Riser, *i.e.* The Morning Star

the Sun's wife, Morning Star's mother. She spoke to Scarface kindly, and gave him something to eat. "Why have you come so far from your people?" she asked.

Then Scarface told her about the beautiful girl he wanted to marry. "She belongs to the Sun," he said. "I have come to ask him for her."

When it was time for the Sun to come home, the Moon hid Scarface under a pile of robes. As soon as the Sun got to the doorway, he stopped, and said, "I smell a person."

"Yes, father," said Morning Star; "a good young man has come to see you. I know he is good, for he found some of my things on the trail and did not touch them."

Then Scarface came out from under the robes, and the Sun entered and sat down. "I am glad you have come to our lodge," he said. "Stay with us as long as you think best. My son is lonesome sometimes; be his friend."

The next day the Moon called Scarface out of the lodge, and said to him: "Go with Morning Star where you please, but never hunt near that big water; do not let him go there. It is the home of great birds which have long sharp bills; they kill people. I have had many sons, but these birds have killed them all. Morning Star is the only one left."

So Scarface stayed there a long time and hunted with Morning Star. One day they came near the water, and saw the big birds.

"Come," said Morning Star; "let us go and kill those birds."

"No, no!" replied Scarface; "we must not go there. Those are very terrible birds; they will kill us."

Morning Star would not listen. He ran towards the water, and Scarface followed. He knew that he must kill the birds and save the boy. If not, the Sun would be angry and might

---

[8] Night red light, the Moon

kill him. He ran ahead and met the birds, which were coming towards him to fight, and killed every one of them with his spear; not one was left. Then the young men cut off their heads, and carried them home. Morning Star's mother was glad when they told her what they had done, and showed her the birds' heads. She cried, and called Scarface "my son." When the Sun came home at night, she told him about it, and he too was glad. "My son," he said to Scarface, "I will not forget what you have this day done for me. Tell me now, what can I do for you?"

"*Hai'-yu*," replied Scarface. "*Hai'-yu*, pity me. I am here to ask you for that girl. I want to marry her. I asked her, and she was glad; but she says you own her, that you told her not to marry."

"What you say is true," said the Sun. "I have watched the days, so I know it. Now, then, I give her to you; she is yours. I am glad she has been wise. I know she has never done wrong. The Sun pities good women. They shall live a long time. So shall their husbands and children. Now you will soon go home. Let me tell you something. Be wise and listen: I am the only chief. Everything is mine. I made the earth, the mountains, prairies, rivers, and forests. I made the people and all the animals. This is why I say I alone am the chief. I can never die. True, the winter makes me old and weak, but every summer I grow young again."

Then said the Sun: "What one of all animals is smartest? The raven is, for he always finds food. He is never hungry. Which one of all the animals is most Nat-ó-ye? [4] The buffalo is. Of all animals, I like him best. He is for the people. He is your food and your shelter. What part of his body is sacred? The tongue is. That is mine. What else is sacred? Berries are.

---

[4] This word may be translated as "of the Sun," "having Sun power," or more properly, something sacred.

They are mine too. Come with me and see the world." He took Scarface to the edge of the sky, and they looked down and saw it. It is round and flat, and all around the edge is the jumping-off place [or walls straight down]. Then said the Sun: "When any man is sick or in danger, his wife may promise to build me a lodge, if he recovers. If the woman is pure and true, then I will be pleased and help the man. But if she is bad, if she lies, then I will be angry. You shall build the last lodge like the world, round, with walls, but first you must build a sweat house of a hundred sticks. It shall be like the sky [a hemisphere], and half of it shall be painted red. That is me. The other half you will paint black. That is the night."

Further said the Sun: "Which is the best, the heart or the brain? The brain is. The heart often lies, the brain never." Then he told Scarface everything about making the Medicine Lodge, and when he had finished, he rubbed a powerful medicine on his face, and the scar disappeared. Then he gave him two raven feathers, saying: "These are the sign for the girl, that I give her to you. They must always be worn by the husband of the woman who builds a Medicine Lodge."

The young man was now ready to return home. Morning Star and the Sun gave him many beautiful presents. The Moon cried and kissed him, and called him "my son." Then the Sun showed him the short trail. It was the Wolf Road (Milky Way). He followed it, and soon reached the ground.

It was a very hot day. All the lodge skins were raised, and the people sat in the shade. There was a chief, a very generous man, and all day long people kept coming to his lodge to feast and smoke with him. Early in the morning this chief saw a person sitting out on a butte near by, close wrapped in his robe. The chief's friends came and went, the sun reached the middle, and passed on, down towards the mountains. Still this person did not move. When it was almost night, the chief said: "Why does that person sit there so long? The heat has been strong, but he has never eaten nor drunk. He may be a stranger; go and ask him in."

So some young men went up to him, and said: "Why do you sit here in the great heat all day? Come to the shade of the lodges. The chief asks you to feast with him."

Then the person arose and threw off his robe, and they were surprised. He wore beautiful clothes. His bow, shield, and other weapons were of strange make. But they knew his face, although the scar was gone, and they ran ahead, shouting, "The scarfaced poor young man has come. He is poor no longer. The scar on his face is gone."

All the people rushed out to see him. "Where have you been?" they asked. "Where did you get all these pretty things?" He did not answer. There in the crowd stood that young woman; and taking the two raven feathers from his head, he gave them to her, and said: "The trail was very long, and I nearly died, but by those helpers, I found his lodge. He is glad. He sends these feathers to you. They are the sign."

Great was her gladness then. They were married, and made the first Medicine Lodge, as the Sun had said. The Sun was glad. He gave them great age. They were never sick. When they were very old, one morning, their children said: "Awake! Rise and eat." They did not move. In the night, in sleep, without pain, their shadows had departed for the Sand Hills.

IF YOU WOULD LIKE MORE

(some of the books listed below are out of print, but they may be available in your local library)

THE ILIAD

The Iliad Done into English Prose, by Andrew Lang (Macmillan 1903)
The Iliad for Boys and Girls, by Alfred J. Church (Macmillan 1907)
The Iliad of Homer, retold by Barbara Leonie Picard (Walck 1960)
A Story of the Golden Age, by James Baldwin (Scribners 1887)

THE ODYSSEY

The Adventures of Odysseus, by Padraic Colum (Macmillan 1918)
The Odyssey; Done into English Prose, by L. H. Batcher and A. Lang (Macmillan 1921)
The Odyssey of Homer, retold by Alfred J. Church (Macmillan 1951)
Odysseus the Wanderer, by Aubrey de Selincourt (Criterion 1956)

THE AENEID

The Aeneid for Boys and Girls, by Alfred J. Church (Macmillan 1908)

ATTILA

The White Stag, by Kate Seredy (Viking 1937)

BEOWULF

By His Own Might; the Battles of Beowulf, by Dorothy Hosford (Holt 1947)
The Story of Beowulf; Retold from the Ancient Epic, by Strafford Riggs (Appleton-Century 1933)

KING ARTHUR AND HIS KNIGHTS

Book of King Arthur and His Noble Knights, by Mary Macleod (Lippincott 1949)
Boys' King Arthur, ed. by Sidney Lanier (Scribner's 1917)
Stories of King Arthur and His Knights, by Barbara Leonie Picard (Walck 1955)
Story of King Arthur and his Knights, by Howard Pyle (Scribner's 1933)
The Story of the Champions of the Round Table, by Howard Pyle (Scribner's 1929)
The Sword in the Stone, by T. H. White (Putnam 1939)

WELSH TALES

The Book of the Three Dragons, by Kenneth Morris (Longmans 1930)
The Fates of the Princes of Dyfed, by Kenneth Morris (Aryan Theosophical 1914)
The Island of the Mighty, by Padraic Colum (Macmillan 1927)
Welsh Legends and Folk Tales, retold by Gwyn Jones (Walck 1955)

IRISH TALES

Cuchulain, The Hound of Ulster, by Eleanor Hull (Crowell 1910)
The Harper's Daughter, by Alan Michael Buck (Walck 1940)
Irish Sagas and Folk-Tales, retold by Eileen O'Faolain (Walck 1954)
The Tangle-Coated Horse and Other Tales, by Ella Young (Longmans 1929)

HEROES OF FRANCE

Huon of the Horn, adapted by Andre Norton (Harcourt 1951)
The Singing Sword, by Mark Powell Hyde (Little 1930)
Song of Roland, translated by Merriam Sherwood (Longmans 1938)
The Story of Roland, by James Baldwin (Scribner's 1930)

THE CID

Tale of the Warrior Lord, by Merriam Sherwood (Longmans 1930)

ICELANDIC SAGAS

Heroes of Iceland, by Allen French (Little 1925)
The Story of Grettir the Strong, by Allen French (Dutton 1908)

SIEGFRIED or SIGURD

Sons of the Volsungs, by Dorothy Hosford (Macmillan 1932)
The Story of Siegfried, by James Baldwin (Scribner's 1882)

THE KALEVALA

Heroes of the Kalevala, by Babette Deutsch (Messner 1940)
Sampo: Hero Adventures from the Finnish Kalevala, by James Baldwin (Scribner's 1912)
Wizard of the North, by Parker H. Fillmore (Harcourt 1923)

HEROES OF THE MIDDLE EAST

The Epic of Kings, by Helen Zimmern (Macmillan 1929)
Romance of Antar, by Eunice Tietjens (McCann 1939)

THE MAHABHARATA

The Five Brothers, adapted from the English translation of Kisari Mohan by Elizabeth Seeger (Day 1948)
The Wicked Goldsmith, by Mabel Ashe Beling (Harper 1941)

THE RAMAYANA

Adventures of Rama, by Joseph Gaer (Little 1954)
Rama the Hero of India, by Dhan Gopal Mukerji (Dutton 1930)

GESSAR KHAN

Gessar Khan, by Ida Zeitlin (Doran 1927)
The Superhuman Life of Gesar of Ling, by Alexandra David-Neel, with Lama Yongden (London, Rider & Co., 1959)

HEROES OF CHINA
Folk Tales from China, by Sian-tek Lim (Day 1944)
The Magic Spear, by Louise Crane (Random 1938)

HEROES OF JAPAN
Benkei, the Boy Giant, by Marjorie G. Fribourg (Sterling 1958)
Japanese Tales and Legends, by Helen and William McAlpine (Walck 1959)
Prince Bantam, by May McNeer and Lynd Ward (Macmillan 1929)

AMERICAN INDIAN STORIES
Blackfoot Lodge Tales, by George Bird Grinnell (Scribner's 1892)
Nine Tales of Coyote, by Frances G. Martin (Harper 1950)

GLOSSARY

' indicates accented syllable
a—as in fat, man
ā—as in fate, mane
ä—as in far, guard
ȧ—as in abait, balloon

e—as in met, bless
ē—as in meet

i—as in pin, it
ī—as in pine, file

o—as in not, on
ō—as in note, poke
ö—as in move
ô—as in nor, off
ōō—as in foot
ŏŏ—as in cool

u—as in hub, hot
ū—as in mute
ü—as in prune
ú—as in sure, urn
û—as in burr, fur

Abs, Tribe of, (*Abz*). *a Bedouin sub-tribe of north Africa.*

accoutred (*a-kōō'terd*). *furnished with dress or equipment.*

adze (*adz*). *a cutting tool having a thin arching blade set at right angles to the handle.*

Alba (*al'ba*). *old Celtic name for Scotland.*

Albertz, Mount. *the Elburz Range in northern Iran.*

Altain-Ula (*al-tā'yan ula*). *mountain in central Asia.*

Althing (*äl'thing*). *national assembly of Iceland. All free landowners were members. It first met in the ninth century.*

anvil (*an'vil*). *a block, usually of iron and steel, on which metal is shaped by hammering or forging.*

Apollo (*a-pol'ō*). *Greek god of the sun, of poetry and music, of oracles, and of healing.*

Aquitaine (*ak'wi-tān*). *ancient name for southwestern France.*

ardency (*ar'den-sē*) *eagerness or zeal.*

Arfon. *medieval name for part of Carnavonshire, Wales, the area between the Menai Straits and Mt. Snowdon.*

Asgard (*äs'gärd*). *legendary home of the Norse gods.*

Athene (*a-thē'nē*). *Greek goddess of war and also of industry. Roman, Minerva.*

aurioled (*ô'rē-ōl'd*). *haloed.*

bain (*bān*). *a bath.*

Baldar (*bôl'der*). *Germanic god of light and peace.*

bane (*bán*). *slayer or murderer, bringer of destruction, ruin, or woe.*

bellows (*bel'ōz*). *an instrument that expands and contracts to draw in air and force it out. Used for blowing on fires to make them burn hotter.*

berserk (*bûr'sûrk*). *legendary Norse warriors who fell into a great rage when they fought and had enormous strength. They wore no coats of mail. (also baresark)*

bolt (*bōlt*). *a short, blunt arrow or dart, shot from a crossbow or catapult.*

Boyne River (*boin*). *river in southeast Ireland.*

Brahmin (brä'man). *a member of the highest Hindu cast.*

Branstock, Sword of the (brän'stok). *sword pulled by the Norse hero Sigmund from a great oak in the hall of the Volsungs.*

Brugh (brōōk). *old Irish term for region or borough—Brugh of Angus, residence of Angus, a Scotch lord.*

Brython (brith'on). *a member of the British branch of Celts, a Welshman, also Wales.*

buckler (buk'ler). *a shield worn on one arm to protect the front of the body.*

burnished (bûr'nished). *polished.*

Cabul (kä'bŏŏl). *city in Afghanistan.*

Cadi (kä'dē). *the judge of a town or village of the Near East.*

Caerleon (kär-lē-on). *town in Monmouthshire, England.*

Cameliard. *Cornwall, the area around the Camel River.*

Candlemas (kan'd'l-mas). *feast celebrating the presentation of Christ in the temple. February 2.*

cankered (kang'kered). *rusted.*

caparison (ka-par'i-sun). *an ornamental covering for a horse, equipment, adornment.*

Carpathian Mountains (kär-pā'thian). *mountain range between Poland and Czechoslovakia.*

cendal (sen'dal). *thin silk fabric used in the Middle Ages.*

Ceridwen (ker'i-dwin). *Welsh goddess. In some legends, queen mother of the world.*

chamberlain (chām'bûr-lin). *a superintendant of a household or a feudal court.*

chin (ching). *chinese stringed musical instrument.*

cohorts (kō'hôrts). *a band or body of warriors; a company.*

coif (koif). *a defensive skullcap worn by soldiers under a hood of mail.*

constable (kun'stȧ-b'l). *a high officer in the Middle Ages; chief officer of the army.*

coracle (kor'ȧ-k'l). *a small boat made by covering a wicker frame with hide.*

Cordova (kôr'dō-va). *a Spanish city known for its fine leather goods.*

Cornwall (kôrn'wal). *a region in southwest England.*

corslet (kôrs'let). *armor for the body consisting of a breastplate and a backpiece.*

covert (kuv'ûrt). *a place that protects, a shelter.*

craven (krā'ven). *a coward.*

Dacians (dā'shans). *ancient peoples who lived in the land west of the Dneister River, east of the Tisa River, and north of the Danube River.*

Dahna or Tuatha De Danann (dänä). *god tribe of the ancient Gaels. The descendants of the goddess Danu.*

Dehstan. *section of India near Afghanistan border. Inhabited by Dehkan tribes.*

diademed (dī'a-dem'd). *crowned.*

diapered (dī'ȧ-per'd). *richly patterned or embroidered.*

disc (disk). *a circular plate of heavy material thrown or hurled.*

dower (dou'ûr). *the portion of a man's estate that the law gives to* his widow during her life. Also the property a woman brings to her husband in marriage.

Druid (drōō'id). member of a religious order in pagan Gaul, Britain, and Ireland. Sometimes priests and sometimes magicians. Also sometimes judges.

Dun (dūn). a fortified house. A prefix in place names.

ebon (eb'un). ebony; a dark, hard, durable wood.

Echetus, King. a barbarous, Greek tyrant.

Emain Macha. The capital of Coiced Uroth (now Ulster); a kingdom of ancient Ireland.

épaulière (ā-pō-lyay'). a piece of armor that protects the shoulder and connects the backpiece and breastplate.

Erin (ar'in). Ireland.

etheling (ath'ŭl-ing). prince or noble.

Euboea (u-bē'a). the largest island near Greece, belonging to Greece.

Fafnir (fau'nir). a giant dragon who guarded a great treasure belonging to the dwarf Andvari.

farsang (far'sàng). Persian measure, equal to 6.21 miles.

fen (fen). low land, wholly or partly covered with water. Marsh.

Ffotor (fō'tôr). also Fotla. An ancient name for Ireland.

fief (fēf). a large estate given by a king to a noble.

fillet (fil'et). a small band encircling the hair.

Franks (fràngks). confederated German tribes who lived along the Rhine River. The Frankish Empire of the fifth to the ninth centuries later broke up into France, Germany, and Italy.

Garuda Bird (gür'ōō-dà). a supernatural animal, half man and half bird with a golden body and red wings.

Gascony (gas'kō-ni). province of southwest France.

Glam (gläm). a godless giant who was slain by Grettir and afterward haunted the farm on which he had been a shepherd.

Goths (gôth). ancient Teutonic race that lived originally between the Elbe and Vistula rivers. Later some migrated to an area near the Black Sea and the rest settled in Spain and southern France.

greave (grēv). armor for the leg below the knee.

griffin (grif'in). a mythical creature, half lion and half eagle.

Hachiman (hä'chi-man). a Japanese, Shinto, god of war.

halberd (hal'bŭrd). a long-handled weapon, a sort of spear.

hauberk (hä'bŭrk). medieval armor: a long coat or tunic of ring or chain mail.

Hefeydd (hē-vāy'th). a Welsh god. Father-in-law of Manawydden.

Hisi. an evil spirit that inhabited the earth. (Finnish)

Hispania (his-pā'ni-à). Latin name for Spain.

Hu Gadarn (hü gad'arrn). chief of the Welsh gods. Sovereign over the gods and the Cymry.

Ida, Mount (i'da). mountain near the city of Troy, from which the Greek gods watched the siege of Troy.

Indra (*in'dra*). *in early times, the great national god of the Hindus.*

Institutional Bard. *a professional poet or singer attached to a specific sect or group.*

Iphitus. *a friend of Hercules who was killed by Hercules in a fit of anger. Iphitus gave a great bow to Odysseus.*

Iris (*i'ris*). *Greek goddess of the rainbow. The swift messenger of Zeus and Hera.*

Jihun (*jē-hōōn'*). *Iranian river.*

Jotunheim (*yō'tōōn-hăm*). *in Norse mythology the home of giants, located where the oceans meet the edge of the world.*

joust (*jüst*). *a mock fight on horses between two knights using long lances.*

Jumna, River. *an Indian river flowing from the Himalaya Mountains to the Ganges River.*

Junala. *from Jumala, god of the sky. The sky.*

kadamba (*kà-dàm'bà*). *an East Indian tree with very hard wood, often used for furniture.*

Kaianides, race of. *dynasty name for a race of Iranian kings. A Kai Oubad (or Kobad) was the first of the line.*

Kalevala (*kä'lä-vä-lä*). *the great epic poem of Finland. Also Finland itself.*

Kalma (*käl'mär*) *the kingdom and castles of the death-land in ancient Finnish mythology.*

Khan (*kän*) *lord or prince: a title of sovereignty.*

kirtle (*kûr'tّl*). *a tunic or coat for a man. Also a woman's gown or dress, or her outer petticoat.*

Kwannan (*kwän'ōn*). *a female spirit worshiped as the incarnation of compassion and sometimes called "The Goddess of Mercy"—Buddhist.*

Lacedaemon (*lās-ē-dē'mōn*). *another name for Sparta, an ancient city of Greece.*

laton (*lăt'on*). *a brass or brasslike alloy metal, used in ancient times for church utensils.*

ledge (*lej*). *in shipbuilding, a supporting timber or beam running across the ship beneath the deck.*

Lempo. *a Finnish evil spirit living on earth.*

lena. *also léine. a large linen smock or shirt, usually yellow, of varying lengths. Worn by the people of ancient Ireland.*

libation (*lǐ-bā'shun*). *act of pouring a liquid on the ground in honor of a deity; also the liquid thus poured out.*

Lotor. *also Loughor. river and valley near Carmarther, Wales.*

Lusk. *town in eastern Ireland.*

lyre (*līr*). *a stringed instrument like a harp.*

mace (*mās*). *a heavy staff or club used for breaking armor. Any club used as a weapon.*

mail (*māl*). *a fabric made of linked metal rings used in medieval armor.*

makars (*mak'ûrs*). *evil spirits or demons in Hindu mythology, usually a combination of several beasts.*

Malltreath. *also Malldraeth. scene of an ancient battle on Anglesey Island.*

Manala. *Finnish name for "world beyond."*

Mananaun. *also Manannán. Irish name for Manawyddan. The son of Lir the sea god.*

mantra (*man'trà*). *a ritual or devotional exercise made up of specific holy words or syllables. Also a spell or charm.*

Meirion. *another name for Cornwall.*

Menai (*men'ī*). *a strait of water between Anglesey Island and Carnarvonshire on the coast of Wales.*

mendicant (*men'di-kànt*). *the act of begging, or a beggar.*

Midna. *Gaelic god of the underworld.*

mid-world. *also Midgard. In Norse mythology the intermediate world between the homes of the gods and the edge of the world. The place where men lived.*

Minerva (*min-nur'và*). *Roman name for the goddess Athene.*

Mon (*mon*). *ancient name for Anglesey Island, Wales.*

mubid. *also mobid. a priest who tended the fires for worship in the ancient Zoroastrian religion of Persia.*

Mycenae (*mī-sē'nē*). *a city of ancient Greece, near Corinth.*

Mysore (*mī-sōr'*). *state in south central India.*

Neptune (*nep'tūn*). *the Roman name for Poseidon, the god of the sea.*

Norns (*nôrns*). *the demigoddesses or giantesses who presided over and determined the fates of gods and men in Teutonic mythology.*

Odin (*ō'din*). *the chief or head god in Norse mythology. God of war,*

wisdom, and poetry. Also called Thor or Woden.

Oriflamme (*or'i-flam*). *a standard or ensign carried in battle. The ancient banner of St. Denis carried into war by old French kings.*

Orion (*ō-rī'on*). *the most prominent constellation of stars in the sky.*

Orkneys (*ôrk'nēs*). *a group of islands north of Scotland and belonging to Scotland.*

Ormuzd (*ôr'mazd*). *in the Zoroastrian religion of ancient Persia, the chief god and symbol of creation and all goodness.*

osprey (*os'prē*). *a large hawk, dark-brown above and pure white below.*

Pair Dadeni. *in ancient Welsh mythology, the caldron of life and regeneration. The brew it contained was full of inspiration and science; it gave all wisdom and knowledge to those touched by it.*

paladin (*pàl'a-din*). *a champion of a medieval prince; a legendary hero.*

palfrey (*pàl'fri*). *a special saddle horse for travel or for state occasions.*

Panchala (*pancha'la or pahn-chah'-lah*). *a kingdom in the north of India, north and west of the city of Delhi.*

parfleches (*par'flēshes*). *a treated buffalo hide. Also a box or a saddlebag made of such hide.*

pavilion (*pà-vil'yûn*). *a tent, or a covering or canopy of some sort.*

paynims (*pā'nims*). *pagans or infidels, especially Mohammedans.*

Pehliva (*pā'lû-vē*) *also Pahlavi. an-*

cient language and peoples of Iran.

Pelion spear (*pē'li-on*). *spear given to Achilles by the centaur Chiron who educated him.*

pemmican (*pem'i-kan*). *lean buffalo meat or venison cut in thin slices, dried in the sun, pounded fine, and mixed with melted fat. Packed in sacks of hide for traveling.*

pennon (*pen'on*). *a long triangular flag or streamer.*

Pentecost (*pen'tē-kost*). *a festival of the Christian Church held on the seventh Sunday after Easter.*

peri (*pē'ri*). *in Persian mythology an elf or a fairy descended from fallen angels. They were originally regarded as evil, but later were thought of as kind and beautiful.*

phalanx (*fā'langks*). *a body of heavily armed soldiers in very close formation.*

piebald (*pī'bāld*). *having different colors, especially two different colors; mottled or spotted.*

Piru (*pi'rū*). *an evil spirit infesting the earth.*

Pohya (*pō'yä*). *shortened form of Pohyola, the legendary Finnish name for Lapland.*

poltroon (*pol-trōōn*). *a coward or sluggard; idle or lazy one.*

poniard (*pon'yûrd*). *a dagger, usually having a slender triangular-shaped or square blade.*

Poseidon (*pō-si'don*). *Greek god of the sea.*

postern (*pōs'tûrn*). *a back door or gate; a private or side entrance. Sometimes a secret passageway.*

Powys (*powis*). *a large landed estate near the present city of Welshpool in Wales.*

Pwyll Pen Annwn. *the prince of Hades.*

Pylos (*pī'los*). *a town on one of the Peloponnesian Islands of Greece.*

quintain (*kwin'tin*). *a medieval game. A post with a crosspiece that pivoted at the top. At one end of the crosspiece was a broad board, at the other end, a sandbag. The object was to hit the board with a lance while riding under and at the same time avoid being hit by the sandbag.*

Rai (*rā*). *a town in North Iran, six miles south of Tehran.*

raiment (*rā'ment*). *clothing.*

Rakshasa (*räk'shà-sà*). *goblins or evil spirits in Hindu mythology. They were monsters who could assume any shape at will.*

Rama Giri. *the Hill of Rama. A mountain in India.*

rath (*rath*). *a hill residence fortified with an earthen wall.*

Rha River. *Ancient name for the Volga River.*

Rhianon Ren (*rē'a-non ren*). *wife of Pwyll Pen Annwn and later of Manawyddan (in some Welsh legends the same person). She was one of the Welsh gods.*

runes (*rōōns*). *the characters or signs of the alphabet used by the early Teutonic or German people. Also used among the Norse and Anglo-Saxon people.*

rushlight (*rush'līt*). *a candle made of the pith of certain rushes dipped in grease.*

Rutya (*Rūt'jā*). *a waterfall in north Finland.*

saffron (*saf'run*). *a variety of crocus with purple flowers, cultivated for* the yellow dye made from the plant. A special shade of yellow, the color the dye produces.

Salamis (*sal'ă-mis*). an ancient city on the east coast of the island of Cypress.

Samatia. area near the Samara River in southeastern European Russia.

samite (*sam'ĭt*). a heavy silk fabric, often interwoven with gold or silver.

samurai (*sam'ŏŏ-rī*). a feudal warrior of Japan; a member of the warrior class.

Sand Hills. in American Indian mythology, the land of the dead.

Saracens (*sar'a-sens*). originally a nomad of Syria or Arabia. Later Moslems who were hostile to Christians.

Sariola (*sär'i-ōla*). same as Pohya or Pohyola, Lapland.

Saxons (*sak'sŭns*). a Germanic people who were masters of most of northwest Germany and, with the Angles and Jutes, conquered and colonized England in the seventh century.

scabbard (*skăb'ŭrd*). metal holder for a sword or dagger.

Scaean Gates (*sē'ăn*). western gates of Troy.

Scamander (*skă-man'dŭr*). ancient name for the Menderez River in Asia Minor.

scimitar (*sim'i-tŭr*). a saber with a curved blade. Used chiefly by Mohammedans.

Scythia (*sith'i-a*). land in southern Russia near Lake Oral.

seneschal (*sen'e-shal*). the steward of a medieval lord or king, the manager of his estate.

Severn. River in southwestern England.

shards (*shärds*). pieces or fragments of a brittle substance.

shee (*shē*). a fairy fort. Usually thought to be a round green knoll, or mound or an island, having a palace underneath.

shieldburg (*shield burg*). a protecting enclosure or palisade composed of shields.

Skylding. one who comes from the eastern part of the Holderness Peninsula.

Slieve Cullion. also The Ben of Cullen. Hill on Cullen Bay of Mory Firth, North Banffshire, Scotland.

Slieve Fuad (*slēē'vēē*). hill near Newtown Hamilton in County Armagh, Ireland. Thought in ancient times to be the home of the sea god, Lir.

Sowan, Eve of (*sō'wan*). Early Irish equivalent of Halloween.

squire (*skwīre*). a shield bearer or armor bearer for a knight.

stanchion (*stan'shun*). an upright bar, post, prop, brace or support as for a roof, ship's deck, etc.

Sumeru. In Indian mythology, a mountain, the center of the universe around which all lands, mountains, and oceans were grouped.

sumpter (*sump'ter*). baggage for a horse or mule.

Sutri (*sŏŏ'trē*). a town in central Italy.

Tajo River (*tä'hō*). the Tagus River, longest in Spain.

Tanais River. ancient name for the Don River of European Russia.

Thlacta. also tallaght. in Irish mythology the earliest plain in Ireland to rise from the sea. Also the death and burial place of the earliest race of Celtic gods.

thrall (thrăl). a slave or bondsman.

timpaun. an early Irish instrument related to the dulcimer; a stringed instrument having a flat, square base.

tonsured (ton'shûr'd). having the crown of the head shaved. A custom practiced first by monks.

torii. in Japan, the pillared entrance to a shrine or temple.

tournament (tŏŏr'nà-ment). a contest between armed knights, usually for some sort of prize or favor.

troll (trōl). a supernatural being; usually either a dwarf or a giant.

truncheon (trun'chun). a fragment of a lance or spear.

Tuoni. the Finnish god of the underworld.

Turan (tūr-ān'). the region north of the Orus River in Turkestan.

Ukko (ŭkkō). chief god in Norse mythology.

Valhall (val-hal). also Valhalla. The hall of Odin into which he received the souls of heroes slain in battle.

Valkyrie (Val-kū'ri). maidens of Odin who hovered over battles to choose the heroes who would go to Valhall.

Vandals (van'dal's). Germanic peoples from the area south of the Baltic who overran Gaul, Spain, and north Africa in the fourth and fifth centuries.

Wainola. ancient name for Finland.

wallet. a large sack for holding the necessary things for a journey; a knapsack.

warden. one who guards or is in command of a town or district.

wicket gate (wik'et). a small gate or door forming a part of, or placed near, a larger gate or door.

wraith (rāth). the ghost of a person, sometimes thought to be seen just before his death.

Wuoksen (vüŏ'ksen). a river in the east of Finland.

Wyddfa, peak of (with'va). Mt. Snowdon, the highest peak in Wales. Thought to be the home of the ancient Welsh gods.

Ynys Wen. Ancient Britain—Welsh name.

yurta (yŏŏr'ta). a circular, movable tent, of skins or felt stretched over a lattice framework.

Zaboulistan (zà-bŏŏl'i-stan). the area around Ghaziri, Afghanistan, in early Mohammedan times.

Zeus (zūs). the chief of the gods in ancient Greek mythology.

INDEX